THE RIVIERA CONTRACT

ARTHUR KERNS

DIVERSIONBOOKS

Also by Arthur Kerns

Hayden Stone Thrillers
The African Contract
The Yemen Contract

Diversion Books
A Division of Diversion Publishing Corp.
443 Park Avenue South, Suite 1008
New York, New York 10016
www.DiversionBooks.com

For more information, email info@diversionbooks.com

Second Diversion Books edition June 2016
Print ISBN: 978-1-62681-129-4
eBook ISBN: 978-1-938120-92-3

PRINCIPAL CHARACTERS

Hayden Stone, former FBI agent, now CIA operative
Hassan Musab Mujahib, terrorist
Contessa Lucinda Avoscani, love interest of Stone
Abdul Wahab, terrorist
Boswell Harrington, head of the Foundation d'Élan
Sandra, CIA operative
Jonathan Deville, FBI agent assigned to Paris
Mark, CIA operative
Charles Fleming, CIA official
Colonel Gustave Frederick, CIA official
David, a writer, scholar
Claudia, CIA official
Margaux Reynard, French employee at the Foundation d'Élan
Rashid, wine entrepreneur
Philippe Monte, consigliere to Countess Lucinda
Dr. Aziz Husseini, scientist
Maurice Colmont, French intelligence
Prince Mohammed Al Tabrizi

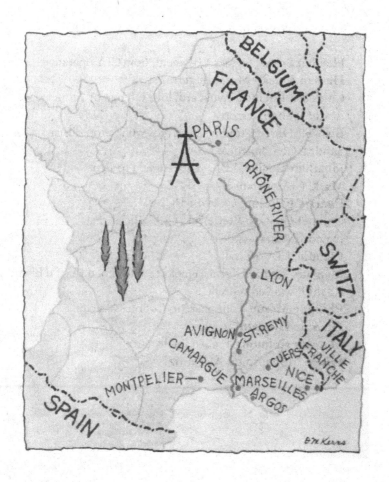

CHAPTER ONE

NICE, FRANCE—APRIL 20, 2002

"Think a lot of yourself, young man? Well, start on your obituary and try to make it interesting."

Barrett Huntington's uncle had tossed out this barb a few months back as the two sat in the dining room of the family's Wall Street investment firm. His uncle had made a call to a friend in Langley, Virginia, to arrange for Huntington to join the CIA. A number of Huntington's New York colleagues had gone to work for the Agency, following the attack on the Twin Towers. The ashes of two fraternity brothers lay in the mound of rubble in southern Manhattan.

Now here he sat, after three days in beautiful Nice on the French Riviera, watching Hassan Mujahid's movements. This morning on the hotel terrace in the shade of a wide-limbed olive tree, his middle-aged quarry quietly ate yogurt and fruit. Finished eating, Hassan leaned back in his chair, unfolded an Arabic-language newspaper from Beirut, and drank two Americanos, wiping his black moustache after each sip. Hassan's body movements interested Huntington. Were all killers so polished? Or just the professional ones?

Huntington was enjoying this, his first operational assignment with the CIA. Who wouldn't enjoy working in Nice, where the sea shimmered and the ochre-colored homes were haphazardly stacked Braque-like up the palm- and pine-covered hills? A twinge of guilt tugged at him. His wife, pregnant with their first child, was alone back in McLean, Virginia. She loved France and if she were sitting there next to him at the quaint wooden table, she would be noting the golden color of the hotel walls and, with closed eyes, breathing in the fragrance from the potted flowers placed in the sun. However, he was watching a terrorist who hadn't changed his attire in three days: tan slacks, white shirt, and a black leather jacket. Huntington spread honey on his warm baguette, content to wait.

After breakfast, Hassan broke from his routine. He skipped his morning swim in the hotel pool set flush against the soaring cliff of Chateau Hill. Instead, at precisely nine o'clock, he slung a travel bag over his shoulder and left the hotel. Huntington followed, maintaining a discreet distance. Turning away from the old town, Hassan sauntered along the road overlooking the sea and rounded the bend toward the yacht basin.

Ten minutes later, on the Quai Cassini, Hassan settled onto the shady side of a long wooden bench. Within minutes an inflatable Zodiac boat piloted by a uniformed man pulled up alongside the quay and took him aboard. As the Zodiac roared off, Huntington saw that Hassan scanned the dock, as if looking for someone he had left behind. Using his monocular, Huntington watched the Zodiac as it headed for a large white yacht. On its stern, the yacht's large gold letters declared RED SCORPION.

Two hours later, faithful to his task, Huntington observed Hassan return from the yacht and start walking toward town. Huntington followed on foot for a half hour until, without warning, a black BMW sedan pulled up to Hassan and he jumped inside. Huntington, with no means to follow, broke off his surveillance. Frustrated by losing his quarry, he was left with only the car's license plate number.

A little after seven that evening, Huntington sat in the hotel lobby and watched Hassan rush down the narrow staircase of the hotel and across the reception area. He tossed his room key at the receptionist and pushed through the front door, then turned right and headed for the old section of Nice.

Huntington folded his *International Herald Tribune* and placed it on the coffee table, where a short red-haired woman speaking German with her companion snatched it up. He watched the second hand on the wall clock advance thirty seconds, then rose and walked to the door. The young receptionist called after him, "Monsieur, your room key?"

"I'm only going for a stroll." His CIA training instructor at the Farm had said to always keep your hotel key to prevent the receptionist from placing it in your mail slot. No need to advertise to anyone that you were out of your room.

"Oh, Monsieur Rowell," she added. "Will you be having breakfast tomorrow morning on the terrace as usual?"

"*Mais oui.*" The name Rowell still sounded odd to him, even after two months on the job. The people at the CIA Headquarters had told him he would receive a pseudonym when he became operational, but they had neglected to tell him that a computer program, not he, would select the name.

From the hotel entrance, Huntington glanced at airport lights blinking from across the dull, choppy bay, and then looked to the right toward the city of Nice. The sun had dropped below the horizon and color was draining from the buildings. Hassan had a good hundred-meter lead. Huntington zipped up his windbreaker and followed him along the *Promenade des Anglais*. The mist blowing in from the bay tasted of salt.

He hoped his target would eat a quick dinner and return to the hotel early. It was difficult to conduct surveillance alone and not be detected. He stepped aside for two lovers huddled under an umbrella. Odd, he thought, as it wasn't raining. The woman's eyes, from beneath a black scarf, met his for an instant too long.

When Hassan turned right, Huntington surmised he was heading for the Cours Saleya, the flower market. For a few seconds he lost visual contact, then spied Hassan wearing a jacket as black as his hair. They had taken this route the night before when Hassan had stopped for seafood in a café on the market square. Tonight he kept walking.

Shop lights turned on as people hurried in both directions along the cobblestone street. Not many tourists were seen in March. The cellphone vibrated in his shirt pocket. Pulling it out, Huntington saw his Paris control's number displayed on the screen.

Hassan took a quick turn up a narrow, unlit alley. Without answering the call, Huntington shoved the phone back in his pocket and followed. The clatter from the market gradually diminished behind him as he moved through the darkness. Ahead, at the far end of the alley, tiny shops lined a softly-lit square. He liked the street lighting in Europe. So unlike the harsh glare found in American cities.

His cellphone vibrated again. Was Paris calling with feedback on the Red Scorpion? He raised the phone to eye level to read the caller's number. It was not familiar. At the same time, he tried not to lose contact with Hassan, moving ahead in the shadows.

A bulky shape lunged from the left and jabbed Huntington hard in the thigh with what appeared to be the tip of a folded umbrella. He felt a sharp prick followed by a burning sensation extending up into his groin. Then numbness quickly set in. He crouched into a defensive position and fumbled for his Glock. The attacker's face morphed into the likeness of the man Huntington had just passed on the promenade. A second figure, a woman, hissed, "*Allons y! Vite! Vite!*"

Huntington stumbled toward where he had last seen Hassan. He forced his legs along in the direction of the square, wanting to get away from the couple. There was no pain, just a soothing relaxation. His mind seemed to be shutting down. His legs glided him toward the pleasant glow of the shops, where he saw Hassan, his back turned, looking in a store window.

The small square glowed soft yellow, whirling all around him. He staggered and swayed. Hassan turned from the shop window and stared at him. The cellphone vibrated in Huntington's hand as he spun around and hit the stone pavement. Strange, he thought, looking up at Hassan. He appears as confused as I am.

Looking down at the body, Hassan was perplexed. What had happened? This young man, who was registered at his hotel under the name of Rowell, had been shadowing him. As a precaution, a member of his cell in Nice had conducted countersurveillance and learned that this man consistently showed up at the same locations as he did. He theorized the young man must be a British agent, as he was too well dressed and mannered for an American. Now he had fallen dead at his feet. Baffling.

He knelt and felt Huntington's throat for a pulse, but found none. No blood appeared on his clothes, but his bowels had emptied. He reached into Huntington's jacket and took out his wallet. Perhaps a card or note would provide some additional information on this man's identity. He removed a hotel key from the pants pocket. The handle of a black Glock protruded from a leather shoulder holster. Hassan reached for it then stopped. He didn't need to take something that the police could trace to this man.

Footsteps echoed from the alley. He stood. The last thing he needed was to be arrested by the French police for robbery or murder. A woman wearing a black scarf, accompanied by a large man, came forward into the light. Hassan stepped back into the shadows, and then headed down a side street at a quick, but controlled, pace. No sense in arousing suspicion on the part of any passersby. He glanced back and saw the large man following him. The woman stayed in the square bent over the body. Two local thieves, he surmised. Most inconvenient.

Hassan pulled a knife from his coat pocket. He thumbed the release button, and the five-inch blade snapped out. The large man continued to close the distance between them. Taking advantage of a nightlight shining from a butcher shop's window, Hassan spun around and faced his pursuer. The large man broke stride, quickly leveled an umbrella, and thrust it toward him. Hassan shifted to the right, sprang forward, and neatly sliced open the left side of the man's throat. The umbrella fell to the ground as the man grabbed at his neck, trying to stem the flow of blood. Hassan lunged, stabbing deep into the front of the man's throat.

From the square, the woman raced toward Hassan holding an automatic pistol. She stopped and slid into a shooting crouch, fumbling the gun with both hands. Hassan took two steps, leaped, and twisted his body in mid-air. His right foot snapped into the side of the woman's head. She fell next to the curb and the gun slid across the cobblestones, clanging into an open sewer. As the woman moaned, Hassan wrapped his arm around her neck and, with a jerk, snapped the vertebrae.

Her partner was knelt as if in prayer, bloody hands unsuccessfully holding back a bubbling flow of blood. Hassan waited. When the man fell sideways on to the street, the air stopped fizzing from his slit windpipe.

Hassan listened and searched the street in both directions. He heard no sound except for the dripping of water from a building's roof. Very well done, he congratulated himself. He paused over the man's body and studied the face. Not French. Algerian possibly … definitely Maghreb. Too bad, killing a Christian would have been more enjoyable. He searched his two victims' pockets and found money, but no identification.

He picked up the umbrella. A needle protruded from the tip. He had seen a picture of a similar poison device in an old Bulgarian intelligence training manual. Whoever these people were, they had killed the young agent and their technology was dated. Perhaps members of some fringe organization from North Africa. He decided to take the umbrella with him. Back at the hotel, he would use the key to search the young man's room.

CHAPTER TWO

NICE—APRIL 22, 2002

Abdul Wahab gazed down at the crew of the Red Scorpion washing down the yacht's decks. Leaning on the brass railing of the upper deck, he tilted his face up to the sun. His trimmed moustache and goatee matched his head of thick black hair. He looked down again and searched the harbor. Below, the yacht's Zodiac tender cast off with a wide-open throttle and headed toward the nearby pier. The prince's guests had lunch reservations at a restaurant in downtown Nice. As usual, the prince stayed aboard.

Wahab entered the pilothouse and walked over to the vessel's wheel and binnacle. His father-in-law, Prince Mohammed Al Tabrizi, had pronounced that, despite the array of high-technology navigation instruments, a helmsman in his gold-braided uniform would stand before the polished oak and brass helm and steer the Red Scorpion. A bit old-fashioned one might say, but it did impress visitors.

The prince owned the three-hundred-foot yacht, a sleek white craft that had three levels extending beneath where Abdul Wahab stood. The large windows of the pilothouse overlooked the bow onto the crowded harbor of Nice. The constant noise of small craft passing close by, as well as the smells from the restaurants along the waterfront, gave some of the guests onboard a closed-in feeling. He mentioned this to the prince and suggested they move around the cape to Villefranche, where an open bay fronted the town lying at the base of a mountain. Also, it so happened that a palace sat halfway up the mountain, which the prince might lease for the ailing bin Zanni, the al Qaeda chief of information.

Wahab stepped past the humming electronic equipment, the green lights blinking numbers and symbols, and went back out onto the open bridge. The report he'd received on the assassination in Nice puzzled him. His two people from Marseille had killed the CIA man, a request from bin Zanni's people. However, later that night someone had killed his two Marseillais. The police had found them lying in the street not far from the CIA man's body. The police were not suspected, as the two had not been shot; the man died from a slit throat and the woman from a broken neck. At first, Abdul Wahab suspected thieves had killed them, but no one had taken their money or jewelry.

Probably the CIA had killed them. He would retaliate; the CIA had an agent in Montpellier. Perhaps he would use the services of that Shiite, Hassan. No. He would save the heretic for a later time.

MCLEAN, VIRGINIA

Hayden Stone went to the hall closet, pulled out his tweed jacket, and walked out onto the redwood deck. He squinted his gray eyes against the late-afternoon breeze and watched the driver toss the last carton in the back of the moving van. The truck, filled with Stone's ex-wife's possessions, eased away from the curb with loud hissing from its air brakes, made a deft turn around the cul-de-sac at the end of the street, and roared by the house with its two tall chrome exhaust pipes belching smoke.

The last time Stone had spoken to his former wife she'd said, without bothering to look into his eyes, that he didn't fit into her career plans. He had known for years he hadn't fit into her life. So now, she lived on the other side of the country, close to their two children's college.

He went back into the house and lit a fire in the hearth. After a few moments staring at the blue flames from the gas burners, he went over to the bar and poured himself a large Irish whiskey. Tonight, he would drink a little too much, not to forget, but to remember.

The fire soon took the chill from the room. The movers had kept the doors open all day while they hauled out the furniture she had claimed as booty from the divorce. Next to his chair sat the whiskey bottle and half-full glass. He tried to think of something good about his marriage, but came up with only sour remembrances.

He shook his head and bent over to pour more whiskey. As he did, his side hit the arm of the chair and a jolt of pain stabbed along his waist. Three weeks earlier in the eastern mountains of Afghanistan, a bullet from a Taliban AK-47 had torn a piece of flesh from his right side. The nurse in the forward camp who had stitched up the wound said that with his "love handle" shot off, he would be unbalanced for the rest of his life. *Apropos*, he'd thought.

Visualizing the brown, hard mountains of Afghanistan, Stone sipped his drink and thought of his colleague, Jason. The two had found refuge in a friendly Pashtun village after Jason had been wounded in the chest. The villagers had declared the two of them "protected guests," the tribal tradition that kept them from the clutches of the Taliban circling the village like jackals.

In the black of night their rescue helicopter came in and hovered over the village square. He dragged Jason from the house and they struggled toward the dull red strobe light pulsating from the nose of the craft. Muzzle flashes from Taliban guns appeared at the edge of the village. Bullets whined past his head and rounds thudded into the dirt around his feet. Streams of red gunfire shot like strobes from the helicopter's guns. From somewhere amid the roar of the helicopter's rotors, he heard, "Fast! Move fast!"

Two Americans in black fatigues grabbed Jason and carried him to the open door of the helicopter. Stone triggered his M4 in short bursts of three and four rounds at the Taliban, coming in from all sides. The helicopter lifted, throwing dirt and dust in his face. He grabbed a nylon strap hanging from the craft and wrapped it around his left arm. As the rising machine jerked him up, he slowly spun beneath it, spraying bullets at the Taliban until the helicopter lifted him into the black.

When the helicopter landed at the forward outpost, he learned that Jason had died en route. The right side of Stone's jacket had been shredded and blood had soaked down to his ankle.

What if he had listened to Jason when he'd wanted to mount their ponies and head back to the village through the mountains? Perhaps they wouldn't have come under fire from the Taliban patrol in the valley.

He drained his glass, got up, turned off the gas to the fireplace, locked the doors, and went to bed.

The next morning, Stone looked out the kitchen window. Early traces of green showed in the backyard lawn and here and there sprouts of crocus and narcissus broke through the edge of the flowerbed. An overcast March sky, gray and listless, dulled the rest of the landscape. He went out to inspect his garden.

The grounds required attention. In the vegetable garden, brown twigs from the former year's tomato plants lay bent alongside dead weeds. No sign of life. By this time there should be movement in the earth along the two asparagus rows. He knelt down, poked with a stake into the dirt, and unearthed an asparagus crown. Gnarled and stringy, it felt cold and lifeless. For thirteen years he had harvested a good crop. Three years before, early in the season, he'd covered the new shoots with hay and produced white asparagus. That year his wife and he had invited friends over for a Sunday afternoon and enjoyed the yield with champagne.

Somehow a garden was no longer important. It was time to move on. He had been thinking about the offer from his friend in Malibu to go in with him on a dive boat. The fellow FBI inspector had promised a lucrative return from well-heeled tourists along with good diving off the Channel Islands. Maybe he'd also open a small restaurant on the beach. Put some exotic dishes on the menu, from Afghanistan maybe. A drop of rain hit the back of his neck. He dropped the dead asparagus crown and returned to the house.

LANGLEY, VIRGINIA—APRIL 23, 2002

Jeffrey looked around the spacious office. The spacious seventh floor office of the CIA headquarters overlooked the expanse of Langley forest. Pines hugged the compound perimeter and oak trees in the distance struggled to open their buds against the chill. Howard, the chief of the European Division, had planted mementos from his many foreign assignments throughout his office for visitors' edification. Soft classical music floated down from the speakers in the ceiling.

Jeffrey, the head of the CIA's Near East Division, had asked his counterpart, Howard, for a meeting. When he entered Howard's office, he immediately recognized Claudia standing at the window, wearing a dark blue dress that had fit better when she weighed less. The three settled into low couches facing a round coffee table. In the center of the table, a large art book from the *Musee D'Orsay* lay unopened.

"Bad business with the death in Nice." Howard sighed. He studied his manicure.

"Barrett Huntington was third generation in our business," Jeffrey said. "He was on loan from me to you, remember?" He waited for Howard to make eye contact.

"Come now, it isn't as if my people in the European Division were negligent, Jeffrey."

"I can barely staff my posts in Lebanon and Cairo." Jeffrey's voice rose. "Then I lend you a good officer and he gets killed."

Howard adjusted his Hermes tie. "We're all stretched thin in resources."

"That's not why I'm here," Jeffrey continued. "The rumor mill all the way to the basement barber shop has it that my division held back pertinent information from the station in Paris. In other words it's my fault that my officer temporarily under your charge was murdered."

"Surely nothing like that would come from this office." Howard glanced over. "Claudia, have you heard anything of that nature?"

Claudia, the branch chief in charge of special projects in Europe had supervised Huntington. She pushed her reading glasses back on her nose and Jeffrey glimpsed a thin layer of moisture on her forehead.

"Certainly not," Claudia said. "We can't put stock in rumors."

"Tell us, Claudia," Howard continued. "What are the results of the investigation into young Huntington's demise? A full inquiry was conducted, yes?"

"Our French colleagues reported his death to our consulate in Marseille." She shuffled papers in her hands. "The French conducted a criminal investigation. He was poisoned."

Jeffrey grimaced. "How long did it take for you to realize that one of your people was murdered? He was one of us, you know, the DO." He looked for some response from Howard, who still cherished the CIA moniker for the Directorate of Operations, even though it had been replaced with a more mundane label. Seeing none, he continued, "My understanding is that it took two days before you knew what happened."

"His control officer in Paris was off meeting with some other operatives." Claudia took off her glasses and stared at the ceiling. "We have a lot going on in the area."

Howard said, "We know you're upset about this case. It is most unfortunate."

"Yes, both for Barrett Huntington and his pregnant wife." Jeffrey took out his pen and pretended to make a note on his pad. "You know he was one of our best picks from the Ivies two years ago. An Arabic scholar."

Howard sighed and turned to Claudia. "Give us a quick wash on what happened."

"Our French colleagues reported that he was stabbed in the leg with a quick-acting poison, a chemical composition similar to that used by the Russians and the Bulgarians. He was found lying off an alley in Vieux Nice. No witnesses. His identification was missing. He'd been issued a sidearm, but the French didn't mention anything about that."

"They probably stole it," Jeffrey said. "How did they identify him?"

Claudia looked at her notes. "He was clutching his cellphone. Whoever killed him didn't notice it in his hand."

"I thought all operational cellphones were non-attributable," Jeffrey said.

"I don't know." Claudia seemed flustered. "Maybe it wasn't through any numbers on the phone that they knew he was—"

"Bad tradecraft." Jeffrey frowned. "I suppose all your contact numbers in France and Italy have been compromised."

"We're attending to that." She scratched in her notepad.

"Well, Claudia, what about Huntington's target?" Howard pressed. "That Arab he was shadowing?"

"No trace of him. He'll surface."

"Is he a suspect?" Jeffrey asked.

"Probably," she answered.

"Christ."

Howard stood and walked to his desk to check his calendar. He looked over his shoulder. "Jeffrey, lunch in the dining room?"

Claudia rose.

Howard peered at her over his glasses. "Claudia, I want a replacement for our young officer. Right away."

"We're in the process of—"

"No CIA staff members. Look into the ranks of the Independent Contractors. Someone seasoned. Not young, understand?"

"We have a number of retired officers who—"

"No one connected with the CIA. Maybe someone with a military or operations background who has seen action." He invited Jeffrey to precede him to the door.

MONTPELLIER, FRANCE

Stacy felt relieved. The meeting at the university in Montpellier had gone well. She had received good information that she knew the CIA analysts back in Langley could use. The golden sun warmed her arms as she drove her Volkswagen back to her flat. She would relax on her patio, enjoy the spring afternoon warmth, and prepare her report.

An afternoon stroll would be perfect, but following the alert from the Paris Station, she had kept a low profile. Huntington's murder in Nice had confounded them all. One did not come to France expecting to be murdered.

One more month and she would complete her tour and return to Virginia. She missed her two daughters; they were growing up, one five years old, the other seven, and she knew they needed her. Ned was a good father, but still, they needed their mother.

At the traffic light, she fumbled in her briefcase and made sure her notes were tucked in the brown envelope. As she returned her attention to the road, a white sedan appeared in the rearview mirror. It had not been there the last time she'd looked. Two men, both unshaven, stared through the windshield. Her hands felt clammy on the steering wheel.

She signaled a right turn and when the light changed, steered to the right. The car behind her did the same. With a quick turn of the wheel, she reversed her turn and went left, cutting across the path of an oncoming truck. She floored the accelerator and glanced in the rearview mirror. The white car followed.

The street turned into a country road with plowed fields on either side. The white car moved up close to her rear bumper, then made a quick move up along the left side of her car. She braked hard and let the car shoot past just far enough that she could bring her left front fender across the pursuer's right rear fender. The white car spun out of control and nosed into a ditch.

She executed a one-hundred-and-eighty-degree turn on screeching tires and sped off in the opposite direction, barely missing a motorcycle.

Reentering the town, she slowed. The car was not in sight, just a lone motorcycle behind her. At a pedestrian crossing, she stopped and rubbed her aching temples. She looked back in the mirror. Still no car.

Then the motorcycle's engine revved twice outside her door. She looked up. The driver was wearing a helmet with an opaque visor. He pulled an automatic pistol from inside his jacket and pointed it at her.

"That's a Berretta," she murmured. "Like the one I carried in Sierra Leone."

AVIGNON, FRANCE

Avignon sparkled in the morning light. On the Place du Palais, the expanse facing the immense Papal palace, Hassan sat at the wobbly table with Rashid, a portly man with a trimmed beard and dark, heavy eyebrows that met over a slender nose. Tourists milled about the outdoor café speaking in a variety of languages.

Rashid waved his hand. "All this belonged to us. From Spain, up across the Pyrenees, into southern France."

Hassan sipped his coffee and watched the crowd from behind his sunglasses.

"Are you a student of history?" asked Rashid, and then answered his own question. "Yes, of course you are. You studied in Baghdad."

"Basra," Hassan corrected him. "I studied in the south of Iraq, in Basra. Remember, I am Shiite."

"Baghdad was the center of the great Abbasid Caliph." Rashid looked over at a German couple arguing noisily two tables away from them.

"It was the Umayyad dynasty from Damascus who conquered and held Al Andalus." Hassan pulled a cigarette out and lit it with a gold lighter. Rashid reminded him of an uncle in Lebanon, overweight much too early for his age, and given to pompous pronouncements.

Rashid smiled. "Yes. You are right. So, you people from the marshes do learn your history."

"There are no marshes near my home in Palestine." Hassan knew Rashid was trying once again to pry into his background. Hezbollah had given Rashid enough information about him. This Sunni bastard need not know more.

"Yes, of course," Rashid continued, touching his nose with his white linen handkerchief. "The Umayyad conquered Spain and then invaded France." Rashid sipped his coffee and sighed. "Look at that fortress, that palace. Home to the Pope, head of the Christians, leader of the crusaders, the despoilers of our culture. They spent their time there with whores."

Hassan regarded the man in front of him, who wore handmade Italian shoes and a jacket sporting a Paris label draped over his shoulders. He thought of his own life in the refugee camp when he was a boy. His father had only one jacket, which he wore every day. He had it on when the Israeli plane bombed their shack.

"What have you learned about the man and woman who killed the American?" Hassan drew on his cigarette and watched the smoke float off.

"They were from Marseille," Rashid whispered.

Hassan waited for Rashid to continue. He had the impression the fat man enjoyed parceling out information.

Rashid bent forward again. "The man and woman you killed both had criminal records and spent time in prison. The man was involved in illegal drugs."

Hassan crushed out the cigarette. "He was a believer ... a Muslim. Whom was he working for?"

"No group we know of. However, there are so many groups, with so many points of view." Rashid smiled again and shrugged. "We, as they say in America, keep bumping into each other."

Hassan did not smile. "I gave you the American's wallet. Was there anything in it that revealed who he worked for?"

Rashid gave a Levantine cluck of the tongue. "The information in it was worthless. He had business cards that indicated he was a wine consultant from San Francisco. There was no money in the wallet. Did you take it?"

"Of course. I will use it to pay for the coffee today," Hassan said. "By the way, do you not own some vineyards near Arles?"

"Yes, that is true." Rashid seemed pleased Hassan knew of his business venture.

"How do you know you make good wine? We Muslims cannot drink it."

Only Rashid's lips produced a smile.

Neither spoke for some time. The sun now was overhead and the shadows across the Place du Palais had disappeared. Hassan breathed deeply and reached into his pocket for some Euro coins. He would leave this man and take a walk along the Rhone River. Perhaps he might take an overnight trip on one of the riverboats. He inched down his sunglasses and studied Rashid. "Why would those two people want to kill me? Did they know who I was?"

Rashid waved his index finger back and forth. "No. No, my friend. You are becoming too suspicious. It was merely coincidence."

Hassan handed the waiter money for the two coffees.

Rashid said, "Before you leave, I wanted to tell you that your meeting aboard the Red Scorpion went quite well. Abdul Wahab was most impressed with you, as I knew he would be. I suspect he will want to do business with you."

Hassan rose and looked down at Rashid. "You and I will meet at the appointed time."

Hassan's shoes clicked on the pavement as he headed for the Rhone. Passing in front of a tourist shop at the end of the Place du Palais, a young woman with white-blonde hair emerged carrying postcards. She bumped into Hassan and her postcards spilled onto the sidewalk. Hassan bent down and helped her pick them up.

"*Pardon*," she said. "*Je regrette.*" She brushed her hair back from her face and looked up with bright green eyes.

The two spoke for a while, laughed once or twice, and then ambled toward the river. There on the riverbank, they sat on a stone bench and watched the boats glide past.

CHAPTER THREE

NORTHERN VIRGINIA

Claudia sped her dented white Volvo out of the CIA headquarters gate, and turned south onto the George Washington Parkway toward Rosslyn. The road was slick from a departing shower that left a raw chill in the air. Through the line of trees on the left side of the parkway, a misty Georgetown appeared across the Potomac River. Two long rowing sculls from Georgetown University glided downstream, the rowers dipping and lifting their long oars in unison. She exited the Parkway at Key Bridge and made her way through Rosslyn toward the Fort Myer military base. If she made all the traffic lights, she would not be late for the Tuesday noon lecture. The Association of Former Intelligence Officers sponsored the monthly gathering, which provided a good networking setting for the intelligence community. Maybe she would spot someone there to replace Barrett Huntington. The morning meeting had not gone well. Knowing her boss Howard, he would hound her until she got the French operation back on an even keel.

Five red lights. She arrived late and had difficulty finding a parking space in the officer's club parking lot. Huffing up the staircase to the second floor dining room, she found a seat next to Rachel, who had been in her new officers training class twenty years earlier. On Rachel's first overseas assignment, she had lost an eye when a terrorist bomb exploded outside her embassy office window; since then she refused all foreign assignments. They began comparing notes on the latest position changes in their respective divisions.

Before the main speaker began his address, Claudia asked Rachel whether she knew of a good replacement for her officer murdered in Nice. At the same time, a tall, dark-haired man wearing an expensive gray suit came in and sat two rows in front of them.

Rachel, transfixed by the man, nudged Claudia. "I recognize him. A few years ago we did business together on a Middle East terrorist case. He works part-time for the Agency."

Claudia gave the man a quick once-over. He had a scar on his left cheek. She leaned over and whispered, "Name? Background?"

"Hayden Stone. Has counterintelligence background," she whispered back. "Retired mid-level executive. Familiar with the Middle East."

"What agency?"

"Hmm ... well, the Bureau."

"I'll find someone else. He's the last thing I need right now. You know I don't trust the Bureau or FBI agents."

The cellphone in Claudia's purse played the theme from Mozart's symphony number forty. She glanced at the phone, pushed back her chair, and hurried out to the lobby where other people paced with cellphones pressed to their ears. Her aide had bad news. Ignoring formalities, and without comment, Claudia switched off her phone. She returned and plopped back into her chair. "I've lost another officer this morning in Montpellier. I need someone *now!*"

Rachel pointed in the direction of Stone and then turned back to Claudia. "He has all our clearances."

"What's his name again?"

WASHINGTON, DC—APRIL 25, 2002

"Good to see you." Colonel Gustave Frederick gave Stone a firm handshake and the two walked up the white marble stairs into the lobby of the Army & Navy Club. The club was enjoying a busy lunch day, a favorite venue for members to conduct low-key, but important business. The maître d' led them across the thickly carpeted dining room to a table adjacent to French doors overlooking Farragut Square. Frederick ordered a scotch; Stone ordered an Irish whiskey, neat.

Frederick had returned from Afghanistan the week before, where he had led a counter-insurgency operation. Stone had been on his team. The drinks came and they ordered lunch. The thick glass in the doors muted the traffic noise outside. Frederick leaned back and grinned. Whenever Frederick lifted his chin, looked down his long patrician nose, and raised his heavy brown eyebrows, Stone knew to expect a surprise.

"I have a feeling you'll enjoy an assignment to the South of France," Frederick said. "Hasn't warmed up yet, but then again, the crowds haven't arrived."

Stone rotated his drink on the white linen tablecloth. "I appreciate your thinking of me, but after Afghanistan I think I'll take a break."

"An acquaintance called me yesterday afternoon on the secure line and inquired about you. It seems his branch has a need for someone with your background. I gave you a five-star recommendation." Frederick paused. "It would be a good change for you, especially now that you're unattached—or do I say single?"

"Divorced," Stone said, repositioning the heavy silver forks to the left of the flowered china plate. "It seems I have a knack for losing partners. Marital and professional."

"Jason's death in Afghanistan wasn't your fault." Frederick leaned forward and looked intently into Stone's eyes. "You could've been the one killed on that helicopter."

"Yeah," said Stone. "Anyway, my golf game needs work. Then again, I may go out to California and try some sailing. I'd be near my two kids."

"Tee-times are hard to get in the Washington area, but the sailing is great along the Côte d'Azur." Frederick leaned back again and took a long swallow of scotch.

Stone cut into his halibut and wondered why he could never prepare fish like the chef did at the club, with a slight crust on the outside and moist within.

Frederick sliced into his filet. "I hope this meal meets with your gourmet standards. Come to think of it, you may pick up a few cooking tips in Provence."

"I think I'll stop cooking for a while. Start eating out."

"Look Hayden, it's been six months since the World Trade Center attack. The new war is the one we're fighting in Afghanistan. Firefights with a touch of the espionage game we played during the Cold War. That's the shadow war you'd go to in the South of France."

"Does sound interesting," Stone said. "However, I'm looking forward to a change."

"My understanding is they will invite you down to the Farm, beat around the bush, then ask if you'll accept the job."

Stone played with his coffee cup. "Where in the South of France?"

"Does it matter?" Frederick smiled. They both looked out the glass doors at the people hurrying along the sidewalk in the light drizzle. "Be very careful with these people," Frederick whispered. "They're nervous about what's going on over there, and nervous people make mistakes. Stay focused. And ask for a big bonus. They'll pay it."

SOUTHERN VIRGINIA—APRIL 28, 2002

The twin turboprop glided toward the deserted runway. Stone peered out the fogged window of the aged plane. Small craft dotted the Chesapeake Bay. At least one, he reckoned, was a CIA patrol boat. The plane braked to a halt and the passengers disembarked from the spartan aircraft used by the Agency to haul equipment and drop new case officers during their parachute training. Stone descended the shaky portable ladder onto the runway and breathed in the smell of Virginia pines. The sun felt warm on his face.

A nine-passenger brown van waited on the tarmac. The driver stood alone and waved them toward the open door. The group hauled their luggage from the plane. No one spoke.

For almost ten minutes, the van creaked over a macadam

road, passing isolated bungalows set back among the pine trees. An occasional pickup truck drove by. At a complex of tired-looking buildings, the driver deposited the group in front of a two-story wooden barracks. A man with a Virginia Tidewater drawl handed out room assignments, keys, and instructions on base rules and procedures. Stone also received a white sealed envelope.

His room on the second floor of the barracks reminded him of the bargain motels in Texas where he stayed when he was on the road as an FBI agent: clean, but providing only the essentials. He threw his suitcase on the bed and opened the envelope. A hand-written note told him to go to building seven. A hand-drawn map was enclosed. They expected him in an hour. He unpacked and then stretched out on the bed. With his eyes closed, he smelled barbecue cooking. The mess hall must be nearby.

After a half hour, he rose, brushed his teeth, and headed off for his meeting. The newly constructed building number seven stood alone in a pine grove. A black sedan with a Washington, DC license plate was parked in the shade. He touched the hood of the car—it felt warm, and he estimated the car had been sitting there for less than an hour.

Let's see what they have to offer, he thought as he approached the door. The only information he had about this assignment had come from Colonel Frederick during their lunch. The day after his meeting with Frederick he had received a phone call from a man who refused to identify himself and who asked whether Stone was interested in a deployment. Stone said that he would like to learn more. The same man called again an hour later and gave him instructions on when and where to meet the plane.

A gray-haired man in the brown suit who had flown on the same plane greeted him at the door. Stone recognized his voice as belonging to the caller. He led Stone down a hallway to a Secure Compartmentalized Information Facility, commonly called a SCIF. Already seated in the tight room were a large woman and two men in dark blue suits.

One of the men, pointing a gold pen, was speaking in CIA jargon. "Claudia, you should not misinterpret our coming down here to assist in the interview. We know your plate is full, and with this recent development—" He stopped, got up, and shook Stone's hand. "I'm Howard." He motioned for Stone to take a seat. Like most Agency people, he had offered only his forename, which might or might not be his true name. Stone surmised that Claudia's bosses had come down from Langley to do a bit of micromanagement.

The room's metal door sealed shut with a long hiss of air. The air-conditioner turned on as Claudia began speaking. Without making eye contact with Stone, Claudia quickly explained that the Agency had brought him to the Farm to determine his suitability for a special assignment. Then she shot off a series of questions about his knowledge of surveillance techniques and Middle East matters. Stone found it difficult to complete his answers before she fired off another query.

At last, she looked up in his direction, but not at him as FBI agents do when they look directly into the eyes of individuals they are questioning, intending to peer into the mind and psyche. She just presented an expression, with eyes unfocused, one aimed at something on his face, the other on space beyond his left ear. Her face was a vague presentation, lacking personality, similar to the faces seen when walking the corridors of Agency buildings and used to mask their identities, if not souls. With only lips moving, she asked, "Have you had a full-scope polygraph examination?"

Howard interrupted. "Claudia, that information is in his file. Let's do move on with the business at hand." He rested his elbows on the table, showing off his gold cuff links, and smiled. "Mr. Stone, are you available to go to France for up to ninety days?"

Stone nodded. He found the tension between Claudia and her superior annoying, but at last he was about to learn what they expected of him in France.

"We have a number of people scattered around Europe who sit and wait for terrorists to pass by. When the bad guys are spotted, you watch them and report their movements. That's the gist of it."

"Where in France will I be stationed?"

Howard let out a long sigh. "Ah … the South of France." He looked down at his notes, then back at Stone. "But don't expect it to be a vacation."

"I won't. I've worked for you people before." Stone leaned forward. "Sounds like a naval picket duty operation. How soon do you expect me to be on station? Will I be operating solo?"

"You don't need to know that now," Claudia said.

"Best we move quickly on this, Claudia," Howard said. "Mr. Stone, we have your background. You are right for the job. You will go to Paris, meet up with your handler, be briefed further, then be sent to your post."

"We have your plane ticket," Claudia interjected. "You leave tomorrow evening. Pack for the long haul."

"Change that ticket for two days from now," Howard said. "I told you, Claudia, tomorrow he has firearms training and the crash-and-bang course." He turned to the gray-haired man. "Please take Mr. Stone to the classroom."

"We've planned an espionage tradecraft refresher session for you," the gray-haired man mumbled.

"Just a refresher, Stone. We know you're a professional." Howard laughed. "I wish I could take the crash course with you. There's nothing more fun than banging up a government car."

"There's one more thing," Stone said. "The question of fees and expenses."

Howard took an exaggerated breath, then removed a three-page contract from his briefcase and pushed it across the table. Picking it up, Stone flipped through the pages. He crossed out the figures for his fee and expenses, carefully doubled the amounts, initialed the changes, and signed the contract. He smiled as he pushed it back to Howard, who, without looking at the new figures, said coldly, "Agreed."

As the conference room door slammed behind him, Howard was shouting, "God damn it Claudia, please try to—"

• • •

The next day's program started early in the morning. On the schedule, it was listed as a course in defensive driving. Stone went out with an instructor in an old, dented car with a well-tuned engine. The instructor made him drive at speeds exceeding one hundred miles per hour and then execute emergency turns and maneuvers. Later on, he and the instructor took turns in separate cars, trying to knock each other off the road.

After lunch in the camp mess hall, he met his firearms instructor, Mark. They drove in a twenty-year-old pickup truck to the firearms range. The sun hovered behind low-lying cloud cover, which Stone figured would dull the gun sights in long-distance shooting. The range was a basic setup, a cleared area with covered shooting positions. Shooters mounted fresh paper targets on fir stakes after each session. Old, warped tables, positioned under metal corrugated roofs, held an assortment of firearms and ammunition.

Stone felt at home. The smell of gunpowder and cordite brought back memories of his FBI training. Under J. Edgar Hoover, guns were an integral part of the FBI culture. All agents, whether a lawyer, accountant, chemist, or linguist, learned how to shoot, and trained constantly throughout their careers.

Mark was a retired CIA operative, rehired as an independent contractor. He walked with a shuffle, his light brown hair falling down onto his forehead.

The first weapon Mark handed him was an M4 assault rifle with a folding stock. Mark explained how even though the weapon was accurate at a distance of one hundred yards it had its drawbacks; very fine-grained sand caused the gun to constantly jam.

Stone smiled. "I'm not going to the Middle East. I'm going to France."

Mark frowned. "I have to make a phone call." When he returned, he said, "Let's take the M4 and the AK-47 back to the gun shack. We'll work with a nine millimeter Glock twenty-six." In the shack he also handed Stone a collapsible automatic rifle that could fold into a shoebox. "The Agency designed and fabricated this baby. A lightweight sniper gun with a Swiss telescopic sight. Takes a 7.62 mm cartridge."

Stone repeatedly fired the Glock at distances of ten, fifteen, and twenty-five yards. He never liked the modern automatics. They were reliable and sound, but guns like the Glock and Sig Sauer lacked the beauty and feel of the Smith & Wesson model 19 revolver he had trained with at Quantico.

His dislike for the weapon showed on the target. The shot holes were scattered across the paper. As Mark handed him a fresh target, he suggested Stone use a two-hand grip. He did and his shot pattern improved.

At last, Mark called a break and the two sat down on the wooden table. Stone took big swallows of water and threw the empty plastic bottle into a trashcan. "So you didn't know I was going to France?"

Mark shook his head.

"You thought I was going to the sand box?"

"The word didn't come down to me that you were the replacement for that young fellow who got killed in France." He slid the bolt action of the sniper gun back and forth. "With all that's going on here, sometimes there's a breakdown in the communication chain."

So, he was replacing someone who was killed. No wonder Howard hadn't flinched when he doubled his fee. Stone waited for Mark to continue.

"I trained that guy in firearms right here. About three months ago."

A seagull cried over the bay. As Mark adjusted the telescopic sight on the gun, he said in a near whisper, "As you know, he was poisoned last week in Nice. So I guess Paris Station will insist you go down there with a sidearm."

It paid to sit and listen. One found out all sorts of information. Stone picked up another bottle of water off the table. "Now that sniper gun you're holding … what's that all about?"

He grinned. "They didn't tell you much, did they?"

"Enough to get me here."

"This is what I know." Mark handed him the sniper gun.

"If certain people from the Middle East pass through your bailiwick down there in the South of France and there isn't time to send in an Ops team to grab them, you're going to be told to take them out."

The two stared at the targets dotted with bullet holes. Mark looked at his watch. "Time for me to check in with my wife." He slid off the table and instructed Stone to break down the sniper gun and then reassemble it. "Oh, I just heard. Another officer got killed. In the town of Montpellier."

As Mark walked away, he called back. "Pull a Colt .45 and some ammo from the shed. See how it feels. If you can get hold of an old Army Colt over there, get one. They pack more punch than any nine millimeter."

"A Colt .45 automatic. Now that's my gun of choice," Stone said. Especially since he didn't know what he was walking into.

CHAPTER FOUR

PARIS—APRIL 30, 2002

The plane from Dulles International Airport touched down at Paris Roissy Charles De Gaulle into a soft, misty French morning. Stone passed through the airport arrival formalities, claimed his luggage, and then hailed a cab. Outside the terminal, the moist chill surprised him; after all, it was April. He tried his French on the taxi driver, who hinted the hotel would be difficult to locate. Stone said he doubted it since the hotel was located in the First Arrondissement, a well-known neighborhood. The driver glared in the rearview mirror, then returned to maneuvering through the rush-hour traffic.

The drive into Paris was not as bad as the last time when he'd visited with his ex-wife. That had been a quick trip. They had both hoped it would restart their marriage. It hadn't. All week it rained. His one good memory of the trip was an excellent spinach soufflé at a restaurant near the American Embassy.

An upscale kitchen supply store and an antique map shop flanked the narrow hotel entrance door. Outside the establishment, people and cars clogged the narrow street. Workers unloaded trucks parked halfway over the stone curb; other Parisians hurried to their jobs elsewhere. Insults in French, accompanied by hand gestures, answered car horns. Stone lifted his luggage up the entrance steps, but had to give way to a group of Americans exiting for a morning bus tour of Paris. He smelled coffee brewing, turned, and saw a brasserie across the street, where he knew he'd find delicious pastries and rolls. Paris churned in the morning light. Too bad he had to leave the next day.

After checking in at the reception desk, he crammed his bags into the tight elevator and creaked up to the third floor, where he settled into his equally confining room. After unpacking he set off for the American Embassy. Pausing on the front steps of the hotel, he looked over at the brasserie. It looked tempting, but his contact at the embassy wanted to meet for lunch. Rue Saint-Honoré was down the street to the left, and it would take him to the embassy.

The street life of Paris fascinated him. People hurried along the narrow sidewalk and shopkeepers occupied themselves with their chores. Young fathers in business suits held their chattering children's hands as they headed for a school located in a grey 18th century building.

The American Embassy sat off the busy Place de la Concorde, where rush-hour traffic sped around the huge plaza. Uniformed police stood beside barricades in front of the embassy with compact machine guns dangling from their shoulders. Stone had to show his passport to a French policeman before he was allowed to pass.

At the gate, a white guardhouse served as a pedestrian checkpoint. Inside, he asked the on-duty US Marine, a lance corporal in a crisp khaki blouse, to call his CIA contact at the embassy, Charles Fleming. The Marine instructed him to wait in the guardhouse.

Five minutes later, Fleming pushed through the heavy security door. He came up to Stone, took his arm, and with a smile, led him out the door. "Let's do lunch."

A middle-aged African-American wearing French designer glasses, Fleming seemed not to have the time to adjust his tie, or perhaps he thought such things unimportant. He led Stone out onto Avenue Gabriel, then stopped under the tall plane trees.

Fleming groaned, "This terrorist business has really changed embassy life. Lucky for us the French have placed the police here full time." He pointed to two green-blue buses parked a few yards away. They resembled armored American school buses.

Stone detected that something was amiss. The purposeful stride of the Parisians he had noted while walking to the embassy was absent. People dashed from the square toward the side streets. Then riot police jumped out of the two buses, assembled, and in a phalanx, slow-marched toward the square. Shouts and commotion came from the direction of the Metro entrance, from which people waving banners and placards were spilling out.

"Well, we're not going to a restaurant in that direction," Fleming said. "Quick, before the cops tell us to go back inside the embassy."

The two hurried across the avenue onto the strip of park that paralleled the Champs Elysées, their dress shoes crunching on the soft gravel path. Fleming motioned to slow down, and they turned toward the roar. Demonstrators poured across the square, disrupting traffic and banging cars and trucks with stakes and rocks. They advanced toward the police line that looked too thin to hold back a mob.

"What the hell's going on?" Stone asked.

"North Africans in from the *banlieues*, the suburbs. I guess they've decided to burn some cars here instead of in their own neighborhoods for a change."

Stone found himself walking backward along the path watching the demonstrators. "Are they pissed off at Americans?"

"Of course, but today they're more pissed at the French authorities. They have no jobs." Fleming looked around. "They're probably heading for the Presidential palace, which is in our direction. Let's go before they catch up." Fleming steered him toward a white, elaborately designed building gracing the park. "That's our restaurant."

The employees at the door of the restaurant were locking up in preparation for the coming horde, but Fleming talked their way beyond the glass doors. He leaned close to Stone's ear. "This is the Pavillon Elysée, one of the hidden jewels of Paris and only a few steps away from the embassy. Great food."

The noise, the color, and motion fascinated Stone. "Let's stand at the door and watch."

"Careful of flying glass. I'll get us a nice table and come back." Fleming asked a waiter whether given the commotion they could still get lunch. The Frenchman appeared nonplussed with the riot outside the restaurant. "*Certainement.*"

Stone watched the rioters, mostly male, bob in and out of the clutches of the police. An individual in a hooded sweatshirt made an ill-timed turn into the arms of two policemen, who threw him to the ground. One clubbed at the man's backpack while the other ground the man's face into the gravel.

"If there are any gasoline bottles in that bag they'll break," Fleming said, who now stood behind Stone. "I think we're safe here."

Only one other table in the establishment was occupied. At the far side of the room two French businessmen, impeccably dressed, talked in low voices with quick hand gestures. Chrome and slate tables covered with pale blue tablecloths stiff with starch held blue vases with two white flowers placed in the center. Muted light came from the skylights above.

"This is probably the best place for us to talk and not be overheard." Fleming smiled. "And as I said, the food is great."

Fleming chose the Paris Deauville—a salad with crabmeat, prawns, apples, and grapefruit. Stone ordered the Paris Oslo, smoked Norwegian salmon in a salad with horseradish.

"I see the menu interests you," Fleming said. "You've come to the right place."

"The cuisine of Provence interests me. I hope to pick up some tips while I'm down there."

"Oh, I see. Someone has already told you where you're headed. Well, just remember to keep your wits about you. Young Barrett Huntington didn't and—" Fleming's eyes clouded.

Stone let a few minutes pass while Fleming took a sip from his water glass. Finally, Fleming gathered himself then whispered, "Your cover is a travel writer. We managed to get you a three-month fellowship at the Foundation d'Élan, an arts institution in Archos, a village near Marseille."

However, being sent out under his true name and not a false identity worried Stone. "What if someone took my picture when I came to the embassy?"

The shouting diminished outside the restaurant. Fleming

looked toward the door. "I think the demonstrators are moving on." He turned back to Stone. "You're a writer sponsored by the American government, so you would naturally stop by and check in."

He went on to discuss his light cover as a writer, details of emergency contacts, arrangements for funds during Stone's stay, and his car in Archos. "You'll receive additional instructions at our meeting in Provence next week."

Carefully choosing his words, Stone asked, "So, what are the details on the death of the fellow in Nice?"

An explosion went off nearby, a muffled pop. It didn't sound like any high explosive Stone recognized.

Fleming looked past Stone. "Molotov cocktail … sounds like they're near the Presidential palace. My wife and I really looked forward to this assignment." With a resigned expression, he gazed down at the table and ran his finger around the edge. "I guess you have to take the good with the bad. Are you married?"

"No longer, but I have two kids. Both in college." He waited for Fleming to answer his question about the murdered officer.

"My wife and I have two kids, also. Getting off the African circuit was a blessing. Here in Paris we have better schools and we don't have to worry about our kids catching malaria, but then this latest problem with two murders—the one in Nice and the other one in Montpellier…"

The waiter came with their meals and poured the wine. Fleming spoke to him in rapid French. He bowed and moved on to another table.

"Who was the officer in Montpellier? And do we have any leads? Do you think the same person murdered the officer in Nice?"

"We have the whole gamut of usual suspects." Fleming forked a prawn from his salad. "The primary suspect in Huntington's death—that's the fellow you're replacing—is a man by the name of Hassan. The female officer in Montpellier was not really tracking any particular individual. She was working on an industrial chemical project. Her spotting function was a secondary duty. Her death is really puzzling."

"So where's Hassan?"

"We've lost track of him. The French are searching for him, too. They're being cooperative. Of course, we do well on the working level with French intelligence. We leave policy and bombast to our superiors."

Stone now heard only faint noises in the distance. He wondered what was burning from that Molotov cocktail. The restaurant had reopened and patrons rushed in talking about the riot. He looked at Fleming. "Do you have a photo of this Hassan or any other information on him?"

"After lunch, back in the office, I'll show you the photos." He continued in a lower tone. "Hassan came in from Marbella on the Italian Riviera. Our people from Milan passed him off in Nice. Huntington followed him around for about a week."

Stone matched the lower level of Fleming's voice. "Did he provide a report of his activities in Nice?"

"He sent us regular reports by e-mail. By the way, you're getting a laptop computer yourself. I'll show you how to transmit your reports securely."

They left the restaurant, and instead of going back into the embassy, they walked around the Place de la Concorde. The acrid smell of tear gas lingered in the air. Parisians had returned to their routines. On the crowded sidewalk near the Hotel Crillon, Stone bumped into an old FBI friend, Jonathan Deville. It had been a year since they'd last met. After a few moments of banter, Deville gave him his telephone number and they agreed to get together.

Stone and Fleming continued down the street. Fleming asked how he knew Deville and, not waiting for a reply, added, "Deville's the FBI's Legal Attaché here in Paris. Now I suppose I'll have to tell him something about your connection with the Agency." He sighed. "You never know if the Bureau can keep a secret."

They turned onto the Rue Saint-Florentin and then through the security checkpoint at the Hotel Talleyrand. The

American Embassy owned the historic building and used it as an annex. Fleming explained that for security reasons most of the American staff had moved to other locations throughout the city. The two walked through the high-ceilinged lobby and passed by visitors attending the annual embassy art show. They rode the elevator to the basement level and Fleming led him through narrow hallways. The smell of heating oil hung in the air. Machinery hummed behind green doors. As they turned a corner, a number of heavy metal doors with narrow grilled windows came into view.

"That's where the Nazis put important *résistance* prisoners." Fleming stopped and opened one of the doors. "During World War II the Talleyrand building was Gestapo Headquarters in Paris."

The cell could hold two people. Stone thought he smelled a hint of sweat and urine, but decided it was only his imagination. They continued down the hallway and came to a door with a black spin dial lock. Fleming spun the combination and pulled open the door. "Our version of a SCIF," he said.

The air inside the room was stale. Stone sat at a grey metal table while Fleming went to retrieve Hassan's dossier. Returning with the folder, a laptop computer, and a cellphone, Fleming instructed him to look through the file while he went back to his office to make a phone call to Washington.

As Fleming left, the door to the hallway opened and a woman with pale-blonde hair wearing a well-cut taupe suit entered. She stopped and looked down at Stone, searching his face with her green eyes. She wore no rings on her left hand.

"You must be Hayden Stone. I arranged for your cover at the Foundation d'Élan. You're a travel writer, who writes under the name of Finbarr Costanza. I suggest you assume a passive role at the foundation. Don't get too chummy with the people there. Maybe grow a beard."

"How come I don't have an alias?"

"No time to go through the backstopping process. Our people at Langley are overwhelmed." She looked Stone up and down. "In situations like yours, it's easier to get on the Internet, block all references to your FBI background, then create some about your writing career." She frowned. "Hope you enjoy your stay on the Riviera."

Hurrying to one of the side rooms, she sat down with her back to him, and turned on a large screen computer. He opened the file folder, and then looked back at the blonde through the open door. Where had she come up with the name Finbarr?

In the file, he learned that Hassan's true name was unknown. His Gulf State passport listed him as Hassan Musab Mujahid. An asset in Beirut reported he was born in one of the refugee camps in southern Lebanon and he spoke with a Palestinian accent. Members of the Shiite terrorist organization Hezbollah referred to him as Abdul Fahad. He attended a university in Basra, Iraq. The photographs showed a well-groomed man in his early forties. Pockmarked cheeks touched the edges of his thick black mustache. His eyes looked empty.

Fleming returned and dropped into a chair across from him. He scribbled a few notes on a yellow legal pad then looked up at Stone. "Did you meet my boss at Headquarters? Ms. Claudia?"

Stone smiled.

"I won't bore you with the conversation I just had with her, except to say you're under orders not to get yourself dead. At least not until I get my ass out of here." Fleming closed his eyes and smiled. "*Comprendez?*"

Stone held up Barrett Huntington's reports. "These are just routine surveillance logs. Did Huntington ever relay any concerns for his safety? Did he come up with any contacts that Hassan met in Nice?"

"His reports are pretty ... thin, but remember this was his first assignment," Fleming frowned. "And no, he never indicated he felt in anyway threatened. It was a light one-man surveillance. We have dozens of these going on in France alone."

"Yes, I understand. Before I forget, there is mention here of a yacht Hassan boarded in Nice harbor. Any follow-up on that?"

"It belongs to a Saudi prince. Real rich and real religious."

"A Shiite hobnobbing with a Sunni?" Stone asked. "Ever since the schism a thousand years ago, the two have been at each others' throats."

Fleming lifted his hands. "Don't know about that, but there is one thing not in the folder that the French told us. Probably doesn't mean anything, but at the same time Huntington's body was found, the bodies of two Algerians, a man and a woman, were found two blocks away." He rose and stepped to the door of his office. "Read over the file again while I check my email."

Picking up a pencil, Stone began making doodles on a legal pad. He wondered whether Fleming had a handle on the operation. Had he done his homework? After what he had said about doubting that Jonathan Deville and the FBI could keep a secret, either Fleming didn't know Stone was a retired Bureau agent or he didn't care. Maybe he had too much on his mind. He recalled Frederick's remark in Washington about how nervous people make mistakes. At lunch, Stone had begun to feel uneasy about the assignment. Already two CIA officers had been killed and the killer or killers were still loose. Was someone planning for him to be next on the list?

CHAPTER FIVE

CÔTE D'AZUR—MAY 1, 2002

An hour out of Paris, settled in a first-class seat on the high-speed TGV train from Paris to Marseille, Stone folded his newspaper and admired the French countryside. Now and then, he spotted villages hosting centuries-old stone churches and chateaux. In the pastures, white Charolais cattle grazed on the lush grass. The pastoral scene and slow rocking of the train relaxed him. His fellow passengers in the carriage, mostly middle-aged French couples, buried themselves in their newspapers and books.

For the first time since his divorce, Stone began to enjoy the relaxed state that comes with having to care only for oneself, especially when traveling. Was it a passing euphoria—or one of the steps in a final separation?

Stone reached into his travel bag and took out a tour book on Provence. The previous night in Paris, he had purchased the stiff green-covered book at W. H. Smith on the Rue de Rivoli before walking to his favorite café, tucked in an alley two blocks from the Louvre. Having a book to read made him feel less self-conscious when eating alone. The meal had been good; he'd especially enjoyed the escargot, moist with a lot of garlic. Nothing like immersing himself in the French lifestyle to get his mind off unpleasant personal matters like a divorce.

He had been staring toward the end of the carriage when he detected a man, about twenty-five with short, medium-brown hair, studying him from five rows away. The man wore a collared shirt under a dark-blue, textured sweater. Stone had seen young French intelligence agents like him a few years before on a trip to Bordeaux. The French used rookies to tail low-level targets, which he now assumed he was. The young man looked away with almost an embarrassed look.

Stone returned to flipping through the pages of his tour book. Through past experience he knew if he were under surveillance, there would be at least two agents on the team. The other agent probably would be about the same age as this fellow. Stone placed the book on the seat next to him and rose. He turned and faced the other end of the car, then started for the lavatory. In the seat directly behind him sat a young brunette who abruptly turned her head toward the window. Stone passed her and went into the *toilette*. He washed his hands and wiped his face with the wet towel. He balanced himself as the train swayed. Easing the door open, he saw the brunette pulling a valise from the overhead rack. Meantime, she peered forward over the backrest as if examining the items Stone had left on his seat.

Stone slipped out of the restroom and came up behind her. Startled, she shoved the valise back into the rack. As she eased herself back into her seat, Stone looked down, smiled, and asked in French, "When will the coffee cart pass by?" She gave a startled shrug. Stone's daughter attending college in California was not much younger than this junior officer. At that moment the snack cart came crashing through the door and Stone said, "Aha. There it is." He took his seat. The young man who had been sitting in front of him had disappeared.

When the cart approached, Stone ordered coffee and a baguette sandwich with thinly sliced ham and cheese. Munching his snack, he reasoned it was natural that he would be under surveillance. Fleming and he had had lunch the day before in a restaurant close to the embassy, and surely the French knew Fleming was intelligence. Despite Stone's cover as a writer sponsored by the American embassy, and despite the fact that he should meet Fleming who was the embassy's cultural attaché for that program, a competent intelligence service would double check. Then again, the French had a lot more on their plates than to investigate some second-rate writer. No. They must have picked up some pattern he had provided them. Maybe his Paris hotel had been used too often by the Agency. Maybe the

Agency had used the Foundation in Archos once too often for cover purposes. Anyway, with these two green agents assigned to him, the French obviously didn't consider him all that important. Good.

An hour later, the train eased into the Marseille station. Stone lugged his two suitcases down from the carriage onto the platform, looked up, and took in the open expanse of the building. Pigeons flapped overhead under the high glass ceiling. Shafts of sunlight angled down on the passengers waiting in the staging area.

Ricard, the driver from the Foundation d'Élan, an older man without a smile, wearing a tweed jacket and nondescript tie, found him at the station entrance. The rosette in his lapel identified him as a veteran of some French military action. Walking from the station to the Renault sedan, Stone didn't detect surveillance. He had either been turned over to more seasoned agents or the surveillance had been paused. No matter. He would ignore them for the time being.

The city of Marseille proved an initial disappointment. The buildings looked neglected, and the streets needed sweeping. Too shabby, Stone judged. However, his mood changed a few minutes outside the city, with glimpses of the sea and a whiff of salty air. By the time the car passed through the Foundation gate at Archos, Stone had absorbed the warmth and earthy smells of Provence. The estate stretched over five acres along a limestone cliff in sight of the fishing village of Archos. Ricard led him to his cottage. Despite a severe limp, he insisted on carrying the largest of Stone's bags.

A tidy flower garden bracketed the front door of the cottage. Stone paused and caught the familiar fragrance of jasmine, last remembered from a stay in San Diego. He pushed open the pale blue door and walked into a bright, open living area. The first floor had a dining alcove, a comfortable kitchen, and a sitting area furnished with blond wooden furniture. A porcelain vase filled with fresh peonies sat on the dining table.

He smiled. Everything was tastefully arranged; even his former wife would be stretched to find fault with the décor.

Upstairs he unpacked his suitcases and enjoyed a long shower. Afterward, he stepped through the French doors onto the balcony. The manicured lawn below extended to a line of bent pine trees that partially concealed the sparkling indigo Mediterranean. Noisy yellow and red birds zipped between the buildings of the Foundation. This had to be one of his best assignments. Then again, what appeared too good to be true usually was.

He had to keep in mind that the man he replaced was murdered. Barrett Huntington had been a rookie, but the kill had the touch of a professional. Worse, the Agency could only guess the assassin's identity, and they had no clue as to what had provoked Huntington's murder. Stone would mind Fleming's warning back in Paris, to keep on his toes.

The wicker chair creaked when he leaned back and lifted his feet onto the balcony railing. Here in Archos, he would read a novel or two but, for cover purposes, he would write. Not bad. Much better than going back into the mountains of Afghanistan, wearing panty hose under his trousers so he wouldn't get saddle burns riding the short Afghan horses all day.

His daydream ended abruptly with a knock on the downstairs door and a mellow voice. "Hello there, new colleague. Welcome to Élan."

Stone went downstairs, opened the door, and was greeted with, "Welcome, dear Finbarr Costanza. Of course, that's not your name, just your *nom de plume*. My name is David. I'm the resident scholar on Esperanto." David's eyes searched Stone's. "The universal language?"

Stone detected a Chicago accent and inhaled a strong whiff of cologne. A slightly built, blond-haired man wearing a khaki sport coat and matching creased walking shorts stood before him. His skinny legs were planted sockless in a pair of worn boat shoes. His blue eyes searched for some response.

After a moment's pause, Stone presented a grin and a handshake.

David took a deep breath and unbuttoned his jacket. "Am I the first to greet you and your—" He looked around. "Are you single?"

"Recently divorced, and I intend to stay that way."

"Sorry. Understand. Don't mean to intrude. I just stopped by to see if I could be of any help." David started to move away from the door.

"That's very kind of you," Stone tried to say in a soft tone. Fleming had cautioned him that among artists he should appear to be sensitive. "Where and when do we eat around here?"

"God, Hayden. May I call you Hayden? Didn't the staff tell you anything? I'll be glad to pass by and accompany you to the dining room. Dinner starts at seven, but cocktails are at six. That's where you'll meet all our interesting people."

"I would enjoy a cocktail. What's the dress code?"

"Riviera casual, and I know you writers enjoy your libations."

Stone watched the man walk away. David had a bounce to his step as if he had found a new friend.

For his initial appearance before his fellow scholars, Stone selected a pair of white linen slacks, an Italian silk shirt, and tan loafers. He wondered whether the CIA had placed any other operatives at the Foundation. When he had posed that question to Fleming in Paris, he received a noncommittal shrug. If he had time, he might play a harmless version of Spot the Spook; the frivolous game practiced by some American Foreign Service people to expose intelligence officers assigned to the embassies. Sometimes their pranks resulted in dire consequences when the cover of those intelligence officers was blown. On second thought, he would just concentrate on his assignment. Besides, odds were the French had planted someone there feeding them information.

A few minutes before six, David dropped by the cottage and the two walked across the grounds toward the dining hall. David pointed out the various buildings and displayed a good knowledge of not only the Foundation's history, but also the backgrounds of the fellowship holders in residence. The community, Stone realized, was not large. Keeping his identity secret would be a challenge.

A woman with short, light-brown hair came from the direction of the administration building and crossed their path. She headed toward the swimming pool. He admired her long tanned legs. An unbuttoned, gauzy shift allowed brief glimpses of a white bikini. She threw them a quick look, nodded at David, then slipped her sunglasses down on her nose. Hayden grinned, recognizing what he considered her very French gesture.

"Hayden, you did say you're single, right?"

Now Stone chuckled.

"That little number is Margaux. She's not one of the Fellows. She's a local French gal who works in the library, so you two will be working together a lot." David motioned for them to take the path to the right. "Also, if you're thinking what I think you're thinking, be forewarned. In the past four months, I've seen two very hearty males, both noted painters as well as accomplished swordsmen, depart for home sorely defeated in their efforts to seduce that fair maiden."

"Perhaps she doesn't care for the artsy crowd."

"She doesn't care for Americans. I don't know why she continues to work here, especially with the exchange rate going south. Then again, few of the French like Americans these days, which delights some of our left-leaning American colleagues." David stopped and turned to Stone. "Hope I didn't offend you. No more politics from me. You'll get enough from some of the people you're about to meet."

"Don't worry, and thanks for sharing your insights."

Climbing the slate stairs to the open patio, Stone looked down on the late-afternoon pastel-colored expanse of the Bay of Archos. Tree-spotted limestone mountains provided a backdrop for the small port with its marina of fishing and pleasure boats. About twenty people in little groups were standing on the patio with drinks in hand, talking softly.

Stone followed David to the nearest grouping. All heads turned toward Stone, the eyes taking in first impressions. As

David made the introductions, Stone attempted to attach names with faces, but after the fifth try, he switched to concentrating on his smile and varying his banal exchanges. When his new colleagues learned he wrote travel stories, they lost interest in him and returned to discussing their own personal artistic issues and challenges. He would use his role as a travel writer, if such a role existed, to blend into the background.

David elbowed him. "That's Boswell Harrington, our esteemed director, who just arrived with his wife. She's quite a handful. He must have hurried back from Nice for something important." David paused. "We'll let him come over and introduce himself. For some reason, he thinks that makes him one of the common folk."

Harrington and his wife glided across the patio exchanging pleasantries with the fellows. When the two paused to speak with a particularly serious-looking group, Stone caught Harrington studying him. Then he leaned over and whispered to his wife. The two left the group and came over to Stone and David.

"Hello and a big welcome, Hayden," he said in a plummy Bostonian accent. "I'm Boswell and this is my wife, Helen." The woman, fighting middle age, wore her pitch-black hair in a bob. Her bright red lipstick overwhelmed a white bland face. "Sorry I wasn't here to greet you upon your arrival." Harrington smiled and looked away. "We had some business up the coast."

Harrington's blond hair, combed back, touched the collar of his dark blazer. The ascot tucked beneath his French blue shirt told Stone that the man welcomed attention.

"Hayden, you come highly recommended by our people in New York." He continued to search the gathering. "I'll have to read some of your work. Meantime, I'll leave you with David, whom I'm sure will tell you all about his very interesting project."

The Harringtons marched off across the patio, stopping to chat with two young women, both braless, wearing sheer white blouses.

"*Kio a kompleta mistifiki,*" David muttered.

"Excuse me?"

"It's Esperanto for 'What a complete ass.'"

Stone grinned. *"Moi?"*

"Of course not. Harrington's the fool … or a fox, I'm not quite sure which."

Stone smiled. Not exactly a congenial group. Best he blend into the woodwork.

The white-coated waiter emerged from the dining room door and announced dinner was being served. Once inside, David hurried off to another table, leaving Stone to sit with the Harringtons and three other Foundation fellows. The Harringtons ate silently. Boswell, his face masked in a slight smile, let his gaze dart around the table from one person to another. Stone had the feeling Harrington didn't consider him important. One of the two young women at the table monopolized the conversation with a not-too-subtle pitch for a two-month extension to her grant. Stone found the meal more interesting than the company.

After dinner, Stone took a stroll along the edge of the grounds, admiring the lights of Archos twinkling across the bay. In the morning, he would explore the town. The cool evening air refreshed him, and as he approached his cottage, he thought he'd relax and listen to some music.

"Mr. Stone?"

He spun around, taking a combat stance.

"Pardon, Monsieur. I did not mean to startle you." The old driver was holding a large parcel. "This arrived during the meal time. I thought it best to wait until after your dinner."

"Thank you, Ricard."

The package was heavy.

"You are a veteran?" asked Stone.

"Oui."

"So am I."

"Bon soir, Monsieur." Ricard touched his hat and left.

Once inside the cottage, Stone switched on the recessed ceiling lights, flooding the interior in a soft yellow glow. At night, the accommodations seemed even more welcoming than in daylight. He placed the package on a table and noticed the French postage. One of Colonel Frederick's pseudonyms appeared on the return label. Carefully, he opened the parcel and unwrapped a pair of litre bottles of Irish whiskey from tissue paper. A box of Cuban Montecristo cigars lay beneath with a note that read:

Thought you would need a Care Package to pull you through your assignment.

It was unsigned. Beneath the cigars lay a blue velvet bag. Inside Stone found an old, but prime, Colt .45 automatic and a box of fifty rounds of hollow-point ammunition.

Back to business. He'd hide the Colt with the Glock Fleming had given him.

David felt a slight glow as he sat at his desk. The two glasses of wine at dinner had hit the spot. Just one more half-glass and he would head for bed. No more Esperanto tonight. He poured some red wine just as two hard knocks sounded on the front door. Probably that new fellow Stone locked himself out of his cottage. David opened the door and saw Harrington with the Algerian.

"Still up, David? Good, thank you for inviting me in." Harrington pushed him aside and entered the room. The Algerian blocked David's escape.

"What can I do for you, Boswell?" David stepped back. He had witnessed Harrington's flushed cheeks and half-squinted eyes before.

"I've been waiting for your report, you little twerp." Harrington moved over to the desk spread with papers and flipped some pages to the floor. "Is this the crap you're working on?"

David hurried over and retrieved his papers. When he stood up, Harrington took him by the collar. The Algerian smiled, and David saw a bright gold incisor among yellow, broken teeth.

"What have you learned about Ricard? Did you follow him like I told you?"

"He is a harmless old man. He does nothing out of the ordinary. Just drives the Foundation's car and delivers packages." David tried to move away. "I told you that before."

Harrington shoved him against the desk. Losing his balance, David fell to the floor with a groan. "Why did you do that?" he gasped.

"It gives me pleasure." Harrington pushed back his hair from his forehead and pulled a cigar from his jacket. He struck a match and held it under the end of the cigar.

"Please, don't smoke that thing. You know I have allergies."

"How do you say 'fuck off' in Esperanto?"

Harrington puffed on the cigar and threw the lit match onto the papers on the desk. David leaped up and slapped the burning match with his hand.

"Lucky for you, I don't have time to stay longer." Harrington walked toward the door and Gold Tooth opened it for him. "Something else I want you to do, you little shit. Find out all you can about this writer, Stone."

CHAPTER SIX

CÔTE D'AZUR—MAY 2, 2002

Bright sunshine spilled through Stone's bedroom windows. He considered turning over and going back to sleep, but the fresh air blowing in from the sea convinced him to stretch and roll out of bed. At the open second-floor window, he leaned out and heard, then spotted, four black ducks sailing by in tight formation. The rich smell of coffee wafted up, and looking down he saw a silver tray covered with a white linen cloth lying outside the front door. Nice touch.

The round iron table with matching chairs on the patio off the kitchen seemed like the perfect place to enjoy breakfast. Coffee, very black, along with crunchy French rolls still warm inside and slathered with rich butter made for a great start to the day. A copy of the *International Herald Tribune* sat on the tray. He scanned the headlines, then set it aside. No real need to be current on the news. Why not just slip into a casual Mediterranean mode?

He took in the scenery, then stopped and said quietly, "Wrong." In the past few weeks, two CIA operatives had been killed. Had they let their guard down? Maybe he needed a shot of paranoia. What about David? He was a bit too friendly. Stone dabbed some jam on a roll. Maybe he was an outsider in a group of outsiders and he needed a friend. Stone could use him as a source of information here at the Foundation, but still he had to be cautious.

As Stone drank his second cup of coffee, he debated whether to stroll down to the village of Archos or drop by the library and give some show of starting a writing project. The arrival of Margaux put an end to his quandary. Dressed in a beige pant suit, she crossed the lawn toward him.

"*Bonjour*, Mr. Stone. Mr. Harrington asked me to drop by to say he is available for your welcome meeting." She inspected his pajamas then looked down at his bare feet.

"Please, call me Hayden." Her tan complexion indicated time spent outdoors.

She didn't smile, just hesitated as if to make sure she phrased properly what she was about to say. "The director is available now, but of course, you are not dressed."

"Would a half hour do?" She wore tan soft leather shoes that matched the brown leather buttons on her jacket.

"He must travel to Marseille this morning, so if you would be prompt. Please."

"Okay. I'll head over after I've showered and shaved." Stone downed the last of his coffee. "After my meeting, I'll see you in the library."

She tipped her head slightly, and then headed back toward the administration building. Her hips had a gentle sway and he guessed she knew he noticed.

Harrington's office was neat and orderly. Stone had expected some degree of academic clutter, with papers and books strewn about the desk and tables. Two large glass doors led out onto a private garden. They flanked an open fireplace decorated with blue Provençal tiles. The faint smell of an expensive cigar, perhaps smoked the night before, lingered in the room. Harrington was reading his e-mail on a laptop and waved for Stone to take a seat. He wore a dark pinstriped suit with a light blue tie. A gold signet ring on his right little finger reflected the sunlight.

"Well, Hayden, have you found everything to your satisfaction?" He shut down his computer. "Your accommodations pleasant?" He glanced at his gold watch.

"Very much so, Mr.—"

"Boswell … Boswell. We don't stand on formality here." He fumbled around his desk and found his car keys. "I had the chance to look through your latest work. Your travel to Yemen. Quite fascinating." His eyes looked up to the ceiling as if pondering a deep thought. "You don't strike me as one of those 'driven' travel writers like that fellow Bruce Chatwin. More on the order of Waugh or perhaps Graham Greene, just looking for a change in scene."

"Well, I just try to write what I—"

"Yes, yes. Seems your publisher gave you a nice advance, so you'll be busy getting that new book out, right?" Harrington winked, then in a confidential tone, "My job is to know all about the Fellows studying here. Listen, I must be off to a business meeting. This director's job is ninety-nine percent keeping the funds flowing, if you know what I mean." Harrington jumped up and headed for the door.

"Thanks for the welcome, Boswell."

Harrington stopped as if he'd forgotten something. "Oh, and by the way, there's a cocktail party tonight at the American consul general's villa in Marseille. That fellow from the embassy, Fleming, asked me to invite you." He winked. "Fleming is an important person for our Foundation. Very important. He has good connections with the money people in New York." He hurried out of the door ahead of Stone and started toward to his Mercedes, then looked back. "Oh, Hayden … black tie. You did bring formal wear?"

"Never leave home without it."

A cleaning woman passed Stone as he entered the cozy library. Bookcases lined two of the walls and there were more book-laden shelves in an adjoining room. The room smelled fresh, but with a comfortable hint of old books. In a side office, Margaux took off her reading glasses and rose from her chair. She walked over and handed him a book. "It is strange you'd want to read your own book," she said.

"I want to make sure they put all the commas in the right places."

She tried a smile while leading him to a long wooden table

with a brass lamp sitting in the middle. As he sat down, she excused herself then hurried out of the room carrying a stack of books.

The book she had handed to him had his name under the title, or rather his *nom de plume*, and a picture of the Marib Dam in Yemen on the cover. Some scholars believed the Queen of Sheba built the dam during the Biblical time of Solomon. The water stored by the huge structure accounted for Roman records of a fertile land in ancient times. Arabia Felix they had called it, where now desert spread for miles. The CIA ghostwriters at Langley impressed him. It had taken them only a few weeks to put the book together and place it in the Foundation's library. Stone had worked in Yemen two years before. Whoever decided to compile this book wanted to stay on territory familiar to him.

On the inside of the dust jacket, he found his photograph and a short biography. It read that he had been a history teacher at a Norbertine Preparatory School in Delaware and enjoyed travel and adventure. Well, the travel and adventure part was on the mark. The photograph came from one of the Agency files. His associate at the time, Tanya, had taken the photograph when they visited Marib. He flipped through the pages then became aware that Margaux had returned to her desk.

Stone plugged his laptop computer into the receptacle next to the lamp and clicked on the Internet icon. Finding no e-mail messages from his two children, he cleared out his junk mail and checked the stock market. He still didn't have the means to send Fleming a secure communication. He would remind him tonight at the consul general's party.

His wristwatch indicated noon. He called over to Margaux, "Do you know a good place to eat in town?"

"Sorry," she said, and without looking at him, got up and left the library again. David stood at the door as she passed by.

When he reached Stone's table, David grinned. "She knew where that line of questioning was going. Listen, she gets hit on all the time."

Stone feigned innocence, but David was right. He found Margaux interesting and he had wanted to have lunch with her.

"Come on, I'll show you around town."

• • •

Reaching the Archos waterfront, David pointed the way along the narrow quay next to small fishing and pleasure boats tied up and bobbing in the water. A row of four-story townhouses, some façades refaced, looked over the harbor. Cafés and shops occupied the ground levels, and table and chair settings extended from their entrances onto the walkway. Fishermen hauled fresh fish from their boats and passed them to cooks wearing stained white aprons. Harbor smells mingled with the scents coming from the kitchens. David pointed to a restaurant with a bright red awning and said he favored the lunches there.

"Let's make sure we sit in the shade," Stone said. "I forgot my hat."

They agreed on a table and ordered drinks and sandwiches. Stone began watching customers whom he assumed were regular patrons heading for their favorite tables. Their only concern appeared to be what was on the daily menu. On the walkway, two Scandinavian blondes giggled by. Damn, Stone realized. While he rode the crowded morning Metro in Washington, these people were enjoying themselves like this every day. He looked over at David. "You know, my grandfather used to say he didn't care how long he lived, as long as it was in a nice place."

"Where did he live?" David asked.

"Philadelphia."

"Your grandfather and W. C. Fields?" David then pointed to a burly man speaking to a seated couple. The man wore a white silk shirt and tan slacks. A heavy gold bracelet hung from his left wrist. "That gentleman is Margaux's father. He owns this place and a vineyard nearby. So, what do you think of him?"

"Looks like he carries some weight in this town," Stone answered as the waiter set their sandwiches on the table. "By the way, I had my meeting with Harrington this morning."

David took a gulp of iced tea and murmured, "How did it go?"

"He seemed a little preoccupied. Had to rush off to a business matter in Marseille."

"He's been running up and down the coast lately." David leaned back in his chair. "At first, some of the fellows thought the Foundation was in trouble, but it seems most of the business he's conducting is of a personal nature."

The lunch finished, and as they were in the process of splitting the bill, Charles Fleming approached their table. "Glad I spotted you two here. Mind if I join you?" As usual, Fleming's tie was loosened. He appeared distracted.

"Have a seat, Mr. Fleming," David said. "What a pleasure. Down from Paris to check up on us?"

"Just drove down to check on an embassy-sponsored delegation at an institute in Marseille, so I decided to pop over and see how my scholars were doing here at the Foundation. Part of my duties as cultural attaché." Fleming ordered a soda with ice. "David, I spoke with the professor at the Sorbonne about your Esperanto dictionary and he was most … fascinated."

"Any indication he would like me to come up to Paris and talk about it?"

"I think he said he would have to check with someone in his department. I'll keep you posted."

"Not very encouraging," David sighed. "Thanks for the information." He threw some euros on the table and left the restaurant, walking away with his head bowed, hands thrust deep into his pockets.

Stone gave Fleming a quizzical look. "What was that all about?"

Shaking his head, Fleming sighed. "Interesting character, David." He downed his soda and suppressed a burp. "Really is deep into that Esperanto stuff. Unfortunately, no one gives a shit about Esperanto. The up and coming dead language is Latin." He dropped some coins on the table. "Let's walk."

They strolled along the quay until Fleming motioned for them to proceed out onto a wooden pier with small craft lining both sides. The two had a clear vantage point to observe anyone on the waterfront who might be watching them. Also, it would be difficult for someone to pick up their conversation even with electronic devices.

"Had a meeting with the director of the Foundation this morning. Evidently, he bought my legend. He mentioned that my publisher gave me a big advance."

Fleming held his handkerchief to his nose, holding it so no one could read his lips. "What's your take on that guy?"

"A tad slippery."

"So I hear. Keep your wits about you and just try to blend in with the woodwork. I'll pick you up about five o'clock today and drive you to the consul general's place for the party." The white of the cloth contrasted with his dark skin, now shiny with perspiration. "Afterward, I'll get a ride to my hotel. You keep the car. You'll need it." He forced a smile. "Consider it part of that big advance your publisher gave you."

"A car will be handy. I'll also need a coding device to attach to the computer."

Fleming reached into his pocket and handed him a USB flash device. "Insert it when you message me, take it out when you're finished. Follow the instructions on the screen." He continued to scan the waterfront and the surrounding boats. "Let's move on. No, wait." He turned back toward the bay.

"What's the problem, Fleming? You're jittery."

"We have a situation. We'll probably need you to go to a town up north by the name of Saint-Remy-de-Provence."

"That's an historic area."

"Stone, this is a job, not a vacation."

"My cover is a travel writer. It's logical I would go to a place with history."

"Sorry. What I mean to say is this is a new situation and it's moving very quickly."

"What's moving quickly?" Stone asked.

"We have a lead on bin Zanni, the Al Qaeda chief of information. He may pass through Saint-Rémy."

"When do you want me to leave?"

"In a day or so. I'll let you know.

CHAPTER SEVEN

MARSEILLE

Hassan rapped three times on the door and waited. A brown eye peered through the peephole. The door opened and a man with only three fingers on his left hand ushered Hassan into the hotel room. A second man with a shaved head and dark complexion was slumped in a chair watching the local news on a battered television set balanced on a bent metal stand. The screen emitted a green-gray glow and shadowy figures. Someone had just used the toilet. Hassan went over to the bathroom door and closed it. Without speaking, he went to the window and inched aside the shade. Delivery vans crowded the trash-laden street below.

His man, Three Fingers, had picked a good location. Anyone watching this room from the street would have a hard time remaining undetected. He turned to Three Fingers and the dark man and pointed around the room. Then he touched both ears indicating someone might be listening. Three Fingers rose and turned up the volume on the television set.

"Any word from our friends at home?" Hassan asked softly in Arabic.

The two men shook their heads.

"Have you detected any surveillance?"

"Possibly a week ago," the dark one answered. "But not in the last two days."

Hassan peered out the window again, looking for the man he had spotted twice that day. There was no sign of him on the street, or anyone else resembling a police agent. He eased into a shaky wooden chair and motioned for Three Fingers to begin his briefing.

"The woman in Montpellier was replaced by a man yesterday. Tall and older than the man killed in Nice. He is very careful. Not like the woman. We saw others interested in him."

"The French are following him?" Hassan found it interesting that people were following the American replacement so soon.

"No. The people are Maghreb, North African."

"And the American who was killed in Nice? Was he replaced?"

Three Fingers whispered, "Soon we will learn who the replacement is. Possibly tonight at the American consul general's party."

Hassan closed his eyes and rocked back on two legs of the chair. His plan appeared at times impossible to pull off. He hoped the simplicity of his vision was its strong point. There were so many unknowns, so many side issues. It was best he move quickly.

Hassan left the hotel and walked down a street lined by six-story buildings. The date of the building, *1880,* appeared on the arch of an apartment's doorway. Vagrant grass and weeds grew out of the façade. He recalled there were similar buildings in sections of Beirut.

Rashid waited for him on the sidewalk. He wore a new dark suit, but the buttons pulled at his ample waist. The two went through the motions of shaking hands while both looked up and down the street. Hassan glimpsed a view of the old port of Marseille three blocks away. The aroma of a mid-day meal being prepared nearby drifted through the air. Satisfied they had not been followed, Hassan allowed Rashid to lead the way through the door.

They started up a wide marble staircase stained by years of use. Rashid's shoes clicked on each cracked, polished step. When they reached the third floor, they entered the office of a wine wholesaler. Rashid stepped forward and exchanged greetings with the fat, balding owner who had come around from his desk. The Frenchman offered coffee and motioned for them to sit. Hassan scanned the office. The top of the owner's desk was stacked with invoices and piles of *bouchons,* corks from wine bottles. With the coffee cups passed around, Rashid began the negotiations. "My friend here from Beirut would like some advice in shipping some wine to the United States. He would like to ship—" He turned. "How many cases, Hassan?"

"About thirty. Ten each to New York, Washington, and Los Angeles." Hassan brushed away an annoying fly.

"So why not go to a distributor, a company here in Marseille that does such things?" asked the wholesaler.

Rashid moved forward in his chair. "I have convinced my friend here that I know where he can get some very excellent wine for his people in the United States."

The owner lit a Gitanes cigarette and the smoke drifted toward the open window. He closed his eyes and hunched his shoulders. "Does not your religion forbid alcohol?"

"It forbids us to drink it, not sell it," Rashid said.

"Convenient interpretation, no?"

Hassan spoke up. "I have funds to invest from a charity in Beirut. The funds entrusted to me must bring back an income for refugees. My cousins have restaurants in these three cities and they desire to become, as they say in America, upscale. Excellent wines from France would help."

The owner continued to smoke.

"I have contacts in the business, as you know," Rashid said. "My friend here needs assistance in selecting only the best vintages. We must ship the cases soon and with no complications."

"It's possible." The owner pointed to Rashid. "You and I will get a selection together." He looked back at Hassan. "I'll need money. As a guarantee. We can call it a no-interest loan, right? You Muslims cannot accept interest, no?" His stomach rolled with a deep laugh.

"My friend will tell me the amount and I will have it delivered to you," Hassan said. "Euros?"

"Very good." The wholesaler mashed out the cigarette.

"Oh, and as Rashid will explain," Hassan added, "I have found some very excellent wine from Cassis. I will be including two cases for each destination."

The negotiations concluded, Hassan and Rashid left the building and walked in the direction of the old port.

"I thought the meeting went well," Rashid said. "But I have a problem. I don't understand why you are sending this wine to America. And if you are sending wine, why in such small lots?"

"I want to learn how it's done, and if it is possible for such a venture to bring money in for our cause." The open area of the port came into view as they neared the end of the street. "I can't be held at fault for wasting our funds from the Persians."

Rashid cleared his throat and spat. "They are not Arab."

"They are our allies in the Faith. We must put some issues aside."

Noonday shoppers crowded the daily fish market and the two began bumping into passers-by. Rashid asked, "Where are you headed?"

"I am meeting someone here."

"A brother?" Rashid asked.

"No ... an acquaintance."

"Is this the friend you met in Avignon?"

Hassan stopped. "Yes. How did you become aware of her?"

"I watched you after our meeting there." He laughed. "And then you were seen having dinner with her in Aix a few days ago." Rashid bid him to continue walking. "She's not American is she?"

"Canadian."

"Ah, that explains why she doesn't display her body for all to see. They are modest, those Canadians, no?"

Hassan put on his sunglasses. "The sun is very bright here in the market."

Rashid agreed. "And the market crowd is too much for me. I will return home to Arles."

They shook hands and separated.

Hassan found the young blonde studying the light blue trays holding the fishermen's morning catch. She wore a flowered skirt that stopped just above her ankles. Her blue long-sleeved blouse was open discreetly at the neck. He walked up behind her and touched her shoulder lightly. She turned, removed her sunglasses, and appeared to want a kiss. Hassan placed his cheek next to hers.

"What a great market." She pointed to a tray stacked with moray eel reaching four feet in length and John Dory, an odd-looking fish with a huge spiny head and long flat body. "And look over here." She stopped before a tray of octopi, one about to slither over the edge and plop onto the ground.

Mingling with the local shoppers, who were arguing with the fishmongers, they debated where they should have lunch.

"British Columbia has a fish market like this one. It has the same fishy smells," she said. "You might not like it there though," she teased. "There is a lot of rain and clouds. Not like here."

The sun warmed the top of Hassan's head and made him sleepy, yet relaxed.

"Were you interviewing the man I saw you with?" she asked.

"Who? Oh, the man in the suit? No, not really. He is setting up an interview for the story I told you about."

"For your newspaper in Beirut?"

"Yes … You know, I love the way you speak … the sound of your voice." He touched her arm for a second and then looked around. "This market area can be part of my article. There are markets like this all along the Mediterranean coastline. They all look alike, and even the catch of the sea is the same."

They had a light meal at one of the cafés along the waterfront. She told him she had to take the early afternoon train back to Avignon to tend to her elderly aunt. After lunch, they walked to a taxi stand. As they waited for a taxi to take her to the train station, he asked, "When will we meet again?"

"You can call me on my cellphone when you come to Avignon. When will that be?"

"Soon, but tomorrow I must go to Nice to write my article."

• • •

It was while having lunch with the woman, as he cut into the ripe tomato covered with oil and basil, that he had spotted the man for the third time that day. From his facial features, Hassan believed him to be an Algerian. The man had stood before the trays of fish in the marketplace, but did not speak to the fishmongers nor examine the fish. Repeatedly he had turned his head in Hassan's direction. After Hassan had put the blonde-haired woman into the taxi, he started toward a quiet section of the city. A few moments had passed when Three Fingers called him on the cellphone. Three Fingers said he was accompanied by the dark man with the bald head from the hotel room. They were three blocks behind Hassan, but only one block behind the Algerian. They had been countersurveilling Hassan from the time he had left the hotel. The Algerian had materialized soon afterward and followed Hassan to the market.

The street Hassan chose to turn into was empty. An abandoned car sat halfway up on the sidewalk. Some of the steel grates on the shop doors were rusty. A thin cat with little fur remaining on its body opened its mouth at him, but no sound came forth. The Algerian could not be a policeman. They traveled in pairs. This man must work for Rashid, or those Saudis, he thought. Or perhaps someone else. No matter, this was an interference with his plan. Before he reached the cross street, Hassan stopped, put his foot up on a step, and pretended to tie his shoe. On the other side of the street the Algerian slowed his pace, then stopped and lit a cigarette. Hassan waited until his two men came around the corner and started down the street, then walked back toward the Algerian.

The man took one step forward, then back stepped, and stopped. Hassan's men quickened their stride and closed in behind the Algerian. Hassan moved up his side of the street and slipped out his gun. From his left pocket, he pulled out the tube-like silencer and began screwing it into the barrel of the pistol. The Algerian turned around and stumbled into Hassan's men. They grabbed him and pushed him into an alley. Hassan ran across the street in time to hear the man curse in Algerian Arabic.

"Hold him," Hassan ordered.

They slammed the man against the wall, but he lashed out with his feet. Kicked in the shin, Three Fingers let out a yell. Hassan took a deep breath, then put a bullet in the Algerian's right thigh. He collapsed into a sitting position, moaning.

"We do not have time to play games." Hassan knelt and held the barrel of his gun on the Algerian's genitals. "Who pays you?"

"Your mother's vagina!"

Hassan shifted the gun and put a bullet in his left thigh. The Algerian screamed and flashed a gold right incisor. He looked to the sky.

"Look at me. Is your master Rashid?"

The Algerian's face dropped for a second, enough to give Hassan his answer. He told the others to move away, then placed a bullet in the middle of Gold Tooth's forehead.

Three Fingers went through the dead man's pockets and handed Hassan a cellphone, who turned it on and searched the list of calls. Rashid's cellphone and home phone numbers appeared. Another number appeared frequently. He did not recognize the area code. When he punched in the number on the cellphone, an operator answered, "Foundation d'Élan."

From the dead man's pocket came a book of matches from a bar known by Hassan's people as an illegal drug dealer's meeting place in Marseille. They also found scribbled notes in Arabic on pieces of paper, some euros, and an identity card. Three Fingers raised the dead man's lip, revealing the gold tooth. He looked up at Hassan, who nodded.

They hurried away from the body and headed toward the retail section of Marseille. Three Fingers bounced the gold tooth in his palm.

"It is almost solid gold," he said. "Maybe one hundred grams."

CHAPTER EIGHT

MARSEILLE

"We should be at the consul general's in about a half hour," Fleming said as he downshifted the Porsche through the tight mountain curves. Despite their traveling at seventy miles per hour, a Mercedes was hugging their back bumper. Finally, Fleming waved the car past. "This car is yours for your stay here. Any trouble, take it to the leasing company in Archos."

Stone liked the feel of the open-air roadster. They rounded a bend in the road and he looked down at Marseille glowing in the golden sunset, stretched along the Mediterranean coast. The cocktail party at the American consul general's residence would start at seven o'clock. Years before, as a young naval attaché, Stone had attended a number of consular social functions at the villa. He wondered whether it looked the same.

"Your FBI friend, Jonathan Deville, came down from Paris. We'll see him tonight." Fleming switched on the car's headlights. "He's investigating our officer's death in Montpellier. There's a little bureaucratic tug-of-war concerning the killings of our two operatives. Since they were American citizens, Deville wants to conduct an investigation. At first, Langley said, no, they were deep-cover operatives. As usual, the Bureau won."

"Any specifics on who shot her?"

"Yes, I meant to tell you. She was shot while driving. A witness told the police a motorcycle came up alongside her car and the driver placed two bullets in her head."

"So that's why I'm getting this fast car?" Stone asked.

"No. Not really. I just enjoyed driving it and thought I'd pass it on to you. The dead officer's replacement is already here, but he's not coming to the party."

"Will I meet him?"

"You've met him already," Fleming said. "It's Mark. Your firearms instructor at the Farm. Langley believes that with all the shooting going on we need some heavy guns."

"Where does that place me?"

Fleming gave Stone a quick look. "Don't play coy. I checked your file this week. It says at one time you were an expert firearms instructor for the Bureau. That, and your counterintelligence background got you here. It blends well with the CIA's ops function." Fleming passed three cars. The tachometer needle reached six thousand rpms. "Back to Deville, I know you FBI guys have that bond, but this operation is on a need-to-know basis, so be careful what you say to him."

"Why is it you people in the DO still call me the FBI guy? How long do I have to work for the Agency to be one of you?"

"Listen, if I went over to the FBI to work, I would always be the CIA guy. One has to be baptized from the start. And speaking about being clannish, you people take the cake."

Stone laughed. "Oh, the DO isn't clannish?" He felt more at ease now that Fleming appeared less jittery than he did that afternoon on the Archos waterfront.

"We've changed. We're not the DO anymore. Now we're the National Clandestine Service. Anyway, after the party, take the car back with you. We'll meet in Saint-Rémy in a day or so."

They pulled up to the entrance of a villa that clung to the side of a hill and overlooked the Corniche Kennedy. The Mediterranean Sea edged the opposite side of the road and the sun was poised for its final dip into the sea. A swarthy young man opened the iron gate and they drove down the driveway. Fleming parked and raised the convertible top. Slate steps led up from the parking area to a patio overlooking the bay. Stone spied Jonathan Deville talking with a tall African-American man wearing wire-framed glasses.

"Hold on a second," Fleming said, adjusting his black bow tie. "I'll introduce you to my buddy over there talking with

Deville." They walked over and Fleming introduced the African-American to Stone as Consul General Brooks. After a few minutes of exchanging pleasantries, the consul general pointed out in his subtle manner where everyone ranked in the evening's pecking order.

When Brooks began talking about office politics, Deville pulled Stone away, and they walked over to the rock-faced balustrade. They leaned against the railing and viewed the darkening city. Deville's brown hair was, as usual, neatly combed. He looked lean and hard, and Stone figured he had not gained an ounce of fat since his Marine Corps days. His courteous Virginia manner served him well at country clubs as well as in diplomatic circles.

"So you landed a grant at the Foundation?" Deville chuckled. "And your cover is a travel writer? Sweet."

"You know I'd like to talk about my assignment, but Fleming said I had to be discreet." Stone smiled and turned around to face the other guests. "So Jonathan, how's your lovely wife?"

"Rhonda loves Paris. Being an artist, she's involved with the annual embassy art show. Her painting is on this year's art show poster." Deville paused. "She wanted me to tell you to get your life back on track. I think she has a girl in mind for you when you come up and visit us."

"Tell her thanks." Stone looked forward to being with a pleasant woman for a change. Whoever was sleeping with his ex must be getting sick of her by now.

"You know the area around Archos could be a good source of material for your travel writing." Deville motioned to a girl carrying a drink tray. "We did a murder investigation near the village of Cuers some time back. Pretty country."

"Cuers," Stone mused. "Where have I heard that name before?"

Deville looked over Stone's shoulder and stiffened. Stone turned and realized Boswell Harrington had been standing behind to him.

Harrington frowned. "Hello there, Hayden. Enjoying yourself? What's this about Cuers?"

Perhaps his afternoon business meeting went sour, Stone thought, then answered, "Mr. Deville here is from our embassy. He mentioned there are some interesting places around Archos that could be material for travel articles. The village of Cuers just came up."

"You're wasting your time if you go there." Harrington turned away and looked in the direction of Fleming, who was being harangued by a short, fire-plug-shaped woman with red hair styled in the shape of a pencil eraser. Straightening his tie, he looked back. "I must touch base with Fleming about some grant issues." He sighed. "I was too hasty about Cuers. You're new here and don't know the lay of the land. I'll tell you what … tomorrow morning I'll see whether the young lady in our office, Margaux, can accompany you for a spin about the countryside. If you happen to pass through Cuers, you'll know what I mean."

As Harrington moved on, Stone remembered that Cuers was the French village where his college roommate, Herb Walker, had died under what he had always thought were strange circumstances. The alumni bulletin provided few details: only that Herb had been cremated and his ashes scattered near a local Catholic church.

Deville laughed. "Harrington is doing Fleming a favor by interrupting that loud mouthed redhead. See her poking her finger in Fleming's chest? That awful woman is in from Washington and she's driving the embassy staff crazy, including the ambassador."

A whiff of floral scent stirred Stone's senses as long fingers slid down the left sleeve of his tuxedo. From behind, a woman glided around into his view. Her hazel eyes bore into his.

"Lucy?" Stone said.

"I always hated that name. It is now Lucinda."

"Contessa, it's a deep pleasure to see you." Deville bowed his head slightly and beamed his first smile of the night.

Stone had last seen her eighteen years ago. His former lover had become more beautiful with time. The green beaded chemise perfectly complimented her auburn hair. She smiled at Deville, then turned back to Stone.

Stone didn't know what to say. First had come the surprise of recognizing her, then a wave of excitement, followed by a wish to flee. They had separated on less than good terms.

"I saw you talking with Harrington and recognized your profile immediately." Lifting her head slightly, she studied Stone's face as if to see what time had wrought. She settled her gaze on the scar on his cheek.

"Would you believe an irate woman did it?" Stone said, his defenses engaged.

"Yes," she said, then addressed Deville. "How are your lovely wife and your adorable children?" She went on to ask how the children were doing in their new school.

Deville repeatedly attempted to get a word in and finally managed, "And how do you two know each other?"

Lucinda pursed her sensuous lips. "The last time I saw Hayden was ... oh, a few years ago ... when you, Hayden, were a Navy officer ... an ensign, no?"

"Yes, I was assigned to Nice when we had a consulate there."

He allowed her to relate the story in the way he surmised she wanted it to be told. Deville continued to smile as he grabbed another glass of wine from a passing tray. Meanwhile, Stone retraced in his mind their affair as he remembered it. Her voice had a slight husky tone that Stone had forgotten.

"Needless to say, Jonathan, I was very young and sheltered by an Italian mother and an Egyptian father. Hayden and I, if I recall correctly, attended a number of formal social gatherings together." She looked at Stone, whose throat had become dry. "I remember at the last function all the officers wore bright white uniforms and we girls were in our party dresses ... accompanied by our chaperones, of course." She stopped and waved to a server to take her empty glass.

"It was a beautiful summer." Stone immediately regretted saying it.

She glared. "So it was." Then she gave Deville a kiss on both cheeks. Stone reached to take her hand, but she moved away, weaving past the guests toward Harrington.

Out of the corner of his eye, he saw Deville grinning. He

waited for the inquisition to begin. Deville surprised him, as he held off his inquiries until Stone feigned going inside the villa to look at the consul general's collection of ink drawings.

"No way, Hayden. I want to know, and I want to know now. All the details. Oh man, your reputation is bona fide!"

"Jonathan, we're gentlemen and gentlemen never talk about their conquests."

"Conquest, you say. I *knew* it! Stone, if this got around you'd be the envy of every man on the Côte d'Azur." He finished off the glass. "Well ... except for Harrington over yonder." Lucinda and Harrington had started a conversation with an older Asian couple, as Harrington's wife watched her husband from the other side of the patio. "Word is the director of your foundation has been trying to score with the contessa for some time now, to no avail. If he finds out about you two, he may slip into your room some night and try to cut off your balls."

"Look, it was a long time ago, when we were young and the world was quiet." Stone thought he recognized Lucinda's emerald necklace, the one she'd worn for her twentieth birthday party. "What's all this contessa business?"

"Hey, it's hereditary from her mother's side. I heard that once she decided on being Roman Catholic instead of an Egyptian Copt, the Vatican gave its blessing."

"Imagine. I could have been married to royalty."

"Yeah, she would have gone down for the count."

"Enough of this sophomoric humor, let's take a look at the consul's art work."

They passed through the open doors and entered the living room. Stone headed for the etchings and Deville peeled off to talk with an acquaintance. Young women passed by carrying hot canapés on oval porcelain trays. Stone put two greasy ones, origin quite unrecognizable, on a napkin. He looked around the room and saw that Lucinda had come in with Harrington. Her eyes met his, and she turned away.

Deville came up with a middle-aged man with graying at the temples, very icy blue eyes, and a red handkerchief stuffed in the top pocket of his tuxedo. He introduced the man as Maurice

Colmont, whom Deville explained he had met the week before at a Paris INTERPOL function. Although Colmont spoke with a pleasant accent and assumed an upper class poise, he had large, calloused hands.

After some banter, Colmont said to Stone, "I hope to see you when I visit Archos." They shook hands and Colmont moved on to talk with Harrington and the contessa.

When he was out of earshot, Deville whispered, "Colmont's our new intelligence liaison contact in Paris."

Stone saw the guests easing toward the buffet laid out on the dining room table. He touched Deville's arm. "I've got to get back to my writing. Time to take a French leave. Walk me to my car."

On the path down to the parking lot, Deville whispered, "Have to tell you, Hayden, keep your wits about you. You're not in the Bureau relying on trusted backup. You're hanging out there alone."

"Thanks, that's the feeling I'm getting. You know, everyone around here seems to be playing parts. No one is really who they seem."

"Neither are you, pal. Oh, be careful around Harrington. We've got some bad reports about him. In fact, I'm surprised the Agency put you up at the Foundation."

"Is Fleming aware of that?" Stone asked.

Deville shook his head. "Don't know. I deal with Fleming's boss, the station chief in Paris, and I haven't told him."

"Hmm."

"Politics, my man. The station chief hasn't been very cooperative lately." Deville shook Stone's hand and headed back to the party.

Stone made his way down the dark pathway. He glanced up at the party guests on the terrace. When he saw Lucinda, he paused. She stood next to Harrington, her hand on his arm. God, she was still a beauty. Who would have thought he'd ever see her again? He continued down toward his car. A push on the button on his ignition key flashed the Porsche's headlights. A dark figure jumped up from the front of the car. Stone challenged him. "What were you doing next to my car?"

"It's only I, sir. I dropped a guest's car keys on the ground and I have found them, see?"

"And who are you?"

"It is I, Ali, servant to the consul," he said, moving toward the gate. "You are leaving the party, sir? I shall let you out."

Stone slipped behind the wheel of his car and checked to see whether the Colt was still hidden under the seat. It was. He watched the little man open the gate. As he drove out, Ali called, "Have a nice evening, sir."

Stone drove the car out onto the Corniche and headed east toward Archos. A faint rose glow lingered on the western horizon. A short distance down the coast, he pulled to the side of the road and lowered the convertible top to enjoy the balmy night.

As the canvas slipped into its folded position, he spotted in the rearview mirror a motorcycle partially concealed behind a parked truck about a hundred meters back. A brief glow from a cigarette revealed someone in the driver's saddle. A car with yellow headlights approached and the figure on the motorcycle leaned farther behind the truck, as if trying to hide.

Decision time. Should he make a beeline back to the party for support and blow his cover? Not a viable option. Besides, this may be the guy who shot the CIA officer.

He reached under the seat and pulled out the Colt. Assuring a round was in the chamber, he laid the gun next to him. With the gearshift in Drive, he pressed the accelerator. The car shot onto the roadway. In the rearview, a single headlight switched on and moved out from behind the truck.

"Let the games begin."

He maneuvered the Porsche in and out of traffic, but not to elude the motorcycle. He wanted to get a feel for how the car handled, for he suspected the person behind him would wait for the twists and turns on the mountain pass ahead before making a move.

The traffic thinned as the residential areas passed by and he began the climb into the Massif. During the ascent and through the first turn, Stone tested the rocker switches on the steering wheel used to shift the gears of the Porsche. The motorcycle closed the distance between them.

Two more turns and the motorcycle was directly behind Stone. It came up along his left side, which he didn't want. He inched over onto the centerline to block the motorcycle.

A few seconds later, with no oncoming traffic, the motorcycle roared out again onto the left side of the road and came up next to the Porsche. Stone downshifted two gears; the Porsche decelerated and the motorcycle flew past. The driver fired twice with his automatic. He missed.

Now in front of Stone, the motorcycle began weaving back and forth. Stone kept his position until the driver moved to the right side, where he wanted him. The motorcycle slowed, nearly touching Stone's right door. Stone grabbed the Colt, shifted one gear up, took a quick look at the driver, and squeezed the trigger twice. A flash hit the top of the handlebar and the motorcycle veered and scraped along the guardrail, throwing off sparks.

Stone saw a curve ahead. He tossed the Colt on the seat, downshifted, and steered the car through the turn, barely sticking to the road. With his eyes fixed on the road, he saw the single headlight come up again in his peripheral vision. At a straight section of the road, the roar of the motorcycle and the glare of a headlight in the left side mirror alerted him that the driver had recovered and was coming in for the kill.

Stone swung the car back and forth. Behind him, the motorcycle did the same. A one-hundred-and-eighty-degree reverse spin at this speed was out of the question. The taillights from a tractor-trailer in the right lane loomed ahead. He floored the accelerator, got a lead on the motorcycle, and passed the truck, braking until he was directly in front of the truck's bumper. The truck driver blew his horn and flashed his headlights.

Veering quickly to the right, Stone turned onto the shoulder of the road and let the truck pass by. From under the truck's raised trailer, he saw the motorcycle pass on the other side.

The low clearance of the Porsche scraped rocks and brush, but he controlled the car and moved back onto the hard surface directly behind the truck's bumper. The motorcycle was now ahead of the truck, looking at an empty road. Stone turned off his headlights.

The driver of the motorcycle weaved in and out of the left lane. After a minute the motorcycle moved over onto the right shoulder, zigzagging back and forth in the gravel. The truck driver drove past, leaned on the horn, jerked to the left, and then sped ahead. Now alongside the motorcycle, Stone fired twice. The motorcycle spun out of control and flipped over the low guardrail.

Stone switched on his parking lights and pulled to the side. He wanted to get a look at the assassin. In the glove compartment, he found a flashlight next to a full magazine for the automatic. He reloaded the Colt.

The gravel gave way underfoot as Stone walked back along the guardrail. Down the slope, among low bushes, the motorcycle's headlight was pointed into the ground. The only other light came from the moon. A moan came from the gulley below, followed by the sound of branches breaking. This bastard was plenty tough.

With his flashlight Stone searched the brush. A face looked up into the light. Stone climbed over the guardrail and slid down the incline.

"I saw you go off the road," Stone said in French. "May I help?" He moved closer.

The terrorist was confused. Blood seeped from a circular burn hole in the left sleeve of his jacket.

"Yes. Please help me."

His helmet came off and Stone saw he had a close-cut beard. "What's your name? What should I call you?"

"Why is that of importance?"

"Because, asshole, you don't look French." Stone brought up the Colt and aimed.

The driver cursed in Arabic and pulled a gun from his belt.

Stone squeezed off two rounds into his chest. "It's not nice to kill a lady."

CHAPTER NINE

CÔTE D'AZUR

Stone made his way back to his car, hugging the outside of the guardrail and hoping to stay out of sight of passing motorists. As he opened the door to the Porsche, the driver of a van slowed down and offered assistance. Stone feigned zipping up his fly and the motorist honked his car horn twice and sped on.

By the time Stone reached the outskirts of Archos, his neck muscles were aching. A stiff drink was in order. He pulled into the parking lot of a café on a hillside overlooking the port. As he exited the car, he looked down. His shoes and the bottom of his trousers were caked with mud. Deciding against going into the restaurant, he walked to the far end of the parking lot and pulled out his cellphone.

On the second ring, Fleming answered and immediately ordered, "Go into secure voice mode."

Stone punched in the code then held the phone screen to his eye until it identified the pattern of his retina. After a few clicks, the amber display indicated their conversation would be private. Stone related the details of the shooting.

Fleming remained silent until he finished, then said, "Let's do a quick review. No one saw you. The assassin is definitely dead. You are unharmed and back in Archos."

"I should have retrieved his gun." Stone kicked a rock with his shoe. "You could make comparisons with the bullets that killed the officer in Montpellier."

"No problem. The French can do that when they find the body. I'll contact them now, before the gunman's buddies find him."

"What will be the French reaction if they find out

I'm responsible?"

"Oh, about the same reaction you would have if some French spy came into your home town and shot up the place." Fleming thought it funny and laughed. "Excuse me, but you know yours is the best news I've heard in a while. I can't wait to tell Claudia."

Stone put the phone in his pocket and returned to the car. Buckling up, he thought about the dead terrorist. It had been nothing more than a matter of self-defense, and he had done well. This was no holiday in the South of France; that's why Frederick had sent him the Colt .45. He turned on the car and listened to the warm engine hum. Odd. During the gunfight it never occurred to him he might end up the corpse. He drove back to the Foundation d'Élan.

The grounds of the Foundation were dark except where the solar-powered lamps illuminated the walkways. He parked near his cottage and checked the outside of the car for bullet holes; there were none. Inside the car, he retrieved three shell casings, but couldn't find the fourth one. At least he'd had the presence of mind to retrieve the two casings at the roadside scene. Tomorrow he might find the missing one in the car, but for now he wanted a drink of that Irish whiskey sitting on the kitchen counter.

CÔTE D'AZUR—MAY 3, 2002

After the short trip from the Red Scorpion, Abdul Wahab jumped from the Zodiac inflatable boat onto the dock and immediately pulled out his cellphone to call Rashid in Arles. "What is happening in Marseille this fine Friday morning, my friend?" Wahab motioned to his driver standing by the Bentley Arnage to wait for him.

"Ah, all is well here," Rashid answered. "As I sit here looking at the vineyards, I expect a fine harvest and—"

"How fortunate for you. I received word this morning from Mr. Harrington that a certain Algerian whose services we lent to you has met with an accident in Marseille." Wahab listened to silence for a minute. "You know who I'm referring to … the man with the bright dental work."

"Yes. Yes. That is very sad." Rashid coughed. "The crime situation in Marseille is getting worse."

"Mr. Harrington is concerned about how this affects his business there. So am I."

"No need for concern," Rashid insisted. "The matter had nothing to do with our business arrangements here."

"So, what was he doing for you when he met his end?"

"Nothing important, really. As they say, he was in the wrong place."

Wahab walked over to the Bentley. The driver opened the back door for him. He climbed in and waited before continuing the conversation, listening to Rashid breath hard on the other end of the line. Wahab continued. "This man Hassan, whom you are helping with a shipment of wine, do you still trust him?"

Rashid coughed twice. "Yes. I think he is someone who can help us … although we must watch him."

"Yes. I agree, but then again we must be careful of everyone." Wahab paused. "Mr. Harrington, who as you know, can be difficult at times, is not pleased with what happened to his man. I can't afford to have Harrington displeased." Again, a long pause. "Understand?"

"Yes, my sheik."

"I want a meeting with Hassan."

"When would be a good time, sir?"

"Today. I want both of you here. We will have lunch."

"But sir, it will take some time to—"

Wahab rang off and slipped the cellphone into the pocket of his blazer. He thought for a moment, then instructed the driver to take him to his favorite museum in Villefranche.

Stone planned to spend Friday morning on his patio, surrounded by pots overflowing with brilliant flowers, reading his day-old newspaper, and drinking coffee. The birds were especially noisy and a soft, warm breeze floated in from the bay. Thin white clouds dotted the sky. He had awakened with a headache, but had no nightmares during the night. Today, he would call Fleming and ask whether the French police had any information on the terrorist he'd shot. Otherwise, he intended to lie low at the Foundation.

Margaux crossed the lawn and stopped before him. She let out a long sigh. "Monsieur Harrington has instructed me to accompany you to Cuers."

"Margaux. Please sit down." He pushed a chair toward her. "Let me explain. Last night, Harrington suggested you might be able to show me around places like Cuers and I agreed."

She sighed again, a bit exaggerated, and eased primly into the chair.

"I don't mean to impose on you," he continued. "It's the weekend. I'll make other arrangements."

"No, no. It is just that I work all week, then I must come to work on the weekend."

"Some coffee?" Stone asked. "Let me get another cup from the kitchen."

She waved her hand indicating no and rose from the chair. "When shall we go?"

"Let's make it at eleven o'clock and find some interesting place to have lunch on the way."

"Why Cuers?" She frowned.

"I want to visit the church where my friend had his last rites."

"So you are taking me to church?"

It was the first time he had seen her smile.

Once they left the motorway, they proceeded north on a secondary road toward the village of Cuers. Margaux's royal blue scarf blew around her head. Gold bangles on her wrist clicked when she pointed out local landmarks. A mile out of Cuers, Stone's cellphone rang. Fleming's number appeared on the display. He pulled over to the side of the road and parked under the shade of a tree. Excusing himself, he stepped away from the car, punching the phone's keys for secure mode.

"Where are you right now?" Fleming demanded. "I need your exact location."

Stone gave his location and added he was with Margaux from the Foundation d'Élan.

"Figures you would be with a girl. I just wanted to confirm that it's you we're tracking on satellite. To make a long story short, a tracker beacon was placed on your car, probably by the same people following you now."

"What people? How far back are they?" Stone searched up and down the road.

"About four miles away. The French picked up the signal this morning and told us about it. They're tracking the people who are following you."

"So let's see … I'm being followed by Hassan's group, the French, and the Agency?"

"It's not Hassan's group," Fleming said. "It's someone else."

"Who are they?"

"We think they're connected with some Saudis in Nice."

"So they're probably al Qaeda?" Stone moved his hand to his shoulder holster.

"Maybe, maybe not."

"That's great. Before you get off the phone, any information on the terrorist I shot?"

"None yet," Fleming said. "By the way, don't try to find your beacon. Leave it. Just have a good time with your friend. And remember we're watching you."

Stone returned to the car. "My editor in New York wants more rewrites on my next book. Time to go to church."

She gave him another smile.

The church in Cuers stood alone, gracefully aged. Stone and Margaux found a side door open and inside the dark interior met a curate with a shy smile who had emerged from the sacristy. He spoke little English, so Margaux asked in French about the American Herb Walker.

The curate took them to an office beyond the baptismal font and searched the records in a thick ledger. Flipping through pages, he found Walker's name and the date of his funeral. Since few Americans had died in Cuers, he said he remembered performing the funeral service. The cause of death was not noted, but a notation reflected that he had been cremated and his ashes spread in a nearby vineyard. They thanked the priest and departed, but not before Stone lit a votive candle before a side altar.

Back at the car, a bony-faced man in clerical garb approached them and tipped his black, wide-brimmed hat.

"Pardon. My name is Father Dominic." He spoke with a stilted French inflection. "I was informed you were inquiring into the demise of an American here in Cuers a few years ago."

After shaking hands, the priest suggested they sit at a table at a nearby ice cream shop. They settled under the faded awning. The cleric placed his large hat on the chair next to him. His haircut looked like a razor cut.

"Did you know my friend?" Stone asked.

"I recall very little about him, except I believe he died of a stroke. He was Catholic and we performed the last rites. Of course, there was a funeral, but I believe the pews were empty. I never spoke with him." Father Dominic looked away from Stone's stare.

The waiter came and asked whether they wanted something. Father Dominic asked for a glass of water and continued. "Now I remember. A friend of his flew in from New York City and handled the funeral arrangements. How did you know him, Mr. Stone?"

"We were friends in college."

"So you are here to pay your last respects, as it were."

"Yes. I lit a candle for him. Do you know what he was doing here in Cuers?"

"He was in real estate investments, I believe." The priest brushed dust from his cassock.

"I guess he enjoyed the wine here in Provence," Stone said.

"I was told he had no interest in wine. A typical American, he liked his beer."

Father Dominic gave Margaux directions to a vineyard where he said he believed Herb's ashes were scattered. Then he put on his hat. A slight breeze lifted the brim as he rose from his chair. Stone looked down at the man's shoes. Strange for a French priest to wear British-made brogues.

Margaux recited the priest's directions as they rode, and eventually they found the vineyard. The surrounding area was hilly and not far from a stand of ancient oaks. During the ride, Stone failed to detect any cars following them, yet he couldn't relax and enjoy the scenery. Where was the surveillance? Why was he of interest to these people? The attack on the road after the Consul's cocktail party nagged at him, and looking over at Margaux he wondered if he was putting her life in danger. They got out and walked along the rows of trimmed vine plants. On the way back to the car, he asked Margaux, "Why were you so quiet when we spoke with Father Dominic?"

"That cleric had a strange accent. He is not from Provence, and he is not from Marseille."

"I found it odd that he sought us out," Stone added. "Also, he didn't know Herb very well. Herb loved wine."

As Stone turned the key in the ignition, Margaux lifted herself off the car seat and removed a brass shell casing. After examining it, she placed it into his palm. "Ah, this is what was pinching me all this time. Yours?"

CHAPTER TEN

NICE

Hassan slouched in the back seat of the BMW sedan, jiggling his *misbaha*, the worry beads his father had given him when he was a boy. Three Fingers sat in the front next to the driver, an Iraqi; the two spoke softly to each other. Hassan had told them he wanted quiet, so he could think. He instructed the Iraqi to remain within the speed limit on the Autoroute to Nice. No need for the police to stop them for speeding. The exit for Cannes passed. It would not be long before they would arrive in Nice and meet with Rashid and the Saudi, Abdul Wahab. Along the way, he studied the clean farms and settlements. In many respects, the countryside resembled Lebanon and Palestine. Once again, the theme played in his mind: His civilization was older than here in the West. His people were as intelligent. Why were they not also blessed? Because the West did not allow it. It was not in their interest. Well, the time had come for change.

His fingers clicked one bead next to another. He wondered if he would detect any anxiety on the part of Rashid, who by now knew his man had been shot while following Hassan. Rashid had set up this special meeting with Abdul Wahab. It was very important, Rashid had insisted.

The last time Hassan had gone aboard the Red Scorpion, Wahab had tried to bribe him to join in an alliance against their mutual enemy, the Americans. As a show of good intentions, Wahab told him an American intelligence officer was following him. Of course, Hassan knew he was being followed, and he supposed the Saudis knew that he knew. Hassan had told Wahab he was appreciative and would think about his proposition. All Saudis, especially this Wahab, thought they could bribe anyone with their money. Apparently, the two North Africans he'd killed that night in Nice were either in Wahab's employ or Rashid's.

"We are only a few minutes from the harbor," the Iraqi driver said.

"Park as close as possible. We will all go aboard the yacht."

The two men in the front seats stiffened and glanced at each other.

"Take your guns," Hassan ordered.

The driver parked near the quay. Few people were walking along the waterfront. The three men found a stone bench next to the landing site and sat down to wait. They watched the Zodiac leave the yacht anchored off the point and head toward them, throwing off a flat wake. A breeze ruffled the water creating short whitecaps. Gulls circled overhead searching for fish scraps.

Hassan thought for a moment, then asked, "That man, Ali, who works for the American consul general … how did you learn he worked for these Saudis?"

Three Fingers spoke. "We contacted Ali after the party at the American's villa. We asked him who had replaced the American killed in Nice. He was jumpy. I laughed and asked if he had to take a piss." Three Fingers paused to light his cigarette. "'Ali, go to the bathroom,' I said. 'Stop shaking.' Ali started to whine like some lamb. 'I am in great danger,' he cried."

"And then?"

"Ali told us he was also working for these Saudis. During the party last night, the Saudis told him to place a tracking device on the car of an American writer. He watched the American leave, followed by a motorcycle driven by someone working for the Saudis."

The yacht's tender approached the quay. On the craft, Rashid sat next to Abdul Wahab, the spokesman for the prince who owned the Red Scorpion.

"Continue," Hassan said, watching the boat approach.

"Ali told us that just before we came, his Saudi bosses had told him the driver of the motorcycle had been killed. They wanted to know if he had told anyone about the tracking device. Ali said he swore to them on his family's name that he had not. He said he was sure they now would return and kill him."

"Ali's family wallows with swine." Hassan rose to greet Rashid, who was standing in the bow of the boat.

"Allah be praised," Rashid called out to Hassan. "Come aboard, we have a meal ready for you on the yacht."

Hassan motioned for his companions to follow him and Rashid held up his hand.

"No. Very sorry. I have an invitation for only you, Hassan."

"Then I will forgo the gracious offer of a feast aboard the yacht, and we will confer over here on the benches." Hassan turned to the driver. "Please, go to that store and get us some cold drinks."

Rashid spoke rapidly with Wahab, who spat out a curse, and then turned back toward the water. He continued to coax him and finally Wahab yelled at the boatman. "Call the yacht and tell them I am staying ashore." Wahab disembarked, presented Hassan with a switched-on smile, and said, "Please, let us sit." Three Fingers grinned as they walked over to the benches.

Hassan, Rashid, and Wahab spoke of recent events in the Middle East. They all agreed the times were bad but, God willing, they were about to improve. Eventually, Rashid eased out of the conversation and let Hassan and Wahab talk. After a time, Wahab unbuttoned his blazer and leaned toward Hassan.

"We need your services. Our friend, Rashid, has assured us that you are not only trustworthy, but very professional." He looked around to see whether any passersby were near. "The intelligence officer we warned you about the last time we met was killed. He has been replaced and we fear this new American is in a position to disrupt our plan."

"What plan?"

Wahab paused. "We have a very important person traveling through this region. We do not want him to be discovered."

"One American can disrupt your plan?" Hassan looked over at Three Fingers, who was listening. "With this plan and this very important man who is coming, how can we be of assistance to you?"

"We must be assured the American does not interfere with our man's travel." Wahab turned to Rashid, who nodded his head. "We intend to be very generous."

"We will need funds now to pay our expenses. Is it in Marseille where we will watch the American?"

"No. It is possible he will travel to a town called Saint-Rémy-de-Provence. We would like for you to go there and look for him." He retrieved an envelope from the inside pocket of his jacket. "I believe the funds in this envelope will be more than adequate to compensate you for this favor."

Hassan looked over at Three Fingers and then at Rashid. "Rashid will be our mutual contact." He saw that Wahab seemed pleased. "Where is the American now?"

"He is staying at a Foundation in Archos, near Marseille," Wahab answered, then handed a photograph to Hassan. "This is his picture."

Hassan glanced at the photograph, and then slipped it into his pocket. The negotiations concluded, all shook hands and Rashid and Wahab boarded the Zodiac. Hassan watched the craft head back to the Red Scorpion. He lit a cigarette with his gold lighter and blew a long stream of smoke into the air.

"Who is this very important man?" Three Fingers asked. "Al Qaeda?"

"I am sure he is, my friend." Hassan handed him the envelope containing the money. "We shall go to Saint-Rémy and find the American ... and the al Qaeda man."

"Do you think Rashid suspects we killed the Algerian with the gold tooth?"

"Probably." Hassan then recalled that the telephone number for the Foundation d'Élan had appeared on the call list of the dead Algerian's cellphone.

Hassan and his two men returned to the BMW. In the front Three Fingers unfolded the yellow Michelin map, while in the back seat Hassan studied the face in the photograph Wahab had given to him. It had been taken close up while the American was sitting alongside a short blond-haired man with a faint moustache. Masts of moored sailboats stood tall in the background. The American looked older than the young man he had watched die two weeks before. It was not the scar on the American's cheek that held his attention; it was his eyes. He remembered other men with that same look in the Afghan training camp.

CHAPTER ELEVEN

CÔTE D'AZUR—MAY 5, 2002

The staff had Sunday off, so Stone brewed his own coffee. He perused the Middle East travel book in the name of his alter ego, Finbarr Costanza. Reading the book didn't help him solve the problem of how he should play the part of a writer. Suppose another writer at the Foundation asked him to critique their work? Could he fake it? Doubtful. His stomach growled and he searched the kitchen cabinets for something to eat. Finding only staples, he decided to go into town to find an open brasserie.

As he approached the town, a change in the wind brought dirty clouds in from the sea and Stone smelled the coming of rain. A few blocks back from the waterfront, he found a table at a café. He had just finished off his croissant and opened the weekend section of the *Financial Times* when his cellphone rang. Fleming wanted to see him at the American consulate in Marseille at eleven o'clock, a forty-five minute drive.

Strong gusts brought a cold drizzle to Marseille. The green neon signs in the pharmacy windows brought no feeling of warmth to the city, now turned dismal. Stone parked the Porsche on a side street off the Rue Armény. At the consulate's front gate, French police checked his passport and allowed him to proceed onto the grounds. The security measures set in place at the consulate general because of the worldwide terrorist threat had changed the atmosphere of the old stone building. Years before, as a naval officer, he could walk up to the front door and ask to speak to an American. Not now.

A locally-hired French guard led him down into the garden

and to the entrance door. Fleming stood in the lobby holding a large paper bag. They shook hands and then rode a two-person elevator to the top floor where Mark was waiting in a cramped office. He had last seen Mark at his firearms training session at the Farm in Virginia. The rich aroma of meats and herbs from the sandwiches in the sack held by Fleming competed with the dry, woody smell of the attic office.

As they ate, Fleming began by saying, "Mark is replacing Stacy, the officer killed in Montpellier. His job is to go there and gather information on a high-level al Qaeda leader. Sensitive sources report he'll pass through the area in the next couple of days." Fleming turned to Stone. "You'll proceed to Saint-Rémy, sit and wait for this al-Qaeda guy, who might use the town as a base of operations. One big problem—to date we have no name or description for him."

Mark seemed to have no problem with the assignment, but Stone was amused. Finally, Fleming had given him a specific task. At last, a job to do besides avoiding getting himself shot. "I'm to go to a little French town and play the tourist?"

"Like I told you in Paris, your cover is a travel writer. So, go travel and write." Fleming handed him a packet. "Here's your itinerary and hotel reservation. We'll be in contact by phone."

Mark looked at Stone. "You put my excellent teaching to good use the other night."

Fleming removed his glasses and cleaned them with his handkerchief. "Yes, that's another topic on the agenda. It's a shame that man had to be killed. Now understand, I'm happy you are alive, it's just ... I may have some difficulty with the authorities. Some French jurisdictions might want to go through the legal process. Just a formality, understand?"

"Bullshit!" Mark exclaimed. "What about our two people who were murdered?"

"My sentiments exactly," Stone added. "Do the cops know my name? Have they been tracking me?"

"No. Yes."

"It's a good thing I got rid of the tracking device yesterday."

"That was against my instructions. Where is the device?"

"On the bumper of a tour bus headed for Rome. When did the French pick up the signal on my car?"

"Yesterday. They followed what they thought were some narcotics traffickers to Cuers. During the surveillance, they picked up two signals and realized that one was coming from your car. Then they realized the drug people were on your tail, so they identified you. They learned you were an American who attended the consul general's party, so they called Jonathan Deville in Paris, who then called me."

"The French are pretty efficient," Stone said. "But then, they have the advantage of working on their own turf." He stood up and stretched. "If they didn't start tracking me until yesterday, how will they connect me with the shooting?"

"I'm not sure they will. I'm just trying to anticipate a problem."

"How do drug dealers fit into all this?" Mark asked.

"Yeah," Stone said. "Yesterday, you told me they could be al Qaeda."

Fleming frowned. "I told you about the bodies of a man and woman found near the body of Huntington, the CIA officer killed in Nice. Yesterday, Deville said the police told him they found a vial of poison on one of the victims. Same kind of poison that killed our man. The two victims were connected to the drug trade in Marseille. Both came from Algeria, and both had connections with al Qaeda. The French told us the people who followed you yesterday were connected with those two."

"So they killed Huntington?"

"Seems that way, but we don't know why. Plus we don't know who killed *them*, or why."

"Maybe Huntington killed them before he died," Mark offered.

"The French investigators doubt it. One was sliced with a knife, and no knife was found on our officer's body."

The three listened to the rain as it hit the roof. Stone thought the unanswered questions were intriguing as well as disquieting. "I'd like to know how the drug people got a lead on me. Maybe someone at the Foundation fingered me?"

"I doubt it. We did our homework. The Foundation appears to be safe."

Stone shook his head, thinking of what his friend Deville told him at the consul general's party about Boswell Harrington being dirty. "Maybe."

"How does this tie in with Hassan?" Mark asked.

"Again, we don't know." Fleming pushed the remains of his sandwich into the bag.

"Any more on Hassan's location?" Stone asked. "And what about the yacht Hassan was seen visiting in Nice? The Red Scorpion?"

"Don't know, but you two should keep an eye out for Hassan both in Montpelier and Saint-Rémy," Fleming said. "As for the yacht, we have someone working on that angle. Stone, as you asked in Paris, what are these Saudis, who are Sunni Muslims, doing hanging around with a Shiite like Hassan? A lot of this doesn't make sense."

Stone paused, then asked, "What did you learn about the guy I shot?"

Fleming rose from his chair and almost hit his head on a low-hanging wooden beam. "The gun the police recovered from the body was the same one used to kill Stacy, our female officer in Montpelier. We assume he was the assassin."

Mark laughed. "Now that's what you call closure. What are you worrying about, Fleming?"

Stone said, "One other thing—that servant of the consul general, the one I think put the tracking device on my car, what are you doing with him?"

"The guy's name is Ali. We're doing nothing for the moment. I told the CG and he agreed that for now we know who the spy is and we can watch him. Take him out and we'll have to start looking for his replacement."

Stone walked over to the window and watched the rain.

Fleming continued. "The terrorist you shot—the police say he was killed with a .45 caliber weapon. I thought I gave you a 9mm Glock in Paris?"

"Yes, you did."

Fleming stared at Stone. "You did a good job for us shooting that man, but still … these complications with the French."

Mark interjected, "Fleming, my man, you're assigned to Paris. The CIA put you in this cozy slot because of your administrative abilities. You can keep Stone out of trouble with the French. If you can't, both of us are out of here."

"Make the problem go away," Stone added. "And don't give them my name."

"Don't worry. Just keep your mind on the job."

Outside the consulate building, Stone and Mark huddled under an overhang. The rain poured and brought a clamminess that went through Stone's thin cotton windbreaker.

"Listen," Mark said. "Fleming is trying to cover his ass. Two people killed on his watch. Career-wise, that's not good. Like a navy captain running his ship aground, no way can you make admiral after that happens."

"I know. I just hope he keeps his bearings."

"He's got a lot of people upstairs, like Claudia, working full time to place all the blame on him."

The rain eased up. Mark leaned closer. "I'll have a packet of exit documents and passports sent to you in case you have to make a quick escape."

"Thanks. I may need them." Stone pulled up the collar of his jacket. "Let's make a run for it."

They shook hands and hurried to their respective cars. On the drive back toward Archos, the rain followed Stone up the coast. Arriving, he made a quick stop in the center of the town and found a *charcouterie* still open. A prepared lamb stew and a bottle of local red wine both looked good and the proprietor packaged up his meal. Stone added a custard tart.

Back at the Foundation, the grounds were deserted. Stone sidestepped the puddles on the walkway to his cottage, as he imagined David sulking in his room about the negative Paris reaction to his Esperanto dictionary. No visit from him.

A visit from Margaux would be pleasant. Still, he hadn't

figured her out. She seemed too interested in his writing. Stone remembered what his father had told him years ago when he learned that his son had been assigned to the Nice consulate. Only French men understood French women. Or they thought they did.

A wood fire in the hearth warmed the living room. Stone made himself a drink. Why do the French insist on having such small ice cubes? He glanced out the window at the rain. After a few swallows of Irish whiskey, he turned on the radio and flopped into the armchair.

He mulled over what Fleming had said about the terrorist he shot. He had been an accomplished killer who had killed a female CIA officer. How many other Americans had he killed? No bad dreams about that bastard. He must clean and oil the Colt.

Since he had to go to Saint-Rémy, he would ask Margaux about the town and the surrounding area. Too bad she couldn't accompany him. She was a pleasant traveling companion. He got up and walked to the kitchen to freshen his drink. He chuckled. "God, my mind is back on sex. The juices are flowing again."

The radio station played light jazz. The wood in the fireplace burned with sharp cracks and put off little sparks. It smelled like mesquite wood, but looked like juniper. A good fire to stare at.

With a topped-off drink in hand, he went to the French doors and peered out onto the wet lawn. The town of Archos was barely visible through the mist. At home on Sunday afternoons this time of year he watched golf tournaments, but the television in his cottage only carried CNN and the regional French stations. One was a TV station from Nice. Lucy lived near there.

Lucy. Now Contessa Lucinda. Funny he hadn't thought about her. Maybe it was the finality in the way she had said good-bye at the party in Marseille. Years ago, he hadn't handled that romance well, but hell, he was a kid just out of college. He had learned a lot since then. Then again, four months ago his wife had walked out on him.

Lucinda. They had met at a New Year's Eve party given by some society group in Nice. Single US Navy and Marine Corps officers assigned to the Nice consulate were invited to attend as escorts for the young French debutantes. Stone first saw her sitting at a table with two older couples and several young women. He had debated whether he should approach and ask her to dance. The people at the table looked important and very rich, and probably one of the couples made up her parents. Just as he decided to move on, the Marine captain standing next to him said that after he returned from the bar he would target the broad with the nice tits. He'd looked in Lucinda's direction.

By the time the Marine captain returned, Stone was dancing with her. She had a beautiful accent and her auburn hair flowed softly over her ears. She kept turning away when she asked short questions about the weather, where he lived in America, and what he had studied in school. When she did face him, for those short moments, she seemed to have trouble concentrating. She clutched his hand and moved in closer as they danced.

The dance ended, and he suggested they walk over to the refreshment table. While sorting through the hors d'oeuvres, the Marine walked up, but before he could say anything, Lucinda took Stone's arm and asked him to introduce the Marine to her. At the same time, she waved to one of her girlfriends to come over.

When her girlfriend walked up, Lucinda said, "This young captain is going to ask you to dance." Turning to the Marine, she added, "Are you not?" Her girlfriend grabbed the Marine and pulled him onto the dance floor. Lucinda looked up at Stone, ran her hand along the single gold ensign's strip on his sleeve, and asked whether he would like to join her for New Year's Day dinner at her parents' villa. Her eyes were a hazel green.

The log fell off the grate in the hearth and scattered sparks onto the floor.

CHAPTER TWELVE

CÔTE D'AZUR—MAY 6, 2002

Stone decided to add physical exercise to his daily morning routine, hoping it would help his mental alertness. He looked forward to taking the trip to Saint-Rémy-de-Provence. A hard knock on the cottage door interrupted his sit-ups. Ricard, the French veteran, stood on the step holding a package. A slight mist hung over the lawn, and Stone asked whether he wanted to come in. He declined, and Stone joked about all the packages he was receiving.

"You have many friends, *Monsieur*. You are lucky."

When Ricard left, he unwrapped the package on the kitchen counter. It contained two American passports under different names with numerous entries and exits stamped in the pages; his photograph appeared in each one. A thin stack of credit and business cards accompanied the passports. The package also contained a pair of French automobile license plates. The short note enclosed read:

To assist you in your travels. M.

Mark had come through with the promised false identification. Just a bit of insurance, in case the assignment turned sour. Colonel Frederick was a good friend for handing him this contract, but Frederick was a realist, and Stone had better become one too.

He shuffled the papers on the table. A disguise would be good to use in Saint-Rémy, just a light alteration of his appearance to confuse his adversaries. He decided not to shave off his two-day-old beard. Already the growth was beginning to hide the scar on his cheek. He must not look American, so he would pack only continental-style clothes, and his footwear had to be European. He packed clothes for three days.

On the way to the Porsche, he stopped by the library to tell Margaux he was going on a research trip. "Up through the Luberon and onto Les Baux. Maybe Saint-Rémy," he told her. No need for anyone at the Foundation to know his exact destination.

She suggested he visit Arles. "Van Gogh lived there," she said. "It has an interesting Roman arena where they have bullfights."

He also needed to switch cars. The Boxster handled well and he would have preferred to keep it, but too many people had the car's description. Fleming had given him the name of the automobile dealer where he could exchange it. In the showroom, another Porsche caught his eye, a black Carrera 911 with manual shift. Once on the highway, he noticed the difference in handling. With a lot more power on the highway he felt in tune with the car as his hand coaxed the gearshift through the positions.

He left the Autoroute and cruised the back roads toward Saint-Rémy. Ancient plane trees, probably planted by Napoleon for the comfort of his marching infantry, bordered the two-lane road. The invigorating smells of awakening vegetable and herb gardens on either side of the road drifted in the open windows and, despite the gray afternoon sky, Stone settled into the world of Provence.

At Saint-Rémy, he parked the car in the treed parking area in front of the hotel where Fleming had reserved a room for him. The white, four-story wooden structure sat across the square from an old church. A café with outdoor tables and discolored umbrellas bordered one side of the plaza. Next to the church, a sign pointed to the walled old town of Saint-Rémy. Townspeople moved about as if determined to finish their tasks before the day ended.

The hotel receptionist wearing black-framed glasses didn't return Stone's cheerful "*Bonjour.*" She demanded his identification and he passed over one of his new passports under an alias. He knew the terrorists had an informal spy network of guest workers in France and he had no intentions of helping them identify him.

The young porter led the way up three flights of stairs and showed him to a room overlooking the square. It was a perfect position to sit and watch. He was glad he'd brought a pair of binoculars. Over the darkening town, steel-colored clouds seeped a soft mist. Lights from building and street lamps started coming on, casting reflections off the wet streets. Passing cars splashed people hurrying home from work. Despite the rain, he decided to take a short walk into the old town and look for the restaurant the concierge had recommended.

By the time he entered the narrow lanes of the old town the drizzle had wet his hair. None of the other men he passed on the narrow streets wore hats. *What happened to the beret?* He pulled the jacket hood up over his head. Darkness dropped on the town. If he continued to wander the alleys he could lose his way. He retraced his steps toward the lights of the square. Dinner would have to be at the hotel. The next day he would carry a town map as he pretended to pursue his travel writing assignment.

Hassan and his two companions pulled up to a two-story apartment house in a simple working class neighborhood of Saint-Rémy. The Iraqi driver parked the BMW in the one remaining space in the back of the building. The three hurried up the flight of stairs and knocked on the first door on the second floor. A bearded man wearing a stitched white skullcap answered and Hassan was met by the sweet smell of moussaka and *Allah, be with you.*

"I have dinner for you, my brothers," the bearded man said, and led them to a wooden table where they hastily ate the meal set before them. Their host returned from the kitchen and told them, "You may sleep there tonight." He pointed to the cushions scattered on the floor.

Hassan asked, "Any luck learning about the important man the Saudis are protecting? The al Qaeda leader?"

"Our brothers are alert. If the Saudis stay here, they will

have to eat. They can eat food only prepared in the permissible manner, *halal*, so our friends in the restaurants are watching for them."

Hassan showed him the photograph of Stone. "I am also looking for this American."

The man studied the face. "There are few Americans in this town, and they come in buses for a day and then leave. This man I have not seen."

"Tomorrow, we will walk through the town and find this 'very important person' Abdul Wahab spoke of. If the American is here, he may lead us to him." Again, Hassan considered it odd that Wahab and his Saudis were so concerned with these Americans.

The next morning, Stone threw back the thin blue blanket from his double bed. In his bare feet, he walked across the cold floor to the bathroom and, after relieving himself, brushed his teeth at the rust-stained sink. In the mirror, the stubble hid his scar. The shower needed a good scrubbing. He stepped into it, closed the torn plastic curtain, and tried to enjoy the hot water.

After drying himself, he dressed and went over to the window, pulled back the curtains, and swung out the shutters. The morning sky was cloudless. Sunlight brought out the earth tones of the town below. Across the square, the old town huddled amid tight, winding streets. The gray church looked like it had planted itself into the ground centuries ago. The people below moved about at a relaxed, early morning pace. His black Porsche was still under the tree where he'd parked it the night before.

At the café on the plaza, he sat in one of the curved wooden chairs with rattan backing and enjoyed coffee and yogurt. Finished reading the newspaper, he returned to his hotel room, pulled a chair to the window, and then watched the activity below. Soon he became restless. The CIA believed the high-level terrorist would travel through the town, but would someone so high profile risk traveling through this busy section of town, or would he hide out in an outlying area? The only face he knew was Hassan's, and he was not part of the Saudi group. He called Fleming.

"Mark and I are on the road now," Fleming answered, sounding annoyed. "We should get into your area by dinnertime." The phone transmission faded in and out. "The rendition team has left from Germany, but won't be in position to act for a day or so."

"What do you want me to do?"

"Walk around. Look for people who fit the obvious profile, like you're supposed to." Fleming hesitated. "And watch out for that guy Hassan. You saw his picture. If you see him, follow him."

"Who are these people from Germany?"

"The rendition team? They're the guys who will snatch this terrorist. Don't worry about them, your job is to spot anyone suspicious." The cellphone faded out for a few seconds. " ... fancy hotel that could hold seven or eight rich Arabs."

"Look for a hotel? Any name?"

"Hang on." Stone heard Fleming talking in the background with Mark, then came back on. "It looks like an old mansion, with gardens and trees. Don't know the name. Ask around. Stay in touch."

Stone shook his head. Soon a horde of armed people would descend upon peaceful Saint-Rémy, looking for a phantom terrorist.

At the front desk, he was given two possibilities that fit Fleming's description of the hotel. One was close by, on the road toward the Roman ruins of Glanum. He decided to walk along the outside of the high wall surrounding the old town to get a feel for the locale and then search for the hotel. The light breeze through the sunlit olive trees caused shadows to dance on the paving stones. On the upper floors of centuries-old stone-faced townhouses, homeowners had thrown open shutters painted blue, green, or maroon. Shopkeepers unlocked doors for customers, who parked and hurried into the shops. Stout older women watered window boxes holding brilliant red and blue flowers.

Stone enjoyed the setting and slowed his pace, but remained vigilant, searching the faces of the men passing him. Before long, he found a hotel that matched Fleming's description. The wide two-story structure looked like a mansion that years before had belonged to a family of importance. It sat back a hundred feet or so from the residential street surrounded by tall sycamores. He crossed the gravel drive and climbed the four worn marble steps to modern glass entrance doors. Inside the hotel, his shoes squeaked on the waxed floors as he approached the unmanned reception desk. Off to the left he saw an unoccupied dark-paneled library lined with bookcases. The only sound came from the slow ticking of an antique clock on the mantle of a stone-faced fireplace. Beyond the reception desk, tables and chairs filled a glass-enclosed patio that overlooked a treed garden resembling a park. A voice came from behind him. "Monsieur?"

The concierge regarded him with an inquisitive look. He wore a pressed suit with a crossed-keys pin, *Les Clefs d'Or*, in his lapel. A gold pen in his right hand tapped the notebook held in the left. In French, he asked Stone whether he required assistance. Stone responded in Italian-accented French, "I am seeking accommodations for myself and my family."

The concierge closed his eyes and waved the pen back and forth. "No. No." He then asked Stone in French whether he spoke English.

Stone continued the charade, answering in English, again with an Italian accent. "I wish to see your hotel. My family will be coming. My wife, children, and I need a nice place for us. Perhaps tonight or tomorrow night."

"Impossible. Very sorry. We are fully booked. Perhaps next week."

"Ah, but you have such a big hotel!"

"A party has reserved the entire hotel for the next four days. They will be arriving this afternoon." He motioned Stone toward the door and then stopped. Three men had exited a BMW sedan parked in the lot and were approaching the entrance door.

"More people to turn away," Stone said. The men wore dark clothes and the one in the middle had a full moustache.

As they came up to the door, Stone pointed to the library and said, "I'll just take a quick look in there while you're taking care of these people." Before the concierge could object, he left. The man with the moustache entered first. Stone listened as he introduced himself to the concierge as Hassan Musab Mujahid. Then he inquired about the party arriving from Toulouse. The concierge advised that the party of seven was expected in the late afternoon.

Stone edged out the side door and hurried through the gardens to the street. He turned left and jogged to the end of the block, then positioned himself where he could spot Hassan and his men when they drove out of the hotel parking lot. Leaning on a tree, he dialed Fleming's number on his cellphone. No answer. The Porsche was a good five minutes away, and even if he ran to get it, he probably wouldn't get back in time to follow Hassan's car. He decided to stay put.

The BMW eased out of the driveway and turned in the opposite direction from where Stone stood. Two men were in the front, but Stone couldn't see whether more men sat in the back. He watched the car drive off, then walked back to the Boulevard Victor Hugo, crossed over, and entered the old town through an arched gate in the wall.

Options came to mind. Get the Porsche and return, sit on the street, and wait for the terrorist group to arrive. Then again, if they're half as good as the CIA believed, they would set up countersurveillance and spot him. No sense being "made" at this point. Better stay away from the hotel. Meanwhile he had to contact Fleming.

Buildings of varying shades of gray and tan defined the narrow winding streets of the old town of Saint-Rémy. The worn tile roofs looked incapable of keeping out the rain. A car occasionally inched past him, barely missing him and the fronts of buildings. From a timeworn marble fountain, water trickled out of the mineral-stained mouth of a stern lion. The fountain clung to the side of a building, and above it ivy climbed to the eaves of the roof. He found Rue Lafayette with its few smart shops lining the street close to the St. Martin church.

His cellphone rang. It was Fleming. "I spotted Hassan," Stone told him, then gave a quick rundown on what he'd learned at the hotel.

"Good work. Now just stand off. We'll handle surveillance of the hotel and the rest of the operation." Stone listened as Fleming related the same information to someone in the background. Fleming came back on the phone. "Your job is basically done, but stay another night in case we need you. Did Hassan see you at the hotel?"

"I don't think so, and I'm out of the area now."

"Good, we'll be in touch."

While Stone slipped the phone back into his pocket, he spotted a boutique displaying men's sportswear. Buying clothes didn't interest him so much as he was curious to see how a French designer would skillfully blend a modern shop with honey-yellow hues into a cold stone building. He walked in and gave a cheerful hello to the proprietor, which was not returned.

Earlier that morning, the bearded man at the apartment house had told Hassan that two local restaurants were to deliver *halal* food to a hotel outside the old town. Hassan decided he would go to the hotel and try to identify the important Saudi, even though members of his advance party might see him. When he had arrived at the hotel, he identified himself as a member of the Saudi delegation and the concierge told him the others would arrive that afternoon. The concierge appeared to feign not remembering any of the names of the people who would be arriving. Before leaving, Hassan casually asked whether many guests had to be turned away.

"No, not many," the concierge replied.

"And who was the gentleman who came in a few minutes before us?"

"Oh, the Italian gentleman. Unfortunately, he and his family must look elsewhere."

Before Hassan had gone into the hotel, he and his two companions had parked on the street for an hour to make sure no Saudis were in the vicinity. While waiting, Hassan had seen the familiar-looking man enter the hotel. Something about the man's motions or body language made Hassan suspect he was not European. When he did not see the man inside the hotel, his suspicions increased. Now, standing next to the car, Hassan showed Three Fingers the photograph Abdul Wahab had given him. "I am certain it was this American. He is on foot. Go into the town and find him."

"And when I find him?"

"Kill him. However, be careful of him. When it is done, contact me."

After an hour searching the narrow lanes of the old town, Three Fingers spied the American inside a boutique. From the street, he watched the American take his time trying on sweaters. One particular light blue sweater seemed to appeal to him. As he replaced it after examining the garment, the proprietor, appearing irritated, refolded it and set it back in its original position. The American continued to select items of clothing, hold them up for examination, then discard them; the shopkeeper closely followed him around the shop, refolding the clothes.

From down the street, an elderly man and woman approached carrying groceries. Three Fingers raised his cellphone to his ear, looked down at the ground, and pretended to carry on a conversation. The couple passed him and he put the phone back in his pocket.

Smoke from his cigarette hung in the still air and he moved a few steps away from the swirl. Hassan expected him to kill the American quickly and without complications. Hassan was that way, very efficient. He would be good in commerce, if he had a place to do business, but who can do business in refugee camps?

Now the shopkeeper seemed to be arguing with the American. These Americans, these crusaders—very difficult people—no one liked them.

Hassan's people had helped his family when they all fled Palestine in 1967. Their two families were close long before they fled their homes. In Palestine they had cultivated citrus groves next to each other. There were no groves as beautiful in the refugee camps. The dirt there was hard and dirty.

He watched the American wave to the shopkeeper and walk out of the shop. Outside on the street, the American strolled with his hands clasped behind his back. He stared into the window of each shop he passed, pausing now and then. Three Fingers watched his body movements. The man was right handed; therefore, his left side would be his weaker side. A narrow alley came up and the American hesitated, then turned into the entrance.

When he looked around the corner, the alley was empty except for the man he was stalking. The American had stopped a few feet ahead and was looking down a slight incline at a house with a low iron fence in front.

It was time.

Three Fingers pulled the knife from his belt and advanced on the balls of his feet, the blade held high in his right hand. Coming from behind, he intended to reach around the right side of the American's head and bring the knife quickly across the throat. If need be, he would follow up with a quick stab into the kidney area, then kick him down the incline.

As the extended knife came around his neck, the American's head jerked back and his right arm swung up, deflecting the knife hand. Three Fingers saw only the American's left hand as it came around and crunched into his right ear. Surprised by the blow, the knife slid from his grasp. It clattered across the alley. The heel of the American's right hand smashed up into his nose. Blood wheezed from his nostrils. His eyes blurred, but Three Fingers rushed forward.

The American jumped back, removed his sunglasses, and placed them in his shirt pocket. His eyes looked like Hassan's, icy. Three Fingers lunged again, but the American grabbed his right arm, yanked it forward, and threw him down the incline.

As Three Fingers flew through the air toward the staked fence, he knew something bad would happen. He landed face down on the fence, the metal stakes penetrating his shirt and into his body. The wounds were serious, but not fatal. He flayed with his hands to push himself off, but then a heavy weight slammed against his back. The American had landed on top of him, pushing his body down six more inches until his chest met the crossbar.

"The end has come," Three Fingers whispered.

An image of his elder son's handsome face came to him as the American yanked up his head by the hair and whispered, "Go with God."

CHAPTER THIRTEEN

SAINT-RÉMY-DE-PROVENCE—MAY 7, 2002

"Did anyone see you kill him? Were you followed? Did you use a gun?" Fleming's questions shot out of the cellphone. "Shit, Stone, how does this affect the operation?"

"As far as I know, it doesn't. The guy was one of Hassan's men. I don't know how he found me."

"Where are you now?" Fleming asked.

"In my hotel room looking out the window. All seems quiet. Have you seen our target?" At that moment, two large sedans drove through the square. "Hold on. The target is here. Two black Mercedes just passed by, heading toward the hotel."

"Wait a second." Fleming was shouting in the background. He came back on the line. "We're on them. Can't talk anymore. Keep out of sight."

The line went dead. Stone hadn't had time to tell Fleming that Hassan's BMW was following the two Mercedes.

His attempt at disguise had not worked, so Stone shaved off his beard. After another glimpse out the window, he lay on the bed. For the first time since he'd come to France, his gun lay on the nightstand next to him. After he had killed the man, he'd returned to the hotel by a circuitous route. He hadn't heard police sirens. Evidently, no one had found the body. Hassan must suspect by now that something had happened to his man. What would be his reaction?

While the soft light of dusk eased through the window, Stone stared at the ceiling. Outside the window sirens wailed. He jumped out of bed and took a look. An ambulance followed by two police cars nosed into the narrow street next to the church and disappeared into the old town. Someone had found the body.

• • •

Dinnertime. Stone needed fresh air and a different scene, something to distract him, to get him out of his sour mood. In the short time he had been in the sunny South of France, two men had tried to kill him. This assignment has major downsides, he thought, taking a deep breath as he looked around the dingy room.

No matter that Fleming had ordered him to stay out of sight—he would take the Porsche for a drive in the countryside. Jamming the Colt into his shoulder holster, he chose his leather jacket to ward off the chill and hurried out of the hotel. It felt good to get behind the wheel. The map showed the town of Les Baux not far away. Margaux had given him the name of a good restaurant there. Too bad she wasn't with him. Every few seconds he checked the rearview mirror. He detected no surveillance. A short distance out of town, he passed Roman ruins. He would visit them the next day before returning to Archos.

Hassan listened to the bearded man, whose dirty white skullcap sat crooked atop his greasy hair. He was relating how the police had found Three Fingers. The apartment smelled of burnt cabbage. Hassan motioned to his Iraqi driver to open a window to let in fresh air.

"My brother, who sweeps the clothing store of a Frenchman, said a young boy found your friend on top of a spiked fence. It was very near the store. Some medical people came, but he was dead." The bearded man raised his arms and looked up to heaven.

"Did your brother see anything? Did anyone notice anything out of the ordinary?"

"No, my friend. He may have fallen onto the fence by accident, but it would have been difficult, my brother said."

The Iraqi driver spoke. "A strange way to die."

Indeed, thought Hassan. His unlit gold lighter lingered at the cigarette dangling from his lips. He would miss his friend.

Three Fingers was someone he could trust, not only with his thoughts, but also for counsel. They were able to communicate without speaking. He looked at the driver, who was picking his nose. It was a wonder the dumb ox remembered to unzip his pants before he pissed.

"I wonder how it was done," the driver continued. "I mean, how did he get himself on the fence? Do you think it was the American?"

"It is probable." Hassan leaned back. "Yes, it was the American." He thought a moment and then asked the bearded man, his host, "How many Saudis are here now?"

"Seven. Two of them, those Sunni pigs, came from Marseille two days ago. It was they who made sure of the hotel and the food for the al Qaeda man, bin Zanni."

Hassan jumped up. "You know the name of the al Qaeda? Why did you not tell me this before? Are you sure?"

"I learned only this morning." The bearded man's eyes pleaded. "My brothers just told me. They overheard the Saudis talking. They were quite excited."

Hassan sat down. The bearded man rose and offered him a tray of bread and hummus, which Hassan accepted and chewed slowly. Could it have been al Qaeda who killed his friend? If they did, they would think he would blame the American. Then he would take revenge and kill the American, leaving them free to take this bin Zanni to wherever they were going.

Hassan asked for more bread and the bearded man placed the tray on the table next to him. Something troubled him. Why were those Saudis so concerned about Americans? Why not the French? Did they hate the Americans so much to have that one killed in Nice?

The two North Africans came to mind, the man and woman he'd killed. Did the Saudis know he had killed them? Was it he they wanted to eliminate?

At a soft knock on the door, Hassan and the driver were on their feet, guns drawn. Hassan motioned the bearded man to the entryway. After a few words, a short man was allowed to enter the apartment. The visitor had a message for Hassan. Abdul

Wahab, the counselor to the Saudi prince, was in Saint-Rémy and wanted to meet with him as soon as possible.

Hassan and Abdul Wahab found a seat in the back pew of St. Martin's church. The only other people in the Catholic church were clustered in front at the altar. Wahab appeared amused by his choice of a church for their meeting. Hassan failed to see the humor.

Wahab bent over and whispered, "Everything is going according to plan. We have encountered no problems. Part of our success is due to your help. We assume the American has been eliminated, and we are most grateful to you."

"I heard the important man has arrived. How long will he stay here?"

"You have good ears." Wahab smiled. "Also, we heard that you thought enough to make sure the hotel was safe for his arrival."

"There are many ears in this town, as well as eyes."

"Thank you for your assistance. I am glad Rashid recommended you to us." Wahab handed Hassan a thick envelope. "This gift is given in the hope we can work together in the future. We will be in touch with you through Rashid."

Hassan watched him get up, walk to the front of the church, and depart through the right side door. He glided more than walked. He was a fop. When was the last time Wahab rode a camel in the desert? He opened the envelope and thumbed the euros. He would give this money to the family of his dead friend.

The next morning Stone broke out of a deep, dark sleep. His dreams usually came in colored images, but this time the dream had been gray and white, with him wandering through his empty home in Virginia. For a brief moment, he forgot he was in Saint-Rémy.

A door slammed in the hallway. He quickly reached for his gun on the nightstand. It sounded like someone was dragging a heavy piece of luggage down the hall, past his door, and then onto the staircase. Whoever it was let the suitcase drop step by step down the stairs, the noise diminishing as the bag made its way down to the first floor. The toilet bowl was trickling from the night before. Sunlight stole its way through the cracks in the closed shutters.

He stretched, rolled out of bed, and went up to the window. With the shutter opened, he looked up at a rose- and pink-clouded sky. Below were the normal complement of sleepy citizens headed for work. In front of the church, farmers had erected stands for the daily market. He detected no sign of surveillance activity.

After settling his hotel bill, Stone packed his car and set off for Archos. On the road south to the Roman ruins of Glanum, trees, pollarded the previous autumn, now burst with clumps of green leaves, which haphazardly clung to the pruned-back trunks and limbs. It took only five minutes to reach the ruins. A few early tourists were wandering around the monuments.

The Roman arch and the tall mausoleum sat somber as they had for two thousand years, testaments of the refusal to bend to the ravages of time and vandalism. He strolled across the road and entered the Glanum ruins. After studying them, he found a level piece of marble in the midst of bright red poppies, where he sat and took in the quiet scene. From the direction of the parking lot, a man in a dark business suit and blue tie headed toward him. The man had a confident walk and a slight graying at his temples. Stone recognized him from the consul general's party. He was the man Jonathan Deville had introduced to him and whom he said was his French intelligence contact in Paris.

"Good morning, Mr. Stone. We met at your consul general's party."

"Of course, Monsieur Colmont. What a coincidence meeting you here." Stone tried to read Colmont's face, at the same time wondering how long he had been under surveillance. Did the French witness the attack in Saint-Rémy the day before?

"No coincidence at all. I wanted to see how you are faring after your short stay in Saint-Rémy." Colmont dusted off the marble slab with his handkerchief and sat down next to Stone.

"The last time I spoke with Mr. Deville, he asked that I check up on you."

"That was kind of him. We're old friends."

"I thought it wise inasmuch as two of your American colleagues have not fared well recently. However, you seem to be more resilient." He slapped both knees with his hands, waiting for Stone to speak, and when he didn't, he continued. "Your colleagues have been working with us. The al Qaeda people are leaving this morning for Nice instead of tomorrow, so plans are a bit ... hmm, in disarray."

Stone did not trust the Frenchman. Fleming had not mentioned a joint operation with the French, although it made sense. You just didn't pull off a rendition operation in France without their concurrence. "I'm heading back to Archos," Stone said. "The stay here was quite pleasant."

Pointing to a broken marble column, Stone mused. "I wonder ... you know, back when these beautiful ruins were a living town, I wonder if the ordinary person knew the barbarians were about to destroy them? Tell me, Mr. Colmont, do you believe history repeats itself? Are the barbarians preparing to get us all again?"

Colmont tried a smile. "Mr. Stone, be careful. You were lucky here. Your people used you as bait to find the al Qaeda leader, bin Zanni. They should have confided in us. We have been tracking him for a month." He pulled out a pack of cigarettes, frowned, and put it back in his pocket. "Your people have to learn to trust us."

"How well do you know Jonathan Deville?" Stone asked.

"We went to school together in Paris. As you know, years ago his father was a legal attaché at the American embassy." Colmont laughed. "And now Jonathan is the legal attaché. A family tradition."

Stone smiled. "The old school ties. Works every time."

"His family has a history here in France, so..." He turned his hand back and forth. "And you, Mr. Stone? You come from the same organization as Jonathan, no?"

"Yes." Stone raised his right index finger and waved it back and forth. "But now I am a travel writer."

"I understand, Mr. Stone." He rose.

"Let me walk with you"

They walked to the road and Stone saw Colmont's black Citroen parked behind his Porsche. Colmont's two men stomped out their cigarettes and climbed into the car.

"Well at least they gave you a nice car." Colmont sighed. "Make good use of it to tour our countryside in Provence. Do you intend to return to Cuers?"

"I don't plan to. My trip there produced more questions than answers."

"Sometimes in life that happens."

Stone glared. "So I was no more than bait?"

Colmont shrugged, and then looked down at his shoes. "I hope we can work together on this operation. You are much more professional than your colleagues."

The two shook hands. Stone watched the Citroen drive off before he climbed into the Porsche. He sat a while and studied the Roman arch. The time he had gone trout fishing in Arizona came to mind. It was up in the Mogollon Rim country. He remembered tying a Royal Wulff wet fly to his line and thinking it was an interesting lure.

That's what he'd been since coming to France: just bait, a lure. A fucking Royal Wulff.

CHAPTER FOURTEEN

VILLEFRANCHE—MAY 8, 2002

Contessa Lucinda always felt relaxed with Philippe Monte, the man her father had hired as consigliere. Her father had fled Egypt after the political situation had made an Egyptian Copt's opportunity for continued financial success difficult. Fortunately, most of her father's holdings were parked in Swiss banks. Following the death of both her parents, Monte had continued to help Lucinda administer the family's finances.

Philippe Monte unbuttoned the jacket of his taupe Brioni suit. "I've always enjoyed this view, contessa. It is one of the best on the Riviera." He swept his hand before him. "From up here on the mountain one can see the bays of both Villefranche and Beaulieu. It is like sitting in an amphitheatre." His trim gray moustache matched his close-cropped hair. "Look at the town of Villefranche down on the right and Cap Ferrat out there."

"Yes, it is gorgeous. I hope we can continue to enjoy it, however, we may need some luck." She closed her eyes and lifted her face to the sun. "Your report shows we are in debt to the sum of twelve million euros."

He nodded, then sipped his cappuccino. The morning breeze ruffled the white linen tablecloth. In the distance, a truck rumbled on the coastal road high up the mountain above them.

Lucinda shifted her legs and adjusted her pleated skirt. "And all because of that unwise investment. Why did you allow Boswell Harrington to talk me into backing him on that Afghanistan scheme of his?"

"I warned you against signing those promissory notes."

"It was your job to protest! For God's sake, this is my *birthright* we are talking about!"

He laid his report on the coffee table. "If you remember, you were more confident of Mr. Harrington's—uh, shall we say, business acumen?—than listening to my concerns about the venture."

"We would have made a tidy profit if it had succeeded." She removed her sunglasses and pressed her palms on her eyes.

"Who was to know?" Monte sighed. "Who was to know one could buy that space age mineral from Angola at a cheaper price."

"I should have been smarter. Who has ever made money in Afghanistan except drug lords?" She pushed away her plate of fruit, then reached back and picked some grapes off a stem. "How much is this castle worth?"

"Contessa! You are not thinking of—" He shuffled the papers on his lap. "You could realize, perhaps, twenty-five million euros for the whole estate here. With the furnishings." He paused and said slowly, "But sales of this magnitude take a long time to find a buyer."

She gazed down at the Bay of Villefranche as she had done from the time she was a little girl. Sleek white boats cruised back and forth from their anchorages out to the Mediterranean Sea. As a girl, she would make up stories about who sailed on the boats and what adventures the seamen had or were going to have. The big American warships would anchor for weeks in the middle of the bay, their little gray boats ferrying sailors to and from the dock.

"My family has lived here for centuries," she said. "We lived here when this region belonged to Italy and, I think, the Grimaldis. I will not sit here and watch it disappear. Never!"

She clapped her hands, summoning the servant, and asked Monte, "Would you care for anything more to eat?" He declined. After a few moments she asked, "Are you positive we cannot sell or lease out the land in Tuscany? Can you not come up with some ideas?" She tapped her shoe, looking for the servant.

"The property in Tuscany is already mortgaged, and then there is the question of your brother's compliance. He, or at least his wife, might protest the sale."

Her brother, who lived in and out of a sanitarium in Livorno, proved to be a financial and emotional burden for her. And his Russian wife tried to intrude in the family affairs. She looked at Monte. "I apologize. Thanks to you, I have final say regarding family enterprises. My brother's compliance is merely a formality. His wife is of no consequence."

The young Austrian servant scuffed in her sandals over to their table. Lucinda ordered her to clear the dishes from the table and bring fresh coffee. The girl arched an eyebrow and then sauntered off with the tray. She pushed the door into the kitchen, and after a brief pause, Lucinda heard a sharp crash of broken china.

"Has the staff been paid their salaries?" Lucinda asked.

"I am pretty sure there were sufficient funds to pay them this month. I will check."

A single cloud cast a moving shadow across the bay toward the white yacht that had anchored the night before. Lucinda then thought of her sailboat tied up next to her beach house. It was a ketch with a teak deck that her father bought and taught her to sail. Hayden Stone had sailed with them that summer. Her father had said that Stone was a natural sailor. "He has salt water in his veins." When the weather improved, she would take the boat out for a sail.

"Does that monstrous white yacht belong to the Saudi prince?" she asked.

"Yes, that is the Red Scorpion. It was anchored over in Nice, but I suppose the prince wanted a change in view."

"Harrington would like to do business with the prince," Lucinda said. "He has asked me to provide an introduction. Therefore, I am planning an affair this weekend. We will hold it down at the beach house."

Monte frowned, then let out a long sigh. "Contessa ... your finances?"

"Please, don't be dramatic. The food will come from our farms up in Provence and the wine from our depleting wine cellar." She looked up at the pink-tinted clouds. "We still have those farms. Perhaps I will end my life as a milk maid."

"And a very elegant one, I must say."

"Perhaps the prince may help me with my finances … directly or indirectly." Monte frowned, and she continued. "Yes, I know, I'm courting trouble, but I do not intend to marry him." She straightened her skirt. The women in her family had a history of marriages of convenience, but not to Muslims. "Harrington wants the prince to finance the purchase of a Turkish shipyard specializing in yachts for wealthy Americans," she continued. "The arrangement is very vague, but I will receive what is called a finder's fee. Is that what it is called?"

"That is the term."

Looking off to Cap Ferrat, she said, "Too bad Mr. Bill Gates is married. He has a lovely house over there on the Cap."

"Not a suitable match for you, my dear. Besides being married, it is reported he refuses to wear a tie."

They laughed and finished their coffee.

"Contessa, regarding your properties in Tuscany—as you know, my cousin works on your vineyards and he has been doing some digging for new vines. He has uncovered a number of artifacts."

"When did this occur?"

"Recently." He pulled out a silver cigarette case and motioned if it was permissible to smoke.

Lucinda nodded.

He lit his cigarette. "You are aware that Italian laws are strict with regard to the sale of antiquities."

She nodded again. "Yes."

"As a result, the prices on the international market of these exquisite pieces have risen in the past few years. My cousin knows one of the last of the respectable *tombaroli*. This man says the vineyard to the west of your farmhouse sits on a Roman villa."

"You are suggesting I allow some grave robber to dig on my property and sell what we find? Which I suppose is illegal?"

"Well, the Italian government says it is illegal. There are those who would contend that what is found on your own property is yours, period."

Lucinda placed her slender, manicured finger to her

chin and thought a moment. "How much can I make selling those pieces?"

"I have another cousin who knows a buyer in Zurich who has seen photographs of the pieces. He has offered to pay up to three million euros for the first lot. That sum would keep the bankers satisfied for a few months at least."

"Good. Tell him to proceed, but I want you personally to supervise the matter. I am not to be embarrassed by problems with the authorities. Moreover, I want to see those photographs." She thought for a moment. "There may be a particular piece I want to keep for my collection. Especially anything Etruscan." She stood. "Now, I must be getting the guest list together. I am inviting Harrington, the prince and some of his retainers, and of course the American consul general. Do you have any other suggestions?"

"Let me phone the consul general. He may have some ideas for the guest list … say some visiting American business people or notables. The bigger the stew, the better the chance of finding the perfect morsel."

She laughed. "Philippe, you just made that up. My dear, I don't know what I'd do without you."

The two walked along the terraced path to where he had parked his car. As they strolled, he told her that because of her cash flow problems, he had returned her Bentley to the dealer, but the manager, a longtime friend of his, had agreed to lend her a Maserati in its place.

She waved as he drove off. On the way back to her library she decided she would phone the manager of her Tuscan estate and get his version of the story about the proposed archaeological excavation on her property. He also may have some idea how much Monte and his cousin expected to realize from the scheme. As for the weekend party, she would extend invitations to her friends Maurice Colmont and Jonathan Deville. With their connections, both could possibly be of help in her financial predicament.

Not until Lucinda had checked off the last name on the guest list did she instruct her secretary to add the name Hayden Stone.

Stone had been in her thoughts since the night at the party in Marseille. Lucinda believed chance encounters, like coincidences, had meaning, just as one's life had purpose beyond mere existence. She would rely on her instincts.

MARSEILLE

The people in Beirut had assured Hassan that the new man, Yazid, would be a good replacement for the deceased Three Fingers. Now here Hassan was, parked on the shoulder of a major highway on the outskirts of Marseille, looking down at this fool Yazid, performing one of his daily prayers.

"How long does he take with his prayers?" Hassan demanded. "We cannot stay along this roadside much longer. We are attracting attention. This is not good." Hassan looked up and down the highway. "In Marseille, we must find someone less absorbed in religion."

The driver answered him with wide eyes. "But he is performing his prayers, sir. He is a holy man."

"Praise be to Allah. We are soldiers, not mullahs." Hassan looked down at the prostrate figure. The man would be good with a bomb strapped to his belly and sent into a government building, but he would be useless on an assassination or a mission that required thought. "After Palestine is free, there will be time for prayer and poetry."

Yazid finished his prayers and hurried to the car, his head lowered. Hassan ordered the driver not to stop the car until they reached their destination. He settled in the back seat and pulled out his worry beads. After fingering them for a few seconds, Hassan shoved them back in his pocket. They were behind schedule with his plan. The brothers in America were impatient to receive the shipment. The next day he would meet with Dr. Aziz Husseini. He would urge him to move faster with his formula. Rashid would return from Nice after sucking the asses of the Sunnis, and then he and Rashid would meet with the distributor again about the wine shipment to America.

He sighed, thinking of his dear friend, Three Fingers, and hoped the brothers in Saint-Rémy had attended to his burial. The two men sitting in the front seat of the car were unreliable; indeed, he needed a trusted collaborator.

The car passed by the Marseille-Provence airport. Soon they would reach the safehouse. It amused him how quickly the Saudi, Abdul Wahab, had left Saint-Rémy with the al Qaeda functionary, bin Zanni. Hassan had caught a glimpse of the fabled terrorist leaving the hotel. Bin Zanni had needed the support of two men to walk the short distance to his car. Hassan stared out the window. Odd. The man was not old, and Hassan had not heard he was ill. And why were they taking him to Nice?

Wahab and his easy Saudi money. Hassan felt the inside pocket of his jacket for the thick envelope of currency Wahab had given to him in the church in Saint-Rémy. Again, the question came to mind: Did Wahab kill Three Fingers to make Hassan believe the American had done it? What purpose would that serve? No. The American had killed his friend. This American was more skilled than the CIA man he'd watched die in Nice. Another puzzle—why did the Saudis kill the CIA woman in Montpellier? Was the CIA getting close to catching bin Zanni? On the other hand, were they onto his own plan in Marseille?

The week before, on the car trip from Nice to Saint-Rémy, Hassan had decided that Wahab planned to use him as a diversion. If something went wrong with the assassination of the CIA man living at the Foundation in Archos, the CIA and the French would be looking for him, Hassan, the Shiite. They were clever, those Saudi Sunnis. No matter ... he would kill the American when the time was right, and then handle this Abdul Wahab.

Yazid in the front right seat chanted a Koranic verse. Hassan went for his beads, thought otherwise, then pulled out a pack of cigarettes.

CHAPTER FIFTEEN

SAINT-RÉMY-DE-PROVENCE

The conversation that morning with Maurice Colmont at the ruins of Glanum continued to nag at Stone. He pulled the car off the quiet two-lane country road onto a dirt farm path and came to a stop. Was the Agency using him as a decoy? The only specific operational instructions he had received since arriving in France were to go to Saint Rémy and look for a phantom al Qaeda functionary and a terrorist named Hassan. The latter may or may not have been responsible for the deaths of the two CIA officers. He was certain the Agency had an anti-terrorist program in place, but the details were being withheld from him. Why? Because people lower on the chain like himself needn't know.

Meanwhile, it seemed as if he had been led into the middle of an open field, while the Agency sat back and watched to see what would happen. Despite being targeted twice, the assignment hadn't been all that bad. After all, he now stood in the quiet Provence countryside, warmed by the Mediterranean sun and taking in the smells of a spring morning.

Back in the car, he turned on the ignition, hesitated, and then leaned back. In Saint Rémy, Fleming's last words were to keep out of sight. Disappear into the woodwork. Okay, that he would do. He decided to phone his friend Jonathan Deville in Paris.

"They let the target get away," Deville said, and Stone could picture him shaking his head. "I wonder sometimes if our colleagues are really serious about all this, or is their fumbling due to resources being stretched too thin."

"Fleming could use more people," Stone said. "and better intelligence. There're too many bad guys running around here, and we don't know who they belong to."

Deville lowered his voice. "I heard you had another nasty altercation. Apparently, you've become a lighting rod. Why don't you lie low for a while? Come up to Paris and stay with us for a couple of days. Paris is good for the soul."

"That's sort of what Fleming suggested," Stone said. He remembered Deville telling him at the consul general's party that his wife wanted to introduce a girl to him. Then Lucinda came to mind. She was on good terms with the Devilles. "Listen Jonathan, I do need a diversion, but I don't know if I can get to Paris." He paused. "You wouldn't have Lucinda's phone number handy, would you?"

"Christ, Stone, I suggested comfort for the soul, and immediately your mind goes carnal." Deville chuckled. "Wait a second." Back on the line, he continued, "From the contessa's reaction at the party the other night, I would say you're heading into more trouble, but anyway, here's her number."

After ringing off, Stone immediately punched in the contessa's phone number. Then, before pushing the Send button, he snapped the phone shut. What would he say to her? And how would he say it? He hadn't thought this out.

He started the car, waited a few minutes, then turned off the engine. The call would be awkward. The win-lose odds were not in his favor. What the hell. If he didn't call now, eventually he would. He had to remember to call her Lucinda, not Lucy. He phoned. Feeling relieved when told she wasn't available, he left his phone number with the woman he assumed was Lucinda's secretary.

As Stone pulled the car out onto the road, he felt a familiar sensation; a sixth sense told him he was being watched. The only other car on the road was behind him, a good mile away. It followed him for a while, then turned off at an intersection. Ten minutes later his cellphone rang. Stone knew it was Lucinda even before he saw the number displayed on the screen.

"Hello ... Lucinda."

"You called me?"

"Please hold on until I pull off the road. I'm driving." Stone eased onto the shoulder of the road. *Give both of us time to catch our breath.* After a moment, he said, "Lucinda, I've been meaning to give you a call." He waited, but she didn't respond. "The party at the consul general's house was a pleasant affair, don't you think?"

"Yes, it was," she said in her husky voice. "As it so happens, I just sent you an invitation for a little party I am giving this weekend."

"How nice. I'll be there."

After a long pause, she asked, "How is it in Archos?"

"I'm on the road right now. Just left Saint-Rémy and am heading back." Stone found himself running out of light conversation. "The weather in Archos ... I heard it's overcast. How's it there in Villefranche?"

"Sunny and warm. I'm watching sailboats down in *La Rade*, the bay."

"Sounds wonderful. Do you still have *La Claire*?"

"I would never part with my father's boat," she said. He detected her voice break slightly. "You are only two hours away. I can have a lunch packed, and we can take her for a sail."

"Great. I'm on my way."

"The boat is tied up at my villa's slip down on the bay. You can find your way, no?"

When Lucinda hung up, he stared at the phone and murmured, "Well, as Mom used to say, life has its twists and turns, doesn't it?"

La Claire's rigging hung smartly and her teak deck shone a golden brown from a fresh oiling. Stone looked over the craft's lines: still long, sleek, and strong. Lucinda's father had loved the boat and had shared the nuances of her personality with him. Stone had considered that sharing by Lucinda's father a generous gift.

"Hello there. You made good time," Lucinda called from the boat. She wore a navy blue turtleneck blouse and white shorts that flattered her long tanned legs. "Come aboard."

Stone hesitated as he realized his dress shoes would scuff the deck. He leaned against a piling and began to remove them.

"We have footwear for you," she said. "Did you bring a bathing costume? Of course not. No problem, you may use my brother's clothes and his shoes, if they fit." She offered her hand. "My brother looks the same size as you, and he will never use them."

Now came the moment Stone had dreaded. During the drive to Villefranche he'd wondered how he would handle the greeting. Would they kiss hello or just shake hands? Lucinda's palm felt moist, and he guessed she worried about the same thing. She solved the problem by giving him two *bises*, the French salutary kiss, one on each cheek, then pointed him toward the forward cabin.

There he found swim trunks and a blue- and white-striped pullover laid out on the bunk. Next to them lay an expensive sweater with tissue paper still in the sleeves. New boat shoes, which happened to be his size, rested in a store box. All he suspected had been purchased that morning from a very expensive local shop.

"My, you do look like you are ready for a sail," Lucinda said when he emerged from below deck. "Let us cast off. We can lunch while we are underway."

"Aye, skipper," Stone said. "It's been some time since I've been on a ketch. Just tell me what to do."

Lucinda used the inboard diesel to ease the boat away from the dock, toward blue water. She killed the engine and asked Stone to pull the halyard to raise the mainsail. She handled the mizzenmast. The craft leaned slightly from the light breeze, and with the trickle from water passing along the sides of the boat and slight creaks from up in the standing rigging, they were underway.

"Please take the helm," she said. "You know how she handles."

The polished wooden wheel felt familiar in his grasp. Images returned, only half-remembered: the helm, wooden and scarred in familiar places along the spokes; the soaring height of the mainmast overhead; the mizzen swinging close in front; Lucinda's father sitting in the cockpit across from Stone, stuffing his pipe with Turkish tobacco and gazing out across the sea.

Lucinda, balancing herself against the boat's tilt, gingerly slipped down into the cabin after saying, "Please do not make hard turns," a euphemism from the days when they were lovers and they sailed alone, and when she went down to use the head. This time, she blushed after she said it to him, as if she did not want to bring up old confidences.

Just within the mouth of the bay, Stone took the boat into the wind and the sails fluttered. Lowering the sails, they slowed to a stall and gently floated. Lucinda came up from below deck carrying a wicker basket holding a long brown baguette and a wine bottle protruding from beneath a blue-checkered cloth.

"You must be hungry, Hayden. When did you last eat?" She placed the basket down and then frowned. "We should not eat here. It is not the right place. A swell is coming in from the sea."

"I remember the spot where we used to snorkel. 'Our place,' you used to say." He thought he detected disapproval for referencing past times.

Lucinda repacked the basket and went to the helm. "Haul up the mainsail," she ordered.

They leisurely sailed toward a cove on the east shore. Perched on a cliff, two terra cotta-roofed homes, walls painted ochre, had not been there the last time. A motorboat with a cubby cabin passed slowly off the cove and, after a second pass, left them alone with the sounds of sea birds and waves gently washing up on the rocks. They dropped anchor and Lucinda allowed the ketch to ease around with the wind so the flukes of the anchor took hold. "The water is cold," she said, pulling out two wetsuits from a locker. "But I think only the tops are necessary." Slipping the top over her head, she added, "We can eat after our dive."

The black wetsuit stopped above her white bikini bottom. Her body had filled out since he had seen it last and now had a mature firmness. The absence of tan lines suggested hours of sunbathing in the nude. Stone zipped up his top, sat down, and pulled on his fins.

When he spit into his mask, she laughed. "You are old

fashioned, Hayden. The glass has been treated with … what do you say? Defogger? You do not have to spit on the glass anymore."

Her smile, with that trace of the innocence he remembered, had at last reappeared. Perhaps he could relax. "I wonder if that old German World War Two plane engine is still down there," he said.

"Let us take a look." She jumped feet first off the side.

He followed and they paddled a few yards from the boat. They took deep breaths and then dove down into the clear, aquamarine water. Inside the sheltered cove, the lack of current from the bay made for easy diving. White and pink shellfish and gently waving marine plants set a background for a quiet world. Lucinda took hold of his arm and pointed to a gray, twisted metal hulk. He indicated he saw it and then gave a thumbs up. At the surface, breathing hard, he said, "The wreck's still there." He blew water out of his snorkel. "Odd, we never found any other plane wreckage."

"Come, I will show you something else I found," she said. "But you must promise to keep it a secret."

She swam a few yards toward shore then pointed downward. Her strong legs took her straight down to an isolated clumping of seaweed at the bottom of a rock incline. Again, she took his arm, pulled him toward the plants, and then pushed the branches aside. Stone moved in and grasped a limb to hold himself steady. Lucinda touched a broken amphora, then swam to the side and brushed sand from the face of a marble goddess. The slanted sunlight from above played intermittent shadows across the statue's profile, chipped and slightly stained, yet still classic. Stone gazed as long as he could withstand the need for air. They popped to the surface at the same time, both gasping. Three times, they returned to look at the statue and at last agreed to return to the boat. Again on deck, pulling off their wetsuits, Lucinda extracted a promise he would not reveal her secret. "Collectors look for artifacts along the coast," she advised. "I do not want them to find her. She has rested down there for centuries in peace."

• • •

The two lay on the smooth wooden deck facing the sun. Stone let the rays heat the skin on his chest. He braced his feet on the chrome wire lifeline. Occasionally, a breeze brought on a slight chill. They had devoured the sandwiches packed in the wicker.

"Do you have a wife?" she asked, keeping her eyes closed, her face lifted up to the sun.

"I just got divorced."

"You left her for another woman?"

"She left me."

"She left you for another man?"

"I don't think so."

She rose up on her elbow and looked at him. "That is something you would know, I think. That is, if you had any interest in her."

Her swimsuit had dried. Her auburn hair, still damp, was pulled back, showing her ears. A little large. Once he had wondered whether they came from her Egyptian father or Italian mother. No matter—on another woman they would have been a distraction.

"Have you been married?"

"No," she said, and lay back down and closed her eyes. "Almost. Two weeks before we were to be married, he was killed in a car accident outside of Monaco."

"Sorry."

"No need. He was speeding with another woman in the car who, at the time of the crash, was performing a sexual act on him." She snorted. "Papa warned me about him."

Raising herself up, she looked down at her breasts and then adjusted her bikini top. For a moment, Stone thought she was about to remove it. She looked down at his body. Her eyes stopped on the recent wound on his side. With an assuredness, she reached over and ran her fingers over the pink scar. A pleasant chill spread over the skin of his chest and arms. He didn't want it to stop.

As if catching herself slipping into another world, she

looked away. "I will go down below and heat some Brie. Would you like to open the Chablis?"

An hour later, after checking the anchor, Stone walked back and sat next to Lucinda, who was gathering the glasses and plates. "You did not care for the wine?" she asked.

"Oh no, I did," he said, picking up the bottle and reading the label. "A Petite Chablis. It went perfectly with the Brie, which tasted of mushrooms. The wine was nice and clean." A bit edgy … just barely made the grade.

"Your director at the Foundation d'Élan gave me the wine," she said, balancing the glasses on the plates. "Now, what is it you do there?"

"I'm trying to write."

"Jonathan told me that," she said. "He thought you wrote travel books." She went over to the open hatch and Stone got up to help her. She continued, "How do you know Jonathan?" Without waiting for an answer, she started down the ladder, still talking. Stone followed. "Jonathan and his dear wife are coming to my party, so you will have someone to talk with."

"Is Harrington coming also?"

She laid down the dishes and glasses in the sink, then turned and looked him in the eyes. "Yes, he is coming with his wife." She stared hard, then she softened. "Boswell Harrington and I have had some business arrangements. You have no doubt heard that he wants to make it more than just business, no?"

"I don't consider that any of my business."

"My dear Hayden, you have become so sophisticated." She touched his chin. "The sun is beginning to set."

"It's a shame we have to go back."

She smiled and motioned him to follow her up on deck. "We have some options, as you Americans say. We can sail over to town and eat dinner there, or go back to the villa."

"Or we could stay here overnight. There're provisions aboard," Stone suggested. "And it's a safe anchorage."

She laughed. "Is it now?"

• • •

After a light meal prepared by Lucinda in the galley, they idled, watching the changing colors of sunset, talking about the deceased Villefranche poet, Jean Cocteau; the onslaught dreaded by the locals of *les aoutiens*, the August tourists; and how the world had changed in recent years. No mention was made of their time as lovers. Stone wondered what the sleeping arrangements would be. He could only hope for the best, but he picked up only vague signals suggesting they would sleep together. At about nine, the waning crescent moon appeared and Lucinda announced she was going to her cabin. "Hope you will be comfortable in the forward cabin," she said. "I put some English books there in case you wanted to read before going to sleep."

"Would you mind if I had a cigar on deck first?"

She didn't mind, which he knew, because her father had introduced Stone to cigars. She handed him a brandy, then said goodnight. Almost as good as a kiss. The temperature had dropped and Stone was glad Lucinda had provided him with a good, thick sweater. Soft twinkling lights dotted the shore of the bay of Villefranche and burst into vibrant whites and reds where the town was coming alive. The ketch rested on the water and stars spotted the sky above the mast. Only an occasional splash a distance off the bow broke the quiet. Perhaps squid shooting up from the depths and breaking the surface. Mediterranean fishermen hung bright lamps over the bows of their boats to attract them. However, all was darkness around him.

He decided against having the cigar and instead took a good swallow of brandy. Then he went down to his cabin and undressed. The books stuck in a cubbyhole were old hardbacks. Stone appreciated that none were erotic novels, the last thing he needed tonight. One of them was a vintage copy of *Travels through France and Italy* by Tobias Smollett. Perhaps the author would provide some ideas on travel writing. Did Lucinda purposely provide the volume, thinking he was now a travel writer?

An hour after he had fallen asleep, Stone woke to hear light footsteps overhead. Was Lucinda checking the anchor? Had the boat shifted toward shore?

He pulled on his swimsuit and sweater and headed for

the ladder leading up to the deck. The ketch's anchor lights provided some reference. He called out Lucinda's name, but received no answer. Holding on to the mainsail boom, he started toward the bow.

Suddenly, a heavy body tackled his midsection and threw him against the lifeline. A blade sliced through Stone's sweater and cut into his shoulder. He pushed against the hand, but the assailant twisted free and slashed back, this time low, and cut him again, this time on his buttock.

Stone realized he couldn't overpower his assailant, so he eased up and yanked the man to the side. Clinging to one another, they fell overboard.

The blackness of night crashed into the blackness of water. Stone had taken a big gulp of air before going into the bay. Now underwater, with his left hand, he grabbed his attacker's hand holding the knife. At the same time, he slipped his right arm under the attacker's arm and brought it around to his other hand, the one holding back the knife. On solid ground and with good traction, Stone could have pushed his opponent's arm back out of its socket, but in the water, the two just spun around. Meanwhile, in rapid gasps the man began swallowing water.

With his knee, Stone dug into the man's groin then snatched the knife. Now Stone slashed back and forth at the man's midsection as they drifted upward. When they surfaced, the man coughed out water and at the same time slugged Stone. The blow snapped Stone's head back. He kicked away and bumped into a hard moving object behind him. He assumed it was another attacker, but as the object passed along his left side, Stone felt the sandpaper scrape from the skin of a shark.

Stone swam hard toward the ketch's running lights. From behind him, the assailant screamed, a flashlight went on, and a beam from a motorboat searched across the water. Looking back, Stone saw in the light the man swimming hard for the boat.

The light beam now played on Stone and he heard the muffled shot from a gun fitted with a silencer. Next to his head, bullets splashed the water. Stone heaved the knife in the direction of the light. The knife rotated in the air and fell short, hitting

Stone's assailant who was still a good twenty feet from the boat.

The light beam now focused on the man, who was flailing and screaming. Stone wondered what part of the body the knife had hit to cause such a reaction when he saw the shark shoot out of the water, bite down on the man's shoulder, and give him two violent shakes. Both disappeared under the surface.

A voice carried faintly over the water from the boat. "Leave him." Stone detected a slight British accent. The engine started up with a throaty roar and the boat spun away, heading for open water.

Stone swam to the side of the ketch and searched for something to grab onto so he could lift himself aboard. The pain in his shoulder now matched an aching on his right buttock. Blood poured from both wounds, which he knew would attract other sharks. He had just thought of the anchor line as a means of getting out of the water, when Lucinda called from above.

"Hayden, is that you?"

"Yes. Quick, throw me a line. Sharks!" As he spoke, something hit his lower leg hard and pushed him away from the boat. "For Christ's sake, hurry!"

"I am. Here is the line."

A heavy nylon line hit him on the head. Stone pulled hand over hand until he was next to the boat. He tried to pull himself up, but Lucinda cried, "The line is slipping!"

"Throw the rope ladder over the side and tie it to a cleat! Quick!" Stone knew the shark would hit again. She yelled that the ladder was secure and dropped it over the side. He climbed, feeling the pain in his shoulder. As he reached the top of the ladder, Lucinda grabbed his sweater and yanked him onto the boat. He had not realized how strong she was.

"What happened? Who was in that boat?"

Stone collapsed on the deck. Lucinda switched on the deck lights and flashed a spotlight in the direction of the splashing. "Don't bother looking," he said.

"What is causing that splashing?"

"The shark found something tastier than me." He stood and pushed his wet hair from his face. "It seems we had an unwelcomed boarder." Had the terrorists found him there? No need to alarm Lucinda. "Are there pirates around here?" he asked.

"No, but there have been some robberies on the yachts and—God, Hayden, the shark bit you!" She touched his shoulder. "Take that off." She began pulling up his sweater.

"It's a knife wound. The robber stabbed me."

"The cut is not deep. No need for sutures, I believe," she said, using the sweater to press on the wound. "Where else?"

"Well..." He turned and pointed to his right buttock.

"Let us go down below to handle that," she said. Stone thought he detected a grin. In her cabin, which had a double bed squeezed fore and aft between the bulkheads, she directed him to the sink and applied an antiseptic to his shoulder. She then placed a thick bandage over the wound. Finished, she raised her eyebrows and pointing, ordered, "Down."

"I think the bleeding has stopped."

"Down with the trunks and lie face down on my ... bed." She gave a bored sigh. "We are adults, no?"

Stone complied and put his face in the pillow. He had made it to her bed, but saw no chance of scoring. He felt the sting of the antiseptic as she dabbed the cotton swab gently on his skin.

"It is not a major wound."

He thought he detected a held-back laugh.

She applied a bandage, smoothing down the tape with her fingers. "Well, your *derrière* will recover." This time she laughed. "It is still as *adorable* as I remember."

She got up from the bed. He turned over and rose to his feet. She stood at the sink with her back to him. He moved close to her and caressed her arms, then buried his face into the nape of her neck. He kissed her for a long time. Then he withdrew and waited.

Lucinda turned slowly, grabbed his waist, and kissed him hard. She pushed him away and struggled with her nightshirt. "Help me get this off. So you can get to me."

The shirt came off and he took a breast in each hand. Again, she kissed him hard, at times missing his lips. As they fell onto the bed, he slipped off her thong. Her fierceness surprised him. No submissive maiden lying back for him to take her. She grabbed and scratched at him. Each time he tried to place her in a position, she moved into one she wanted. Finally she took his face in her hands. With a slight shriek, she bit into his neck. Stone stopped thinking.

At last, exhausted, they lay under the sheet, looking at each other. Both were tired, yet they couldn't sleep. After a while, Stone whispered he was going up on deck to make sure everything was secure. Also, he wanted to see if any boats were lingering nearby. The people in the speedboat might decide to return. She threw a leg over him and held him tight.

"I'll be gone for only a few minutes."

She moved closer and snuggled her head on his chest. She jerked up. "Your wounds," then rolled over and switched on the light.

Stone looked down. "Shit. There's blood on the sheets."

"No matter," she said. "Just some blotches."

He let his eyes search her body as if studying a Greek statue in an Athens museum. She tilted her head and grinned as if to say, "enjoying the view?"

Stone chuckled. God, he loved being in bed with a woman!

"I shall come up on deck with you. There is a jacket in your cabin." She rose, then exclaimed, "You did not use protection!"

"Ah, no. Sorry, but I'm clean, trust me."

"Same with all you males, 'I am clean.'" She huffed. "I could become pregnant!"

"Ah, the chances are very slim—"

"Slim! Hah! Like I always told my girlfriends, you come like a racehorse."

"Lucinda, who did you say that to?"

"Oh, be still. What a prude. Go put on your trousers."

• • •

When they returned to the stateroom, Lucinda slipped on a top, placed a blanket on the bed and invited Stone to join her. Soon, she was breathing in the long and steady rhythm of deep sleep. Stone pressed his face against her arm and laid his hand on her waist. With half-shut eyes, he listened for any sounds not consistent with the boat's movement caused by the sea and wind.

Had Hassan tried to kill him again? Of course it was Hassan. Stone had killed one of his men. One of the men he had seen accompanying Hassan to that hotel in Saint Rémy. How did he find Stone? What made Stone such an important target? Tomorrow, Fleming had some answering to do.

Lucinda stirred and gave a fitful moan, then went back to sleep. He had put her life in jeopardy. Best he stay away from her, but ... He moved his lips slightly across her arm and his tongue tasted her supple flesh. The taste brought back the time she had surprised him with a visit to his apartment on an early rainy morning. He remembered having to call in to the consulate and tell his boss he was taking the morning off.

They slept until eight in the morning. The rocking of the boat from swells rolling in from the Mediterranean awakened them. The stab wounds were sore, but otherwise Stone felt good. His mind was clear and he seemed to be viewing the world from a different perspective. Lucinda slid out of bed and went to the head. She called from behind the door that she had to get back home. He rose and went forward to his cabin and brushed his teeth, washed, and started to put on his clothes. She came in and told him to wait until she changed his bandages. During the procedure, she avoided looking into his eyes and said little.

Afterward, as she dressed in her stateroom, he ground coffee beans and brewed a pot of coffee. She emerged from her cabin wearing white slacks and a beige pullover with no brassiere. Again, she said little. After they had filled their mugs with hot coffee, they went up on deck and viewed the bright sky and the bay sprinkled here and there with whitecaps from the breeze. Stone wondered what was wrong, but years before his father had told him, that at times like this it was best to keep your mouth shut. In the past when he had violated that rule, which was often, it had always proved disastrous.

So, of course, after a few more sips of coffee, he blurted, "Lucinda, is everything all right?"

She went back to the stern and sat looking out to the sea. "I have many things to do back at the palace. We must call the police about this incident."

"I know a policeman, but I don't know his number. An Inspector Colmont."

"Oh yes, Maurice. He is coming to the party." She handed him her cellphone. "His number is on my contact list." She looked at her watch. "We must set sail. The party, by the way, is what you Americans call black-tie."

"I remember going to parties here wearing my uniform," he said, regretting the statement immediately.

She got up and went forward to the bow. "I could use help hoisting the anchor," she called back. As they pulled on the line, she said, "The Navy dress uniforms always look better on younger men."

The *La Claire* rested, securely tied to the slip next to Lucinda's bayside villa. Stone picked up a hose to wash off the salt water from the deck. "No need," Lucinda called. "I'll have her cleaned later." Her dour mood had vanished once they had hoisted anchor and caught the morning breeze in the ketch's sails.

At sea, Stone hadn't been able to connect with Maurice Colmont to report the attack from the night before. He asked Lucinda for her cellphone. This time Colmont answered and listened while Stone related the details of the attack. Colmont interrupted, "What time of night did this occur? Were you and the contessa the only ones aboard?"

"It must have been about ten o'clock and just Lucinda—the contessa—and I were aboard." Stone answered, while watching Lucinda gather the wicker basket and her overnight bag. "Do you think it was more than just a random robbery attempt?"

"Tell me, Mr. Stone, what do your instincts tell you?"

Stone thought for a moment, watching Lucinda handing the food basket to a woman on her staff. "I think it was deliberate ... and if so, I've put Lucinda's life in jeopardy."

"Well, you may be right, but life is in many ways a gamble," Colmont said, after a pause. "I will have the local authorities look into the matter, and then after speaking with my superiors I will let you know if we have learned anything of interest. You will be at the contessa's party this weekend, yes?"

God, the French were as bureaucratic as Americans. "Yeah. I'll be there. Perhaps you'll have some information for me." Stone rang off.

Lucinda came over and, taking her time, gave him a warm kiss. She touched his shoulder gently. "I must attend to my ... other affairs."

Stone put his traveling case into the front trunk of the Porsche and wiped sea spray from the windshield. As he opened the car door, a young staff member ran from the villa carrying a round pillow.

"Sir, the contessa wants you to use this for your ride back. She wants you to follow me to the doctor's office. It is over there." He pointed to a two-story building a few blocks away.

"I don't think—"

"Sir, please, if you do not allow the doctor to examine you, Madame will be quite angry with me."

CHAPTER SIXTEEN

THE CAMARGUE—MAY 9, 2002

Early in the morning with the sun trying to break through a layer of low-hanging clouds, Hassan slumped in the back seat of the BMW as it headed west from Marseille to the salt marshes of the Camargue.

Dr. Aziz Hussein had suggested to Hassan that they meet at a place midpoint between Montpellier, the location of his university, and Marseille. This time of year few tourists visited the Camargue, a remote wildlife preserve.

Hassan remembered meeting Dr. Aziz in Brazzaville, Congo two years before. The scientist was working on disease control and spent most of his time in the jungles northeast of Brazzaville studying monkeys. A Palestinian brother had introduced Hassan to Aziz as they shopped for groceries at Brazzaville's only supermarket. After the introduction, the three had walked along the street toward the Sofitel Hotel and passed the abandoned American embassy. An old French colonial mansion, the embassy showed damage to the façade and roof from one of the recent riots.

"Would that all the American embassies look like this one!" Aziz had exclaimed, who stopped and smiled at the gray, dilapidated building.

At the hotel restaurant, the three had relaxed over glasses of iced tea and gazed out the windows at the swift, muddy Congo River, carrying flotsam and broken trees toward the rapids. Kinshasa, the capital of the other Congo, Zaire, sat a mile across the river and, at least for a while, the two Congos were not exchanging artillery rounds back and forth. Hassan sipped his drink and listened to Aziz expound upon his work with the contagious diseases of central Africa. Aziz had impressed him with his scientific knowledge, but mostly with his zeal. The man fervently believed they lived in the time of Arab civilization resurgence. Hassan hoped so.

"What are those lesions?" Hassan had asked, pointing to Aziz's arm. "Are they from your work? Are they from some disease you contracted from the jungle?"

"No. No. They are from the tumbu fly. They lay their eggs on laundry hung out to dry. You put your clothes on and the larvae then penetrate the skin." He rolled down his shirtsleeves. "An American businessman I met told me I should iron my clothes before I put them on. It kills the eggs."

They had all laughed when Aziz had added that it was wise to take good advice even from your enemy. Hassan also had thought this was a man he could use someday for his plan.

The BMW pulled into the parking lot of the Camargue Information Center; Hassan emerged, surveyed the surroundings, and then took the footpath that led away from the information center toward the open water of the Étang de Vaccarès. Aziz had told Hassan that he had visited the site a week prior specifically to look over the area for this meeting. He had sent written instructions to Hassan on when and where to meet. At one of the viewpoints overlooking the lake, Hassan saw Aziz with a heavy camera equipped with a long telescopic lens taking photographs of flamingos. The sun had warmed the lake water, which now gave off a heavy, tangy marsh smell.

Hassan stopped and instructed Yazid and the driver to split up and meander around the area to look for anyone appearing suspicious. Then he approached Aziz and exchanged greetings, after which the two strolled along the path bordering the lake.

"Did you see the white horses as you drove into the preserve?" Aziz asked. "They are wild horses. It is said our brother Arabs brought them here centuries ago when this place was ruled by our people."

"How much longer will it take to have the virus ready for shipment to America?"

"Praise to God, it will be ready soon," Aziz said, and continued to discuss the ecosystem of the Camargue.

Aziz had lost weight since the last time they'd met. His face held a gaunt, faraway look. Very few of his sentences did not invoke some form of prayer. He had promised delivery of the virus a month ago. Hassan pressed him, tugging at Aziz's sleeve. "I must know the quantity. Is it in liquid form?"

Aziz stopped and whispered, "God willing, you will get the virus in fine powder form."

"But I'm sending it in wine bottles, you fool!"

"It is so fine that it resembles liquid through the glass. Much easier to handle. It is my own design."

"No! It must be liquid!" Hassan moved quickly down the path.

Aziz called after him, "Powder is much better to handle. Our people in America who receive the bottles will be better protected."

"Who cares if they are protected?" Hassan spit the words out. "They are soldiers! Especially when true martyrs wrap explosives around their bellies."

Hassan turned and rushed back to Aziz. "Give me an idea when you will be ready. I must have a time frame. The bottles have to be labeled and filled. It will be a delicate procedure to fill the bottles without spreading the virus. Then I must ship the cases to America." He could feel the beginnings of a headache.

"Do not be concerned, my brother, I have thought that part out. Have patience. I will be in charge of filling the bottles myself. I know the cautionary procedures. There will be no mishaps. Within the week, maybe two weeks, God willing, I will be ready."

"That's what I mean! One week, two weeks, God willing this, God willing that … I cannot operate under conditions like this!" Some spittle flew from his mouth and landed on Aziz's jacket.

Aziz glowered. "If it were not for me, there would *be* no plan. Using my knowledge of genetics, I have engineered and replicated the virus." Aziz pushed Hassan back. "I, with God's help, have managed to isolate and stabilize this strain of virus. I avoided contamination and detection by the authorities. I did all of this *alone*."

Hassan put his hands in his pockets and walked over to the lake. Flamingoes and egrets were stepping carefully in the water. He suddenly wished he could enjoy this peaceful scene. Instead, in addition to his headache, he had a growing pain in his stomach.

Aziz came up behind him. "You will be patient. You have no recourse." Aziz's breathing became heavy. "When the virus is ready, and God willing, it will be ready soon, I will notify you. Then you will proceed with the plan."

Hassan took his hands out of his pockets and placed them on the shaky wooden railing separating the path from the water's edge. He had no choice but to wait. Aziz was in control, so he must bide his time. Aziz had possession of a virus, one of the most deadly known to science. If indeed he had reproduced it and they could transport it successfully to America, all would be well and good. If Aziz failed in the mission, Hassan would kill him.

CÔTE D'AZUR

In the shade alongside the swimming pool at the Foundation d'Élan, Stone relaxed in a deck chair next to David, who busied himself editing his Esperanto manuscript with a red ink pen. Stone thought it odd that only a few of the fellows from the Foundation ever used the pool, so the tranquil setting allowed for reading and contemplation. The air smelled fresh from the surrounding pines and the salt air from the sea.

The drive back from Villefranche had been uneventful, and the pillow Lucinda had insisted he take had eased the pain in his backside. Her physician had redressed the wounds, never asking the cause of the cuts. Stone did notice a number of sideward glances that suggested he was suspicious, but evidently Lucinda carried a lot of weight in the town.

Stone tilted his cap down over his face and closed his eyes. What a night. Putting aside the unpleasantness with the would-be assassin, sleeping with Lucinda had been unexpected and fantastic. What had he been thinking when he dumped her eighteen years ago? He had given up an easy lifestyle on the beautiful French coast, married to the most exotic woman he had ever known. Since he'd left Villefranche, images of running his fingers through her soft, auburn hair kept returning.

"Damn!" David exclaimed, jarring Stone from his daydream.

Stone took a quick look from under the brim of his hat. Seeing David engrossed in editing his manuscript, he returned to his thoughts. Maurice Colmont's remarks the day before at the Roman ruins still nagged at him. Perhaps the French intelligence officer was right; maybe he had been used as bait in the operation against bin Zanni. So what? He followed orders. Being a decoy was part of the job. He needn't know all the details. The "need to know" policy was necessary in case of capture by the enemy. Yet even knowing and believing this, Stone realized he had not relinquished control of his life; he carelessly had let it slip away.

Colmont was clever, trying to sow seeds of doubt. Maybe it was part of a recruitment approach by the Frenchman. Stone had used the technique numerous times in the past in attempting to recruit spies. Perhaps this weekend at Lucinda's party, he'd try a pitch on Colmont. Come to think of it, how did Colmont know the contessa? Are the social circles along the Côte d'Azur so closed? Then again, she knew Jonathan Deville. A nice little network. If it wasn't for people trying to kill him, he could get to like this place.

He turned to David. "Wasn't it about this time of day when we saw Margaux heading for the pool?"

David replaced the top on his pen. His Panama hat sat low on his head. "I see. Instead of working on your new travel book, you're mentally reviewing the attributes of that French maiden."

Stone grinned. "Just want to do my part for international

relations. My contribution to the 'People to People' program."

"My God. I last heard that phrase from my mother. How old are you?" David sat up. "I give you fair warning, that French lady is not to be had."

Bruises appeared along the left side of David's chest. Stone wanted to ask him about the marks, but thought he might come back and ask about the bandage on his shoulder. Then he'd have to come up with some story. No need to bring up last night's attack. Perhaps a subtle approach. "How are things with you?"

"How do you mean?" He looked away.

"I mean … with your Esperanto? Any encouragement from that academic in Paris?"

David lowered his head, concealing his face under his hat. "Not from the people in Paris, nor from anyone here at the Foundation."

"How much do you have invested in the project?"

"Everything. My life." David set his manuscript aside. "I'm counting on being published in order…"

"In order for what?"

"I teach at a prep school outside Philadelphia. If I get published, I'll stay employed." He set his jaw. "If I don't, I may end up a Dharma bum here on the Riviera."

Shouts came from the direction of the walkway leading from the Harringtons' residence. Trees and bushes hid the owners of the voices, which grew louder as they approached an open flight of stairs. Stone realized that they belonged to the Harringtons.

"Oh, Lordy! Here we go again." David jumped up and gathered his papers.

Boswell Harrington popped into view. He raced down the stairs with his wife Helen following him. He'd just paused to steady himself using the pipe rail when she gave him a roundhouse blow over the head with a wooden-handled handbag. Stumbling down the next two steps, he turned and threw his arms up to ward off another bash.

Stone shook his head. Here were the two paragons of the Foundation, impeccably dressed, screaming, and battering one another. Next to him, David said something about wishing he were somewhere else. The argument continued, and Stone picked up verbal clues as to the cause. Helen sputtered the words, "Villefranche! Weekend romp! She's nothing but Euro-trash!"

Harrington yelled back, "For God's sake, *you'll* be there! Your hysteria has turned into paranoia!"

She placed a well-aimed kick to his groin and he bent over. Groaning, he fell forward onto his wife and knocked her onto the steps. Stone jumped up and ran over to grab Harrington to prevent another blow. Both Harringtons turned on him.

"Back off!" Harrington growled. "This is of no concern of yours!"

"You heard him!" his wife yelled. "Mind your own business, you hack writer!" She pushed herself up from the stairs and started for Stone. Blood dripped from her left nostril.

Stone backed away. "Just thought a bit of arbitration might help."

She caught Stone blindside with her bag and he felt a welt rise on his left temple. He ripped the bag from her hand.

Harrington pointed at Stone. "Don't you ever again interfere in our business! If you do, I'll send you packing!"

Mrs. Harrington scoffed, "This person obviously doesn't know his place!" She wiped blood from her nose with the back of her hand.

"I do know, Madame, that this is not the place for such nonsense." He threw the bag to Harrington and back-stepped toward the pool. "And the place for foreplay is in the bedroom."

As Stone returned to the pool, he saw David heading for his cottage, who called back, "I can't afford to get into any more trouble." Then he rushed off.

Now the pool was deserted. Stone picked up a towel and pressed it to his head. On inspection, the towel showed no blood.

Margaux materialized from behind the vine-covered gazebo next to the stairs. She peered up the stairs at the Harringtons marching back to their villa. Her abbreviated top revealed a well-formed navel. At birth, did French doctors give an extra twist to girls' umbilical cords to form such delicious bellybuttons? She ambled over to him wearing a smile that said—you got yourself into trouble. She delicately took the towel from his hand and examined the welt with her dark brown eyes. Then she looked at the bandage on his shoulder. "Tut-tut."

Stone breathed in her familiar scent. "What is your diagnosis, Mademoiselle?"

She took his arm. "You certainly must be more careful. Let us go to your cottage and put ice on your head."

"You get hit in the face a lot?" Margaux had found an ice bag in the medicine cabinet and filled it with ice cubes. On the couch, her body touched his side as she pressed the ice bag to his head. After a bit, she let him take the compress from her. She stayed next to him and traced the long scar on his cheek with her index finger. Still examining his face, she ran her finger back and forth along the mark. Stone knew she was deliberately ignoring his eyes. At last, she said, "You must learn to duck your head."

They both laughed and as he moved his arm around her shoulder, she pulled back and moved to the far end of the couch. She brought her legs up and discreetly tugged her shirt down. With her arms wrapped around her ankles, she placed her chin on her knees. He let himself enjoy her coquettishness, while they made small talk as the late afternoon sun slipped through the French doors, casting streams of golden light across the rug.

"You know, I enjoyed our trip to Cuers," she said. "How did you fare in Luberon?"

He smiled. "My meal at the restaurant in Les Baux you suggested was excellent. I had wild boar." He wouldn't mention his trip to Villefranche.

For the first time since they had met, he found himself studying her face. She had high cheekbones and a straight nose, not too long. Her full eyebrows were a shade darker than her light brown hair. "On my next trip, perhaps you would like to come along?" he suggested.

"How do you say it? We shall see."

"What's going on with the Harringtons? Is there a problem

with the Foundation finances?"

She moved her legs off the couch and, with a slight pout, faced the fireplace. "That is not a good question to ask of me. He is my employer and there is a confidence."

"You're right, but obviously the Harringtons are having a hard time and they aren't keeping that in confidence." He pointed to the bruise on his head. "Maybe it's something other than finances?"

"You Americans are strange ... I mean annoying ... at times. You think you can fix everything that is wrong with the world." She shook her head. "Excuse me. What you tried to do, stopping the Harringtons from fighting was good. Everyone else just ran." She wiggled two fingers to illustrate a person running. "But sometimes it is not good to act on impulsion?"

"Well, my dear, my *impulse* now is to eat dinner. I would cook for you, but there is no food in the refrigerator." She appeared to interpret what he said as a hint that she should leave, so he quickly added. "Let's go into town and have dinner at your father's restaurant."

Margaux laughed and threw back her head. "Have you met Papa?"

He told her David had pointed out her father when they had lunch the week before.

"He will be very interested in meeting you," she laughed. "He knows we took a road trip together and has asked many times, 'Who is this Yank?' I told him you were an old sailor—I read that on the back cover of your book—and he does not like sailors." She waved her index finger back and forth.

"Oh great!" As the words came out, he thought of his daughter in her first year of college.

"Do not frown, Hayden. I will take care of you."

"I was thinking I should be watching over my daughter like your father watches over you." Her raised eyebrows indicated that his being a father was new information. "I have a son and a daughter. The twins are in their first year at university. Who is there to question her suitors? Young university men can be as dangerous as sailors."

"Your son can watch after his sister. They are lucky. They are not alone."

"You're right."

"So." Margaux caught his hand. "Off to my family's restaurant."

Archos had only a few cafés and the loyal patrons of Reynard's restaurant were filing in to occupy the few remaining tables. Animated conversations competed with the clatter of dishes and silverware. Margaux had reserved a table immediately outside the restaurant under an expansive canvas awning. The chairs were painted the same shade of orangey red as the tables and the awning. Their feet rested on the smooth cobblestones. They had a clear view of the harbor, and fifty feet away sailboats, tied up to the quay, rocked gently. In the near distance, high limestone cliffs, grasping scrubby Holm Oaks to their sides, formed a semi-circle around the village. Dusk retained the day's spring warmth.

Margaux agreed with Stone that a white wine would be perfect, and she went into the kitchen and returned with a chilled bottle of Cassis with beads of sweat running down its side. He filled their glasses and she raised her glass to him. "*A votre santé.*"

The wine was cold and crisp, and the sunlight glimmering through the clear tulip-shaped glass gave off a pale green tint. He tasted a hint of rosemary.

Her father, pulling a chair from the next table, joined them. With trimmed gray hair, combed back, he looked about ten years older than Stone and gave the impression of a man confident in life. He had a firm handshake. In French, he told Margaux the kitchen was busy and suggested the *rascasse* for her and her American friend.

Stone said, also in French, "This wine is delicious, Mr. Reynard. Is it from your vineyard?"

"Yes it is, Monsieur Stone," he answered in English, his eyes traveling over Stone.

Margaux watched her father pull out a pack of cigarettes.

"Papa, they are not good for you." She put her hand on his arm.

"Do you smoke, Mr. Stone?" Reynard slipped the pack back into his shirt pocket.

"A cigar now and then. I should have brought a couple with me tonight."

"Ah, Madame Reynard forbids cigars in the restaurant." Reynard smiled at Margaux. "Yes, my dear?"

Margaux waved at an attractive woman at the far end of the room standing next to the maitre d'hôtel. "I must go talk to Mama," she said and got up.

Stone glanced over but couldn't see her mother clearly. He turned back to Reynard who watched his patrons while tapping his fingers on the table. His heavy gold bracelet clicked on the surface. Stone waited for him to speak. Reynard turned abruptly in his chair and faced him. He started to speak, but stopped, searching Stone's face. "I see some American writers get battered."

"Only when they let their guard down."

"My daughter told us you have written books. Are you a serious writer?"

"Some say I'm too serious."

"You people who study at the Foundation stay for only a short time. Then you move on to some other place, no?"

Stone nodded.

"Are you married? Do you have a wife back in the United States?"

"No. I'm divorced." Stone set his glass down and leaned back in his chair. "You know, I really like it here in Archos. Perhaps I'll stay a while ... maybe write a book about Archos and all the friendly people who live here. What do you think?"

Margaux slipped back into her chair and anxiously searched both men's faces. "What were you two discussing?"

"We were discussing how writers get banged-up faces." Stone grinned.

"I must go back to work." Reynard bowed slightly. "A pleasure to meet you." The two men rose and Stone observed they both stood at equal height and had the same build. Reynard looked down at his daughter. "Margaux is, as you say, the apple of my eye." He quickly shook Stone's hand and moved off to speak with a group of customers seated at a long table.

Stone sat down and smiled. "Now, I thought that went quite well, don't you?"

"Hayden." She turned and blinked. "You have a lot to learn about the French and my father. Next to inspect you is Mama."

Mrs. Reynard came to the table with the fish stew. Her name was Juliette and she had the same dark brown eyes as her daughter and the same color hair, except for a few strands of gray. Her eyes ran over him, and when she finished her inspection, he felt as if he had been sized up for a new suit.

"I see good looks run in the family," Stone said.

Juliette faced him, arms akimbo, and shook her head. She turned to Margaux and in French said, "Remember what I told you about older men." Then she gave an exaggerated sigh. "But, you will not listen." She walked away shaking her head.

"I think your mother liked me," Stone said, sinking into his chair.

"Perhaps, but I can tell she does not trust you. She will give me a long talk tonight about older men and their tricks." She picked up the serving spoon. "Let us eat. The rascasse is a fish stew with what the English call scorpion fish." She served him a steaming portion of fish chunks and vegetables smelling of leek and fennel.

The stew provided constant subtle surprises in flavor, and the Niçoise salad differed from what he remembered from home, obviously due to the freshness of the olives and the anchovies. He asked Margaux where she lived, expecting her to say her family lived in an apartment above the restaurant.

"Outside of town," she said. "In an old house next to the vineyards."

Of course, and no doubt the family home was decorated in exquisite taste and reeked of history. Stone let himself relax. He looked away. Across the water, lights became visible as the sun inched toward the cliffs. Over the bay, the colors in the sky had changed. The appreciation for the Mediterranean style of living that had washed over him as a young man had returned. A comfortable world, vastly different from the Washington life he now realized he wanted to leave behind.

His musings were interrupted by loud voices coming from a restaurant two storefronts away. The stridency of one voice distinguished it. The voice sounded familiar. Margaux stopped eating, her eyes intent, as if straining them helped her hearing. She looked at Stone and both realized the voice belonged to Boswell Harrington.

"Don't turn around," Stone whispered.

At the same time, Reynard came back to the table. She looked up at her father and put her finger to her lips. Reynard bent down. The two whispered and gestured toward Harrington. Stone got the drift of their conversation, then she pointed to Stone's bruise.

Reynard's moustache turned up in a smile, and he grabbed Stone's arm. "Your director often eats over there in my competitor's bistro. Tonight, he is with some tough customers from Marseille. From the look of it, he is having big problems."

"Those two thugs he's with—what line of business are they in?" Stone asked.

Reynard whispered something in his daughter's ear. She looked at Stone, then at her father and nodded.

"Maybe illegal business," Reynard said. "I know this is not good for the reputation of the Foundation."

"We all have skeletons in our closets." Reynard had not quite caught the meaning of the phrase. "Does it have to do with narcotics?" he added.

Reynard shrugged and moved away. Margaux pushed her plate aside and leaned back in her chair, tilting her head in the direction of Harrington. Stone studied the faces of the two men from Marseille. The big one had the look of a North African, and the other one, wearing a well-tailored suit, could have been from the Levant, maybe Syria or Lebanon. Both appeared agitated.

• • •

Harrington pushed back his chair and walked out onto the sidewalk. There, he folded his arms over his chest and looked out at the harbor. The man in the suit threw some paper money on the table and joined him. The North African remained in his seat and sipped his coffee. Eventually, it appeared that the man in the suit had reassured Harrington on whatever problem had caused the row and the two started to stroll away from the restaurant. The man at the table got up and followed them.

"I'll be right back," Stone said. "I want to see where they go."

She touched his arm. "I will go with you." Before he could object, she said, "I know this town better than you."

As they hurried out of the restaurant, Stone glimpsed Reynard scrutinizing them. He didn't look happy.

They slowed down when they were about one hundred meters behind Harrington and the two men. Whatever had triggered the argument apparently had now been mollified. He and his two companions meandered along the quay. They turned left and headed up a tree-lined street.

Margaux pulled Stone's jacket sleeve and led him up an alley that ran parallel. "They are on Olive Street. We can go this way. I will show you."

The perspiration from Boswell Harrington's armpits spread into his dress shirt. Tonight, at the restaurant, Rashid had proven to be a problem. Arguing in a public place, especially in Archos, wasn't wise. Twice today, Harrington had lost control. Not good, especially with business associates. Obviously, Rashid was intent on taking over Harrington's sources in Marseille. It would not happen. He had worked hard to create his little network. Haphazard as it was.

"How far away did you park your car?" he asked Rashid.

"On the street up to the left. I do hope we are still friends. Disagreements always occur now and then." He touched his heart with his right hand in the Middle East gesture of asking for pardon.

Harrington had seen this gesture many times and knew when it was accompanied by insincerity. This fat, unctuous man and his ugly companion had no chance getting what they wanted. Harrington's contacts in the Marseille drug world were his, and if Rashid persisted in demanding to know who they were, he might have one or two of those contacts pay this bastard an unexpected visit.

"Rashid, my good friend, we deal in weighty matters, so tensions can arise," Harrington said. "We will talk of this later."

Rashid turned left onto a side street. "Our car is down the street, Boswell. May I call you Boswell?"

"Not many people do, Rashid." Harrington slowed his pace. He wanted to leave these two annoying people and return to the Foundation. "This weekend at Villefranche, I will speak of these matters with your boss, Abdul Wahab."

Stone and Margaux had reached an intersection and turned right. She pointed down the darkening street to indicate that they would see the men as they walked by. Harrington and the two men appeared, but instead of proceeding straight, they turned the corner and headed toward Stone and Margaux.

Stone took her hand and pulled her into the narrow, enclosed entranceway of a dress shop. The three men continued to walk toward them on the other side of the street. Dusk had not progressed enough to conceal them in shadows. They huddled next to the door.

"I don't want him to see me," she whispered.

Of the same mind, he moved her up against the door, and stood with his back turned to the street. Margaux stood facing him and he felt her firm breasts brush him through his open jacket. His impulse was to kiss her. "Let's pretend to be lovers."

She gave him a look that could be interpreted as both unease and alarm. Her cheeks flushed and he caught her perfume.

"We're only acting," he said softly. He kissed her cheek, then rubbed his nose into her hair. Damn. Another night, another woman. Who did he think he was?

Her body moved, first toward him, then away. She began to say something, but stopped and kissed him on the neck. Her hand ran through his hair.

"They have stopped," she said, and she shifted her body to the right. "They are getting into a car, I think."

Stone could not look around and had to depend on her eyes. He kissed her forehead and moved his hands below her waist.

"One is getting into the car. The ugly one."

"What about—"

"Wait … the other one is getting in. Harrington is waving good-bye." She touched her lips to his neck. "Don't move now."

He had the perverse urge to lick her ear, which he realized would make her jump. He forced himself to concentrate on the charade. "Can you see the license tag of the car?"

"No. Harrington is walking away."

The engine started and the car pulled from the curb.

"I have the number," she said, and closed her eyes while her lips repeated the numbers.

Stone gave her a light kiss on the lips, and she pushed him away. "Why did you do that?"

"Couldn't help myself."

"It is over. Look, he is returning to the waterfront." She peered down the street. "Let us go back to the restaurant."

Stone's euphoria deflated. She squeezed past him and went out onto the sidewalk. In the distance a cellphone chimed and both looked to the right in the direction of Harrington. His voice echoed off the buildings' masonry fronts. Stone heard the name Lucinda. He moved forward and crouched next to a parked truck to listen.

"Come, let us go back," Margaux urged.

"Let's listen for a second." Why was Lucinda calling Harrington?

"No. It is not right to listen to someone talk with his—" She looked around and then motioned for him to follow her.

"In a second." The lovely Margaux had become annoying.

"I am leaving!"

Stone heard Harrington tell Lucinda he would see her

that weekend. Something was said about a business deal, but a car approached from behind him and he no longer could hear the conversation. Harrington approached Olive Street with the phone pressed to his ear and made a right turn toward the harbor. Stone stood and looked around. Margaux had gone.

He hurried back to Reynard's restaurant and found it packed with patrons, the waiters running from table to table, balancing drinks and plates on trays. He couldn't find Margaux. Had she made it back safely? Then she emerged from the water closet. When she saw him, she motioned for him to follow her. The restaurant was larger inside than it appeared from the street. It had the warm, comfortable feel of a Parisian bistro on a rainy night. They stopped next to an old-style coin telephone attached to the wall.

"You have no manners! No couth!" she scolded. "That was 'not cool,' as they say in America!"

"I only kissed you lightly on the lips."

"No. No. No." She shut her eyes and shook her head.

"Well, I smelled your hair and also kissed your forehead." He grinned. "Which one is frowned upon in France?"

"You know what I mean. Harrington was speaking with the contessa. That is a private thing. It is ill-mannered to listen in on something like that."

"Oh. Well, I couldn't understand what was said, so I didn't hear anything."

"It does not matter. You tried to listen."

"So you know Harrington is involved with Lucinda?"

Margaux walked away and then pivoted. She rested her hand on the table next to the phone. An elderly female customer walked by and Margaux exchanged quick pleasantries with her. When the elderly woman passed, Margaux moved closer.

"Lucinda?" She pursed her lips and tilted her head. "So that is why you were so interested in the conversation?" She took a deep breath, her eyes moist. "Well, it seems *Lucinda* is also interested in you. Today, *Lucinda's* secretary called with an invitation for you to attend her party in Villefranche. It is on Saturday. I left the message for you in your mailbox."

She turned and headed for the kitchen, and then Stone remembered the license number. "Margaux, please write down the license number of that car."

She stopped, gave him a long look, and said, "I have forgotten the number."

Stone had just passed through the side gate of the Foundation when his cellphone rang. Lucinda, he hoped, but no, the voice belonged to Mark. "Hey, Pal. I'm here in Nice with Fleming and the team. We're covering the Saudis, hoping to get a lead on bin Zanni." It sounded like he was catching his breath. "Claudia has arrived from Washington to take charge of the operation."

"What should I do?"

"Well, Fleming thinks she's come to town to break up all the furniture. If I were you, I'd lay low. On second thought, I've planned a surveillance on Hassan tomorrow in Marseille. I could use your help."

CHAPTER SEVENTEEN

MARSEILLE—MAY 10, 2002

The thirty-two foot cabin cruiser, moored in Marseille's crowded inner harbor, rocked gently in the wake of a passing fishing boat. Stone and Mark had settled themselves in the galley and, from a distance of fifty meters, had a clear view of the fish market set up along the edge of the quay. Fishmongers with their collapsible aquamarine-colored tables spread out their daily catch of fish, shellfish, conger eels, and other staples for the kitchens of serious Marseille cooks. By eleven in the morning, the inspecting, judging, and deciding for the evening meals was now at full tempo.

Inside the cramped cabin Stone relaxed on a canvas chair, gray from years of weather, his bare feet propped up on a box of spare parts for the boat's marine diesel engine. Through an open side window, he scanned the colorful parade with binoculars. He felt a certain contentment with the moist warmth on his skin, feeling the rhythmic motion of the boat under him, and hearing the caws of the gulls overhead. He was at home with the deep smell of sea and fish.

"There's beer in the fridge," Mark said.

Mark arranged a series of eight by ten photographs on the table. Gray hairs speckled his three-day growth of beard. One by one, he picked up the photographs and studied them. Stone had concluded that here was a guy who felt comfortable in situations like this. Typical of someone who had risen through the CIA's paramilitary division.

"These were taken yesterday at about the same hour," Mark said, almost as if he was examining a scientific specimen. "It's the best template we have, given the time constraints." He restacked the photos. "What we want to do, is spot people who don't belong out there."

In a half hour, Hassan and a blonde-haired woman were expected to appear in the market area. Mark and Stone would take photographs of the two and, more importantly, take pictures of any suspicious individuals in the vicinity who might be interested in the couple.

"I can't believe the Agency conducts surveillance with beer on the menu." Stone shook his head, got up, and reviewed the photographs. In his thinking, it was a long shot to find anyone out there on the quay who didn't match with the people in the previous day's photographic mosaic. For him, the photos were of minimal help. All the people he saw through his binoculars looked like they belonged.

"You FBI folks have a reputation for being tight-assed. Go have a beer and bring me a sandwich, will you?" Mark laughed, and then, through the cabin's mesh-covered front windows, searched the crowd. "Imagine all the good meals that are going to be cooked tonight in this town. This is a gourmet's paradise."

"I'm getting to like Marseille. It has a certain charm." Stone agreed, pulling two sandwiches out of the small refrigerator. He passed a beer to Mark and took a bottle of water for himself.

Mark mused. "It's a tough town, but the people have a good, earthy sense of humor."

Stone unwrapped his sandwich and climbed up to the semi-enclosed bridge to get some fresh air. Puffy white clouds blowing in on a soft sea breeze spotted a royal blue sky. Images returned of his navy days, the visits to the ports along the Côte d'Azur and, of course, Lucinda. He should have called her when he returned to Archos.

Stone frowned and took a bite of his chicken sandwich. Kissing Margaux had been a dumb move. She was young and would probably get the wrong impression. It was all he could do to handle Lucinda. He smiled. That is, if anyone could handle her. And why did Lucinda phone Harrington? What was that all about? Stone laughed. What the hell was wrong with him?

Mark looked up from the cabin. "You okay, Partner?"

"Yes. Yes. My new life as a single man has fascinating complications."

Mark shook his head. "No lurid details, please. I'm happily married and will be away from my wife for at least another month. Don't get me thinking about sex."

"Tell you what, I'll lend you one of my travel books. Reading it will dull your senses."

Mark went back inside and a few moments later called out, "Show time!"

Stone jumped up and slipped down into the cabin. Through the binoculars, he recognized Hassan moving with athletic grace from one vendor's table to another. He wore a leather jacket, a white, open-necked shirt, and tan slacks. At his side sauntered a tall blonde about thirty years old. She was talking with Hassan and gesturing at fish on the trays. Her face looked familiar. The two continued to pass along the line of tables, examining the displays of seafood.

Mark phoned Eric, the surveillance agent positioned on the wharf. Then, with his camera, equipped with a long telescopic lens, he snapped every two seconds. Stone searched the crowd for anyone looking out of the ordinary. Finally, Mark stopped taking pictures. "If you see anyone who looks suspicious, let me know."

"Right," Stone said, scrutinizing the blonde. He had seen her before. "Hey, I know her."

She was the CIA officer he'd met in the American Embassy in Paris, the one who had created his legend at the foundation and gave him the name Finbarr Costanza.

Mark whispered, "Yep, she's one of us."

Hassan found himself following the blonde and trying to keep track of her chattering. He had never met a Canadian woman before and wondered whether they all talked as much as she did. He found her slight lisp intriguing. It was good to be away from his comrades and the worry about whether Aziz would come through with the virus.

"Do you do any cooking, Hassan?" she asked, as she looked at a particularly odd fish with a large mouth.

He shook his head. "Back home, the women cook."

She would be good in bed, what with her strong back and solid legs. He wondered why he did not think more about having sex with her. Maybe he just enjoyed the change in routine she provided. Since they had met in Avignon, when they sat along the Rhone River and chatted, he'd considered her merely a pleasant diversion.

"How did the story you were working on in Nice go?" she asked. "Did it get published in your Beirut newspaper?"

"The story?" He studied her. "Oh, it will be published next week."

"I would like to read some of your work."

He smiled. "Do you read Arabic?"

"Afraid not. Will you return to Nice?"

"No time soon. I will stay here in Marseille for a while." He put his hand on her shoulder as they squeezed between two large women with sacks of fish. "When do you have to return to your aunt in Avignon?"

"After lunch." She spun around. "Oh, let me pay this time."

He shook his head. "Arab men do not allow a woman to pay for a meal. It is tradition."

"Hum, I'll have to remember that. Did you have some good meals in Nice?" She pulled back her long blonde hair with both hands and looked up at the sun.

"Yes. The food is good there."

Why was she asking all these questions about Nice? He pretended to be interested in some painted clay pots placed next to a tray of mussels. What was it about Nice that aroused her interest? It was very peculiar.

"Look, there's a seahorse on this tray."

He studied her eyes and her mouth for some sign of deception he hoped not to see. It would be good to trust her.

The seahorse dropped onto the ground. "Damn." Her movements were controlled and quick in a way that surprised him. She picked the seahorse up and threw it back onto the tray.

• • •

Stone picked up the change in Hassan's body language. "Shit. Something's up." His body had stiffened as he looked down at the CIA woman when she bent over and picked something off the ground. The stare lasted a second longer than normal.

"What you got, Partner?" Mark shifted from scanning the crowd to Hassan and the woman.

"He looks like he didn't like something he heard. He's acting different."

Mark watched for a moment. "You're good. Yeah, where's that big-toothed smile?"

"Should we do something?"

"Not yet. She still has a task to perform. I'll call our legman and give him a heads up."

Mark phoned Eric, the operative positioned a block away, and told him to enter the market area.

"Look," Stone said. "I think she picked up on Hassan's change in mood."

The CIA woman pulled her cellphone from her purse and appeared to try to make a call. After a few moments, she banged the phone shut in her hand and then looked at Hassan with exasperation. She handed him the phone.

Hassan took the phone and pushed some buttons, put it to his ear, and then shook it. With one hand raised in resignation, he returned the phone to her and she let him drop it in her purse. He offered his own cellphone to her, but she waved him off. They walked off toward the row of outdoor cafés.

"Bingo," Mark said. "We've got his fingerprints. Now I'll signal her."

Mark pulled a silver flashlight-shaped instrument from a box and aimed it at the CIA officer.

"I'm directing a laser beam in her direction. It should set off a vibration on her ankle bracelet. Two pulses indicate a warning." Mark pressed the button twice.

"What if she's in real trouble?"

Mark looked around, "I hold it down steady and hope she

runs faster than he does."

Hassan and the female agent strolled to a restaurant facing the north side of the old port. Mark put down his binoculars. "I'll go ashore and move closer to them in case she needs assistance."

"Wait a minute," Stone interrupted. "We've got a bogey … no, two bogeys." Stone focused on two men standing at the edge of the market.

"Where?"

"Look straight ahead, over that blue and orange striped umbrella with Orangina printed on it."

Mark searched with his binoculars. "Yeah. Okay, but what two guys? There're a hell of a lot of people out there now."

"One's dressed in a coat and tie. The other guy, as a lady said last night, is pretty ugly."

"Oh yes. I see them." Mark aimed the camera and started taking photographs of the men. "Do you know them?"

"They were pointed out last night as bad guys. I think illegal drugs. They're hooked up with the director of my foundation at Archos."

Mark phoned Eric, instructing him to follow the new two targets, then said to Stone, "I'm heading for the restaurant to make sure our gal's safe."

Stone stayed with the boat and acted as command control. Eric surveilled the two men, while Stone watched Mark position himself near the restaurant. An hour later, Stone got a call from Mark. "Hassan and our blonde are leaving. Our guy seems to have settled down. If things go according to plan, she'll take the bus back to Avignon."

A few minutes later, Mark called again. "Hassan split and is headed for the commercial section of town. I'm going to get on the bus and ride with her to Avignon. Call Eric and get his location."

The call to Eric went unanswered, but a few moments later, Eric called back. His two "rabbits," as he called his targets, had followed Hassan from the restaurant for three blocks and then broke off. "Now they appear to be splitting up. Which one should I follow?"

"The man in the suit."

Five minutes later, Eric called and said the man wearing the suit had gotten into a Renault sedan and was heading out of town. Stone told him to get the license.

"I'm doing better than that. I'm shadowing him."

"How will you do that?"

"I'm on my motorcycle. I'll call later." The line went dead.

After a bit, boredom set in and Stone started some housecleaning. Beer and soda cans, in addition to paper wrappings, littered the boat. Finished, he sat down and let out a sigh. No use in delaying the call to Lucinda.

"How are you?"

"I am fine. Also, I am very busy," Lucinda said, and then called out to one of her staff to chill the wine. "The party is tomorrow night, you know. So much to be done."

"That's right. I'll have to get my tux shirt cleaned."

"I am glad you are coming," she said, almost inaudibly.

"Harrington will be there?"

A pause and a long sigh. "Yes, and he is bringing his wife."

"Good."

"I know what you are thinking, Hayden. You are acting silly, like you used to years ago. Be prepared to be my escort."

The mobile phone on the boat's table buzzed. Stone recognized Mark's cellphone number.

"That's great, dear," Stone said. "I'll let you get back to your chores."

"Hayden, please come early."

Stone picked up the mobile phone. Mark was outside a hamlet near Avignon. The CIA officer and he had gotten off one bus. Now they were on another one heading back to Marseille. He had talked with Eric, who had followed the Renault sedan to a chateau outside of Arles. Eric had spotted a single-engine plane he suspected was surveilling the Renault. "Our allies, the French, seem to have joined in on the fun," Mark said. "By the way, did you ever submit a contact report to Fleming on that

Frenchman you met in Saint-Rémy? You know, your meeting at the Roman ruins?"

"How did you know about that?"

"I always keep tabs on my students," Mark answered. "Remember, Claudia is in town and she runs a tight ship. Don't give her an excuse to fire an old FBI agent."

"I'll message the report to Fleming on my computer tonight."

"Thanks for your help," Mark said. "By the way, the name of our blonde is Sandra."

CHAPTER EIGHTEEN

PROVENCE, FRANCE

Claudia jerked her head around and hollered at Fleming, who was sitting in the back seat of the SUV studying a crumpled French roadmap, "How long before we reach the highway?"

Fleming studied the open map on his lap as he rocked back and forth with the movement of the vehicle. Hanging from his ears were two white buds connected to a cellphone. He pointed to the cellphone. "I'm getting a message from the Major."

Fours days before, Major Simon, in one of the sedans of the four-vehicle convoy, had flown down from Germany with members of his extraordinary rendition team. The team had previous experience working with the CIA rounding up leading Islamic radicals throughout Europe and spiriting them to locations where they could be interrogated. The last snatch Simon had orchestrated led to information that prevented an attack on the Oscars ceremony.

Message received, Fleming pulled one of the buds from his ear. "We're about five miles from a major intersection. The road winds down through this forest. We have a drop of about fifteen hundred meters."

"We should take them down," she shouted, then turned around and faced front. "Tell the Major to start making a move."

Fleming closed his eyes, shook his head in disbelief, and then radioed her instructions. The combined military and CIA operation consisted of twelve people in three sedans, and the Mercedes SUV in which he was riding. The two BMW sedans they were tailing held at least eight members of al Qaeda, and one of them was their target, bin Zanni.

"We haven't seen any oncoming traffic for about ten

minutes," she shouted. "This is a perfect place. What's holding him back?"

"He's waiting for the drone to gain enough altitude to see whether the road behind us is clear."

The four vehicles drove in close formation down the two-lane blacktop. Patches of dirty snow under Alpine brush hugged the edges of the road. Around a sharp bend in the road, Fleming glimpsed the two BMWs. They appeared to be slowing down.

"Tell that man we're going to commence the operation *now*!" Claudia pulled a Glock automatic from her black handbag.

Fleming complied. The response from the Major was as expected. "Tell her to get fucked. I'll decide when we move."

"What did he say?" Claudia turned completely around in the seat, bumping the driver. "I heard something coming out of your headphones."

"He's checking with his people," Fleming answered. "Also, he's getting input from the drone overhead."

"Bullshit!" She turned back in her seat and ordered the driver to speed up.

Their SUV closed the gap, and the other CIA vehicle moved up behind them. Fleming glanced back at the cars. The two sedans with the military contingent were lagging behind. He was about to tell Claudia that the formation was separating, when the Major yelled, "Slow down! Slow down! The drone spotted two more vehicles joining our targets."

"There are now four al Qaeda cars ahead!" Fleming yelled. "They have four cars!"

"So do we. Let's take them!" Claudia yelled.

The driver looked over at her and then back at Fleming through the rearview mirror. He took his foot off the accelerator.

"What the hell are you doing?" Claudia glared at the driver.

Just then the "abort" signal came from the Major and Fleming reached forward and tapped the driver's shoulder to slow down.

Claudia yelled, "Don't countermand me!" Spittle flew from her mouth.

"Mission is aborted," he yelled. "The Major has aborted."

"He's not in charge here! Keep driving!" She leaned forward in her seat.

Accelerating, the SUV twisted down the mountain road. Warm air from the valley flew in from the open window. They came down out of a thicket of pine trees and leveled off onto the valley floor. Now fifty meters separated them from the terrorists' sedans. As the al Qaeda cars neared the intersection, the last car in the al Qaeda group braked hard. Smoke came from its tires as the vehicle spun and halted sideways in the road.

Fleming yelled into the phone that they had a "situation." Bearded men in dark clothes leaped from the car and opened fire. Claudia crouched against the door. The driver slammed his seat back, and with his head lowered, peered over the steering wheel.

The front windshield exploded and a piece of glass gashed the right side of Fleming's forehead. Claudia fired her automatic through the shattered windshield. Fleming grabbed his machine gun and lowered the back window.

The driver accelerated and drove onto the right shoulder of the road. Clangs and pops came from the body of the car as terrorists' bullets found their mark. *Only 9mm rounds*, Fleming realized. *Thank God.*

The SUV fishtailed on the gravel and sped past the terrorists' car. As they passed, Fleming shoved his machine gun out the side window and raked the terrorists with a steady stream of fire. He did not release the trigger until the magazine emptied. A loud ringing pained his eardrums.

The driver slammed to a full stop. Fleming fumbled for a full magazine and reloaded. The three leaped from the car shooting, using the car as a shield. The team cars pulled up and the members emerged firing, laying down a withering crossfire. In less than a minute, the shooting ended.

Fleming looked around as the al Qaeda sedans reached the intersection, then sped off in three separate directions. With one hand holding a handkerchief on his forehead to stop the bleeding and the other pointing his machine gun, Fleming approached the terrorists' car. He coughed on the lingering gun smoke. His ears continued to ring. Bullet holes riddled the car doors and fenders. Escaping air hissed from the engine compartment.

All four al Qaeda were dead. On inspection, none fit bin Zanni's description. The team took photographs and fingerprints of the dead, then dispersed.

On the way back to Nice, Claudia refused to speak to Fleming.

NICE, FRANCE—MAY 11, 2002

Claudia glared at the soldiers sitting on the floor of the safehouse. The military people looked at each other, and took their time getting up. The Major asked whether he could use the Agency satellite phone to call his headquarters. Fleming handed him the phone, but Claudia grabbed it from him. "We'll need this phone, Major."

The team filed out. The last one slammed the door. The meeting had gone as well as expected, Claudia thought. These military types had to be kept in their place. Know who's boss.

Fleming rose from his chair, went to the window, and opened it. Claudia lowered the volume on the radio. She'd never believed in the sound-masking technique of using radio noise to block hostile eavesdropping. Most of what the CIA's Office of Security came up with she considered just gimmicks to make a case officer's life miserable.

She looked over at the blonde officer from Paris. "So tell me what happened in Marseille while we were trying to capture bin Zanni."

Sandra leaned her head back and looked at the ceiling. She described her meeting with Hassan. "He seemed suspicious at first, but eventually he settled down. He revealed little about his trip to Nice, and never mentioned going to Saint-Rémy. My sources advised that he showed a lot of interest in wines and vineyards recently."

"Is that all you came up with?" Claudia huffed. "Seems like a waste of time."

"This operation is being run by the Station in Paris. It has nothing to do with your mission."

"How so? Your man, Hassan, was in Saint-Rémy and in contact with bin Zanni's babysitters. It definitely has a connection."

"What I meant to—"

"Anything else to report about the Marseille meeting?"

"We picked up two people either surveilling Hassan or countersurveilling Hassan's meeting with me. We're close to identifying one of them. French liaison is working with us on that angle."

"We have to keep the French out of this. This is our show." Claudia stifled a yawn. She still had jetlag.

"My station chief doesn't see it that way. Our liaison with the French is delicate and—"

"Anything else about Marseille?" Claudia asked, tapping the armrest of the chair.

"Nothing, except that the man, Stone, from Archos was a great help."

Claudia looked at Fleming. "Is Stone that trigger-happy FBI cowboy I met at the Farm?"

"That's a gross exaggeration," Fleming said. "He's *retired* FBI. He's now one of our Independent Contractors. Our division chief at Langley approved him?"

"Fire him. He's a loose cannon. Get someone else." Claudia turned to her assistant. "You start working on a replacement for him, and make him an Agency veteran." She turned to Fleming. "I want Stone out of France by the weekend."

"Hold on there," Sandra interjected. "We have cover considerations. We can't pull him out of that foundation. I spent a lot of time and used a lot of influence placing him there."

"I don't care."

"Paris Station cares. I suggest you speak to my station chief about this first."

Sandra impressed Claudia. She appeared smart and someone had told her she'd gone to an Ivy League college, or was it one of the Seven Sisters. The Agency needed people like her.

Claudia had sat for over an hour. "That's enough for now.

I'm going back to my hotel to make some calls." She pushed herself out of the chair and headed for the bathroom. "Fleming, locate bin Zanni," she called back. "Sandra, you and I will have an early dinner tonight. Find a nice restaurant. I like mussels."

Claudia took a cab for the short distance to her hotel. She walked into her room and headed for the glass doors leading to the balcony. The doors opened onto a view of a black Mediterranean Sea. The operation had been a disaster. No doubt, some people at Langley would use it as an excuse to criticize her. Neutralize her.

CHAPTER NINETEEN

VILLEFRANCHE

The contessa glided across the sun-dappled patio wearing a black off-the-shoulder gown. The Harringtons were standing next to the wrought iron railing, admiring the panoramic view of Villefranche below. The two were still dressed in casual clothes.

"Helen, dear, I am so happy you two pulled yourselves away from the Foundation to attend my little get-together." She gave Mrs. Harrington a two-cheek kiss, which Helen accepted with a forced smile. "I trust your rooms are satisfactory. I put you up on the higher level."

"Thank you for the invitation," Helen said. "You're most gracious."

Taking Boswell Harrington's hand, the contessa said, "You are wearing a new ascot. Very becoming." She motioned for the two to sit and summoned the young Austrian servant to take their drink orders.

The late-afternoon sun bathed the stone walls of the palace and warmth radiated back onto the patio. Shade from the Aleppo pines smoothed the glare from the low-hanging sun. After the girl took the drink orders, the contessa sat in the chair next to Harrington, who occupied himself with adjusting the ascot tucked under his cream-colored shirt.

"Let us discuss our business deal before we drive down to the villa for the party," she said, as she smoothed the shoulder of Harrington's blazer. "I am confused about some of the details." She smiled at Helen. "Do you mind if your husband and I talk business?"

Helen shook her head. "No."

Harrington spoke. "Our business plan involves purchasing

a Turkish shipyard that builds yachts for the world's mega-rich. A yacht like the one down there, owned by the prince." He pointed to the Bay of Villefranche, now a mosaic of soft and hard blues formed by cloud shadows and shallow depths. "We want the prince to provide the financial backing for the deal."

"You don't know anything about shipbuilding," Contessa Lucinda laughed.

Helen leaned forward. "How would you know that? He sails my father's boat at Nantucket all the time."

"Yes, of course, dear Helen, but we are talking about running a boatyard, not sailing off for a cocktail party at sea." She tightened the clasp on her emerald earring. "You are not leaving the Foundation and heading off for Turkey are you?"

"No. The idea is to buy the shipyard, then flip it over to another buyer." Perspiration formed on his upper lip. "I know one of those Silicon Valley-types who is having a yacht built there now. It is a year overdue and he's quite anxious to take delivery." Harrington took the martini from the Austrian girl, picked out one of the olives, and popped it into his mouth. "He's one of your guests tonight. I'll approach him and plant the seed about buying the shipyard."

"Well, that should prove interesting." The contessa toasted the two with her flute of champagne. "Now, and I hate to be boorish, but what is my finder's fee?"

"I think you will be very happy with the arrangement. I worked it out with Abdul Wahab, the prince's ... oh let's call him, major domo."

"I wish my major domo, Philippe Monte, was here while we are discussing money. But do go on."

Helen rose from her chair. "Excuse me. I suppose we'll be heading down to the party soon. I want to change, and since you two are talking business…" She strode off to the guest room.

Harrington waited a few moments until his wife was out of sight and then moved his chair closer. "Lucinda, any chance of us being alone this weekend?"

"You are here with your wife. I have over fifty guests coming to the party down at my villa. I do not want to discuss our 'getting together.'"

"Damn it, you know how I feel about you."

"I believe your wife knows also. Our relationship, dear Boswell, is strictly business." The contessa moved her face closer to his. "How much money am I going to make out of this deal?"

"You'll get from three million to four million euros."

"That is vague. Please explain."

"Well, the deal is complex."

"Go on."

"In order for me to get the financial backing from the prince, I agreed that I would convince you to lease your palace to the Saudis. We'll discuss it tonight at the party. Abdul Wahab is most anxious to move on the lease." He gulped his drink.

The contessa placed the flute on the table next to her, sat back in her chair, and stared at Harrington. He was grinning at her in that ridiculous manner, his upper lip almost touching his nose. This fool with his receding hairline, sitting across from her and drinking her liquor, and having been responsible for losing twelve million of her euros, now has hatched a plan to move some Arabs into her family's palace.

She fantasized inviting an aroused Harrington to her bedroom where, when they were *in flagrante delicto*, she would put a knife to his balls. She blinked twice and then delicately lifted the flute from the table and took a sip of champagne. "Please explain this little idea of my moving out of my palace."

"They want to use your palace to hold some sort of conference. All you have to do is move down to your villa on the water for a month, maybe two. You certainly can use two or three million euros."

"Yes, thanks to you. And I thought you said it was three to four million?"

"Lucinda, you must trust me."

There was a long pause. "Of course, darling. Tonight Philippe Monte and I will discuss this with—what's his name, Abdul Wahab? You be there to make the introductions."

"Of course. Damn it, I thought you'd be happy. And after the party—"

"Oh, here comes my escort for tonight." The contessa rose. "You know Hayden Stone." She glided up to Stone and kissed him gently on the lips. "Hayden, you look splendid in your tuxedo." She glanced back at Harrington. "Are you dressing, or are you going 'as is'?"

Dusk brought enough chill to the air that Stone appreciated the comfort of his jacket. He and Lucinda strolled along the open promenade that separated her villa from the bay. Strings of white lights stretched along the masonry wall overlooking the water. The whole staff had come down from the palace. Attired in their black and white uniforms, waiters carried silver trays filled with drinks and canapés for the arriving guests.

"Do you remember your way around the villa?" Lucinda asked, and then stopped a young man, inspected the quality of the shrimp, gave her approval, and the man moved on.

"It's as I remembered it." Stone thought of the last party he had attended at the villa years before. At least four times this number of people had been invited to Lucinda's eighteenth birthday party. Her father had spared no expense for his only daughter. Stone had always liked the old man, and he believed her father liked him.

They paused at the marina next to the seawall. Two bearded men were waiting at the slip for the prince's launch to arrive from the Red Scorpion. Stone looked up the mountain and saw, in the distance, the contessa's palace, sitting alone on a treed ledge, a dull buff mass of stone turned to rose in the last of the sunset.

"Lucinda, I always wanted to ask your father why your place up there on the mountain is called a palace."

"Centuries ago, it was one of the Pope's palaces. He gave it to my family for their backing in some war."

"It resembles one of those mosques in the Middle East," Stone said. "You know, ones that were formerly churches."

"Maybe that is why the prince wants to rent it." The contessa pulled her black lace shawl up over her shoulders, partially covering her emerald necklace.

"You've rented your palace!"

"Yes, and as you Americans say, to make a long story short, he will pay a lot of money to rent it for a month. He wants it for some conference he is having." They circled back toward where the guests had gathered. "Harrington has made the arrangements." She stopped and looked at him. "Do not be so surprised. I need the money."

"Do you trust Harrington?"

"Of course not, I do not trust any man." She smiled. "You know, Hayden, your cold gray eyes fit you perfectly."

Philippe Monte approached and she took Stone's hand. "I have to consult with my consigliere. Please Hayden, while you are playing my escort, call me Contessa."

Stone stood alone and wondered whether the contessa's demeanor would thaw before the end of the weekend. The kiss on the lips back at the palace was for Harrington's benefit. *Just what is my role here tonight?* No doubt, she was distracted with the palace lease deal.

He looked around for familiar faces. Half the men had come in formal dress, the others wore blazers or, in the case of the rich Americans, jeans and turtlenecks. Conversely, all the women appeared expensively attired. He'd overheard that the casual Americans were members of the dot-com crowd from California who were wise or lucky enough to have sold their companies before the Wall Street crash of 2000.

Jonathan Deville passed through the gilded iron gate accompanied by his wife, Rhonda. The two looked lost. Stone hurried over and gave Rhonda a hug.

"How have you been?" she asked. "I haven't seen you since you and Patricia—oh, I am sorry ... I forgot, your divorce." Rhonda was French, plump, and always appeared happy to see him. "Tell me, Hayden, is there any chance you and Patricia will get back together?"

"Very unlikely."

"You are sure? Good. Then I will say, I never did like her. She was not for you, but back in Paris there is a perfect woman for you. Cultured, rich, and, of course, French. The perfect distraction for you."

"I told you, Stone," Jonathan laughed. "She started plotting the minute I told her about your divorce."

Rhonda discussed their children and their plans for when Jonathan retired; they wanted to live in France as long as the dollar held up to the euro. "Tonight we're staying in the palace in the room next to you," she said, and pushed her finger in his chest. "I'll be listening to hear if you have any midnight guests."

Before Stone could retort, Maurice Colmont joined them.

"You met Maurice at the consul general's party last week," Deville said.

"We met again this week in Saint-Rémy."

"Yes, we did, Mr. Stone, and I see that you managed to return safely."

Stone motioned for a waiter to bring drinks. Colmont gave his attention to the Devilles, yet repeatedly glanced back at him.

"This is proving to be an interesting evening, my friends," Colmont said. "A royal prince in attendance at the party."

"Exciting, no?" Rhonda gushed. "With a prince and a contessa in our midst?"

"The prince will be glad to get off his yacht." Colmont looked hard at Stone. "What with all those people on board."

"How so?" Deville asked.

"Tuesday, a large delegation flew in from Riyadh and boarded the yacht. Then the yacht moved from Nice harbor around the cape to anchor here."

"Maybe that's why the prince wants to rent the contessa's palace," Stone said.

"I was not aware of that, Hayden."

"The contessa told me a few minutes ago." Stone looked at Deville. "I guess when we check out tomorrow, the Arabs will move in."

The waiter arrived with champagne and they decided to move on to the long table holding assorted hors d'oeuvres and rich-smelling canapés. The china and silverware reflected the flames from the candelabras. The American Consul General came by, spoke briefly, then became distracted by a group of boisterous Californians.

The contessa slipped in between Rhonda Deville and Colmont, but before she could speak, a waiter rushed up and told her the prince's launch had arrived. She addressed the group, "Please come help me greet the prince and his entourage."

Colmont lagged behind, pulling out his cellphone. At the same time, he motioned to Stone to join him. Completing his call, he clicked the phone shut. "Most interesting. Why would the Saudis rent the contessa's palace at this time?"

"And why would all those people come from Riyadh?" Stone added. "Any connection with that fellow we've been chasing?"

"Very possible," Colmont said. "Let us keep our ears open tonight, yes? Meanwhile, the contessa could use our help."

"Before I forget, Maurice … any information on the man who tried to kill me on the yacht?"

"None," Colmont answered. "And no body has been recovered from the bay."

As they headed toward the dock, Colmont whispered, "It is good that you are here at the party."

Stone wondered why he thought so.

Boswell Harrington watched as the contessa, with Stone at her side, formally greeted the prince as he came up from the dock. The prince wore a flowing white *thawb*, the robe touching the ground, and a matching *kuffiyah* draped over his head. He spoke English with an Oxford accent. A black, spade-shaped beard grew on his puffy, pale face. After the requisite introductions, the Saudis separated in stages and mingled with the other guests. Harrington stood aside and waited for an opportunity to pull Abdul Wahab away from the prince. He wanted to firm up the details of the palace lease.

Harrington had noted that initially Stone had been at the contessa's side, but when the Saudis joined the other guests,

Stone melted into the background. Now the contessa's soirée took on the appearance of a business meeting. When he saw his chance, Harrington approached Wahab and suggested they converse privately. He pointed to the covered observatory atop the villa. Wahab agreed, and the two climbed the outer stairs and found themselves alone with the twinkling lights of Villefranche spread around them. A cruise liner had anchored in the bay and displayed a line of white lights strung from the rigging stem to stern. The party guests milled below them while Vivaldi strings played from hidden speakers.

"I believe one could call this observatory a belvedere," Harrington remarked, sipping his scotch on the rocks.

"Please stop playing the pundit." At least a foot taller than Harrington, Wahab glared down his long nose. "Has the contessa agreed to lease her palace to the prince?"

"I talked with her, and she's inclined to let the prince move in. It's only a matter of the amount of payment." Harrington wanted to light up a cigar, but couldn't remember whether Wahab objected to tobacco.

"I told you the price is five million for one month and two more for an additional month if it is required." Wahab sipped a ginger ale. "Time is of the essence. When will the palace be available?"

"The contessa is conferring with her consigliere now and plans to discuss it with you tonight. I see no problem." Harrington looked out at the bay and decided to bring up his own project. "About the other matter ... the financing for my deal?"

"My friend, first, if the prince is denied the palace, there is no, as you say, deal." Wahab leaned over, staring Harrington in the eye. "Also, this is *my* money we are talking about. I have decided I will finance the opium coming from my old Afghani war comrades. I will ship it to Marseille." He looked hard at Harrington. "You will get a generous finder's fee for making the arrangements with those people you know who take delivery in Marseille."

Harrington walked over to the railing, thinking. *Count to five before you say anything.* He drained his glass. "That wasn't our agreement. That's not the deal."

"My money. My deal." Wahab placed his drink on the railing and adjusted his black tie. "Your last deal ended up a fiasco. You lost the opium and the money to the authorities. The money belonged to the contessa, yes?"

Harrington turned away. This was unexpected. The money he'd counted on to retire to Carmel, California had just evaporated. That morning, his wife had told him his horoscope for that day looked ominous. He said, "This isn't, as you Cambridge graduates say, cricket. Perhaps I should look for other financing."

Wahab scanned the guests below him. "Does the contessa know her money was lost in an illegal narcotics transaction? I am under the impression she thought you were bringing in rare ores from Afghanistan. Is that not so?"

Harrington wanted another drink. He had to accept the situation. He had no leverage. The contacts in Afghanistan belonged to Wahab. Question was, how much would he get? Odd, a Saudi with all his money and connections wanted to get involved with illegal drugs. For what purpose?

Wahab interrupted his train of thought. "Who is that man down there with the contessa?"

"Oh, that's a new fellow at the Foundation," Harrington answered. "Some hack travel writer."

"The two of them seem to be getting along quite well." Wahab stared hard. "You led me to believe she was your paramour."

"They're just old friends."

"Does that writer have a scar on his cheek? And did he take a trip to the countryside this past week?"

"Yes, on both accounts," Harrington answered. "Why do you ask?"

"Because he is CIA, you bloody fool!" Wahab took a deep breath and moved away. "And he is supposed to be dead," he whispered. He came back to Harrington. "You can make up the money you lost on this deal by killing him. One hundred thousand euros. No, I'll be generous. Two hundred thousand!"

Harrington felt a sharp pain in his stomach. "What do I look like, a hit man?" He shook the ice in his empty glass and looked at Wahab out of the corner of his eye. How dare he? Fucking raghead! They pantsed his kind at prep school!

"I have no time to play games," Wahab said through his teeth. "We must close the lease arrangement with the contessa. This will not be the first American agent you've killed. Three years ago you killed, or had killed by heroin overdose, that American agent at Cuers, the one who got too close to your little drug operation."

"How did you—"

"The person you had administer the heroin told us." Wahab straightened up to his full height. "Kill Stone, and make it quick. Now let us go down and start the negotiations for the palace lease."

Harrington followed Wahab toward the stairs. He tried to think how this man knew about him killing the agent in Cuers. He must have an informant in his organization.

At the top of the landing, Wahab paused and turned back to Harrington as the Devilles mounted the stairs behind him. Wahab repeated to Harrington the sum he was willing to offer the contessa for use of the palace. His carelessness surprised Harrington. Jonathan Deville's facial reaction showed that he'd overheard Wahab.

Once again down among the guests, Harrington touched Wahab's arm and suggested, "Why not just make the check out to me? I'll make sure the contessa gets a fair sum."

For the first time that night, Wahab laughed loudly. "Harrington, Harrington … you are incorrigible."

An aide to the prince rushed up and announced that the prince was about to depart for his yacht. Wahab and Harrington looked at each other, then hurried over to the contessa, who was conferring with her consigliere and the two Devilles.

"Contessa, excuse me, if I may?" Wahab interrupted. "Have you reached a decision on the lease of your palace to my prince?"

"Is there some urgency involved?" she asked, slipping her

hand under Jonathan Deville's arm.

"I'm sure the prince would like to know your decision on the lease before he boards his launch."

"Tell me the arrangements as you see them and the fee you propose."

"Contessa, please let me handle the fee matters," Harrington urged. "All you need to do is agree. Abdul Wahab told me the prince wants to move in Monday, if that suits you?"

Philippe Monte coughed and gave Harrington a skeptical look.

Wahab smiled. "As Mr. Harrington indicates, time is of the essence."

The contessa paused for a few moments. They all looked over at the prince, who had completed his farewells and was heading in their direction. She took a deep breath, nodded to Monte, and then addressed Abdul Wahab. "As soon as my consigliere here, Monsieur Monte, receives the check for seven million euros, I will move down here to the villa. That sum is for five million the first month and an additional retainer of two million for the second month."

"But contessa, did not Mr. Harrington tell you the sum was—" Wahab said.

"Here comes your prince to bid farewell," she smiled. "And you have such good news to tell him."

CHAPTER TWENTY

VILLEFRANCHE

Following the departure of the prince and his retinue to the Red Scorpion, the soirée quieted down. Stone strolled back and forth along the veranda with the Devilles and Maurice Colmont.

"The contessa seems to have been successful with the lease arrangement," Rhonda Deville said. "Although I sense she is concerned about something." She searched in her purse. "I'm going off to freshen up before we drive up to the palace."

The three men moved away from the other guests. When Stone thought he could speak privately, he asked Colmont, "Who was that tall man with the prince? The one who seemed to be his confidant?"

"You must be referring to Abdul Wahab," Colmont said.

"He's a wealthy Saudi who is married to one of the prince's daughters," Jonathan Deville added. "Obviously, he's in charge of the lease negotiations for the palace."

"Evidently he and Harrington had some misunderstanding," Stone ventured. "I saw the two of them up in the observatory having an intense conversation."

"Most observant, Hayden," Colmont said. "I also watched them."

"I don't trust Harrington," Deville said. "Our office has gotten rumors that he's dirty. He doesn't seem to have the contessa's best interests in mind."

Deville then related that he and his wife had overheard Wahab and Harrington on the staircase discussing the terms of the lease. He had let the contessa in on how high a figure she could demand.

"Mr. Harrington has many faces," Stone said.

"Or a face that changes, like a chameleon," Colmont added.

"I agree, Maurice," Stone said, then faced Deville. "Jonathan, you did the contessa a good turn and she certainly needs friends." Over Deville's shoulder, he saw Lucinda talking her way past a group of guests and heading toward them. "Before she gets here, what do we have on this Wahab?"

"He's well-connected with the Saudi establishment, but it seems he's trying to polish up his Islamic fundamentalist credentials," Deville said. "He has terrorist connections."

Colmont leaned forward. "Somewhere I believe I read he was in Afghanistan last year. Hayden, you have been there, no?"

"Why, Maurice Colmont, are you sharing intelligence with us?" Deville laughed. "Now who said our governments didn't cooperate?"

"Wahab has a certain presence, doesn't he?" Stone said. "He looks familiar."

"We find it interesting that the prince is so intent on leasing the palace," Colmont said, taking Stone's arm. "Another matter—yesterday, north in the mountain region, your people tried to capture the al Qaeda functionary, bin Zanni, and failed miserably. People were killed. Paris is very upset."

"I was in Marseille."

"I am aware of that."

Stone paused, wanting to change the subject. "Do you see a connection between bin Zanni and the lease of the palace?"

"There is some speculation—" Colmont stopped as the contessa joined them.

"Well gentlemen, did you enjoy our soirée?" She moved in between Colmont and Deville. "Before I forget, thank you, Jonathan dear, for that—how do you say? —financial tidbit?"

A strained smile crossed her lips as she avoided Stone's gaze. The music selection coming through the loudspeakers had changed. An old song by Johnny Mathis replaced the concert strings of Vivaldi. A few couples started dancing.

How would she react if he asked her to dance? Oh, what the hell. "Contessa, as your escort, may I have this dance?"

"Just one dance, Hayden. I must attend to my guests."

Stone guided her to where the other couples were dancing. The lights surrounding them appeared softer. Images of past dances on the veranda with her in his arms flashed in his mind. It would be comfortable to return here. Oh, so comfortable.

She spoke before he could. "Yes, I remember this song. I remember all the times we danced to it." She looked away. Gently, he steered her from the other couples and then slowed the pace of the dance. His lips came close to her face, but she turned her head away.

"The song is almost over," she whispered, and then her body stiffened. "God, here comes Harrington." Her voice broke and her eyes welled up. They stopped dancing.

"Contessa, we're heading up to the palace," Harrington said, as he bumped into Stone. "Oh, sorry about that Stone, didn't mean to interrupt your dance, but my dear wife is feeling a bit under the weather."

"Of course. It appears everyone is leaving," Lucinda observed. "I think I will let the staff handle the clean up. Tomorrow is moving day for me."

As Harrington left, he glowered at Stone. Colmont and the Devilles came over and thanked the contessa for the evening. She let out a deep sigh, and then said to the Devilles, "I will drive you back to the palace in my car." She took Rhonda's arm. "You and your husband are such good friends." Slipping her other hand through Jonathan's arm, they started toward the exit. She looked back at Stone. "And you still dance well."

"Be careful, Boswell, there's a curve ahead." Helen Harrington grabbed the armrest of the Mercedes. "How much have you had to drink?"

"I'd be glad to pull over and let you drive. Otherwise, be quiet. We're almost to the palace."

"Just be careful."

Lately, it seemed she had to do most of the thinking for them, at least with respect to the Foundation's business. Other matters had preoccupied her husband, one being the contessa.

Obviously, the bitch continued to rebuff him. Helen recognized his moods: edgy, whiny, and mean. "Just how much will we get from your Arab friends?"

"At least two hundred thousand euros," Harrington said. "Probably more."

"Christ, Boswell, you talked millions, not thousands!" Helen leaned toward him. "Get this straight. I've had enough of this place, enough of the Foundation, enough of—" She stopped, leaned back, and looked out the passenger window.

"Abdul Wahab has gotten obstinate," Harrington continued. "He reneged on the deal. He won't give me the money to finance the transaction." Harrington eased up on the accelerator as the car approached the palace. "I'll get only a finder's fee for providing the contacts in Marseille."

"Two hundred thousand euros?"

"No. That's a separate deal." Harrington pulled in front of the palace. An elderly man emerged from the front door and walked toward car. "Abdul Wahab wants me to kill Hayden Stone."

"Really. When?" Helen's throat muscles tightened, making it difficult to breath. The muscle spasms had been occurring a lot lately.

"The sooner the better." The old man offered to open the door for Helen, but Harrington motioned him to wait. "Oh this is rich, my sweet. You'll enjoy this bit of information, being an alumna of the New Left. Stone's a CIA agent."

Helen took deep breaths. She looked out at the darkened palace, with only a few dim lights coming from windows scattered on the face of the massive structure. She wanted so much to return to California, but how would they be able to afford it? "Boswell, you're becoming an assassin? Or is that too nice a word for a hit man?" She looked at his face, which seemed to be aging more each week. In college, when they'd crashed in that apartment on the hill above Haight-Ashbury and spent the long afternoons lying naked, smoking dope, and discussing Marxism, his features were crisp and sharp. So much for youth and dreams.

"You said two hundred thousand to kill Stone?" she asked. Maybe they could kill that little slut Lucinda along with the fascist pig Stone.

Stone climbed the palace's marble staircase to the second floor and found the door to his bedroom. The contessa's staff had turned on the lamps and readied his bed. The ice bucket was full, as was the wooden liquor cabinet. All the furniture, nothing newer than one hundred years old, sat in the same place he remembered the last time he had slept there years before. Palaces and castles do not change much over time.

The smell of age hung in the room, yet he saw no dust. The polished wood floor bordering the edges of the frayed Persian rug reflected light from the lamp. An original print by David Roberts hung on the wall next to the door. The scene, the contessa had told him, was in the Middle East, a place called Gaza. In the picture, ruins lay in the foreground and a bleached town spread out on a hill in the distance. He had seen a copy in a London shop and it, like a whiff of perfume evoking the memory of a past lover, had brought him back to this room.

He hung his tuxedo on the wooden clothes valet, slipped into his pajamas, and put on his robe. Finding his slippers, he walked over to the paned-glass door leading onto the balcony. With a cigar and a brandy in hand, he pushed the door open and stepped out. The balcony faced the mountain, and above his head, a waning quarter-moon and traces of constellations glimmered in the cool night air. Before he lit his cigar, he breathed in the cool air flavored with Mediterranean spices. The last time he'd stayed in this room, he had smoked inexpensive cigarettes from the navy commissary. Years later, when he started jogging, he quit.

At nights, when they were young lovers, Lucinda had come to this room. The first time, on her eighteenth birthday, she had taken the hidden passageway, entering through a moveable panel in the closet. He had checked. The panel still opened. Perhaps she would visit him tonight. He turned away from the mountain and leaned back against the banister. The romance had lasted almost a year. She was eighteen, he twenty-two. Memories returned of the last summer they'd spent together.

Why had he left her? Maybe he believed that with little money of his own and unsure of his future, he would lose her. It was less painful to end the romance before she did. *Strange, some of the decisions you make, even knowing at the time they're wrong.*

Some pebbles dropped on his hair. He looked up, but it was too dark to see from where they came. A bird or bat moving up in a parapet? He took a long puff from his cigar and wondered how at this time of his life he'd found himself invited to stay the night in a palace and hobnob with the glitterati of the Côte d'Azur. During the party, he'd had a difficult time taking his eyes off Lucinda. She was no longer a young girl, but quite a woman. Her auburn hair had darkened over the years, but it still had luster. That black dress, cut snug, ever so slightly revealed her tanned breasts. She played the role of a contessa quite well.

Again, some pieces of rock dropped from above. As he looked up, he heard his suitcase in the bedroom fall to the floor. Taking two steps forward, he peered through the glass doors into the bedroom. Lucinda passed in front of the table lamp. He smiled, tossed the cigar over his shoulder, and moved toward the door.

From behind him came a crash. Jagged pieces of granite hit the back of his head. He dove past the door into the bedroom and landed on the floor at Lucinda's feet.

"Good God, Hayden, are you all right?" She knelt at his side.

"What the hell happened?" He stood up and pulled her next to him.

They inched toward the door. He turned on a floor lamp and positioned it so they could survey the damage on the balcony. A large block had fallen and crushed a six-inch hole in the terrazzo at the spot where Stone had been standing.

"That has never happened before," she exclaimed. "Not even during earth tremors."

"Thanks for coming. If I hadn't seen you in the room and moved away from that spot, I'd be dead. You saved my life." He went to kiss her, but a loud knocking at the door interrupted him.

She ran to the closet, turned back, and motioned to answer the door. He waited a moment for her to close the panel, then opened the door to find two of the contessa's employees next to the Devilles, all asking at once about the noise. Invited into the room, they went to inspect the damage on the balcony. Stone opined that a piece of the palace's façade had come loose. Lucinda now appeared at the door. It hadn't taken long for her to climb the passageway back to her room and return by the hallway.

Jonathan asked Stone to come out with him on the balcony. Outside while they looked up into the darkness, Jonathan whispered, "Seems a bit of a coincidence, don't you think?"

"You're right. Let's go up and take a look."

"If there had been someone there, they'd be gone now," Deville countered. "We couldn't do a good job of searching in the dark. We'll wait for daylight. By the way, who's staying on the upper floors?"

"The contessa and the Harringtons," Stone said. "Also, the staff has the run of the place."

"Harrington, you say?"

"Yes."

A half hour passed before they all left Stone's room. The contessa's employees, who seemed perplexed, promised that the next morning they would investigate what had caused the block to fall. Finally, alone, Stone refilled his drink and closed the door to the balcony. The night air blew in through the broken panes of glass in the door and chilled the room. He lit the wood in the fireplace and turned off the lights. From his bed, the low flames crackled off a soft glow and created shadows on the walls.

He put his hands behind his head. So far, the gods were smiling on him. Then, he remembered that Lucinda had come to his room to see him. He closed his eyes and waited.

The rustle from the clothes on the hangers in the closet didn't come as a surprise. The contessa emerged quietly, walked over, and stopped a few feet from the bed. She let her gown slip from her shoulders and the firelight revealed her long body in a short black negligee. He pulled the covers back from the bed, and she climbed in and knelt next to him. They did not speak. Her rich perfume came to him in complex waves, which he breathed in deeply. He took her hand and slowly drew her to him.

After dozing for a time, he stirred. When he inched away, she moved closer. She whispered she was warm. He removed one of the blankets.

"I was not going to come to you." She lifted up on one arm and faced him. "Mainly because I knew you wanted me to visit and make love with you."

"So why did you?"

She moved closer and put her face on his chest. "Things are not going well. I told you I must lease the palace to the Saudis because I need the money."

"I wish I could help you."

"Let me finish, please. I need the funds because Harrington, supposedly my friend, talked me into lending him money. He lost it all and put me into debt. Then there is my brother and his family. They are all more of a problem than a help. And my consigliere wants me to sell antiquities on the black market."

"You, my dear, are in a bind."

"Yes, I am. But with you I can escape reality for a few hours."

Stone reached around and embraced her. He held her for a long time, until his arm started to go numb. When he moved, she sat up and crossed her legs.

In her low, cognac voice she said, "So let us talk about what will happen tomorrow." She let out a long sigh. "I will have to get the staff organized for the move down to the villa." She pointed to the balcony. "In addition, that has to be repaired."

He ran his fingers across her belly. "You don't think someone wants me dead, do you?"

"Very strange. This palace is well built. Remember years ago when I showed you the foundations?"

She had taken him into the bowels of the building and showed him ruins on the floor of a large cavern connected to the basement of the structure. She had pointed out walls and marble columns that archeologists had identified as ancient Greek and Roman. A tunnel ran from the basement under the mountain ridge and emerged about a mile from the palace, dug by a medieval lord during the time of seaborne raids by the Moors. One day they had explored the length of the tunnel and had come out onto a thicket of bushes and trees that clung to the side of the mountain.

"It's amazing how many people have lived here. Right on this spot," he said.

She had turned slightly toward the fire, and he studied the outline of her breasts. He looked for the mole under her left nipple. "I wonder what happened to that religion," he continued. "You know—people who believed in Zeus, Neptune, and all those gods in mythology?" He rubbed his hand along the smooth skin inside her thigh. "Do you think our religions will pass away some day?"

"Enough." She took his hand and pressed it down on her stomach. "You are the same after all this time. After making love, you like to lie on your back and talk philosophy, or make jokes. At least now you do not smoke a cigarette afterward." She crawled over and straddled him, her thighs pressing against his sides. Apparently comfortable, she began pulling at his chest hairs one by one. "I have a busy day tomorrow. And what will you do? Go back and write your book?"

"I suppose. Is there anything I can do to help you here?"

She shook her head, caressing his chest. "I will have to read one of your books." A moment's silence. "I wanted to ask, how do you know the Devilles? Rhonda Deville mentioned that you and Jonathan had worked together on something."

"We did, some years ago."

"So you were a policeman like Jonathan?"

"FBI. I'm retired, and now I write."

"And you know Maurice Colmont?"

"We've met. I can't say we're friends."

She leaned down on him and he hugged her. She stretched back and looked at him. Although he could barely see her face in the dark, he felt her staring.

"It would be so nice if I could trust you, Hayden. But of course I cannot." She ran her right hand through his hair. "Why did your wife leave you?"

"She said I bored her to tears."

She threw back her head and laughed. "That is hard to believe." She kissed him hard and said in his ear, "One more time and then I go. Tomorrow is a busy day for me."

The next morning the palace was in turmoil. The contessa's staff rushed about moving furniture and packing objets d'art. Holding a cup of coffee, Stone explored the first floor level and found himself in the library. He read the titles on the shelves. The framed old maps held his interest for a while, and then he thought of the ruins down in the lower level.

He descended a set of stairs to the basement and passed through a door to the cavern. Switching on the lights, he saw before him the columns and relics as he remembered them. Evidently, the contessa took guests down there on tours, because the lighting system appeared modern.

Before he returned to the main floor, he searched for the entrance to the tunnel. He found it in the basement behind a huge water-stained breakfront that looked at least three hundred years old. It blocked the door leading to the tunnel. Pushing hard with his back, he managed to budge the cabinet a foot from the door. An open padlock hung from a clasp, which fell apart when he touched it. He tested the door and it creaked open. It was difficult to close. Losing interest, he threw the broken padlock behind the breakfront and returned to the main level of the palace.

Jonathan approached as Stone put his suitcase in the Porsche's trunk. "Hey buddy, I found out something interesting this morning. I accompanied the workmen up to the roof to find out why that block came crashing down." He turned his face up to the parapet above Stone's room. "The workmen are still puzzled. However, I saw gouges that would indicate that someone pried the block off its base, like with a crowbar." He squeezed Stone's arm. "You know, pal, you've got to stop pissing people off around here."

The contessa stood by the palace front door, giving instructions to a member of her staff who was loading a painting into the back of a van. She looked over and waved at Stone. He blew her a kiss, slid into the seat of the car, and turned on the ignition. The low, throaty rumble of the exhaust sounded good. In the rearview mirror, he glanced back at her. She was still watching his car. The bright sun brought out touches of red in her auburn hair and, for a moment, in her white slacks and tan polka dot blouse, she looked eighteen again.

CHAPTER TWENTY-ONE

NICE—MAY 12, 2002

The chimes from nearby church bells drifted into Claudia's hotel room along with the sun-warmed sea air. Charles Fleming sat in one of the red and white patterned armchairs next to the door of the narrow balcony where Sandra sat, gazing off to the distance, a cappuccino in her hand.

Seated at a russet desk, Claudia wrote nervous scribbles on a notepad embossed with the hotel's hallmark. With the secure satellite phone to her ear, she listened to her boss, Howard, who had called from CIA Headquarters. It was early Sunday morning in Washington, DC, so he considered the call important.

He rambled on, as the people who worked for him were accustomed to. Claudia made hard doodles on the pad and at one point, ripped off the page, and started scribbling on the next one. Between sharp, hacking coughs, Howard said, "A Colonel Frederick will arrive in Nice tomorrow. For your information, the colonel's office is on the seventh floor at Langley. He's attached to the Director's staff."

Swiveling around from the desk, Claudia looked out through the open balcony door at the sun-splashed sea. In the distance, a small fishing boat passed with a lone man standing on the open deck tending the tiller.

Howard droned on. "My counterpart in the Near East Division called me a few hours ago and registered concern that multiple threats in the South of France were not being addressed."

Claudia rose from the chair and paced. It had been five minutes since she had managed to say anything. Fleming, who she knew had a sort of sixth sense for situations like this, had begun to fidget.

Addressing the attempted capture of the al Qaeda terrorist, bin Zanni, Howard emphasized each word. "I'm displeased with your team's *failure* to capture him. The military in Frankfurt, Germany registered a complaint directly to the Deputy Director of Operations. But what's most disturbing is that I received a report from Paris Station indicating our liaison with the French has broken down."

Whenever Howard used the word "disturbing," smart people in the CIA ran for cover. Claudia stopped pacing and, rubbing her stomach, felt the beginnings of a severe stomachache. Apparently, Howard was not interested in hearing her version of events.

Before signing off, Howard said, "Just be sure to arrange for Colonel Frederick's arrival in Nice. And by the way, Claudia, give my salute to that fellow, Hayden Stone, who has evened the score with the opposition."

Claudia switched off the phone and tossed it to Fleming. "Call Paris and find out when Colonel Frederick arrives to assume control. Make appropriate hotel arrangements for him. He's very high up, a super grade."

She stared out to the balcony and studied Sandra drinking her coffee. When did Sandra call and report on her to the Paris station chief? Before or after last night's pleasant dinner together?

VILLEFRANCHE

Under the canvas-covered fantail of the Red Scorpion, Abdul Wahab reclined on an embroidered Turkish cushion. Across from him, the prince sat gazing at Villefranche. As a slight breeze from the sea gradually swayed the anchored boat to the right, the town and the mountains behind it slipped by like a panning cinema shot. The clear air and yellow sun invigorated Wahab, and he wished he were riding his favorite Arabian in the mountains above the town.

Thick steam rose from a pot of black tea sitting on a low round table of intricate marquetry. The prince gracefully pulled back the white sleeves of his robe, picked up a cup and saucer from the engraved serving dish, and took a sip. "When will these people from Riyadh move into the contessa's palace? Tomorrow?"

"It will be Tuesday before they can move in, Excellency," Wahab answered. "The contessa must transport her personal belongings down to her villa. As it is, her staff is moving in haste."

"That man, Harrington, is very foolish. He reminds me of those so-called scholars running about the town of Boston. Why do you bother with him?"

Wahab leaned over and selected a honeyed fig from the tray. "In life one becomes involved with fools. He is useful for some of my business dealings."

"I am not impressed with your dealings with the poppy growers in Afghanistan."

Leaning back on his cushion, Wahab sucked honey from a fig. Next, he would receive a soft admonishment about the welfare of the prince's daughter, Wahab's first wife, who lived in Jeddah. All the while, the prince's unasked question hung there: Why did he, his son-in-law, take another wife, that English woman he kept in London?

"They are Taliban. Our brothers," Wahab said. "They receive money for their crops, poison is sent to Europe, and I have money to finance the infrastructure of my new network."

The prince studied a passing sailboat. "I need not know the details of your network." He paused. "These people from Riyadh are anxious to take their medical equipment to the palace. The men from the interior ministry will go with them. I will be happy to see them leave the Red Scorpion."

The prince set down his cup and his servant poured fresh tea. He then waved the servant away. "I am not comfortable with this escapade, but an important member of the royal family has seen fit to assist bin Zanni." He peered over his wire-framed glasses. "Of course, bin Zanni is a brother Saudi and a believer in the true faith of the desert. We must support him against the infidels, polytheists, and heretics, even if he considers you and me to be corrupt."

"Bin Zanni's handlers sent me a message asking assistance," Wahab said. "He escaped capture two days ago. The CIA and the French know he is in France."

"That is not good news."

"He and his people are in the mountains near the Swiss border. They will stay there until it is safe for them to move to the contessa's palace." Wahab looked up at the mountain and tried to pick out the hulking mass of stone that comprised the palace. "They say they need help getting bin Zanni to the palace."

"They should go on to Switzerland. All these people on the yacht could follow them there," the prince huffed. "It would solve a lot of problems."

Wahab dabbed his beard with a linen napkin and looked at the prince, who started moving his eyeglasses up and down the bridge of his nose as he did when he felt uncomfortable with a political predicament. The prince's instincts were unequaled.

The prince studied him, then asked, "What form of assistance did they request?"

"They want the CIA and the French intelligence to be distracted when they make their move. A distraction will cause the CIA to concentrate their forces away from this area."

"And of course, you have an idea."

"Yes." He did not want to elaborate, and tried to think of another topic to discuss, but the prince continued to stare. "We made arrangements for an attack on the American consul general in Marseille."

"Why are we involved in all this?" The prince put his cup and saucer on the table.

"We must be involved in this wave of the future or become irrelevant," Wahab said, folding his napkin.

The prince rose from the cushion and stretched. He went to the brass railing. "Once when I was young, I swam in the surf. Swimming back to shore, and believing I had mastered the ocean, I stepped through the water toward the beach, elated, when suddenly from behind a huge wave knocked me down and pushed my face into the coral sand."

He looked across the bay, removed his glasses, and again wiped the lenses. Keeping his gaze on the white sailboats skimming across the water, he replaced them, carefully slipping the earpieces under his *kuffiyah*. "I remember many years ago, my father introduced me to my first American. The man was from Oklahoma and he called himself an oilman. He wanted my father to grant him a concession to drill oil and he promised that if my father fulfilled his wish, both of them would profit. My father said he was true to his word. I liked that American. He, my father and I went out in the desert many times and hunted with falcons."

MARSEILLE

Hassan sat at the sidewalk café in the old port of Marseille waiting to meet Rashid. Sunday morning brought out the city dwellers, strolling along the docks and enjoying their breakfasts with friends and family. Dogs sat under their master's tables. Hassan was paging through a local newspaper when Rashid approached.

"A fine morning, Hassan. The drive from Arles was quite pleasant."

Without speaking, Hassan motioned for him to take a seat. A waiter immediately came up and took the order for two coffees.

Rashid settled himself, then spoke in Arabic. "Our friend in Nice has sent me with a message. He has a proposal for you, a most important assignment."

Before he could continue, Hassan said, "I do not take *assignments* from him or his people."

The waiter returned with two coffees. When he moved off to serve another table, Rashid pushed his chair closer. "Pardon. An unfortunate use of the word. I meant to say, a request." He poured three spoonfuls of sugar into his cup and then mixed it in, clicking his spoon. "We must talk, but not here. Perhaps we can walk around the dock next to the water."

"We will discuss the matter tomorrow," Hassan said.

"It is an urgent matter. Please, after our coffee, let us take a leisurely walk?"

Hassan spoke in a low voice. "What about *my* urgent matter? Are we not going to the wine wholesaler tomorrow? Am I not traveling up to Arles to look at the wine bottles and the cases?" He moved his face closer to Rashid's. "Well, my friend?"

Rashid looked off toward the moored fishing boats crowding the inner harbor. Slowly, he nodded.

"Very well then," Hassan said. "After our coffee, we shall take your leisurely walk around the harbor."

As Rashid paid the bill, Hassan watched him leave too generous a tip. Along the quay they stopped where the fish market set up during the week.

Hassan lit a cigarette and faced the water. "So what is this urgent matter Wahab is concerned about?"

Rashid looked around and spoke quickly. "A few days ago, bin Zanni barely escaped capture by the CIA. His group has him hidden, but he must travel to Nice very soon." He continued, whispering in Hassan's ear, "Abdul Wahab wants you to create a diversion here in Marseille. He suggests you kill the American consul general. That would cause the crusaders to draw off their forces and bin Zanni can travel to Nice."

"Kill him, or attempt to kill him?" Hassan asked.

"Either way, it would be a major distraction. The consul general is an easy target ... only one guard according to our source."

"Why is Wahab asking me to do this?"

Rashid thought a moment. "I suppose he trusts you." He looked around. No one was near. "Perhaps his people are all occupied with bin Zanni."

Hassan turned from the water and looked hard at him. "And perhaps ... what else, my friend?"

"Abdul Wahab said he paid you to kill that American in Saint Rémy and was astonished to learn last night that the American is still very much alive. He will accept the American consul general as a substitute."

CHAPTER TWENTY-TWO

CÔTE D'AZUR

Heading back from Nice on the Autoroute in only light Sunday morning traffic, the Porsche hummed along at eighty-five miles per hour. In less than two hours, Stone eased through the narrow streets of Archos. After squeezing into a tight parking place, he headed toward the waterfront. From the gray stone church perched on the side of the hill, bells tolled for the last mass.

He wanted to avoid meeting Margaux. At the opposite end of the quay, he spotted a bistro sporting a blue awning and matching shutters on the upper floor windows. He found an unoccupied table facing the harbor. A young waiter, after taking his time arranging a new place setting two tables away, came over and took his order for a café au lait, rolls, and goat cheese. He suggested a side dish of assorted olives and smoked peppers.

A French family sat at the table next to him, the father and mother doting on the boy and girl. The girl, about six, practiced her French wiles on her father, who pretended he didn't notice. Stone thought of his daughter and wondered what she was doing at that particular moment. How were she and her brother coping with their parent's divorce?

The boats tied up along the quay creaked as they rose and fell on the soft harbor swell. The meal came and Stone concentrated on the cheese, which had a smoky flavor that complemented the red and green peppers. The olives were big and not too meaty.

On the drive back to Archos, he had thought about Lucinda and relived the moments they had shared in bed, surrounded by the glow from the burning logs in the fireplace. He accepted the fact that her face and husky voice would reappear in his daydreams, at least for a while.

Now as far as Margaux was concerned, the next time they met, would she suspect he had slept with Lucinda? Would she care? They were merely acquaintances. So what was the problem? There was none. The cellphone in his breast pocket vibrated. The number on the display belonged to Fleming.

"How was the party in Nice?" Fleming asked. "Hobnobbing with the rich and famous?"

"Your sources are very good."

"Just talked with Jonathan Deville and before that with your new buddy, Maurice Colmont, but that's not why I called," Fleming hurried on. "Someone by the name of Colonel Frederick from the CIA Director's office has replaced Claudia. Frederick arrives in Nice tomorrow and wants a meeting of all the operatives." He gave Stone the location of the meeting. "It appears you and Frederick are old chums," added Fleming. "You know Claudia wanted to fire you, over my objections of course, but it seems you're back big time thanks to the colonel." He paused. "See you tomorrow."

Stone wondered what had triggered Claudia's animosity. Something he had said? Maybe she didn't like his looks—reminded her of someone? As in many times in the past, he probably would never know. Still, it would be worth looking into for future reference.

Stone thought of Harrington as he waited to pay his bill. The man didn't fit into the mold of the director of a distinguished arts foundation. At Lucinda's party, Deville had mentioned that Harrington's reputation was spotty. In addition, Harrington had lured Lucinda into leasing her palace to the Saudis, no doubt for his own personal gain. Lastly, the bastard wanted to bed Lucinda. Had Harrington pushed the building block off the parapet? If so, was jealousy over Lucinda the only motive?

Stone left the restaurant and headed for his car. As he inserted the key into the ignition, he decided to keep an eye on Mr. Harrington.

• • •

Stone rounded the flagstone path to his cottage and halted. Harrington and a stocky man emerged from David's house. The door slammed behind them as they hurried in the opposite direction, toward the administration building. He let them gain some distance, then continued toward his cottage. Harrington had been wearing the same tight grimace he had during had the altercation by the pool. David's door stood ajar, and some cursing came from within. Stone walked up to the door and listened. The swearing was accompanied by the sound of furniture being moved. He pushed open the door.

David looked over. "Please go away." He knelt on the floor, and started gathering papers.

"What happened to all your documents?"

"What does it look like? Our esteemed director paid me a visit."

"Just what is that man's problem, David?"

"You're part of his problem. Another is he likes to take out his tribulations on other people. Like me, for instance."

"Explain."

David went over to the couch and slumped down. "He doesn't like you. It's more than that ... it sounded like ... well, he thinks you're spying on him." He cocked his head. "Are you reporting on him to the Foundation's board of directors in New York?"

A carved wooden cuckoo clock on the wall came to life and chirped eleven times. Stone walked to the window and looked toward the administration building. After a moment, he turned. "Harrington is involved in some dirty business. He's a dangerous man."

"Tell me about it."

"Tell me everything he said when he was here." Stone eased himself into a chair.

"He wanted to know what I had learned about you."

"He had asked you to report on me?" Stone asked.

"Yes, last week, but I never told him anything, because I had nothing to tell him."

"That was when you got those bruises on your body, right?"

Stone asked. "What was he looking for? What did he want to know? Did he mention the contessa?"

"No, he never mentioned her. He wants to know about certain people here. For instance, he's suspicious of that fellow, Ricard ... you know, the driver." David's leg began a nervous twitch. "He came in today with that troglodyte thug of his and was incensed about you. For some reason, you've become his *bête noir.*"

"I'm sorry, David. I think he's pissed off because I'm friends with the contessa, whom I gather he wants as his lover. You got caught in the middle."

"He hates you, but—" He thought for a moment. "At the same time, today it seemed as if he feared you."

"Let me suggest you avoid him," Stone said, to which David gave him a "no kidding" look. "Maybe I can give you some information you can feed to him. It may keep him off your back."

"Okay," David said. "Harrington wanted to know who you were friendly with. I told him Margaux." He lowered his head. "He also asked where you went on Thursday. You were gone all day. I didn't know."

Stone thought a moment while studying the man sitting in front of him. "You know, we can help each other. Keep me informed about Harrington and those thugs of his." Stone got up and walked to the door. "And I'll talk with Fleming in Paris about getting that manuscript of yours published."

MARSEILLE

The cabin cruiser bobbed at its mooring in the Marseille Vieux-Port. Inside, on the galley table, Mark fiddled with the controls on the voice recorder attached to the parabolic microphone. That morning he'd used the device to pick up Hassan and Rashid's conversation while they stood on the quay. As he replayed the disc, he strained to understand the words, pressing the earphones to his head, hoping that would help.

Unfortunately, Hassan and Rashid had spoken mostly in Arabic, a language Mark didn't know. A few words and phrases were in French, which he did understand, and from those he tried to make sense of the conversation. In frustration, he threw the headphones on the table and decided to send the recording to Paris for a complete transcription. He'd clearly heard the words: Saudi, American consul general, Abdul Wahab, Nice. He would phone Fleming this bit of information.

Fleming answered on the second ring and immediately interrupted Mark. "A meeting is scheduled for tomorrow in Nice." Fleming went on about the importance of the meeting. Mark finally managed to tell Fleming about the surveillance and the conversation he had recorded.

"It doesn't sound like much, at least from what you've told me," Fleming said. "Send it to Paris by the courier who's passing through Marseille this afternoon."

"I wish we could get a translation now," Mark said. "There's something about the words and the way they said them."

"Look, the important thing is the meeting tomorrow. The word I get is that this Colonel Frederick likes to kick ass, so let's not offer ourselves up."

After the call, Mark prepared the computer disc for delivery to Paris Station. He had forgotten to ask Fleming about Rashid. Eric, the CIA operative, had identified Rashid after the last surveillance when he'd followed the man to his estate on the outskirts of Arles. Rashid lived in a mansion surrounded by a large vineyard, which Paris Station considered odd, with the Muslim restriction against consuming alcohol. The station had queried French intelligence about him, but they had yet to receive any feedback.

After their meeting at the Vieux-Port, Hassan and Rashid had separated, agreeing to meet the next day, Monday, at the wine wholesaler's office. Hassan strolled out of the port area of Marseille toward the Palais du Pharo. Ten minutes later, he found himself looking up at the edifice standing high on a bluff at the entrance to the harbor. The sun was overhead. The days were getting warmer and longer.

Sandra was waiting for him in front of the Palais, sitting on the edge of a low wall with a 35mm camera dangling from her neck. A narrow black felt band fixed her blonde hair back into a ponytail. She was swaying her white running shoes back and forth. He approached and she jumped down from the wall. The top three buttons of her white blouse were unfastened displaying a deep cleavage. Hassan took note. He kissed her on the cheek and detected a different scent of perfume. A touch of vanilla?

"We will have a wonderful view of the city on the other side of the building." She took his arm. "I want to take some photos for my aunt in Avignon."

He searched for the subtle change in her demeanor she had displayed during their last time together when she had shown too much curiosity about his work as a journalist and his travel to Nice. But today, he found her changed again. No longer was she the virginal young Canadian. She was, as the British said, "fetching." The complications and delays in his plan, plus the problems with Dr. Aziz, had made him tense. It was natural for suspicions to follow, he reasoned.

"This building is not old," she said with her slight lisp. "Napoleon III built it, but he never lived here. It has a fine auditorium. I've attended some of their seminars."

They found their way through the interior of the Palais and emerged on the north terrace, which provided a high vista above the harbor. Sailboats and fishing skiffs dotted the choppy waters farther out on the Bay of Marseille.

She pointed. "Over there is the Saint-Jean Fort, and behind it is the La Major cathedral."

"What is the name of the fort?" he asked.

"Saint-Jean. The Knights of Saint-Jean built it in the Twelfth century. And over there—"

"Ah yes, before those crusaders sailed off to pillage Jerusalem," he interrupted.

She took a few steps away and focused her camera on some sailboats. After a few photographs of the Vieux-Port and the city, she turned back to him. "I don't suppose you'll want copies of these photos for your album then?"

Now rankled, he started along the path on the north side of the Palais. Today, she seemed coquettish, and he had not had a woman since the whore in Athens. That had been an unpleasant experience. The woman had been a favorite of his, and he'd slept with her on his last three trips to Greece. Then the brothers had told him she was reporting to the police. She had to die, but knowing she had three young children, he had left a good sum of money on the table next to the bed—after he strangled her.

Sandra caught up to him. "You know, Hassan, until recently we in the West never realized that your people in the Middle East were so bitter about the crusades. Be truthful … is this something your people recently conjured up as offensive, or have you always held a grudge?"

How dare she! He had an urge to beat her, then take her forcibly. He looked away to the spires of a church on top of the hill looking over Marseille. She was exquisite, and an infidel. Sweat formed on his forehead and he felt a hardness forming in his groin.

"Come on now, don't take it personally. I think it's a legitimate question." She moved next to him and he glanced down the front of her blouse—noticing her lace brassiere. "I mean look at the cathedral over there. How many in the world are now mosques? Hey, you guys did away with the whole Byzantine civilization."

"Did you see a restroom in the building?" he asked.

"Yeah. Let's go, enough of the scenic vistas. Besides, the wind is picking up."

Inside the Palais, groups of people were wandering toward a meeting room. Outside the room, a handmade poster announced an underwater archaeological seminar. Beyond, along a hallway the rooms appeared unoccupied. She led the way down the corridor, then stopped and looked around. Undecided and a bit nervous, she said, "I'm sure this is the right way."

As he followed her, Hassan reviewed the events of the past hour. They had encountered few people during their walk around the grounds. No one had seen them take this corridor. As far as he could determine, no one could place him here with the girl.

Now, no one was in sight. Their footsteps echoed down the hallway. The men's restroom came up on the right. She said she would wait for him outside.

Inside, the lavatory had three toilet stalls and two urinals. The bright white room smelled of disinfectant. The stalls were empty. Quickly, he relieved himself at one of the urinals, then went to the washbasin and splashed water on his face. In the mirror, he watched himself slip off his belt and wrap one end around his left hand.

He eased the restroom door open and stuck his head out. Sandra was alone in the hallway. She was putting her cellphone back into her purse.

"Please come here and look at this," he said. "It is very strange."

"Really, I'm not interested in…" She hesitated and slowly moved to the door.

"Come, come," he entreated. "It is most interesting."

At the door, she leaned forward and peered in. At the same moment, he wrapped the belt around her neck and yanked her into the lavatory. Kicking the door shut, he dragged her by the neck and pulled her across the white tiled floor to a urinal, slamming her head against the porcelain.

She resisted forcibly and her strength surprised him, but with the pressure on her throat, she would soon lose consciousness. She repeatedly tried to hit him in the face and kick him in the shins. He applied more pressure to the belt, just enough to cut the flow of blood to the brain. He wanted her to be alive when he raped her.

Using both feet, she kicked away from the wall. He lost his footing on a wet spot on the tile floor and both fell. She flailed with her arms and elbows. He rolled on top of her, but the belt came loose and she let out a yell.

The scream startled him and he tried to cover her mouth, but she flipped him over. As she scrambled to her knees, her cellphone dropped out of her purse. She grabbed it, and by the time she pressed the third button on the phone, he was on his feet. A hard blow to the side of her head, and her body rolled over twice on the floor, stopping at the brace of a toilet stall.

Hassan crawled over and turned her over on her back. Tiny wet bubbles puffed from between her lips. Pausing to make sure she was unconscious, he ripped her white blouse open, retrieved his pocketknife, and cut the front band connecting the cups of her brassiere. Pulling the brassiere aside, he groped her breasts with both hands, and then jerked up her skirt.

It was then that a thin three-inch silver wire attached to a very thin metal cylinder inside the right cup of her brassiere caught his eye. He reached down and fingered the apparatus.

Then all went black.

"Sandra. Wake up." Stone patted her face with a wet paper towel. She opened her eyes and mouthed some words Stone couldn't make out. He helped her sit up and held her as she stared at Hassan lying on the floor, a splatter of blood on the white tile next to his head.

Finally, she asked in a hoarse voice, "Did you kill him?"

"No," Stone said, as if it hadn't been the right decision.

Standing, she took off her blouse, removed the torn bra with the listening device, then rolled it into a ball.

"Thanks for saving my life ... now stop looking at my boobs." She put on her blouse. Fastening the two buttons Hassan hadn't ripped off, she adjusted her skirt. He reached out to help. "Christ, I can do it myself! Go over there and search him, before he wakes up."

"Here, put on my jacket. Good thing you signaled me on the cellphone," Stone said. "And that Mark asked me to run over here to Marseille to do a countersurveillance of your meet with this son of a bitch."

Stone went through Hassan's pockets, removed a black automatic pistol, and placed it on the floor. By the time Sandra had composed herself, he had laid out Hassan's identification, a number of calling cards, and some notes scribbled in Arabic next to the gun.

"Let's copy everything down," he told her.

She knelt next to him. "If the asshole stirs, please hit him again. Harder."

"We're not letting this guy walk, are we?" Stone asked.

"We don't know what he's up to, only that it's big." Sandra covered her face with her hands. "If he's loose, we have a better chance of finding out..." She started to tremble.

"Okay." Stone put his hand on her arm. "Help me with this stuff."

With both of them copying the information, it took only a few minutes, even with tracing the Arabic script. Finished, they replaced all the articles in Hassan's pockets.

"What about his gun?" Stone asked. When Sandra shrugged, he suggested, "It's a Russian make. I know how to mess with the firing pin."

"Do it, Sport. Then let's get out of here."

It didn't take long for Stone to alter the firing pin and put the gun back in Hassan's jacket. Meanwhile, she had gotten up and was leaning against the wall next to the door with her eyes closed. She breathed deeply.

"We're all set to go," he said. "Are you okay?"

"Yeah. One last thing." Sandra took two quick steps toward Hassan's inert body and placed three hard, accurate kidney kicks. She stood back, took a deep breath, and then added two more for good measure deep into his groin.

CHAPTER TWENTY-THREE

NICE, FRANCE—MAY 13, 2002

In the living room of the safehouse, Stone leaned back in a padded armchair and stretched out his six-foot-two inches. A strong wind had blown in from the north, and thin gray clouds hid the sky. Pressure from the wind thumped against the apartment windows.

He planned to enjoy the performance he knew his friend, Colonel Gustave Frederick, was about to deliver. Frederick had left his pinstriped suit in Washington and dressed down for his trip to Nice: English cavalry twill slacks, a dark blue Italian turtleneck sweater, and a lambskin leather jacket. He had even modified his waspish nasal tone, used for the conference rooms at Langley, to a harder military voice, more appropriate for field operations.

With the wall to his back, Frederick looked over the group while slapping a notepad in his palm as if it was a swagger stick.

"Please address me as Fred, unless you are more comfortable with my military rank, Colonel."

The major in charge of the rendition team nodded, then turned to his men and smiled. Like a fisherman, Frederick was reeling in his audience.

"We have had a change in operational structure. Claudia had to travel to Paris for a briefing and will stay there to handle the most challenging task of operations logistics. Our meetings in the future will include our French colleagues." He waved the notebook in the direction of Colmont. "Namely Monsieur Colmont and his deputies. Let us not forget that this is a Franco-American effort, and a successful outcome is in the interests of both our republics."

Stone smiled. Fred hadn't changed over the years. He still seemed to enjoy the sound of his own voice.

"Now, we must discuss yesterday's incident. Mark, Stone, and Sandra have been working a separate counterterrorist operation in Marseille. Yesterday, during surveillance, the target, Hassan Musab Mujahid, attacked one of them. He may have identified that officer as CIA. We allowed him to escape so we can continue to identify his network. Agreed, Monsieur Colmont?"

"Agreed, Colonel. I believe we are coming up with some valuable information."

Fred continued. "However, the immediate problem facing this task force is to locate the al Qaeda information minister, bin Zanni, and then capture him."

Colmont spoke up. "I have been told that bin Zanni and his henchmen are in the alpine district near Grenoble."

At that moment, Fleming's cellphone rang, and he hurried into the kitchen. Fred had just asked Colmont to discuss some of the political problems he faced with the bin Zanni operation when Fleming rushed back into the room. "Excuse me! I just talked with Claudia in Paris." He read from his notes. "Mark, that conversation you intercepted yesterday at the Vieux-Port? Paris was able to transcribe it. Bottom line, there's a plot to kill our consul general in Marseille."

Colmont jumped up from his chair. "Pardon. This is a French criminal matter. I must know the details and inform the authorities in Marseille."

"Roger that," Fred said. "We'll head over to Marseille immediately. Major, you stay here in position with our French counterparts in case bin Zanni is located."

MARSEILLE

This time Hassan decided not to wait for Rashid outside the wine wholesaler's building as he had done at the last meeting. Instead, he entered the vestibule of the tired Marseille building and found a worn wooden bench with yellowed newspapers stacked to one side. To lessen the pain, he kept his legs spread as he gingerly eased himself down. The air smelled of cooked fish. The sun pierced through a window above, capturing specks of floating dust.

That morning Hassan had done his best to do a countersurveillance, but his head throbbed and his genitals ached. He had difficulty urinating and when he did, blood appeared.

After waking up on the lavatory floor of the Palais building the day before, he had limped in a daze back to his hotel room. He explained to Yazid and his driver that he had taken a bad fall. The Iraqi driver had bandaged the cut on his head and Yazid had found a pharmacy to buy pain medication. At one o'clock in the morning with his mind a bit clearer, Hassan had taken a shower. It was then he remembered the short, thin silver wire and cylinder tucked into Sandra's brassiere. The soap had dropped from his hand as panic set in.

From out of the bright sunlight, Rashid entered the building lobby and came over to him. In a whisper, he said, "So, have you set your plan to…" He stopped, stepped back, and stared at the bandage on Hassan's head. "What happened to you, my friend?"

Hassan rose and motioned toward the stairs. They started up, but after a few steps, Hassan became nauseous. At the first landing, he excused himself and limped into a restroom.

A stream of pink urine dripped out into the urinal, accompanied by a burning sensation. That morning he had thrown up his breakfast of bread and cheeses an hour after he had eaten. The pain in his head returned.

Zipping up his fly, he went over to the basin and washed his hands. In the mirror he saw his face covered with sweat. The tap provided only tepid water. When the sink filled, he put his face down into the water, and held it there. He lifted his head. Even though his body ached, his mind seemed clearer. Where was that Western bitch now? For whom did she work? It had to be the CIA. They knew about him. He must move fast.

• • •

The top button of the bald wholesaler's gray shirt had not seen a buttonhole in years. From behind his desk, he slouched his ample body into a chair and dragged on a cigarette. A crumpled pack of Gitanes stuck out of his shirt pocket. He acted as if he had trouble remembering Hassan and Rashid, even though their previous meeting had been only a week before. This time they sat without being offered a cup of coffee from the stained pot on the credenza.

"You're the ones who want to send a few cases of wine to the United States. How many? Twenty, thirty?"

Hassan said, "I want to send thirty cases of wine, ten each to New York, Washington, and Los Angeles. We should have the cases ready in a few days. We need to know where to deliver them."

"There may be some problems." The bald man leaned forward and waved his cigarette back and forth. "The *flics* are looking at all the shipping of wine lately, especially to the United States. I do not want to get caught in some illegal business."

"Excuse me," Rashid said. "What are these *flics*?"

He threw his hands in the air. "The police."

Perspiration oozed down the back of Hassan's shirt. His head ached at the thought of another problem. The vision in his right eye began to blur. He hoped Rashid would allay this pig's concerns.

"We assure you, sir, this is a legitimate transaction ... small, but quite legal." Rashid leaned toward the man. "If there are those who engage in illegal enterprises, that is no matter to us."

The fat man stabbed at them with his index finger. "What is on the labels of your wine? How old is it? Are you sending rare vintages?"

"They are *nouveau* wines," Hassan spoke up. "They come from near Marseille, from a village called Archos." He put his mind on alert. The wrong word spoken now could ruin the whole plan. "I do not understand about these 'rare vintages.'"

The bald man slumped back in his chair and began rotating the seat on its creaky swivel. He looked up at the ceiling and Hassan expected a lecture.

"The big scam today is selling rare vintages of French wine to rich Americans." The bald man used his hands again for emphasis. "Those fools will pay thousands and thousands for a bottle with the labels of a 1784 or 1787 Chateau Lafite or a 1961 Petrus filled with nothing but six-day-old wine. Do they know? Of course not. They are collectors, not drinkers."

Hassan relaxed, and the dampness in his shirt settled into a not uncomfortable chill. Turning to Rashid, he suggested they show the bald man the labels they would use.

"Here, see the label for yourself," Rashid said. "We will even give you a complimentary case of wine for your own inspection."

On that note, the bald man sat up and scribbled notes on a pad, then threw the pen down. "I will ship the wine for you." He handed Hassan a piece of paper with an address. "This is where you deliver the cases. Oh, I must add some additional handling charges. You understand?"

Hassan and Rashid descended the two flights of stairs to the lobby and stopped at the doorway. Each one took turns leaning out the door and looking up and down the street. They saw no one who appeared suspicious.

As Hassan started out, Rashid grabbed his sleeve. "I do not understand all this. Why are you so intent on sending this wine to America? How much can you or your organization expect to make from all the trouble?"

Hassan wiped his brow with a handkerchief and, seeing it soiled, shoved it back into his pocket. He did not need a debate with Rashid now.

Rashid continued. "The important thing is what you plan to do about the American consul general. Abdul Wahab is very intent about this, and I told you he says that you already have been paid—"

"My people are in contact with a man who is employed at the consul general's home. I do not want to be specific, but the results will please Wahab." Hassan leaned against the doorway. He handed Rashid the piece of paper the bald man had given him. "Send twenty-four cases of wine to the wholesaler today." He pulled a card from his shirt pocket. "Now, here is another address. Today, send six cases of the green labeled Cassis wine to this location."

"This address you give me for the six cases is in Montpellier," Rashid exclaimed. "I do not understand. Why not ship these six cases with the rest of the lot?" Rashid traced the address with his finger.

"I want them to go separately. After my friend has inspected the wine, he will send them to the wholesaler. It is something I want to do."

Rashid looked at Hassan and shook his head. "*Habibi*. My good friend, you have taken a bad fall. You really should go back to your hotel and sleep. You have much to do in the next few days."

Hassan said, "*Shukran*. Thank you. I agree." They left the building singly and disappeared in opposite directions.

Hassan wandered back toward his hotel. He did not relish sitting in a cramped room with four other men, watching a badly-tuned television. The day before, two more men had arrived from Syria to bolster his team. These two Syrians would go to Montpellier and follow up on the delivery of the six cases of bottles to be filled with the virus. Yazid would continue contact with Dr. Aziz in Montpellier, and the Iraqi driver, as incompetent as he was, would unfortunately remain his right-hand man.

At a brasserie, he stopped and ordered an espresso and a pastry. For almost ten minutes, he sat and tried to relax, hoping the throbbing in his head would cease. He sniggered when he recalled telling Rashid that he had an informant at the consul general's residence. The source, Ali, was in the pay of both him and Wahab. When Wahab learned that bit of information, he would begin wondering what other mutual sources the two had in France.

Afternoon pedestrians crowded the streets. Hassan left the brasserie and continued on to his hotel. He wondered what progress Aziz had made with the virus fabrication. The espresso seemed to have relieved his headache and the pain in his groin hurt less when he walked slowly. Also, his stomach had calmed. He rounded a corner and spotted the front of his hotel two blocks away. Good. The bandage on the back of his head needed changing.

"Hassan. Hassan!"

He stopped and looked around.

"Here! Come in here!" Yazid stood in the door of a *pâtisserie* and motioned for him to enter.

"What is the urgency?"

"The police are at the hotel. They are all over." Yazid spoke in Arabic, causing the French proprietors of the shop to dart quick looks from behind the glass display case. "When I passed, I saw one of the police looking out the window of our hotel room."

"What can we get for you?" shouted the storeowner, his pencil-thin moustache arched in suspicion.

Hassan pushed Yazid toward the shopkeeper and told him to buy two pastries, but Yazid's body trembled. Hassan cursed low and pushed him aside. He pointed to two honey-covered rolls under the display counter and asked the shopkeeper if they could sit at one of the two tables. The man scowled and suggested they also order coffee.

Hassan led Yazid to the table and sat him down hard on the metal-framed chair. In a low voice, he said, "Repeat what you just told me." Hassan listened carefully. "So have the police arrested our comrades?"

"I do not know." He glanced out the window. "But there are police heading in our direction."

"Do you have a gun?" Hassan asked, feeling for his own gun in his jacket.

Yazid nodded.

"Drink some coffee and take a bite of the pastry," he ordered, and glanced out the shop's glass door for signs of the police. "We must be calm. It is important I escape and go to Montpellier. Do you understand?"

Yazid could not steady his coffee cup, and let it drop back in the saucer.

"Forget about the coffee and take a bite of the roll. It is honey and sweet." Hassan lifted his own cup steadily to his lips. "You must act as a decoy for me. This is your calling. Remember, this is jihad."

Tears flooded Yazid's eyes. He began stuttering. Hassan realized he had to get him out on the street before he collapsed like a sobbing fool, or worse began yelling, "Praise be to Allah!" and waving his gun in the air. Hassan rose, yanked Yazid from his chair, and pulled him toward the door.

A hard-looking French woman with a flattened nose led Stone, Frederick, and Mark up to the third-floor apartment that served as the French police lookout post. Colmont opened the door and made perfunctory introductions to members of the French surveillance team clustered near the windows. The hotel entrance lay directly below the apartment's middle window. Stone looked around at the cameras, radios, and empty coffee cups. He smelled the acrid odor from the old cigarette butts in the ashtrays. Just like his surveillance days with the FBI when he had spent weeks on a stakeout.

"The arrest team has three men in custody," Colmont said, looking out the window. "We want to hold off bringing them out of the hotel until we get a fix on the other two men."

"Do they have Hassan?" Mark asked.

"No," Colmont answered. "We thought they were all there, but Hassan and another one are missing. We are searching the entire hotel in case they are hiding."

Colmont spoke rapidly over the radio in French with a man who answered in a slow monotone. Stone gleaned enough from the radio traffic to learn that uniform and plainclothes police had fanned out for two blocks looking for Hassan and the other terrorist.

A cellphone rang and the French surveillance team leader barked an answer. After a few seconds, he turned to Colmont and told him the team had found explosives in Hassan's room. They were evacuating the hotel. As Colmont shook his head, the radio blared, "Two suspects just came out of a *pâtisserie!*"

On Hassan's side of the street, two uniformed gendarmes intently searched the faces of pedestrians as they strode in his direction. Walking away from the policemen, Yazid, close to Hassan, breathed hard and muttered a prayer. Hassan tried to stop him from turning his head back in the direction of the police.

"Walk steady, next to me," Hassan ordered. "Do not look back."

When they neared an intersection, Hassan paused. If Yazid went left and he went right, the police might think they were just two friends off on their separate ways. He knew he had a better chance to escape on his own. His companion could explode at any moment.

"We will shake hands now," Hassan said. "Smile, so people will think we are relaxed. I will be in contact with you by cellphone." He turned and started across the street.

"Wait! Hassan, where shall I go?" he shouted after him. "Let us stay together!"

Hassan cursed and looked back at the two gendarmes, who had stopped. One grabbed the sleeve of his partner and pointed in Yazid's direction. Both started running toward him, one with a cellphone to his ear.

Hassan moved quickly across the intersection, using three schoolgirls in blue uniforms as a shield. The shouts from the police stopped as Yazid fired off a shot.

People around Hassan began running. Some dropped down on the ground and covered their heads with their arms. Hassan tripped over an elderly woman who had fallen on the curb. Pushing past a young couple huddled against a building, Hassan looked back and watched Yazid fire his automatic pistol at the police. He did not aim the gun, just pointed it with a wavering hand, shooting and screaming.

The two gendarmes crouched behind a car and had yet to return fire. A man with a military-style haircut and wearing a dark suit brushed past Hassan and leaped into the intersection. He extended his revolver, aimed, and fired two quick shots. Yazid's gun flew into the air and he spun around, staggered, and faced the shooter. Yazid looked over the shooter's shoulder and caught Hassan's eye. As Yazid's lips formed a question, the shooter placed two more bullets in his chest. Yazid lurched backward, landing on the paving stones. His body jerked for a few moments and finally stopped.

A police car with siren blaring and blue light flashing skidded to a stop in the intersection. People picked themselves up off the ground and ran. Hassan fled into the crowd. Three blocks later, he saw an entrance to an underground Metro station. He descended the stairs and hopped on a crowded train that had just arrived. After the fourth station stop, his breathing returned to normal. He pushed his way through the standing passengers to the large Metro map posted next to the car door. Somehow, he had to find his way to Montpellier.

CHAPTER TWENTY-FOUR

VILLEFRANCHE

The prince floated into the mahogany-paneled salon of the Red Scorpion wearing a white, full-length *thobe*, a Bedouin cloak that touched his ankles. Abdul Wahab tried to gauge his mood as he rose to extend greetings to his father-in-law. A servant in a starched white jacket pulled out a dark wooden chair. Now seated at the head of the marble-topped table, the prince's robed body enveloped the entire chair and he appeared suspended in space. Wahab wondered whether it ever occurred to the prince to forego his Arab dress, at least in his private quarters, and perhaps slip on a pair of jeans and a sweatshirt.

"The contessa has moved the last of her personal belongings down to her villa." Wahab took his seat. He sipped the hot tea, watching the prince drum his fingers on the hard surface of the table. Wahab went on. "The palace is ready for bin Zanni and the medical people from Riyadh. We have hired two trucks to transport them up to the palace."

"It is a shame we could not convince bin Zanni to return to Riyadh for his treatment."

Wahab lifted his hands. "If he had, he would face more than just medical problems."

"Precisely." The prince touched the delicate teacup sitting before him, and then withdrew his hand. "When will these people from Riyadh depart the Red Scorpion?" the prince asked.

Wahab rose, went to the large window, and looked out. "They are stacking their equipment on deck now, Excellency, and in a few minutes the first group will cast off in the launch."

"And bin Zanni? Where is he now? How sick is he?"

"My understanding is that he is growing weaker." Wahab

replied. "He is in transit, and he and his al Qaeda people should arrive at the palace early tomorrow morning. Neither the French nor the CIA have detected him." He resumed his seat.

"Are they still coming by helicopter?"

"By a chartered tour bus. Who would suspect a tour bus? It is really quite clever." Wahab smiled. "The little diversion in Marseille worked. My people reported that the CIA and the French shifted their attention away from Nice to protect the American consul general."

"Did you kill the consul general?"

"No, Excellency." He hesitated, becoming uncomfortable with the prince's choice of words. "The plan did not work as envisioned, but the result was satisfactory."

The prince looked at him for a long moment through a pair of tinted glasses. "Please do me the courtesy of being more specific."

"Of course, my Emir." Abdul Wahab had realized years before that he would never gain the prince's full respect because he had placed his first wife, the prince's daughter, in a secret sanatorium near Jeddah. He had no recourse; she had become deformed in both mind and body.

"Well?" the prince pressed.

"I engaged the Shiite, Hassan, to make an attempt on the life of the American consul general." The prince continued to stare, waiting for him to continue. "Apparently, somehow the French learned of the plan and intercepted Hassan and his group. I received a call just before I came here. There were arrests and shootings in Marseille."

"So the CIA is not that foolish after all. The authorities in France take shootings as a serious matter. Can they trace Hassan to you?"

"Not very likely. Only in this matter—"

"In this matter where Hassan was doing *your* bidding, let us hope the French do not follow a trail to you, especially at this time." The prince started to rise from his seat, but settled down again. "I explained to you that I am uncomfortable with my involvement in this al Qaeda matter. Bin Zanni has become a burden … a dangerous one."

Wahab leaned forward. "Please be assured the rest of the plan is, as they say in the West, on track. Once bin Zanni is in the palace, the medical people will begin administering to him. In a few weeks, he will be well again and he will depart from France." He sat back in his chair. "And we will be able to relax."

The prince pushed the checkered silk *kuffiyah* from his face and draped the headscarf back on his shoulders. "He will not be cured, as you well know. He has the same kidney problem as Osama bin Laden. The illness runs in their tribe."

Wahab nodded. Illnesses ran through the generations of the tribes, including his father-in-law's. That is why the prince's daughter had given him sick children. That is why he had married an Englishwoman with clean blood.

The prince continued. "If bin Zanni is not stabilized quickly, he will have to stay here longer than we want."

"That is why we paid the contessa for a two-month lease of the palace."

The prince spoke softly. "We don't want him to stay that long. But then again, if he is very ill … Perhaps it is time for him to be called to Paradise."

The covered afterdeck of the yacht provided fresh air from the evening breeze coming off the bay. Abdul Wahab stood alone at the brass rail and looked down into the indigo water. After a few moments, he looked up at the mountain. In the distance, he detected lights coming on in the upper windows of the contessa's palace. Soon bin Zanni would be housed securely within its stone walls and the doctors would begin their treatments. He thought about the prince's last words and wondered whether he'd interpreted them correctly. Had he really suggested killing bin Zanni? Pacing the deck, he decided to see what the doctors accomplished.

The Marseille diversion had not worked as planned. Still, it had shifted the attention of the French and CIA away from Nice and Villefranche. Bin Zanni's people would be able to transport the ailing man undetected to the palace. Out in the bay, a buoy tilted in the wind and its bell clanged intermittently. He stopped pacing. Had the French known about Hassan all along? Had they known about the assassination plot? Did they observe his meetings with Hassan? What about that fool Harrington?

He shook his head, went to the starboard side of the ship, and squeezed the railing. Had Harrington killed Stone yet? He had managed to kill an American agent in Cuers some years before, but Stone was another matter. Strange ... everything was working smoothly before Stone came on the scene. He had a habit of showing up at the most inconvenient times.

MARSEILLE

At the entrance to the restaurant, Stone met Colmont, who gave him a firm handshake. "Hayden. I suggested this restaurant because it serves a classic Marseille bouillabaisse." Colmont looked very pleased with himself. "With your people and mine we have enough for such a celebration."

Stone agreed the arrest of Hassan's people had accomplished something, but Hassan had slipped out of their net. The French recovered explosives from Hassan's hotel room and three terrorists were under interrogation. As a bonus, the two captured Syrians were on the French wanted list for the bombing of a French consulate in Cameroon. Colonel Frederick told him that Colmont's stature would definitely climb in the eyes of his bosses in Paris.

A waiter cracked open the side window to clear the air of cigarette smell that Stone figured was left over from the luncheon crowd. He chose a chair at the large oval table set with a light blue tablecloth, then spotted Sandra. She stood at the door, hesitating. Stone waved to her, at the same time searching for any change in demeanor due to her ordeal the day before. He detected none. Either she was a good actor, or just philosophical about the perils of her job. She came over and sat next to him. Her voice cracked. "Hi there."

Both watched Colmont vying with Colonel Frederick at the other end of the table over the preparation of bouillabaisse. Finally, Sandra shook her head. "How well do you know Frederick?"

"We were both in Afghanistan last year. Before that we worked on a number of joint task forces."

She leaned toward him, her arm touching his. "He's a breath of fresh air and your star has seen a change for the better. Claudia wanted to fire you. She called you a 'trigger-happy cowboy.'"

"Apparently my charm was wasted on her."

Sandra's eyes lacked their normal sparkle. "I saw her this morning in Paris. The station chief has her under tow, except for her three-hour lunches."

"I thought you were … well, taking it easy after yesterday's experience." Seeing her eyes moisten, he changed the subject. "Try the wine?"

She took a sip. "It's passable." She sighed. "And I'm okay. I flew to Paris this morning to see the shrink. The policy in the Agency is, if anyone has an experience like I had, we have to talk with a staff psychiatrist." She rotated her glass on the tablecloth, then looked at him. "Did you get to talk with anyone after the shooting?"

Stone laughed. "Remember, I'm not staff, so I guess my mental health isn't all that important."

"Bullshit. It was Claudia's responsibility to see that you talked with someone. You know, she really lives up to her reputation."

Colmont stood and asked the people seated to observe the owner leading two waiters into the room carrying tureens of steaming broth. "Ah, here is the first course," Colmont announced. "First, we have the fish broth with some sauce rouille spread on the croûtes, no?"

The waiters ladled the broth into everyone's bowl and the smell of leeks and fennel rose with the vapor. Frederick remarked to Colmont that he had enjoyed a great bouillabaisse some years back at a restaurant up the coast at Cap d'Antibes, but Colmont dismissed any suggestion that it could compare with anything created in Marseille.

Sandra nudged Stone. "I think we're in for an evening of gastronomic sermons." She laughed softly then asked, "Seriously, how are you doing? I mean after your two ... encounters?"

"You mean the gunfight after the party and when I threw that killer onto a picket fence?" He frowned. "I'm okay. Maybe I'm supposed to have nightmares or feelings of guilt, but nope, I don't." He sipped some wine. "I'm always happy being the one left standing."

Stone watched as Sandra concentrated on her broth and wondered how she could be thinking of his problems after what she had gone through. Her spoon wobbled ever so slightly when she brought the liquid up to her lips. Then he tried the broth and noted a lingering taste of saffron.

"And you," he whispered. "How are you *really* doing?"

"It'll take time." She paused. "I'm never without my gun."

Once again, Colmont addressed the group to say that the second course consisted of an array of a half-dozen fish, which came to the table whole. The waiters spaced four platters along the table and commenced to bone and cut the fish. Two serving dishes filled with steaming buttered potatoes were set at either end.

"You know," Stone said. "I always thought bouillabaisse was a fish soup."

He spooned chunks of bass, red mullet, John Dory, and conger eel onto his plate. Sandra asked what kind of fish she had on her fork and he told her he recognized it as a scorpion fish, the same he had eaten in a fish stew at a restaurant in Archos. As he refilled his glass with a chilled chardonnay, he overheard Mark and Eric discussing what they expected to find when they arrived in Nice the next day.

He interrupted them. "What are your plans now?"

Mark answered. "Tomorrow morning Fred and I are heading back to Nice. We haven't heard anything from the Major about our Arab friend, so we have to stay flexible."

"I'm staying here with Eric," Sandra said. "We'll try to get a lead on Hassan. We'll find him. What about you?"

Stone leaned back, having finished his second helping. "I'll go up the road to Archos for the night, and then head to Nice and join the group." He thought for a moment. "You know, I don't get Hassan's role in all this. He didn't kill the Agency man in Nice, nor the woman officer in Montpellier."

"We're not positive about our officer in Montpellier," she corrected. "He could have been responsible for that killing."

Stone shook his head. "Hassan shows up in Saint-Rémy while bin Zanni passes through and sends one of his henchmen to kill me. What's he up to? He's a Shiite working with Sunnis. It doesn't make sense."

"He may be doing them a favor, or maybe it's a marriage of convenience." She put down her fork, dabbed her lips with her napkin, and spoke close to his ear. "We've been tracking Hassan for some time now. He has contacts with a research institute in Montpellier. He also is interested in wines, in fact from your Archos area. We're getting chatter from sensitive sources about some big attack."

Stone chewed on a succulent portion of conger eel while letting that information settle in. This was turning into a serious operation. Did everyone involved have a grasp on the situation? Stone went on, "Then there's bin Zanni and his group. What's going on there? You know he's al Qaeda's second in command." He tilted his head in Colmont's direction. "Will the French allow us to grab him?"

Sandra frowned. "If he lives long enough."

"How's that?"

She whispered, "I'll explain later."

He could take that bit of information a number of ways, but wouldn't pursue it at present. The two of them already had violated the rules of tradecraft by discussing business in a public restaurant. Only remnants of fish remained on the platters. The tablecloth, once spotless, showed the stains and spills of a relaxed and enjoyable meal. Stone had overindulged and now faced a sleepy drive up the coast to Archos.

• • •

After a pleasant drive back, Stone parked the Porsche and walked along the quiet, lighted path to the cottage. A thin sliver of moon hung low over the pocket-sized Bay of Archos. The cicadas' stridulations had increased in the past few days. He attributed it to the warming weather along the coast. He looked forward to getting out of his clothes and having a nightcap.

When he slipped the door key into the lock, he could feel that the bolt didn't disengage. The door was unlocked. Had he forgotten to secure the cottage door that morning as he hurried off? Not likely.

With a finger touch, the door swung in. He placed one foot inside, grasping the handle of his gun with his right hand. He slid his left hand along the inside wall and found the light switch. Twice he flipped the switch up and down. The lights didn't go on.

Perhaps it was a movement in the dark, or instinct, but he sensed a presence. He stepped back, but large hands grabbed the collar of his jacket, yanking him into the room. Flying through the air, he stopped when a blow to his nose rocked his head backward.

As he lay on the floor, the crunched cartilage in his nose caused his eyes to tear. Blood seeped down the back of his throat. A classic first hit, one that both stunned and bloodied.

With no light, his assailants couldn't see any better than he could, but he had one advantage: the room was familiar to him. He pulled out his gun.

An attacker's kick caught the side of Stone's head, and he rolled over just as a body thumped down on the floor next to him. Stone's gun slipped from his grasp. A hot garlic breath told him that the man's face was next to his. Stone unleashed a karate blow with his elbow that connected. A curse in French followed.

Someone else grabbed his left foot, dragging him along the floor. The man yelled something in English to the one Stone had just struck. Stone kicked his foot free, scrambled to his feet, then backed away until he felt the wall. Crouching, he spun and delivered two karate kicks. The second connected in the midsection of his attacker, who let out a loud gasp. Stone jumped toward the door.

An arm snaked around Stone's throat in a chokehold. He delivered a solid back kick to his attacker's shin. Both fell to the floor. The attacker's head brushed his face and a fleshy protuberance passed his mouth. Stone bit down hard. The man screamed, *"Merde,"* and pushed him away. Stone spit out a piece of the man's nose.

A light from outside the cottage flashed in one of the living room windows, allowing Stone to gather his bearings. He jumped over the bar separating the kitchen from the dining area and searched for a weapon. A wooden block holding carving knives sat next to the sink under the kitchen light switch.

He lunged forward and flicked the light switch. The kitchen lights went on. With a knife in each hand, he turned to face his two assailants, but saw only one. The Frenchman with the torn nose rushed him, going for Stone's right hand that held a bread knife. With his left hand, Stone thrust the short boning knife under the Frenchman's ribcage.

As the man with the knife in his side collapsed, a solid object grazed the left side of his head. Stunned, he managed to spin around. He saw a face he recognized. The second priest he'd met in the village of Cuers. He deflected a second blow by thrusting the bread knife up through the man's forearm.

The phony cleric screamed and held his bloodied arm. As Stone felt himself losing consciousness, the cleric pulled out a gun and pointed it at Stone's gut. "Die, bastard!" Then *thunk!* The cleric's head jerked forward and he collapsed onto the kitchen counter.

Stone lost consciousnesses as he saw the blurred image of Ricard, the French veteran, clout the phony cleric a second time with a shovel.

When Stone gained consciousness, he found Ricard assisting the local police as they took the attackers into custody. Two gendarmes lifted Stone and helped him out to their patrol car. Placing him in the back seat, they drove to a clinic in the center of Archos. On the way, the driver turned around and yelled to Stone, "Do not bleed on the car seat."

On arrival, the gendarmes and the medical staff began arguing over how much questioning Stone should be subjected to given his condition. Stone remained silent while the doctor set his nose and applied antiseptic to his cuts.

Meanwhile, one of the policemen answered a call on his cellphone. "*Oui*, Monsieur Colmont." After a few moments of speaking in a hushed tone, he flipped his cellphone closed and informed a medical staffer that he and his companion were leaving.

Stone let himself succumb to a deep, dreamless sleep.

CHAPTER TWENTY-FIVE

CÔTE D'AZUR—MAY 14, 2002

The morning sun angled through the tall windows into the bright hospital room. An African nurse with tribal scars ridged horizontally across her cheeks came in and walked over to the two windows. Before opening each one, she threw a long, hard look at Stone lying in the bed. Cool air filtered into the room. Task accomplished, she marched out, all the while maintaining a steady visual contact with him. The door slammed shut.

Stone took a deep breath. He must really look bad.

He didn't feel severe pain, but a wide bandage covered the bridge of his nose, and the side of his head ached where the blow from the blackjack had left a swollen knot above his left ear. He realized he was medicated and let himself enjoy the remnants of the soft feeling it provided.

The door flew open and Harrington and his wife, Helen, rushed in. A young doctor carrying a clipboard tagged along. The Harringtons sat down next to his bed while the doctor felt Stone's pulse and listened to his heartbeat with a stethoscope. He then told the Harringtons in rapid French that they could stay only five minutes.

"Hayden, how are you feeling?" Harrington leaned forward and with false sincerity said, "My God, we have never had an incident like this at the Foundation. I had to report this to the board in New York."

"Does your head hurt much?" Helen asked, her head tilted in sympathy.

Stone shot a look at one face, then to the other—what gall!

"Those two thieves are in custody," Harrington stuttered. "Actually, they are in a guarded wing here in the hospital." He straightened. "Helen, we can see that Hayden will survive, so we must let him rest."

"Anything we can do, please let us know," she said.

"You both are very kind to visit me. Do you have any idea why they attacked me?" Stone raised himself up on one arm. "I don't believe they were there to steal anything."

Harrington stiffened. "I'm sure the police are working on that as we speak." He stood up. "Now, we must go and let you rest."

"I feel lucky. I've missed getting killed twice in the last two days."

With frightened smiles, the two hurried out of the room as the doctor, accompanied by the nurse, returned.

"My nurse is very curious about you, what with all the police attention," the doctor said. "She doesn't know if you are the hero or the villain."

"There are people who think I'm both."

The doctor replaced the bandage on Stone's nose and remarked that the Harringtons had left after only a few minutes. "I gave them five minutes, but they didn't even take that. An odd sort of visit by those two." When he finished his examination, he said, "Your nose looks promising and should stop swelling. Meanwhile, you have two other guests waiting to see you."

The doctor departed and Colmont breezed in. He stopped halfway into the room, lifted up his hands, and blew out a laugh. "You look awful, my friend!" he said, and turned to the door. "Come in, dear, and take a look."

Margaux eased through the doorway. She looked him over, shook her head, and approached. Stone tried to sit up. Colmont reached over and pushed the button on the bed mechanism to elevate him into a sitting position. The two then sat down on either side of Stone's bed.

"So, my friend, you survived, *non*?" Colmont unbuttoned his coat. He glanced at his wristwatch then looked back at Stone. "We passed the Harringtons in the hallway. You had a pleasant visit?"

"They were checking the damage."

"These two men we have in custody, you have met them before, *oui*?" Colmont asked.

Stone pointed to Margaux and then to Colmont. "You two know each other?"

Ignoring the question, Margaux said, "I looked in on the two prisoners. The one with the knife wound in his chest is one of the men we saw with Harrington the other night when we were at the restaurant."

"And the other is the priest we met in Cuers," Stone added.

"Yes. The one who had the strange French accent."

"He is an Englishman who learned French in Belgium," Colmont advised. "He has a long history in drug dealing. Both men are being interrogated. When we get enough information, we will arrest Harrington. Meanwhile, we will watch your director and his wife."

Stone asked again, "You two are working together, right?"

"Of course." Colmont fidgeted.

"And Ricard?"

"Yes, he has been cooperating with us for some time. Now tell me, why do you think Boswell Harrington wants to do you harm?"

Stone raised his hand. "I'm not sure. Why would he be interested in my trip to Cuers? Maybe the other night he saw Margaux and me follow him from the restaurant. Maybe, he thinks I'm involved with—"

Colmont moved forward. "Maybe, *Cherchez la femme*? The beautiful contessa, he is jealous of?"

Margaux arched her left eyebrow.

"I have no idea why he would be jealous," Stone said quickly.

Colmont and Margaux looked at each other as if they were interviewing a reluctant witness. Margaux's change in demeanor especially intrigued Stone. A bit fussy, he concluded.

"Monsieur Boswell Harrington has been of interest to us for some time," Colmont said quickly. "He has been involved in drug smuggling, a minor role in the past, but a lucrative one for him. He is now working with Abdul Wahab and those Saudis whom we met at the contessa's party."

Margaux added, "Monsieur Colmont told me it was one of Wahab's men who tried to shoot you after the consul general's party."

"Harrington knows you have his two boys in custody. He must be very nervous."

"As I said, we will watch him." Colmont rose. "Sorry, I must depart. I must return to Nice and confer with Colonel Frederick."

"Does Frederick know about last night?"

"Yes. I briefed him early this morning. This Harrington business has Frederick puzzled." Colmont started toward the door. "He expects to see you in Nice tomorrow, so I will leave Margaux here to nurse you back to health. Tough boss, this Frederick." Colmont waved goodbye to Margaux, pointed to Stone's nose, and laughed.

After noon, Margaux drove Stone back to the Foundation in her Citroen. She appeared to enjoy the role of nursemaid. They entered his cottage and she shook her head at the disarray before her. Upended chairs and tables lay on the floor. She began setting the furniture back in place, standing back now and then to inspect her work, then rearranging a chair or table she apparently thought not just right. Satisfied, she went into the kitchen and fussed about the bloodstains on the counter.

"I'll get a cleaning crew in here to handle that," Stone said. "Come over and sit down."

She came into the sitting area and sat next to him. They talked awhile until he stifled a yawn.

She stood next to him and patted his arm. "I will return with some dinner."

The light jazz on the radio relaxed him and he closed his eyes. Good to take it easy, for tomorrow, Frederick would have him on the run.

Stone awoke to a knocking on the front door. Opening it, he found David standing on the step holding a bottle of chilled white wine, staring at him.

"Something wrong?" Stone asked.

David entered the cottage. "Hope your nose grows back." He retrieved a corkscrew from the kitchen, handed a glass to Stone, and poured the wine. "The word around the Foundation is that you foiled a robbery."

"It wasn't a robbery."

David sipped the wine. "Hmm. Not bad wine." He studied Stone. "Of course not. Harrington paid you a visit."

"Two of his goons tried to kill me." Stone studied his reaction. One could talk with David for an hour before realizing he had a light-colored moustache. It was debatable whether its absence would change the appearance of his face.

David set his jaw. "Mauling people seems to be a pastime around here."

Stone let a few seconds pass then asked, "What's Harrington up to today?"

David swirled the wine in his glass. "The Harringtons appear to be packing for a long trip."

"Is he cleaning out his office?" Stone asked.

"Not yet. His wife has him packing dishes."

"I think it would be interesting if we got a look in his office, especially his desk," Stone said.

David's eyes widened.

"What are our chances of getting in there?"

"Find yourself another accomplice," David said. "Harrington plays too rough."

Margaux came through the door carrying a wicker basket. She invited David to stay for dinner, but he declined. Stone walked David to the door and said, "Keep me informed about Harrington, and thanks for the wine."

David nodded, then left.

The boxed dinner from Margaux's family's restaurant consisted of an assortment of roasted meats, vegetables, and potatoes. Unfortunately, Stone's broken nose, along with the medication, muted his sense of taste. The cold white wine refreshed his tongue, but again, no flavor.

"Does my voice sound different?" he asked. "I mean with the bandage on my nose?"

"Yes. You sound like a *sirène de brume*." She had changed into a light cotton skirt and a pink polo shirt.

"I sound like a fog horn?"

"Yes."

He laughed. "The Harringtons appear to be planning a departure."

"Colmont is watching them," she said.

They sat at the kitchen table and leisurely ate.

"So you work for Colmont? Are you an officer in the service?"

She looked at him. "I am not like you, a professional." She paused. "Colmont attended a family wedding two years ago. My mother and his mother are cousins. He asked my father if I could work for him. My father said no, but I said yes. Colmont has been suspicious of Harrington since your American friend, Herb Walker, died in Cuers two years ago. He thinks he had something to do with his death."

"It seems there's a lot more to Herb's death than I knew." Stone put down his fork and dunked a piece of bread in the dark gravy. "When did you find out what I did for a living?"

She hesitated. "I told Colmont about the shell casing I found in your car when we drove to Cuers. He told me then about you." She waved her fork. "I sort of suspected all along. I never see you writing."

"So Colmont told you. Why did you get so angry? You know, when we were following Harrington the other night?"

"Because Harrington was about to see us, spot us." She speared a slice of potato. "All because you wanted to hear what the contessa and Harrington were up to." She shook her head. "You are a very curious man. Maybe *you* are the jealous one."

He would change the subject before an argument ensued. Harrington's interest in their trip to Cuers now made sense if Herb had been investigating Harrington. Stone was about to ask Margaux whether she knew any more about Herb Walker's death when she blurted, "How long have you known the contessa?"

"I knew her when both of us were very young. I was in the Navy, assigned to the consulate in Nice."

"You say you were young. How old were you?"

"Twenty something."

"And she was how old?" Margaux looked him in the eye.

"Oh, something like eighteen."

"Ha. So that is it." She began poking at her food, then pointed her fork at him. "You were her first love and you abandoned her."

"What?"

"It explains everything." Her head tilted. "You deserved what you got."

"My broken nose?"

She threw the fork down to her plate and looked up at the ceiling. "No. You abandoned the contessa. Now years later, your wife abandoned you." She raised her hands. "See? It all works out."

Stone stared at her. She apparently had arrived at the conclusion that part of the world had just been rebalanced. It was best to say nothing.

After dinner, while sitting close on the couch, she told him he looked tired and that he should go to bed. He stared at her until she flushed.

"You're right. It's been a long day," he said. "Thank you for helping me."

The house phone rang. Usually, the calls he received were from the Foundation front office or from David. However, his two children also had the number.

Margaux snatched the handset before Stone could. "Hello?" When she heard the voice on the other end she straightened up and looked wide-eyed at Stone.

In French, she said, "Yes, this is the cottage of Mr. Stone. My name is Margaux." She hurried over to him. "I will pass you on to Mr. Stone." She paused while she tried to detach herself from the caller, then said, "Yes. He has returned from the hospital. Here he is." She handed the phone to him, and with her hand over the mouthpiece, mouthed the words, "The contessa."

"Hello, Lucinda. Thanks for calling. How on earth did you hear about my being in the hospital?"

"Is that really you, Hayden?" Lucinda asked. "Your voice sounds funny."

"My nose is broken. I have a big bandage on it."

"I talked with Harrington," she said. "He said he saw you in the hospital and his *fetching* assistant, Margaux, was attending to you."

Stone mulled over Lucinda's words. "Strange, that he called to tell you."

"I called him. There were some details about the palace lease and I couldn't get hold of that man, Abdul Wahab." She paused. "Are you seriously injured?"

"No." Stone hesitated. "Sounds like Harrington is trying to stir up trouble between you and me."

"Why did you not call me?" Lucinda said, in a low tone. "I can come there if you need me."

"Thanks, but I don't want to put you out. I know you're busy."

A long silence.

"Yes, of course. It seems you are being well taken care of. Goodbye."

"Lucinda…" The line went dead.

Stone sighed, then said, "The contessa thinks you and I have something going on."

"But yes, I would feel the same way." Margaux's cheeks flushed. "That is, if you and I were—"

"That bastard Harrington. I have to admire him in a way. Here he is about to lose a prestigious position, all his money, and probably go to jail, yet he finds time to be jealous of a woman who won't…"

She smiled. "It must hurt him to know that the contessa has turned her attention elsewhere."

Stone got up and slowly climbed the stairs to his bedroom while Margaux went to the kitchen to clean the dishes. He paused at the top landing.

She turned from the sink and looked up at him. "I will lock the door behind me. Tomorrow, I will make sure your coffee and newspaper arrive at the usual time."

"Great. Thanks for dinner and ... everything."

In his bedroom, he cracked open a window and crawled into bed. Margaux had been a comfort. She seemed to continually surprise him. The front door shut and all was quiet. He checked to make sure his gun was under the pillow.

He closed his eyes. Why had Harrington tried to kill him? Was it jealousy over the contessa, or had Abdul Wahab put him up to it? And if so, why did the Saudis want him dead? Maybe Frederick or Fleming had some intelligence they had neglected to share.

Then there was his relationship with Lucinda. That had taken a quick turn for the worse. Tomorrow, he would call her. Before he fell asleep, he wondered whether someday his life might become less complicated.

CHAPTER TWENTY-SIX

MARSEILLE

Hassan's train from Marseille to Arles took a little less than an hour. By the time he emerged from the station, the sun had set and the air had begun to cool. He debated whether to call and ask Rashid to pick him up, but decided against it. Certainly, the police had a telephone tap on Rashid's home phone. Instead, he searched for a car rental company and found an open storefront operation. The lone woman attendant was attempting to handle four impatient customers queued in front of the counter.

Standing in the back of the line, he realized he had only one passport and an assortment of credit cards, not all in the passport's name. All of his other forged documentation had been abandoned in the hotel room and now were in the possession of the French police.

An American middle-aged couple, both large in girth, were arguing with the attendant. The disagreement concerned the mileage on the car they had just returned. Finally, the attendant came from behind the counter, marched out of the office with the couple in tow, and headed for the car parked outside the entrance. Hassan followed at a discreet distance. She opened the door and pointed to the mileage indicator on the dashboard. They all went back into the office, the couple now subdued. The car's keys hung in the ignition. Hassan calmly walked over, got in, and drove off.

The fuel gauge read less than a quarter tank, but that was enough to reach Rashid's residence. The CIA and the French will certainly watch his villa, he reasoned. Perhaps the French already had Rashid in custody.

As he eased past the entrance to Rashid's estate, he searched for surveillance. If he drove by again, he would definitely arouse the suspicion of any lurking policemen. Then by chance he spotted a gray van backed up into the trees about one hundred yards south of the entrance gate. A mile farther down the road, he pulled over and checked the map he'd found in the glove compartment. It showed a winding road some distance on the other side of the villa. He would drive there, hide the car, and walk through the vineyards to Rashid's main house.

Hassan crept up the stairs to the second floor of the villa and found Rashid's study. He peered into the dark-paneled room and saw Rashid at a large oak desk, working numbers in a green ledger. Next to him a computer screensaver displayed colored fish swimming in random directions. Hassan caught the faint smell of a tomato-based casserole in the room. An empty dinner plate sat on a long credenza against the wall.

Startled when Hassan dragged an armchair up to the desk, Rashid gasped and slid back in his chair. "How did you get in here?" He drew his black silk robe over his white pajamas. "Why did you not call? What—"

"I came in the back way. You should lock your doors." Hassan unzipped his jacket and sat in the chair. He spread out his legs and let out a sigh as the pain in his groin and side subsided. "Police are watching outside on the road."

"Why are the police watching me?"

"No more questions." Hassan readjusted the position of the gun in his belt and quickly relayed the story of his men's arrest in Marseille that afternoon. "The police must know we have been working together. That is why they are out there watching you."

"I do not know how they could—"

"Obviously, they have been following your Saudi friends." He pointed. "You were the one who involved me with bin Zanni and al Qaeda. Now the police know about me."

Rashid pulled his robe tight around himself, and then covered his face with his hands. "This is not good." He paused a moment. "We must get you out of here, out of the country."

"I need money," Hassan said.

Rashid opened his desk drawer and pulled out a bulging envelope, then shoved it back. He grabbed his wallet.

Hassan rose, took the wallet from him, and emptied it of bills. "Where is bin Zanni now?" He reached over, pulled the envelope from the desk drawer, and thumbed through the euros.

Rashid raised a hand in protest, then dropped it. "I just heard he is going to a palace in Villefranche. He will be there tomorrow morning." He began to rise, but was pushed back into the chair. "You are not taking all of my money, are you?"

"What palace?"

"The prince has leased a palace from some contessa."

"Were the six cases of wine delivered to the address in Montpellier?" Hassan asked.

"Twenty-four cases were sent to the wholesaler earlier today. The six cases you're concerned about are going by truck to Montpellier tonight."

Hassan stuffed the money in his pockets, went to the window, and pulled back the heavy draperies. Down below, a panel truck was parked outside a two-story barn a few yards from the main house. Ancient trees with wide-spread limbs shielded the chateau from the road. "Is that the truck going to Montpellier?"

"Yes, it is."

"Call the driver and tell him he will have a passenger with him tonight."

Rashid obeyed, and when he hung up Hassan returned to the desk. "You involved me with this Saudi, Abdul Wahab, who wanted me to kill the American agent, Stone. I wondered why he did not kill Stone the same way he killed the other two CIA agents. Why have me do it?" Hassan sat on the edge of the desk. "Then I realized he wanted to shift the attention of the Americans to me and away from him and al Qaeda."

Rashid protested; said that he was unaware of any such plan on Wahab's part.

"It was the same with him wanting me to kill the American

consul general. Have the CIA and French come to Marseille and look for me." He looked down at Rashid and said softly, "Where does this Stone live?"

"At the Foundation d'Élan in Archos. Where that man Harrington is the director."

"I suppose you know Harrington." Hassan pulled out his automatic and released the safety. "I want you to call the Foundation."

"But I do not know the number. Who would I ask for?"

"Ask the operator for the number." Hassan waved his gun back and forth. "Then, when you reach it, ask to speak to Mr. Stone."

"What do I say when he answers?"

"Tell him bin Zanni is going to the palace of a contessa in Villefranche." Hassan pointed the gun at Rashid's face.

"I cannot do that! Wahab will kill me!"

He placed the barrel of the gun to Rashid's forehead. "I will kill you if you do not."

Rashid fumbled for the phone. The operator gave him the phone number, but he had to dial three times before his nervous finger got all the numbers correct. It took a few minutes for the operator at the Foundation to connect Rashid to Stone's cottage.

"Are you Mr. Stone?" Rashid asked.

Hassan motioned with his gun for him to continue.

"It is of no importance, who I am." Rashid then relayed the message to Stone. After repeating it, he hung up.

Hassan looked down at him. "Now the French and CIA will be heading back to Nice." He raised the gun high above Rashid's head. "And the police will be knocking on your door."

He hit Rashid hard on the top of his head with three blows from the butt of the gun. Rashid fell forward, his smashed head landing on the ledger. The heavy bond paper slowly absorbed the blood oozing from his scalp.

The phone rang and Hassan froze. He picked up the receiver and listened as the truck driver said he was waiting down in the driveway. Running down the stairs, he went out the front door and crossed the gravel yard to the truck, where the driver stood smoking.

"Is the wine loaded?"

"It is." The driver turned his back, opened the back of the truck, and pointed to the six cases. Hassan pulled out his gun and slugged him. He then dragged the man into the barn. Donning the driver's coat and beret, he drove slowly out the gate and headed down the road for the Autoroute to Montpellier. He felt relief when the surveillance van remained motionless.

At the kitchen sink, Stone splashed water on his face. He thought about the call he had just received. At first, the brief message hadn't made sense, so he'd asked the caller to repeat it. Not only was the message puzzling—that bin Zanni was heading for the contessa's palace—but also the caller had a thick Middle Eastern accent. He thought for a moment. Trick or no trick, Frederick has to know right away.

CHAPTER TWENTY-SEVEN

NICE—MAY 15, 2002

Stone drove from Archos to Nice through an early morning mist. He parked a block away from the safehouse. Entering, he found the place deserted, so decided to search the team's computer for any messages on bin Zanni. He found none.

An hour later, Frederick and his group stormed in and suddenly the apartment felt claustrophobic. From the second floor, Stone looked down on the outline of a Roman ruin adjacent to the Matisse Museum. Light drizzle spotted the window, obstructing his view. Behind him, a dozen CIA and military people from the rendition team mingled, speaking in hushed tones. Maurice Colmont and his deputy from DST, French Intelligence, conferred with Frederick at the kitchen door. The meeting would begin in a few minutes, so Stone went over to the faded couch and sat next to Mark.

"You remind me of a boxer who leads with his head," Mark said, as he examined Stone's bandaged nose.

"You should have seen me yesterday."

Frederick broke away from Colmont and moved to the center of the living room. He announced that Colmont would present an update on bin Zanni's whereabouts.

Thumbing through an assortment of notes, Colmont turned to his deputy, spoke with him for a second, then announced, "I wish to provide you with some background information on how we located bin Zanni. Last night, Mr. Stone here received a call from a man named Rashid, who said bin Zanni was going to a palace in Villefranche." He scanned the faces in the room. "My people listened to the same conversation. Because of Rashid's connections with Hassan, we had put an electronic listening device on his telephone. This man Rashid also did business with Abdul Wahab, the spokesman for the Saudi prince, whose yacht presently is anchored in the Bay of Villefranche."

Frederick interjected, "We think we know why Rashid called Stone."

"Correct," Colmont said. "Shortly after the telephone call, my agents entered Rashid's villa. We found him bludgeoned to death. Outside the villa, we found one of Rashid's employees unconscious but alive. He told the agents that a man matching the description of Hassan attacked him and stole a panel truck. We think Hassan had Rashid make the call. Why? Because we think he wanted to divert us from Marseille."

"Any lead on Hassan's whereabouts?" Stone asked.

"We have a clue," Colmont answered. "The workman said that before Hassan knocked him unconscious, he asked if six cases of Cassis wine had been loaded in the truck. The wine was to be delivered to an address in Montpellier. After this meeting, I will fly there and join two of Colonel Frederick's associates to search for Hassan." Colmont took a deep breath. "Hassan is a very dangerous man. We suspect he may be engaged in … well, as you Americans say, 'we shall see.'"

Frederick looked at Colmont. "As for bin Zanni?"

Colmont put his notes in his pocket. "We have multiple contacts who have reported that a tour bus arrived at Contessa Lucinda's palace early this morning. As some of you know, the contessa leased the palace for two months to the Saudi prince. My sources report that the palace is full of medical people and armed men. Lights were on in the palace until dawn. All is quiet now."

"Can we be assured bin Zanni is still there?" Stone asked.

Frederick spoke up. "Headquarters advised that yesterday sensitive sources overheard bin Zanni has kidney stones and an enlarged heart. That's why the medical people are there. I would say he's being treated as we speak."

"Any plans to go into the palace and extract him?" asked the major in charge of the rendition team.

Colmont spoke up. "Absolutely none. My orders from Paris

are that we are to watch and keep bin Zanni and his people under surveillance." He shook his head. "That is all that is permissible. Under no conditions are we to launch an assault."

The members of the rendition team looked at each other in disbelief. Mark groaned and Frederick looked at the floor. Heavy drops of rain pelted the window.

"That's the situation," Frederick said. "We'll stay on an alert status until further notice."

"One more thing," Colmont said. "We have the palace under observation both from lookouts in villas owned by cooperative citizens and from a camera aimed at the only road leading to the palace. We will know if anyone leaves the palace."

"And he'll know if we try to get in," Mark murmured to Stone.

After the meeting, Stone, Frederick, and Mark left the apartment and meandered through the Cimiez gardens next to the museum and across from the safehouse. The rain had let up to a fine drizzle that beaded Stone's jacket. He breathed in the fresh smell of rainwater dripping from the pines. The three stopped under the shelter of a large olive tree and studied the walled ruins of the Roman public baths.

"Damn French."

"Mark, trust me," Frederick assured. "Colmont would love to go in there and wreak havoc, but Paris is wary of the Middle East reaction."

"If we can't do anything here, we may as well go to Montpellier and help Sandra," Stone said.

"No, I want you two to stay here. Maybe poke around the neighborhood of Villefranche and see who's coming and going from the prince's yacht. Your FBI friend, Jonathan Deville, is returning from Paris. He may have received some guidance from his headquarters." Frederick motioned for them to continue walking. "The Bureau and CIA don't want bin Zanni to get away, but they don't necessarily want us to capture him. It would present problems, to say the least, to keep him in prison."

"Let me know if you decide to act unilaterally," Stone said. "I know of a way to get in the palace without going in the front door."

"I figured you did," chuckled Frederick. "Why don't you give your friend the contessa a call? However, be careful ... she's been working with Colmont and French intelligence for years."

Stone stopped and shook his head. Why hadn't he realized that? "She's a spy?"

"No," answered Frederick. "She's what we call an 'agent of influence.' A good contact for the French, especially since she travels in high circles."

Stone remembered saying to Jonathan Deville at the consul general's party that everyone around there seemed to be playing parts and no one was really whom they appeared to be.

"Can't blame her," Frederick added. "She needs all the friends she can get."

VILLEFRANCHE

When Stone approached Lucinda, waiting in the marble foyer of her villa on the Bay of Villefranche, she moved gracefully toward him, came close, kissed his right cheek, his left, and then brushed his lips with hers. He detected a new perfume. Flowery, with a touch of lavender. She studied his face and touched the bandage on his nose.

"Harrington sent two of his thugs to kill me."

"That is preposterous! Why would Harrington want to kill you?"

"He's jealous. I'm sure he knows about us." He winked.

She tossed her head. "What about *us*?"

Her eyes shot from him to the boats in the bay. She sniffed. "Perhaps that was one of the reasons, but it must be more than that. Harrington is a desperate man. He has been dealing with that cunning Saudi, Abdul Wahab." She moved closer. "Are you are telling me everything?"

"Have you been forthcoming with me, Lucinda?

Have *you* told *me* everything?"

Pushing him away, she said in her husky voice, "I want to go to town and have lunch." She went out the entranceway and upon seeing his Porsche, added, "I like your car."

The Porsche hugged the narrow mountain road that curved around the bay from the contessa's villa to the town of Villefranche. She had asked Stone to take this road so she could admire the view and he'd obliged. The rain had passed and the countryside glistened. As he shifted through the gears, he tried to gauge her mood.

"It would be nice to go to the little place we frequented years ago. When we were young," she said, holding her hand out the window as if she wanted to catch the air. "You mentioned that Jonathan is coming down from Paris. Tell him he can stay at my villa." Her jeans matched her pale-blue sweater. He always liked it when she didn't wear a brassiere. Around her head, she had tied a Hermes scarf, heavy with French blues and yellows. Large sunglasses hid her eyes. She turned to him. "Are you here to write your book?"

"I'm not here to write," he answered. "Surely, Colmont told you that the last time you two spoke?"

She heaved a sigh. "Monsieur Colmont indicated that you are a spy. I am surprised you did not tell me that when we had our talk. You know ... after we made love."

"That was one thing that didn't come up." He looked over. "All right, I did say I was writing a book. I did say I was a writer. Who's to say I'm not?"

"You have a hard time with the truth."

He pulled the car off the road and parked under a twisted cedar tree. A goshawk screeched, flapped off, and glided down toward the bay. The town of Villefranche glimmered below along the shore. Lucinda lifted her face and looked out the open sunroof.

"Would you please take off your sunglasses?" he asked, as he removed his own.

She turned to him and gestured "why" with upraised shoulders.

"So I can see your eyes. I want to know what you're thinking."

"I know what *you* are thinking, Hayden Stone, even with your sunglasses on." She slid her glasses off. "You think because we have slept together that things are back as they once were." She shook her head. "They are not. Maybe if you had been honest with me—"

"The girl, Margaux, means nothing to me. She is only a friend."

"Probably. Besides, she is too young for you."

"Then it's because Colmont told you I was a spy?" Stone laughed. "A spy doesn't go around announcing 'I'm a spy.' That can backfire on you." He pushed his head back onto the headrest. "Actually, I'm not a real spy ... just sort of a consultant. I'm retired from the FBI. I told you that the other night, right? Besides, you work for French Intelligence, don't you?"

"It matters not, really," she spoke softly. "I want you to know you may stay anytime you want at my villa, but I will never visit your room again." She slipped her sunglasses back on. "Are you still taking me to lunch?"

The Red Scorpion eased around on its anchor with the changing tide. A flock of screaming seagulls circled above the fantail, waiting for the ship's cook to throw the remnants of breakfast overboard. Abdul Wahab gazed across the bay to the port of Villefranche. How nice it would be to have a relaxing lunch over there, perhaps with a lovely woman?

That morning a frantic call from Harrington had added to his problems. Once again, Harrington had failed to kill Stone, and the attempt had resulted in the arrest of two of Harrington's henchmen. His voice frantic, Harrington had said he did not know how long his men could resist police interrogation. If and when they talked, Harrington would be implicated.

Wahab tried to calm him, advising that he should return to the United States, but Harrington had argued that it required a lot of money. Finally, Wahab agreed to send one of his men with a suitable payment. It crossed his mind that a bullet in the head would have been a more suitable payment.

At the contessa's party he had remembered the effortless way Stone had moved from one person to another. That man, Stone, was a form of *djinn*, an apparition, always showing up at awkward times and seemingly impossible to kill. He must find that photograph of Stone and study his face. Without a doubt, he had seen Stone before, but where?

Harrington, on the other hand, was a minor problem compared to the prince, who had grown irritable since the arrival of bin Zanni. He should not have told the prince that bin Zanni's men had barred the two of them from visiting the palace. To complicate matters, those same men constantly flowed back and forth to the yacht to use the communication gear. He suspected that the prince believed he was being used by bin Zanni, and the prince was not a man to be used. Worse, the prince surely blamed him, Abdul Wahab, for this quandary.

The open-air restaurant Lucinda had suggested sat above a woman's boutique having a sale. On the sidewalk below, the shop displayed clothing tagged *en vente*. A smoky glass partition shielded the luncheon patrons from the noise and fumes from the few passing automobiles below. Down the street, Stone saw the landing where the motorboats picked up and discharged passengers for the yachts anchored in the bay. He had watched the Red Scorpion's launch depart, carrying a group of bearded men in dark suits.

Despite Stone going through his repertoire of jokes and *bons mots*, Lucinda maintained a detached air. The only emotion she showed during the lunch was when she complained about strangers living in and soiling her palace. Resigned to her mood, Stone settled back and nibbled at his disappointing salad. It was enough to be in the presence of a beautiful chic woman. More than one man at the adjoining tables had turned from his companion to eye her.

The waiter had gone for the check when Stone's cellphone buzzed. Colonel Frederick was brief. He wanted Stone to return to the safehouse now.

"Business." He put the phone away. "I have an important meeting."

She looked down to the street as if something had attracted her attention.

He leaned next to her. "It's a secret mission." She continued to look at some tourists walking along the street. "I wanted you to know."

She glared at him. "I do *not* care."

"I do *not* believe you."

Lucinda pressed her napkin on the table. Her dark hazel eyes bored into his. "I want you to understand something." She paused for a moment. "My father truly liked you."

"I liked him. He was a good man."

"He told me you would come back. I think he expected to see you again. He, of course, never did."

Stone squirmed in his chair. His mind churned. How long would it take to return Lucinda to her villa and then head off to the safehouse?

She looked down at her empty plate. "Remember when we would go to the cinema and see the films of Jean-Luc Godard? You told me I reminded you of the actress, Jean Seberg. Remember?"

"Yes."

"I read in the newspapers that your FBI people in Washington were not nice to her. She finally killed herself. Did you have anything to do with that harassment?" Shaking her head, she forced a laugh. "Of course, would you tell me if you did?"

"I had nothing to do with that. Most of us in the Bureau didn't even know the program was going on." Stone glanced at his watch. He had become uncomfortable. "Lucinda, I'm sorry for coming back into your life and bringing up bad memories for you. That was not my intention, but you're right. I'm sort of a bastard."

"Ah, you are much more than that. Shall we go?"

CHAPTER TWENTY-EIGHT

NICE

A burly army sergeant with a red crew cut ushered Stone into the safehouse, where Colonel Frederick stood flipping through a black folder. Frederick looked up. "We're taking down bin Zanni. I just got the green light from Langley. We need help with the attack plan on the palace."

The assault team milled about the safehouse, checking their weapons and radio equipment. One of the military women cracked her knuckles every few minutes. Stone sat down at a table covered with maps and drawings. This was all a step-up from a police raid, but the same basic scenario. He picked up a pencil and began drawing. Tossing down the pencil, he placed his hands over his eyes and tried to visualize the layout of the palace.

In time, his rough sketch revealed that the inside of the structure was not as large as it appeared from the exterior. Most of its bulk consisted of thick stone walls attached to a tall, crenellated keep. His big problem was that he couldn't remember the locations of all the hidden passageways winding throughout the palace.

Frederick called everyone in the room to order. "Colmont and his men are busy in Montpellier, looking for Hassan." He scanned the faces before him. "Meanwhile, the television is plastered with news about the attempt on the American consul general in Marseille." He paused. "We may assume bin Zanni and his henchmen believe our attention is directed there. If they're going to let their guard down, it's now."

"So, what do we do?" Mark asked.

"The Major and I came up with a basic plan. Stone is

fleshing it out." Frederick grabbed a chair, turned it around, and straddled it, hanging his arms over the slatted back. "We want to keep it simple. We don't have time for a complicated strategy. Thanks to Stone, we don't have to go in through the front door. He knows of a tunnel from the outside that leads into the basement. We can sneak in and have the element of surprise."

"How do you know about a tunnel?" asked one of the Major's men.

"I discovered it some years ago."

"Not good enough." Mike sat down next to Stone. "It could have collapsed. It might be blocked now."

"That's why I'm leaving after the meeting to do a recon," Stone answered. "While I'm there, I'll place a series of electronic markers along the path to guide us at night."

"There will be ten people going in." Frederick turned to Fleming. "I know you want to go in with the team, but I need you here to handle the command post. Also, if the situation goes south, I can trust you to finesse the French." Fleming didn't look happy.

Frederick turned back to the group. "Stone will lead us through the tunnel until we get into the building. Then the Major leads with four people, followed by me with Stone, Jonathan Deville, who should be here soon, then Mark and Sergeant Wilson. We all will have night-vision equipment, firearms with noise suppressors, flash grenades, and medical gear." Frederick stood up. "We go in together, we go out together."

The Major spoke up. "What about explosives?"

"No high explosives," Frederick answered. "Stone isn't certain about the stability of the structure."

Stone leaned back and folded his arms. Not to mention what Lucinda would do if she learned he had blown up her palace.

Frederick looked at Stone. "Map all the pathways to the most logical rooms where we'll find bin Zanni." He turned back to the others. "Remember, bin Zanni is our target. You all have his description and photo. Anyone else we get is a bonus."

"When do we go in?" asked someone in the back.

"Tomorrow morning at zero two hundred." Frederick

looked at his watch. "That's about eight hours from now. The operation is to take no more than twenty minutes. We leave no evidence that points to us."

Stone looked out the car window at the Bay of Villefranche a thousand feet below. "We're lucky. There'll be little moonlight tonight."

Mark guided the Porsche along the narrow mountain road overgrown with grass and brush. When Stone saw a dip in the road a few hundred yards ahead, he told him to slow down. "Leave me off at the bottom of the hill. That way when I get out, no one at the palace will see me." He checked his flashlight to make sure it worked, then counted the electronic markers in his backpack.

"Only a handgun?" Mark asked.

Stone nodded.

"You have a silencer and extra magazines?"

Again a nod. "I'll call you in about an hour for the pickup." The car eased to a stop and Stone jumped out.

As Mark turned the car around, Stone stood in the silence of the empty hillside, then jogged along the road until he found a path leading down the hill. He recognized the scat along the trail. Goats had passed by recently. The landscape had changed over the years. Even though trees grow and bushes die, rock formations usually remained the same. He searched for the white ledge that he remembered extended downhill, looking directly over a pink hotel down by the bay. He saw no pink hotel. Now numerous condominiums and villas crowded the water's edge.

After ten unproductive minutes, he started sweating. The sun sat on the horizon. If he returned unsuccessful, Frederick and the rest of the team would not be happy. A noisy dove flushed by his approach through the grass directed his attention to a low coppice of trees. Behind a scrub under one of the trees, he spotted the cave entrance. He could have easily passed it by. Now behind schedule, he checked to make sure no one was in sight. He pushed the bush aside and slipped into the dark entrance. His flashlight shot a beam of bright light down the length of the tunnel. The air felt cool.

A few feet into the tunnel bats hung from the ceiling. They had not been there when he and the contessa had explored the tunnel years before. He progressed at a steady pace. Rocks littered the floor. A moment later, he stumbled and fell forward. He got up on his knees and took deep, steady breaths. Slow down. Concentrate.

He continued down the tunnel, the rubber cleats on the bottom of his boots gripping the damp, hard surface. Years before, when he and Lucinda had searched the tunnel, it had taken about thirty minutes to travel from one end to the other. However, they had made their way carefully, stopping now and then to debate whether they should continue. This time, he figured it would take him only ten to fifteen minutes.

The passage twisted and bent along the way, something he had forgotten. The dank, cool air chilled his face as he pushed deeper into the tunnel. At last, he reached the corroded steel door leading into the basement of the palace. By his watch, it had taken twelve minutes.

He pressed his ear to the cold metal. No sound from the other side. He switched off the flashlight and looked for light coming though the cracks. No light.

With his hands flat on the door, he pushed. It didn't budge. He remembered that when he had opened the door from the other side, he'd found it hard to pull. Also, it had creaked.

Again he pushed, this time with more force, and the door scraped along the floor. It opened two inches. Still no light came from the other side. He pushed the door until it hit the antique breakfront. Debating whether to turn on his light, he decided against it. Still, one goal was to pick up the broken padlock he had thrown on the floor a few days before. Just in case someone noticed it and slipped it back on the hasp.

As he searched along the floor, a furry object brushed past his hand. Jerking back, he slipped and hit the tunnel wall. "Damn!" came out before he could stifle it. Seconds passed. He remained motionless. No sound came from the basement.

He moved to the door again and turned on his flashlight. A fat black rat ran beneath the breakfront, then scurried off. On the floor, the rusty padlock looked dull in the beam of light. As he picked it up, the basement lights went on and excited voices speaking Arabic came from the top of the stairs. He extinguished his light and pulled the creaky door shut as quietly as possible, but it jammed.

For a minute, he listened to the men thump down the stairs, arguing. Stone detected three distinct voices. They spoke in rapid Arabic, punctuated with the words "medical" and *Inshalla*, God willing. Finally the name bin Zanni was mentioned in a reverential tone.

Stone pushed his face against the door and tried to see the men inside the basement. As he did, the door creaked. The men stopped speaking. He held his breath.

A long moment passed. Then someone with a deep voice hollered from the top of the basement stairs. In subservient tones, the men in the basement acknowledged the order and rushed up the staircase.

After the last man closed the door behind him, Stone yanked the steel door shut. He switched on his flashlight and double-timed it back through the tunnel to the exit.

CHAPTER TWENTY-NINE

VILLEFRANCHE—MAY 16, 2002

A waxing crescent moon hung low in the sky, just enough to require a slight uplifting of the eyes to see it. Now and then, Stone referred to the electronic markers he had positioned along the trail. The attack team followed close behind. They slipped through the underbrush, careful not to break or stir the branches. Halfway to the tunnel entrance, a covey of black grouse flushed to the right. The team dropped to the ground and froze. A balcony light went on in a whitewashed villa sloped on the hill a hundred meters away, and a man in a blazer emerged through a sliding glass door and came to the railing. He looked over the edge and searched the landscape, then lit a cigarette, waved out the match, and went inside. Frederick, who was kneeling next to Stone, motioned to wait. When no further sound was heard, he used his clicker to signal "resume advance" and they continued toward the tunnel.

At last they came to the tunnel entrance. The team gathered inside and Frederick whispered, "Everyone check your equipment. Make sure your radios are on. Stone, take point."

They hurried single-file through the tunnel. Stone switched on the micro-light attached to his headband. The rest of the team followed, each holding on to the person's shoulder in front of him. After two minutes, Stone passed the order down the line for all to switch on their flashlights. In less than ten minutes, they reached the steel door. Stone whispered over the radio, "Flashlights off. Go to night vision."

Two men eased the door open until it hit the old breakfront. A strange odor came from the basement that Stone had not detected a few hours before. After a pause, they screeched both the door and breakfront aside.

Stone slipped past and entered the basement. Through his night-vision display, he noted the stairs leading up to the main floor of the palace then scanned the room through the eerie green and strangely two-dimensional glow from the screen. "Shit!" He crouched and aimed his MP-7 assault weapon toward the far end of the room. In his radio microphone, he said, "There are five people on the floor, bound and gagged." He rose and crept forward. "Three more in the corner." He paused. "They've been decapitated. Heads are lined up on a table." Bile rose from his stomach. He swallowed hard.

"Holy shit," muttered the Major over the radio. "Hostage situation?"

"No, appears to be some internal cleansing," Stone offered.

Frederick broke in. "Squad Two, we're going in. Quiet."

The five live captives struggled in their restraints. He concentrated on inspecting their faces, trying to avoid looking at the severed heads. The bound men had long beards and the Semitic features of men from the Arabian Peninsula.

Stone then studied the heads on the table. Their long hair and beards draped into the blood pools on the table.

Frederick and the team filed in through the door. In night-vision display, the black-clad group resembled panthers stalking a meal. Frederick came to his side.

At the foot of the stairs, Frederick held up an arm to halt. He tapped Stone. "Take Mark and Deville and use that hidden passageway. I'll take Squad Two up the stairs."

It didn't take long for Stone to locate the arched entrance to the passageway at the far end of the basement, behind a furnace. As he was about to enter the staircase, the door at the top of the main stairs banged open and the basement lights snapped on. Frederick pushed aside his night-vision screen and watched a bloodied-faced man tumble down the stairs. Two armed men wearing black business suits followed. Halfway down the stairs one gave out a shout when he saw the attack team at the bottom of the stairs. Then came the muffled popping from the Squad Two's MP-7 silencers. The two terrorists tumbled down the stairs. Members of the team threw the bodies aside and scrambled up to the main floor.

Stone hurried Deville and Mark into the hidden passageway. He used the micro-light to guide him up the narrow, winding steps, his shoulders brushing against the stonework. A flash grenade exploded from somewhere above them. When they reached the exit panel that led into the library, Stone heard shots and yelling coming from the other side. He slammed open the wooden panel and rushed into the library. Four men were looking the other way out the door leading to a hallway. All were armed.

One of the terrorists spun around and saw Stone. He opened his mouth to yell. Stone and his companions opened fire. All four collapsed to the floor, but not before one of the terrorists put a bullet in Mark's right thigh.

Mark grabbed his leg. "Son of a bitch! That burns like hell."

Stone and Deville scrambled over the dead terrorists and peered up and down the hallway. Two of the Major's men in the kitchen area signaled that the hallway was clear. Stone reloaded as he absorbed the noise and smells of combat.

The library's back door banged open and two terrorists stormed in, spraying bullets. Calmly, Deville dropped the two with short accurate bursts from his machine gun.

Stone looked down at the round, jagged hole in the front of his bulletproof vest. Only a bruised rib. No broken flesh.

Deville ran to the door and looked out. Without turning his head, he gave the "all clear" sign.

"Keep an eye out!" Stone yelled. He knelt next to Mark and started wrapping a compress on the wound. "We'll get the medic to look at this."

Frederick rushed in, breathing hard. "The medic is dead. These bastards are tougher than I expected." He yelled into his radio microphone, "Squad Two leader! Situation report!"

"Main floor is secure," the Major reported. "Target not located. We've found no medical equipment."

Pushing aside his radio microphone, Frederick searched Stone's face. "Any ideas?"

"He's got to be upstairs. The most logical room large enough to handle a lot of medical gear is the contessa's bedroom, on the third floor."

"Fuck! We've got to shoot our way up the main staircase to the second floor, clear it, then move up to the third floor."

"Not necessarily," Stone said. "If I can get to the second floor bedroom I stayed in the other night, I can use another hidden passageway that leads to the contessa's bedroom."

Frederick half-smiled. "I'm sure you can find your way to her bedroom, but what's the best way to take control of the second floor?"

"The back staircase," Deville said. "It's narrow, but a flash grenade should clear away any bad guys."

The Major stuck his head in the door and shouted, "Let's go! We're behind schedule!"

"Mark, you stay put," Frederick said. "Cover our escape route." He looked at Stone and Deville. "Let's get this over with."

Stone looked around the library. Bullets had pierced two of the antique maps hanging on the wall. He recalled studying them the morning after he had slept with Lucinda. Good thing her father was no longer alive to see the damage to his palace.

It took two grenades and wounding of two more of the attack team to make a bridgehead on the second-floor landing. Stone raced up the stairs and waved Deville on to the bedroom, firing his machine gun down the hallway. Slamming through the door, Stone lost his balance and fell to the floor. Two terrorists with handguns began firing, but Deville came in from behind him and leveled them.

Stone shouted to Deville, "Make sure the balcony is clear!"

He entered the closet and slid open the panel, then when Deville returned, they scrambled into the passageway. They squeezed up a circular stone stairway that ended at a door without a handle.

"How does it open?" Deville asked.

"There's a recessed lever above the door." Stone's throat was dry. He repeatedly swallowed so he could speak, then pointed his flashlight upward. "There."

He pushed the lever and the door swung open into a large

closet. Some of the contessa's dresses had been left hanging in a corner. As he brushed past her clothes, he detected her perfume. Shouts came from the bedroom through the closet door. He tried to radio Frederick that they were prepared to enter the bedroom, but the stonework in the palace interfered with the radio transmission. "Damn," Stone said. "We may have to go it alone."

"Not good, pal. We don't know what's behind this door."

Stone moved around in the large closet until, after three more attempts, his radio message got through.

Stone whispered to Deville, "Better have fresh magazines in our guns." He slipped in a forty-round magazine. "Okay, good buddy ... open the door carefully on the count of three." He held up one finger ... two ... three.

They eased into the enormous, high-ceiling room. Stone went right, Deville left. They encountered a bizarre scene. On a bed in the middle of the room, a body lay wrapped in a white shroud. Medical instruments and paraphernalia lined the right side of the room. Some of the equipment lay on its side. An odor of gunpowder and feces hung in the air.

Three terrorists knelt behind an engraved desk, turned over to act as a barrier. Lucinda had mentioned to Stone years before that the desk was an eighteenth century antique. The terrorists were aiming at the hallway door. Stone caught sight of two more terrorists pacing outside on the balcony.

Unaware of Stone and Deville, the terrorists continued to shout among themselves. The situation felt surreal. Stone motioned to Deville to take out the men on the balcony. He stepped forward, waited until Deville was in position, and then opened fire.

Stone emptied his magazine and then used his Colt .45. A few last shots came from the balcony and Deville came back. "All taken care of."

While Deville gathered the weapons on the floor, Stone radioed Frederick to come in. He looked at Lucinda's shattered antique desk and sighed. Then he went over to the shrouded body. With his knife, he slit the cloth away from the face and stood back. Deville came over and stood next to him. The two stared down at the face. The left side showed damage from a gunshot wound, but the right side was identifiable. It was the al Qaeda leader, bin Zanni. Someone had gotten to him first. Frederick and the Major burst into the room. They went to the bed and looked down at bin Zanni's body.

"I hope he's in hell, not paradise," Frederick spat. "Damn it! All this for nothing!"

The sound of approaching police sirens came from the balcony door. Stone yelled, "Let's get out of here!"

Over the radio, the Major ordered the extrication phase. Team members snapped digital photographs of the terrorist's faces, took DNA samples, and then scrambled out the room.

Stone was the last to leave the contessa's room. He lingered, surveying the damage. Lucinda would blame him. He'd never see this room again.

Frederick popped his head back in the door. "Move it, Stone!"

Pockets of terrorists remained on the third floor. The attack team sprayed bullets as they descended the three floors to the basement. Once there, the Major took a quick team head count. With everyone accounted for, they helped the wounded and carried the dead medic into the tunnel. Stone closed the door behind them.

CHAPTER THIRTY

CÔTE D'AZUR—MAY 17, 2002

On the empty road overlooking the gleaming lights of Villefranche, not far from the tunnel entrance, two vans pulled up to the spot on the mountain road where the attack group waited. Colonel Frederick shook the hand of the Major, who took one step back and saluted. All extended quick farewells, and then boarded their respective vans and sped off in opposite directions. The Major took his people to Beaulieu, where a speedboat was waiting to take them to a submarine lying offshore. Stone rode with Frederick, Mark, and Deville back to the safehouse.

Charles Fleming greeted them at the door. He still appeared miffed about being left behind. He and Stone helped Mark into the kitchen where a doctor and a nurse were waiting. They lifted him onto the kitchen table and the doctor began working on his leg. After a few minutes, he said, "Lucky for you the bullet passed through. A few damaged muscles, but they'll be able to take care of that out on the naval hospital ship. It's standing offshore."

"Good for you, old buddy," Stone said. "The CIA takes care of you staffers."

"Stuff it, Stone," Frederick quipped. "We take care of *all* our people. Even you independent contractors."

Once assured Mark would recover, Stone and the other two let the doctor finish bandaging his wound and filed back into the living room.

"It seems while you and your people were en route to the palace, bin Zanni had visitors," Fleming explained. "We intercepted a radio message that the palace was under attack. At first, we thought they were referring to you guys, but we knew you couldn't have gained entry that soon. After a few more messages, we realized that other Saudis were attacking them. We tried to contact you."

"We were probably in the tunnel," Stone said.

"Whom were they sending the messages to?" Frederick asked.

Fleming shrugged. "Anybody who would listen, I guess."

"Did they get any response?" Stone said.

"Just one. Something like, 'Burn in Hell.' Our directional finder indicated it came from the vicinity of the prince's yacht." Fleming walked over to a table and picked up the report. "We should have more information after we've done some traffic analysis. Meanwhile, we also got a call from our friend, Monsieur Colmont, in Montpellier."

"This should be good," Deville murmured.

Fleming continued. "It helps explain what I just told you. Colmont's people, who were stationed in the lookouts, spotted about a half-dozen men coming ashore from the prince's yacht. They drove up to the palace and barged in. That's when the French heard shots. After about two minutes of gunfire, everything went quiet. The men from the yacht never came out."

The colonel asked, "Did Colmont say anything else?"

"Yes. He said his people reported that about twenty minutes later all hell broke loose inside the palace. Machine guns going off. Explosions. I guess that was when your team went in." Fleming threw the report on the table. "When the gendarmes arrived and tried to go in, they were met by a few of bin Zanni's people, who decided to shoot it out."

"That's it?"

"Only that bin Zanni's body was found. Oh, another thing—Colmont said he was puzzled about some of the events. He asked that you give him a call. He figures you may be able to help him sort out some of the details."

Two hours later, Stone and Frederick walked out of the safehouse into the fresh dawn air. "Are you heading back to Archos, or are you going to drop by and see your contessa?" Frederick asked.

Stone considered the remark snide. After all, they had wrecked Lucinda's palace and the colonel well knew their relationship. "After a couple of black coffees, I'm leaving for Archos," he answered. "Any objections?"

"Just stay here at the safehouse. Get some shut-eye. Later today I want you to fly to Montpellier and give Sandra a hand."

"Okay, but let's go over what just happened," Stone said. "We were in one hell of a firefight, our people got shot up, and for what? To take a look at a dead man. Where was our intelligence on this operation?"

"Take it easy, pal. We had bin Zanni located and we moved in. That was the objective. Mission accomplished."

"But why did the prince or someone from his yacht have bin Zanni killed?" Stone pressed.

Fleming came out of the safehouse and joined them, lighting a cigarette—the first time Stone had seen him smoking. "Maybe I can answer that." He waved out the match. "From what our Intel has picked up, and this just came in, the prince was the one who ordered bin Zanni killed. Seems it was more of a preemptive strike. The prince got bin Zanni before bin Zanni got him. Among other things, it seems bin Zanni liked the prince's yacht and wanted to use it for some suicide attack."

"Satisfied, Stone?" Colonel Frederick growled.

"Okay, so it was a matter of timing. The prince got to him before we did." Frederick and Fleming exchanged glances. Stone continued. "Now, about the two CIA officers who were killed? Who killed them? And why? It wasn't Hassan."

Fleming took a drag on his cigarette. "No, we don't think Hassan killed them or ordered them killed."

"You got one of the assassins, Stone," Frederick said. "After the consul general's party."

"But what would be a motive for killing the two officers? If we learned that, we could identify the ringleader."

"You're thinking like a cop," Frederick huffed. "We're in a counterterrorist war."

"Damn it, I'm bringing logic into the equation, Fred." Stone

ARTHUR KERNS

turned to Fleming. "Harrington, the director at the foundation, is involved in narcotics. He tried to have me killed. Would he have anything to gain in killing CIA people?"

"Nothing that we know of," Fleming answered. "However, he's been working with the prince's right-hand man Abdul Wahab, who has been trying to get in on the drug trade in Marseille."

"Jonathan Deville told me Wahab was involved with terrorists. Also, we know from the contessa's party he and Harrington have some business arrangement." Stone thought for a moment.

Colonel Frederick had become quiet and looked at the ground.

"Wahab could easily talk Harrington into killing me," Stone said. "He knew Harrington was jealous of me because of—"

"Your lady friend," the colonel said, without looking up.

Stone glared. "Wahab is the logical suspect. He's the one we should get, but he's probably out to sea on that yacht. One more question—Hassan's man tried to kill me in Saint-Rémy. Why?"

Fleming cleared his throat. "Maybe Wahab had something to do with that, too. Hassan met with him in Nice just before the two of them went to Saint-Rémy."

Stone stared at Fleming, then looked at Frederick. He shook his head. "So you had a surveillance on Wahab?" he snapped. "Am I part of the team or not? That information would have been useful to me."

Frederick straightened up and put on his enough-of-this-discussion look. "Abdul Wahab has been on our screen for some time. The Agency got interested in him when he was in Afghanistan last year … same time you and I were there."

"So now what?" Stone asked. *You two pricks!*

"As I said, Hayden, I want you to go to Montpellier and assist Sandra and Eric. They're zeroing in on Hassan. They could use your help."

• • •

At exactly three forty-five in the morning, an hour after the police had entered the contessa's palace, Abdul Wahab, sleeping fitfully in his hotel suite, received a call from his aide. Half asleep, he instructed him to call back in a half hour. The dinner at the German restaurant had disagreed with him. Even the sedative had not settled his stomach.

In a semi-sleep, the dream returned. In the shimmering desert, he floated toward the expansive black tent of the prince. A group of sheiks gathered in flowing white robes, their backs turned to him. When he approached, they closed ranks and would not respond to his entreaties.

The phone rang again, pulling him out of the dream.

The aide pleaded, "I must speak with you, sir. It is most important."

"Bring me coffee."

Slipping from beneath the silk sheets, he turned on the lights and put on his paisley robe. The aide knocked on the door and rushed in from the sitting room. "Sir, please come out onto the balcony."

Wahab obliged and the aide pointed to the nearby mountain. Blue lights flashed around the palace and a string of ambulances snaked up the road to its entrance. Sirens wailed singsong fashion in the distance.

He tried to clear his mind. "When did this start?"

"About an hour ago, sir. The gunshots have stopped."

"Gunshots?" Wahab eased into a deck chair. A servant appeared, carrying a tray with a serving of coffee.

"One of our men heard gunshots coming from the palace. They lasted for some time before the police came." The aide paused. "All the lights in the surrounding villas came on, as they are now."

The servant poured Wahab a cup of steaming coffee. After a moment, he instructed his aide, "Give me some time. Pack my clothes and then return. We go to the yacht."

"Too late, sir. See? The yacht is leaving."

Wahab rose and went to the banister. The Red Scorpion had hoisted anchor and, with its running lights on, was heading out toward the open sea. He looked back at the palace and let out a slight belch.

"One other thing, sir. Mr. Harrington called and said the police were about to place him under arrest. He needs your help."

Damn! Wahab straightened his back. The police would trace the call to his suite, and soon they would be knocking on the door. "Pack my things, and purchase a ticket for me to London, first-class."

The lights from the police cars and ambulances flashed continually, making the palace resemble a gaily-colored resort. He sat down again and picked up his cup of coffee. It tasted burnt.

"Begging your pardon, sir … one more thing." The aide stood behind him.

"What, for the sake of Allah?"

"I received a call from Marseille. The French port authorities confiscated the opium shipment from Afghanistan."

His mind numbed, Wahab waved him off and watched the fading running lights of the Red Scorpion. The faint crescent moon hung over the bay, to the left, a faint glow appeared along the eastern horizon. Pockets of mist appeared here and there on the mountain. At Cambridge, he remembered his Don referring to this magical time of dawn, known in Middle English as *uht*. He bit his lip. From his pocket, he took a sterling silver case. He pulled out a cigarette and lit it with his lighter. The sharp Turkish tobacco made him cough.

Now he remembered where he had seen Stone. While in Afghanistan, during an attack on his Taliban encampment, he recalled seeing a bearded American with strange eyes, wearing Afghan garb. This American had jumped his horse over the perimeter walls of the hamlet, shooting and killing his Taliban brothers.

The cigarette smoke drifted up in the direction of the palace. Wahab had managed to escape that attack. As he fled the battle, he'd glanced back through the dust and smoke, but the American had disappeared. That man had been Hayden Stone, the cause of all his ill fortune. Certainly, he was a *djinn* … an evil spirit.

CHAPTER THIRTY-ONE

MONTPELLIER

During the short flight from Nice to Montpellier, Stone tried to nap. He had as much luck as he had in the lounge sitting in the Nice Côte d'Azur Airport. "Let's wrap up all the loose ends as soon as we can," Colonel Frederick had said back at the safehouse in Nice. "I think we've about worn out our welcome here in France." Being kept out of the circle of trust by those two men still angered him. "Frederick and Fleming." He snorted. Sounds like a law firm.

Sandra and Eric met him at the airport terminal. They appeared relieved that he had joined them. On the way to the stakeout on Hassan, the city of Montpellier appeared less trendy than Nice. It had a small-town look, similar to one found playing host to a New England college: lots of trees along the streets, many conservatively-dressed pedestrians.

Eric drove the Peugeot sedan and Stone sat in the back. Sandra, up front, turned around to face him. "That address the French got from Rashid's workman belongs to an automobile repair garage. An immigrant from Tunisia owns it. This morning, one of Colmont's agents caught a glimpse of Rashid's panel truck parked inside."

"So they invited us in on the stakeout?"

"Yes. You and I will sit in a surveillance van while Eric goes to the police command center. Say, Colmont seems pissed about the palace business. Did you guys wax bin Zanni?"

"No," Stone said. "We got in and mixed it up a bit with his thugs, but apparently some of his compatriots killed him. Don't know the whole story. Frederick's working on it."

"Well, anyway, Colmont's keeping us on a short leash."

Sandra turned away.

"Should I drop you two near the surveillance van?" Eric asked, easing down a tree-lined street.

"Yeah, but slow down," Sandra said. "I want to tell Stone about Hassan." She talked quickly. "More important than Colmont's hard feelings, we have two concerns. First, this wine business that Hassan is involved in. A week ago, the French followed Hassan and Rashid when they went to some wine wholesaler in Marseille. Afterward, Colmont's people interrogated the guy, who told them he suspected Hassan wanted to play a swindle against Americans with bogus vintage wine. The wholesaler said he finally believed the deal seemed legit, except that Hassan wanted to ship only a few cases to three American cities. Not enough to make a decent profit."

Sandra said, her lisp now returning, "Anyway, this morning some guy drives up to the garage. He's well dressed and apparently doesn't have car problems. He goes inside the garage and shortly afterward, two men, one resembling our man Hassan, come out. They lug chrome canisters, six of them, from the car into the garage. Tried to conceal them with towels, but the French got photographs while they were lying in the backseat of the car."

"Some form of explosive, perhaps?" Stone suggested.

"One would imagine, except when they traced the license tag, they found the car was registered to a Dr. Mohammed Aziz, a scientist at a research center here in Montpellier. His field of expertise is pathology, specializing in the study of African diseases."

"Why does that make me feel very uncomfortable?" Stone muttered.

The Peugeot sedan pulled up in front of a brick apartment house. "I'll drop you two off here," Eric said.

When Stone and Sandra got out of the car, Maurice Colmont suddenly materialized.

"Hi, Maurice. Seems you found Hassan and now have good surveillance underway."

"Mr. Stone, I want a word with you. Alone." Colmont turned and walked away from the car.

"I'll meet you down the block," Sandra whispered, whose big eyes and barely held-back smile broadcasted, you're in for a Colmont lecture.

When Stone caught up with him, the French intelligence man stopped and then stared ahead. For a long while, Colmont avoided eye contact. Finally, he said, "Mr. Stone, I'm disappointed with your actions."

Good God! Stone held back a laugh. He truly was going to give him a lecture. Colmont seemed to be controlling his words. Spinning around and bringing his face close to Stone's, a little too uncomfortable for Stone's liking, the Frenchman said through clinched teeth, "I thought you and your colleagues had more of a sense for politics!" He shook his head and turned away. "You all have put me in a very bad position with Paris. I had assured my superiors we were dealing with competent allies."

"Get to the point, Monsieur Colmont."

"Your raid on the contessa's palace was *stupidité*. Idiocy! I had told Colonel Frederick that we, the French government, opposed such action. The authorities in Paris were against it for many reasons ... reasons that we did not wish to share with you." Colmont took a deep breath. "What did you accomplish? *Rien!* Nothing! Just the ruin of our cooperative efforts against the terrorists."

"Look Maurice—"

"You are a good friend of Frederick. He is a military man. Military men think in very direct ways. If you had thought about the potential consequences of such an action, you could have influenced him to hold off. Instead, you used your muscles instead of your brains."

Stone put his hands in his pockets and started to walk away.

"I am not finished, Mr. Stone! As I say, I thought you were different. You have a sensible friend in Jonathan Deville. He is a good man." Colmont moved closer. "How do you think your actions will affect his professional future in Paris? French doors will be closed to him now."

The tone in Colmont's voice concerned Stone. This was the Frenchman's turf. Colmont could make life very unpleasant.

Stone was accustomed to putting people in jail, not sitting in one himself. Any defense of the CIA's attack on the palace was out of the question, and doing so would admit complicity.

"You know, Mr. Stone, we believe the United States is too old to still act the innocent. Recently, you Americans have lost a lot of your charm."

"Okay, Monsieur Colmont, point taken. Where does that leave us?"

"No, where does that leave France? We have a terrorist problem here that grows each day. We must work with our allies to combat it, just like you need your allies."

Stone spoke in the same measured cadence that Colmont used. "We had an al Qaeda leader in our sights. We were not going to let him escape to have another chance to kill Americans. Good allies would realize that."

Colmont waved his hand and shook his head. "Go sit with Sandra and watch your good allies stop Hassan from killing Americans."

Stone wanted to tell Colmont to shove the favor, but he decided to end the conversation.

"Oh, by the way. Tell Colonel Frederick we could have told him that bin Zanni would be dead when you found him. If he had talked with us, he could have prevented some fine Americans from getting shot. We knew bin Zanni was marked for death by his own people."

Stone stopped. "You still could have told us."

"You are on my country's territory, so we decide when you should be informed." As Stone walked away, Colmont said, "What's more, it was not gentlemanly to use the contessa to further your foolish aims."

"Up yours, Colmont."

Stone shifted his position on the hard metal floor of the stuffy police van. Using a pair of binoculars, he studied the garage through the one-way window. The single-story building had two large bay doors in front for vehicles and on the left side, a smaller workers entrance. The heavy traffic on the street in front of the garage concerned him. "It would be good to wait until things quieted down along the street before we go in," he said to Sandra, crammed in next to him. She didn't appear uncomfortable having her body touch him, and from her he caught a whiff of jasmine.

"Colmont doesn't want us in on the attack," she whispered. "He's really antsy with our presence here. So, how did it go?"

Stone looked at the French intelligence man sitting up front behind the wheel of the van and spoke quietly in her ear. "I don't know about you, but I'm on his shit list."

"Now that wouldn't be the first time for a guy like you, would it?" She touched his leg. "You seem like someone who's bent a few rules in his career."

"Who, me?" He grinned. "Colmont pissed me off." That wise prick had brought up Lucinda. "I think he's agreed to let us observe just so he can keep tabs on us. After this operation, I'll probably be escorted to a plane headed for the States."

Sandra shrugged.

"Meanwhile, we have a problem here," Stone said. "Colmont let it slip that he thinks Hassan is out to kill a lot of Americans. Whatever Hassan is playing with is headed for the USA." He laid down the binoculars and shifted his cramped legs to a new position. "My guess is that right now they're filling those wine bottles with the stuff."

Sandra squirmed her rear until she seemed comfortable. "Eric is checking to see if the French have contacted their biohazard people. If any of that stuff spills, it could be a disaster."

The Frenchman in the driver's seat answered a call on his phone. He turned around and handed the phone to Sandra. She listened, said "*Oui*" a couple of times, then exclaimed, "Holy shit!" She handed the phone back to the driver. "Colmont's people are about to go in."

"What about us?"

She shook her head. "We stay here. Here's the story. Colmont's people went to Doctor Aziz's lab and looked at his research papers. He's been working on a strain of Ebola."

"Ebola! Hassan must be mad! Sandra, do you realize what that can do?"

Stone recalled images of the village of Mnemdo, on the border of Sudan and the Congo. Three years before. His team hadn't needed map coordinates to find the sad collection of huts, they'd just headed toward the circling vultures. He remembered standing in the center of the village and feeling the eerie silence broken only by the scavengers arguing over the corpses scattered on the hard-baked ground. The three CIA technicians, one still barely alive, lay in a low-hanging thatched hut. Blood flowed from all their orifices: even, it seemed, from the sockets of their eyes. Before the last man died, they watched him go through mental and physical convulsions. He had pleaded for them to shoot him. Instead, they'd waited for him to die, then burned the village and all the bodies.

"I understand it's bad shit. No cure, right?" Sandra asked.

"So far, no. In Africa, some say it's bad Juju. Even the scientists don't know where it originates, only that if a person touches or eats a piece of contaminated bush meat, say a chimp, they can catch the virus."

"What are the chances they'll spill some of it?" Sandra said, more to herself. "Best for the French to wait for those biohazard people."

"Handling Ebola is tricky. All research is done in a maximum biological containment setup known as Biosafety Level Four."

She studied him. "You know a lot about it."

"I was exposed to it, so I learned all I could." Stone thought for a moment. "The way I see it, Hassan plans to ship the virus to the States and then spread it. God knows how. Can you imagine the number of deaths? *Horrible* deaths? And we wasted our time going after bin Zanni. Hassan's the threat."

"He's a scary bastard," she agreed. Then she returned her attention to the scene on the street and yelled, "Colmont's not waiting! There they go!"

The police came out from the side of an adjacent building. Four groups, two men in each group, wearing military-style fatigues, moved quickly toward the garage. One pair went to the front door, two groups went to the side door, and one held back with Colmont as a reserve force.

Sandra pointed. "Look! Gendarmes are blocking off the street at both ends."

Police cars maneuvered into blocking positions. With the last car in place, Stone heard a long shrill from a whistle. The police crashed through the side door of the garage and disappeared. The whistle blew again and the reserve unit moved in. A few seconds later, Stone heard a series of single shots, followed by short bursts of machine gun fire. Colmont's men rushed out of the garage. The last gendarme emerged and turned to get off a shot. A bottle thrown out of the open door hit him, but fell unbroken on the ground. He was not so lucky when more shots came from the garage and he fell to the ground.

The French agent in the van jumped out and ran to assist his comrades, now in the process of backing away from the garage. Stone watched as Colmont shouted in his hand-held radio and waved his men back. Sirens wailed in the distance. The two men stationed at the front bay doors advanced. One smashed the pane glass window in one of the doors and the other tossed a concussion grenade through the opening. The front bay doors shook from the blast. He threw in another grenade, which again shook the doors.

"Good God!" Stone said. "They're going to scatter the virus into the air!" He slid toward the back door of the van.

Sandra yelled, "Hassan's coming out from the other side of the building!"

In the garage, Doctor Aziz had filled only two wine bottles with the Ebola virus before the police barged in. Hassan raced to the end of the building, looking for his Uzi machine gun. Meanwhile, the Tunisian garage owner had pulled out his automatic pistol and began firing at the police. Hassan found the machine gun and started spraying shots at the gendarmes, almost hitting Aziz. The police retreated out the garage door. Screaming oaths, Aziz threw one of the bottles filled with the virus out the door at the retreating police officers. Then a grenade came through the garage front window. The blast threw Hassan to the ground. Dazed, his eardrums ringing, he picked himself up, seeing Aziz also struggling to get to his feet. The second wine bottle filled with the virus lay on the floor and as Hassan reached over for it, another grenade exploded inside the garage.

Hassan shook his head and saw, through the smoke, Aziz lying on the ground. The wine bottle now lay next to him. He snatched it, then crawled over to a side window. He broke the glass, climbed out, and dropped to the ground. The Tunisian followed him. The two ran toward the street and turned the corner. A gendarme with a drawn pistol emerged from behind a police car and ordered them to stop. Hassan pointed his automatic and squeezed the trigger, but the weapon failed to fire. He tried again, and then yelled to the Tunisian, who raised his gun and dropped the gendarme. From behind them, a short burst of machine gun fire from the French hit the Tunisian and he slumped to the ground, blood coming from the back of his right shoulder. He cried to Hassan, "Help me!"

"No time," Hassan shouted, yanking the gun from his hand. Throwing off shots in the direction of gendarmes crouching behind cars, he raced through the blockade. Taking long strides, he almost ran into a police car pulling up to the curb. The occupants looked confused as he passed by. Good, Hassan thought as he bumped aside frightened pedestrians, the more confusion, the better.

Shouts and footsteps came from far behind, and Hassan pushed his legs to go faster. He had to get off the street, out of sight. Across an intersection stood a large, two-story stone building, the word *École* etched on its façade. He crossed over and headed for the school's entrance. Once inside, he caught his breath and peered through the window. He saw a man and a woman cross the street and head in his direction. The man he recognized as the American agent, Stone. The woman was Sandra. So the whore was a CIA agent.

He spun around and faced what looked like a group of

women teachers backed against the wall staring at him. Through an open door to his right, he saw stairs leading down. Waving his gun at the women to back away, he took the stairs.

Half way down he paused for his eyes to adjust to the darkened basement. Hassan inched down the next few steps, then rushed the rest of the way down. An old black boiler dominated the open room. A single light bulb hung from the ceiling, giving off the dim light.

"Who are you? What are you doing here?" asked a bald man wearing dirty grey coveralls.

Hassan demanded, "Give me your car keys."

"*Fous le camp!*" Fuck you!

Hassan pistol-whipped the man and the gun went off, striking the man in the chest. He collapsed on the floor. In the man's pocket, Hassan found an old set of keys he recognized belonged to a Citroen deux chevaux. Not exactly the fastest get-away car, he thought.

As Stone and Sandra burst through the door, the frightened schoolteachers screamed, one telling Sandra a man with a gun had descended into the basement. Stone ran to the far end of the school hallway and found another door leading down into the basement. He shouted back, "I'm going down to get Hassan! Tell Colmont!" Then he proceeded down one stair at a time, holding his gun out with both hands.

The high ceiling of the basement was crisscrossed with rows of pipes and vents. The low hum of machinery back-dropped a slow drip landing in a dirty metal basin. The smell of heating oil mixed with the warm, stuffy air.

Oil stained the floor. Be careful, Stone told himself. Don't slip. He tried to control his breathing so he could hear better.

From above the ceiling, came shouts. Colmont had arrived with his men. One foot at a time Stone moved along the side of the large boiler. He stopped when he saw a body dressed in a coverall lying on the floor. That would be him if he were careless.

To his right, he glimpsed Hassan cut across an open area

throwing a shot in Stone's direction. The bullet glanced off the side of the boiler casing with a clang. Hassan disappeared into a storage room. Slipping behind the boiler and using it for cover, Stone looked past the metal plates and saw the door Hassan had entered. The wall with the door was set at an angle. Then Hassan's face appeared from around the doorway. He fired another shot at Stone.

The bullet hit the wall behind him and pieces of plaster fell on his shoulder. He crouched alongside the boiler. His heart pumped hard and no matter how he tried he couldn't slow his breathing. He had to forget it. Accept how his body reacted. Hassan was a pro. Trouble was a stray bullet could break the bottle Hassan was holding and spread the virus. Then they'd all be dead. Still, the bastard had to be taken down.

As Stone inched forward, Hassan popped from behind the doorjamb and fired another shot, then withdrew. Stone raised his gun and aimed where Hassan's head had appeared. He moved the gun sight slightly to the right so that his bullet would hit the wall an inch from the door. Given the angle, he figured the slug would ricochet along the wall and strike Hassan in the face. Hassan's gun appeared from behind the doorframe. Stone paused a second, and then squeezed off a round just as Hassan's face appeared. Chunks of the wall splintered into his face. He let out a curse in Arabic, then jumped from behind the doorjamb and fired two shots at Stone, missing again.

"You're trapped, Hassan! Give up!" Stone felt more confident knowing Hassan was hurting. He started to move to the other side of the boiler. Bullets skimmed along the floor in the exposed area below the boiler, barely missing Stone's feet. Leaping, Stone grabbed onto a valve pipe, and hung to the side of the boiler. He heard Hassan run toward the other end of the basement and open what sounded like a metal door. Stone dropped to the floor and rushed along the boiler. He spied Hassan staring down the lighted hallway, took quick aim, and squeezed off a round. The bullet blasted through the wall next to Hassan.

"Don't move!" Stone ordered.

Hassan turned slowly and held up the wine bottle. Blood ran from a long gash down his cheek.

"It's over! Drop your gun!" Stone yelled. "Place the bottle on the floor!"

"This is a school with hundreds of children," Hassan said with a smile, lifting the bottle for Stone to see. "Here is enough poison to kill them all."

"I don't care about French kids," Stone said. "I mean it, Hassan! Lay the bottle on the floor!" Stone aligned the sights of his Colt .45 on Hassan's forehead.

"Tell me, Crusader, do you have a family? Do they own an olive grove?" Hassan started toward the blower for the ventilation system.

"Don't give me that crap! People like you gave all that up for the Islamic jihad!" Stone's finger tightened on the trigger, and he lowered the gun sights to Hassan's chest.

"I am not one of those al Qaeda, who are the living dead. I am a Palestinian!"

Salty beads of sweat burned Stone's eyes. "If that's true, I'm sure we can make a deal. You people will do business with anyone, won't you?"

Hassan's face twisted in hatred. His gun swung up, but not fast enough. Stone's two slugs hit the middle of his chest and shoved him back through the doorway. The bottle slipped from his hand and, dropping on Hassan's shoe, rolled unbroken across the floor.

Hassan didn't shake or convulse like other men who had died at Stone's feet. Instead, he lay still and muttered, "The smell of an orange grove in spring." Then he let out a long sigh. Stone reached for the wine bottle, but stopped before touching it. He backed away, and then realized Sandra and Colmont were standing next to him.

DENOUEMENT

CÔTE D'AZUR—MAY 18, 2002

In the dark of Saturday morning, Stone had a vivid dream. At first, he though he was in Southern California, because he was standing in bare feet next to a pleasant ocean. Bent pine and cypress trees lined the shore. Around his dwelling grew orange and lemon trees. Then he saw broken Doric columns and what he took for as Roman ruins scattered in his citrus grove. An elderly man in a faded, blue suit drifted toward him, a man with fierce almond eyes that matched his dark, pockmarked skin. The face became familiar the closer he came.

With a bloody hand, Hassan offered him a lemon.

Stone awoke with a start, then lay sleepless for two hours. Eventually, he threw off the sheets, went downstairs, and searched for soft music on the radio. His skin tingled. Too wired to sleep, he stood at the French doors to watch the sunrise.

Dreams or no dreams, Hassan no longer posed a problem, at least not in this life. However, Abdul Wahab, last seen in London, was another matter, and his folder remained open.

Morning light brightened the inside of the cottage. Slowly, his surroundings became a warm yellow. A long shower helped relax him. While toweling, he phoned the Foundation's administrative office and asked them to send over his usual coffee and rolls.

The coffee arrived, rich and strong, the way he enjoyed it. Today, he found on the tray freshly baked croissants that flaked in his fingers. No newspaper came, but it suited him just to sit in his robe outside the kitchen door in the dry, clear air. On his second good swallow, his cellphone rang.

In a high-pitched voice Lucinda asked, "Hayden, is that

you? Do I have the right number?"

"Yes, dear. How are you?"

"Do not, 'yes dear' me. *Ever.*" Her voice went up what seemed a few decibels. "Where are you right now?"

"I'm sitting outside my cottage in Archos having coffee. Why?"

"My palace is a shambles! The police are all over!" She caught her breath. "They are still carrying out dead bodies. They will not allow me to go inside my own home!"

"Have you contacted the prince about this? He rented the place."

She answered slowly. "He is gone … his yacht is gone…"

"Is your consigliere there? Do you want me to come and help?"

"He will be here shortly." She paused. "Tell me, and do not lie—did you have anything to do with the police raiding my palace?"

"Lucinda, the last thing I would want is for the French police to raid your palace. I swear."

After a moment's silence, she said, distinctly, "I do not believe you." Again silence. "Never write me. Never call me. Never even wave to me if you see me in a café." The line went dead.

With a long sigh, he took the phone from his ear and clicked it off with his thumb. A breeze from the sea whistled through the pink oleander.

"Trouble at the palace?" Margaux stood with the sun behind her, revealing her long legs through her sheer white-linen skirt.

"If you would like to hear my sob story, I'll go into the kitchen and get you a cup."

"No coffee for me." She sat in the other wrought-iron chair. "But I'll have one of your croissants."

"I don't think I'm going to get any more weekend invitations from the contessa."

"She will be lonely without you and without Mr. Boswell Harrington. You have not heard the news?"

Her lips had a trace of gloss, her hair pulled back in a

chignon. "You look ravishing this morning," he said, and wondered what likelihood the special attention to her appearance was for his benefit.

"Thank you, but I must tell you. Monsieur Colmont called me at home. The police arrested Boswell and Helen Harrington last night for dealing in illegal drugs. I just left my office. The Foundation is in turmoil."

"That's a surprise. I figured he was too clever to ever get arrested."

"Both Harringtons are going to be in our French jails. Oh, and Colmont said you were a big help to him with the Ebola terrorist plot. He said he admired your professionalism. The whole episode is on the television." She broke off a piece of croissant and waved it in her hand. "Today, I look for another job in Toulon. It is not too far away. Everyone in the office believes the Foundation will disappear."

He tried to assure her it wouldn't, that important people in New York would not allow it.

She disregarded his assurances. "When do you plan to leave now that your work is done?" She crossed her legs and began swinging her foot. She had applied fresh polish to her toenails.

"I suppose I must leave in a few days, but I want to return. Would you like me to come back?"

She concentrated on her fingernails and shrugged.

"The real estate market in Washington is very good now. I can sell my house, make a lot of money, and move here to Archos."

She arched one eyebrow and asked in French. "What would you do here?"

"I could write."

She looked up to the sky and laughed.

"Or I could be a travel agent."

She puffed at the sky. "Not many English speakers come here. No, I think maybe you would come here for a reason that might not end well." She shook her head. "I am fond of you, Hayden, very much, but at heart you are still a sailor." For the word, *you*, she used the familiar French, *tu*.

"Margaux, I have changed since coming here, believe me." He grinned. "I think maybe I'm ready to stay ashore and not go to sea."

She rose from the chair and pointed her finger. "See, *mon chéri*?" she said, then in English. "You said maybe. When it is not maybe, I will help you find a home here." She thanked him for the croissant and waved good-bye. After a few steps, she turned back. "David has left the Foundation. He asked me to tell you he was grateful. His book has been accepted. Evidently, Monsieur Fleming made some calls on his behalf."

"I'll have to buy his book when it comes out."

Margaux smiled. "And will you read it? An Esperanto dictionary?"

"Maybe I'll wait for the movie."

As she walked away, he admired the sway of her hips. Now why had she used *tu* instead of *vous*? What had she meant by that? Some private code there? Damn, two beautiful women had said good-bye to him before he was able to finish his first cup of coffee.

He gazed about the grounds of the foundation. The various greens of the trees and the pale-stone color of the surrounding buildings had a particularly strong glow. Luminous reds, blues, and yellows sparkled from the flowerbeds alongside the cottage. Everything seemed alive. Everything seemed to be the way it should be.

The cellphone rang again. He hoped to see Lucinda's telephone number on the caller identification, but it was Colonel Frederick's number.

"I'm at the Nice airport, walking to my plane," Frederick shouted above the noise in the background. "Something very interesting has come up. Right up your alley. You know your way around Africa, don't you?"

THE END

GLOSSARY OF TERMS

Agent/Asset - Person who is recruited by a case officer to obtain intelligence

Blown/Burnt - Spy who has been exposed

Brush Pass - Momentary person-to-person contact to pass intelligence

Bug - Covert listening or recording device

Case Officer - Staff officer of an intelligence agency, handles agents

COS - Chief of a CIA station posted to an embassy

DST - Direction de la Surveillance du Territoire, the French National Police who conduct counterespionage and counterintelligence. Equivalent to FBI.

Dry Clean - To evade surveillance by hostile intelligence service

Extraordinary Rendition - Kidnapping of spies or terrorists for interrogation

Legat - Legal Attaché, FBI agent attached to a US embassy

Legend - Life story created for a covert officer or agent

Mossad - Israel's spy agency

MI5 - British Secret Intelligence Service (Internal)

MI6 - British Secret Intelligence Service (External)

NOC - Non-official cover. CIA equivalent of Russian deep cover spy. They have no diplomatic immunity.

Parole - Password used to confirm identity between agents

Safehouse - Place where spies can hide from hostile security services

Sleeper - Deep cover officer/agent

Target - Person, place, or thing of intelligence interest

Tradecraft - Mechanics of/proficiency in espionage

ACKNOWLEDGEMENTS

I want to thank the members of my writing group, the Sheridan Street Irregulars, especially Betty Webb, for their support over the years. My ongoing thanks to my readers Judy Starbuck, Deb Ledford, Virginia Nosky, and Marty Roselius, who read and critiqued every page of the completed manuscript. Also, a note of appreciation to the late writer Sam Orlich, who championed this story.

Of course, thanks to my agent Elizabeth Kracht of Kimberley Cameron & Associates, who has so worked hard on my behalf.

Finally, I want to express my gratitude to my wife, Donna, for her constant help and support.

9 781626 811294